Is he worth the heartbreak? At nearly forty, Julie isn't so sure she'll ever find a man who is, so she's vowed that all her big 4-0 decisions will have zip to do with relationships. A successful theater manager, she agrees to travel to North Carolina and help a friend put her erotic performance theater on its feet. Julie has always been curious and drawn to the BDSM world, and now she can safely explore that world in the environment she knows best.

Desmond Hayes is the roofing contractor repairing their rundown theater building, but he's also a rigger, well-known in the BDSM world for his rope artistry. He's not just a top, though; he's a Dom whose unexpected quirks mesh too well with Julie's eccentric personality and awaken her submissive side.

From the time he was born, Des has been fighting the odds against him. Because of that, he's kept his relationships inside the BDSM scene, with clear boundaries. While Julie has almost given up on finding a person worth loving through better or worse—or pleasure and pain—Des never expected to receive that gift.

He's not letting that treasure get away—no matter how much rope he has to use to bind her to him.

Worth The Wait

The following material contains graphic sexual content meant for mature readers. Reader discretion is advised.

Digital ISBN: 978-1-942122-48-7

Print ISBN: 978-1-942122-47-0

Acknowledgments

This book presented a couple of research challenges for me. As always, I am indebted to readers, friends and many online and book sources for helping me round out Julie and Des's story:

To Andy for his community theater management insights. Also, Bo Metzler's wonderful book *What We Do* turned out to be a godsend for a clueless author writing about theater.

To Jeanie, for inadvertently striking the spark that spawned Des's character.

To the many wonderful BDSM groups that provide access to hands-on information that inspires and enriches scenes in my books. Those who teach workshops for these groups often have very specific scene names, so I want to respect their privacy by not citing them here. However, my thanks to the presenters who demonstrated creative options for liquid nitrogen, fire and wax play.

I also offer a tremendous thanks to the presenter of a rope bondage class I saw in 2015. He brought such personal enthusiasm and charisma to the workshop, Julie's hero evolved from a spark into a three-dimensional character during it. This presenter showed me the type of rope artist Des would be.

I also want to thank my invaluable volunteer editing team of Lauren, Judy, and Terry for their beta reads of the final galley. Thank you also to Angela and Sheri for their professional critiques of the book. You all made the book shine! Any mistakes remaining are all mine.

Then there's my wonderful husband, whose graphic and technical expertise has made it possible for me to include self-published books as part of my offerings to readers. He's navigated all the aggravations of that path so I can continue to focus on the writing. Plus, we get the chance to work and be with one another every day, which I love! Twenty-seven years, and it only keeps getting better, darling.

One final BIG thanks. Thank you to all my readers, new and existing, for taking the journey with my characters, and for giving me the support and encouragement to continue creating new ones. I cannot thank you enough for that.

Author's Note: In the Afterword at the end of this book are further acknowledgements, but since they also provide significant spoilers as to where the story is going to go, I've put them there so you can enjoy the unfolding of the story as it is intended.

Worth The Wait

A Nature of Desire Series Novel

Joey W. Hill

Prologue

She was naked, and curled up on her stomach like a trusting child. Her cheek was pressed to the floor, her knees folded beneath her, her arms threaded under her body between them. A double strand of rope ran over her hips, bisecting the tattoo of a flower at her lower back, just above the pale pink thong she wore. That rope connected to the wraps around her ankles, as well as to her bound wrists, folded prayerlike between her feet.

A man wearing jeans and nothing else rested on his bare heels next to her. His fingertips trailed along her spine, questing, seeking response. Her lips parted, her eyes lifting to his shadowed face. His dark, close cropped beard had threads of silver. She had blue eyes. They were pretty any day of the week, but when she looked at him, the emotions that filled them were what every woman held deep in her heart. Those feelings couldn't be summoned at will, consciously given. They had to be earned, with trust and love.

The blue became the bluest possible blue, the shine in them like the light of a temple.

"Master," she whispered. When he touched her mouth, he had a belt folded over in his hand. Her lips pressed against his knuckles, the strap. She had no fear. Only desire, and a craving to feel his touch, the strike of that need...

Julie paused the video on her phone. Madison had sent it to her months ago, to give her an idea of what she wanted to accomplish with Wonder, her erotic performance theater. How many times had she watched it since then?

The Dom in the video was never clearly in the camera, but he was as strong a presence as if he were center screen. Whenever his submissive looked at him, Julie felt what she felt. That aching yearning, the edge of all she wanted, just beyond her bound fingertips.

Only she wasn't the girl in the video. She merely wished she was.

"I'm almost forty, and no one has ever fallen in love with me." Her voice echoed against the concrete walls.

Julie put her feet in the hotel's indoor pool. The Hampton Inn outside Wytheville, Virginia was a quiet place on a weeknight, so she had the space to herself. A glass wall allowed her to see the faint outline of the rolling hills behind the hotel. In daylight, she'd probably see the details: green pastures, farmland and forest. Maybe a hint of the distant mountains of West Virginia, through which she'd passed on the winding turnpike to get this far from New York City in one day.

What incredible stillness. Where she lived in New York there was always noise. Cabbies honking at all hours, and an undercurrent of movement, people, and energy. Here there was the distant trundling of the elevator, the occasional murmur of voices, and this. Tiny ripples of water echoed against their wavy reflection on the gray satin painted concrete wall.

Her whispered words joined the echo. She'd never said them aloud, and she'd definitely never say them to anyone else. Emotional masturbation was best done in private. Though it hadn't been reciprocated, she had considered herself in love, several times. But tonight she was wondering if that was really true.

Julie folded her ankle socks into snowballs, as she liked to call them, and put them in her canvas sneakers. She aligned them with toes out, because shoes spent most of their lives having to point toward one another. At least when hers were off, they could see what else was out in the world. Though there were worse things than always having to gaze at your other half, if you were lucky enough to find him. Shoes came predestined as couples.

Yeah, she was in one of those kinds of moods. Dramatic

melancholy, a permanent side effect of working in theater.

"He has to make my knees weak when he kisses me. Not just when we first start dating, but after a hundred years together. And he has to be able to make me laugh, even when my heart is breaking. Why is finding a man who can meet those two simple requirements so freaking hard?"

She moved her feet back and forth slowly. The water was cool but not cold. She liked that. Extremes no longer interested her. The cold icy water of a lake, the powerful heat of summer, used to seem so exciting. Backdrops against which she could push herself to the limit of experience, daring the cup of life to overflow like a waterfall. The roaring, Niagara Falls kind.

She rotated her feet in opposing circles, watching the ripples drift out, collide. When she'd embraced those extremes, she'd wanted a passionate love story. She'd sought out the cruel, beautiful men who had passion for certain, but no love to give. They were more than willing to take all she had to offer, though. An endless, painful well.

Now she wanted a passion that started as fire and melted into warmth. A steady heat, holding fast for a lifetime against the coldness of the world. Without that hearth, small disappointments could magnify and link, forming a chain that could strangle the heart.

She remembered being a child and summoning the courage to sled down the hill behind her house. Reaching the bottom, heart pumping and her face wreathed in smiles, she turned to see if her mother was still at the window watching. She wasn't.

Her phone buzzed across the concrete like an irritated mosquito, bringing her back to the present. He'd already left three texts. If he was resorting to a call, he was getting pissed and insistent. She sighed and reached for the phone.

"Are you calling to wish me a happy birthday?" she asked.

"We were coming over to take you out for a magnificent night on the town. Dinner at a restaurant you can't afford, dancing at a club you can't get into if you're not with someone important—like me. We were going to finish it off with a midnight boat ride around Lady Liberty so you could

3

do your usual ritual of tossing a coin and making your wish for the coming year."

"It sounds wonderful." She was so maudlin, the thought that she'd hurt her best friends' feelings choked her up. "You guys are wonderful. I love you both. You know that, right?"

"Thomas, she's telling me she loves us and she's about to cry. Find out where she is so I can go get her."

"No, Marcus—"

"Where are you?" Thomas took the phone, all calm and concerned. His soothing Southern tone was as dear as Marcus's sharp New Yorker impatience. Different versions of the same love and care.

"I left. I need you guys to water my plants and watch after my place while I'm gone. I don't know for how long. I'm on my way to North Carolina. I'm going to take Madison up on her offer to be managing director for the first couple shows at her erotic performance theater. It's my birthday present to me."

She'd turned over the running of her current community theater to her very capable stage manager, Belinda. After getting over the initial shock of hearing about her promotion via ten p.m. phone call, Belinda had been unable to contain her excitement. The Juilliard graduate had been ready for some time to move into the managing director role. Sheila, her assistant stage manager, could move into Belinda's shoes capably. Julie estimated six months on her return, but with Belinda, she knew she didn't have to worry about it. The dusty hole-in-the-wall Julie had turned into a community theater in her little corner of the big city had evolved into a recommended attraction for the niche fans of amateur and avant-garde performance. Belinda would tend to it well.

In a matter of hours, she'd turned her life upside down. Julie was sure this sounded like madness to Thomas and Marcus, but she wasn't stopping the train. She had to do something different, or nothing would change. Somehow, something had to change. She was going to explode out of her skin otherwise.

A significant pause conveyed a lot. Or rather, they'd

noticed her state of mind these past few weeks, confirmed by Thomas's next words. "We know you've been restless. If this is what you want, what you need, we're behind you all the way. Charlotte's only a couple hours from our North Carolina house. My Mom would welcome you at her place. Any time you need feeding and mothering, she'd love to have you come stay overnight. And it goes without saying Daralyn and Les would be thrilled to see you."

Daralyn was a family friend and Celeste was Thomas's sister. Julie always had primo girl talk time with them whenever she visited. Thomas had once said they considered her like their big sister.

Tears stabbed at her again. Thomas's family had made her feel welcome from her first meeting with them. They'd offered her a sense of belonging, one of life's true treasures. She wanted it to be enough, and sort of despised herself for wanting, needing more. For longing for her very own just-for-her person. Other women went through life without this craving. Maybe she'd read too many romance novels as a teenager.

Yep, that's what she'd do. She'd blame it on the romance industry. Maybe she'd gather together a million sad, lonely women still waiting for Prince Charming, thanks to Harlequin and *Pretty Woman*, and bring a class-action lawsuit. Maybe Richard Gere would appear at the trial and they could have dinner together...

"When you don't talk, the gears in your mind are going full throttle. Grunt so I'll know you're there."

She summoned an unladylike, pig grunt and heard Thomas chuckle, a deep, sexy sound that gave her vitals a little spin. Damn him and Marcus for being so decidedly gay, and rabidly monogamous on top of that. Another of life's little 'fuck you, Julie' messages, without the literal and very pleasant *fuck you*.

"We'll be back in North Carolina after we get this next gallery tour out of the way," Thomas continued. "We'll come see you then."

Please, not too soon. She took a breath. "I love you guys for caring about me, but don't worry, okay? And don't take this wrong, but unless you and Marcus convert to bisexualism and decide I'm the answer to your threesome dreams, don't call me for a few weeks. I depend on you two too much, and I'm too raw right now. I don't know if it's having another birthday and I'm in the grip of some tediously typical analyze-my-whole-life crisis, but I need some alone time in my head. Without someone who knows me better than I know myself interrupting the flow. I need to recreate myself. You know how it is when you're painting."

"Creative space. I get it." The gentle note in his voice said he did. She needed to get off the phone. It was time for a really ugly, cathartic cry. "But promise to text us every couple of days so we know you're okay. Proof of life. Send us Madison's phone number so we have a backup emergency number."

"Okay, Dad." But she would, because they watched after her, as she watched after them. It's what the people who cared about you did. "Love you guys."

She was choking up, so she disconnected, hoping he would understand.

She wished that her entirely interesting and fulfilling career, and the many wonderful friends she had, could be enough for her. Most of the time she convinced herself it was.

This was not one of those times.

Squeezing her eyes shut, she let the silence wrap around and hold her as she forced optimism into her bleak mind. Change was good. If she couldn't have what she'd always dreamed of having, maybe running an erotic performance theater in North Carolina would help her. She could immerse herself in sex. Not sex for herself, but the artistic expression of it.

Sure. Seeing beautiful, idealized depictions of erotic intimacy was a great plan to end her clawing, aching need to be in love.

She was going to add Disney to that lawsuit. She'd been duped into thinking of romantic love as Cinderella with a happy circle of blue birds chirping around her. It was more like a circle of vultures, ready to tear out her heart with their sharp claws.

"Ugh." She groaned, bending over at the waist to press her face into her knees and link her hands over the back of her head.

Dramatic melancholy. Its vivid imagery never let her down. She was going to snag a fresh baked chocolate chip cookie from the front desk and go to bed. The smell had been assaulting her since she'd arrived. Maybe she'd have two, and imagine having someone in the room with whom she could share them, touch his mouth if some of the melted chocolate smeared it. She'd collect it on her finger and try to taste it, but he'd grip her wrist and draw her finger to his mouth, sucking on the digit and then clasping her around the waist to bring her close. He'd turn that tease into a mouth-to-mouth transfer of fresh baked cookie and chocolate scent, heat and pleasure.

Body-wise, her fantasy lover was always a compilation of the best parts of Thomas, Marcus and assorted Hollywood stars. Yet his face remained shadowed, because the eyes, the clichéd windows of the soul, had to be real, not fantasy. If they couldn't be, the best way not to disrupt her fantasy was to keep them hidden.

Yeah, thinking about sex was sure to make her feel better. *Not.* She wasn't above using an intense workout with her vibrator to help put her to sleep, though. It wouldn't be the first time.

Oh, crap on Crisco, enough of the wallowing. She was starting a new chapter tomorrow. It would be the turning point in her personal story, the post-intermission act where things started to go in the right direction. This was going to be her best year yet. Fuck love, fuck dating, fuck Cupid. She had a great life.

She'd never needed a partner to dance wide open under the stars, and she wouldn't let a few minutes of moping change that.

North Carolina, watch out. Here I come.

Chapter One

Six weeks later

The radio beeped. "Julie, the roof contractor is here to discuss those leaks."

"Great. I'm in front of the stage. Send him down, Harris."

Putting her hands on her hips, Julie rocked back on her heels. It was coming together. The load-in for the first production was scheduled for next week. That meant the much-anticipated arrival of rented sound and lighting equipment, the building of the scenery, the run-throughs with the cast, the tedious yet essential technical direction.

Today, another milestone had been reached. The fire-retardant curtains had been delivered and installed, a particular thrill. Madison had purchased a traveler curtain with a border and a simple fly system, the typical choice for a community theater with limited funds. Narrower curtains, the "legs," shielded the wings of the stage. The acoustic panels for the walls surrounding the audience were also in place. Julie could already tell the difference in the sound, one of the biggest challenges in adapting a building to a theater purpose.

A whisper at a key moment in a BDSM session could change the whole mood and direction of a scene, so it was important that whisper be heard.

When Julie closed her eyes now, she could already see the set pieces. Lighting and sound set-ups, dialogue and visuals, were tools that could bridge the distance between audience and players. They'd balance powerful drama with touches of levity, and take the audience surfing on a wave of erotic discovery and emotional exploration.

Typical for amateur theater, the individuals Logan and Madison had auditioned were not, for the most part, experienced actors. However, they were confident and passionate about their skills in the BDSM world, and those core talents would drive this first offering.

Consent would be a montage of BDSM skits and skills, a tempting glimpse at what they'd be offering at Wonder.

As Julie considered the dark blue color they'd chosen for the pleated velvet traveler, and how all the curtains made their playhouse look even more like a theater, she heard an exchange of voices, Harris's and another man's, the tone deep and even. It distracted her, because the unknown person had an excellent stage voice. Compelling and intriguing, especially when combined with the unexpected appearance of the man who possessed it.

She'd never met a professional roofer, but her assumption of what one of them would look like was set by the subcontractors she'd seen when driving by construction sites. Rangy, sun-darkened men in old clothes, with bill caps pulled down low over their stubbled faces. Cigarettes often dangled from their lips.

The man striding down the aisle toward her had the same body type, but there were key differences. He wore a long-sleeved T-shirt with a Celtic knot design printed on the front against a black background. The words "East Coast Riggers Hotlanta" curved along the edge of the design. The shirt was loose over jeans faded to a thin softness that hugged hips, groin and thighs. He was slim without seeming insubstantial. She noted he moved like a rock star, with a hint of a saunter that wasn't cockiness exactly, but as if he was moving to music in his head. Heavy on the bass, with heart-accelerating drums and the occasional piercing strike of a guitar.

Several rope bracelets were knotted on his right wrist. The tattoo on his forearm, visible because he had the shirt sleeves pushed up, was Marilyn Monroe, restrained in a complicated design of rope that made the most of her voluptuous figure. On the opposite arm was Betty Grable in a different pose, but also an erotic arch, legs tied ankle to thigh, thighs spread and arms behind her, head falling back and full lips parted. Betty wore a dark green dress and Marilyn a gold one, both clinging to curves that were fully articulated.

"The ladies tend to be distracting. A friend was practicing her craft on me Friday night. They're temporaries. They should wash off when I'm in the mood to give them a good scrubbing, but I haven't had the heart to do that yet."

When her gaze slid up to his face, she changed her mind about rock star. He was more like the guy in charge of all the roadies. She could see him in the shadows, absorbing the vibe, his sharp eyes, extensive experience and fully tuned intuition pulling in every detail. He was the guy who elevated the show from merely good to fully awesome.

He had dark brown long hair, loose around his tanned face. The natural curl in it made it thick and touchable. While a woman would despair of that thickness in the Southern humidity, Julie expected he tied it back with insouciant care and let it be a contained chaos of waves.

His face wasn't classically handsome, nor pretty, but it was charismatic, interesting. He had a scar on his chin, it and his jaw layered by a couple days of dark stubble. A good jaw, strong, not weak. Great cheekbones enhanced it.

When she reached his eyes, she wasn't sorry to have saved them for last, because she might have been caught there and missed all the rest. The irises were like the bands of a Grand Canyon wall. Shades of brown, gold and rust with a dark ring around the irises. The longer she looked, the more earth colors she saw, shifting with the light as he moved to stand before her.

"Your eyes detract from the ladies," she said practically. "If someone looks at your face first."

"Yet you didn't."

"You were coming down the aisle. I started with what I saw first." She considered his work shoes. "You need new laces." She counted three knottings where the strands had broken.

"These still work." His deep set eyes lifted from the

laces. As he traveled to her face, she realized he was giving her as studied an appraisal as she had given him.

That was unexpected. An auditioning performer was used to her scrutiny, but when she unconsciously did it to a lay person, usually they became uncomfortable. They'd snap her out of the habit by shifting, or launching into purposed discussion. He did neither. He simply kept looking at her.

Well, she wished him joy in his perusal. The building in which they were standing had at different times been church, private school, homeless shelter and haven for victims of domestic violence. Madison had done a great job renovating the main areas before Julie arrived, sending Julie pictures of the layouts for her step-by-step input. But yesterday Julie had decided two small rooms that had been administrative offices for the school would be perfect as conference rooms for read-throughs, meetings with investors or between production staff.

However, since the rooms hadn't yet been cleaned out or prepped, she'd been up since four, painting, sanding and hauling trash. She probably smelled like a teenage boys' basketball team after practice, and looked like she'd been dipped in a glaze of sweat and rolled through dust, cobwebs and God knew what else. *Contain your lust or take me now, honey.*

Her hair was scraped into a ponytail. She too had naturally curly, thick hair, which turned into a rat's nest without the aid of more hair products than she had time or patience to pursue.

"Are you scared of spiders?" He asked it in a conversational tone, but she noticed his glance had stilled on her shoulder. It reminded her of how her old cat, Meteor, would look when she saw a cockroach scuttling across the ceiling.

She would not look. She would *not*. "No. As long as it's no bigger than a pencil tip, legs and all. If there's something bigger on me, you're about to see me freak out." Okay, she was going to look.

He lifted a hand, drawing her attention, and caught her in his extraordinary gaze again. "Don't freak," he said in that same casual voice. "And don't look away from my face. Even if I'm not looking at you."

"Why?"

"Why not? It's a pretty face, isn't it? Prince Charming material, right?" He stepped closer. "I'm going to let him crawl onto my hand so the two of you can part friends."

"You have an extraordinary voice." It was like Heath Ledger's, she realized. That oddly deep voice coming from a slim body that radiated strength and charisma.

He nodded. "So I've been told. I'd ask forgiveness for this, but my purpose is entirely appropriate, I promise." He pressed the side of his hand against the top of her breast. She was wearing a baggy, soft T-shirt with the logo *Small Town Theater, NYC* curved over the pocket, along with the suddenly rather disconcerting motto: "Take a bite out of my Apple."

"This is the most elaborate excuse a guy has ever used to touch my boobs," she informed him. His eyes were concentrated on his task, his firm lips curved in a far too appealing way. The faint resulting smile was controlled enough to give them a sexy intensity. "If there's not really a spider on me," she added, "you better pull a big one out of your ass, or I'm going to sock you in the nuts with a broom handle."

He stepped back then, showing her a dark brown spider the harrowing size of a silver dollar running over his fingers as he turned them to coordinate with the creature's alarmed movement. "It's just a wolf spider. Hand me that cup on the stage, love. Unless it still has coffee in it."

It didn't. She'd left it there after she'd finished her morning dose of caffeine. "Just put him on the ground and stomp him."

"Uh, no. I did say I wanted you two to part as friends."

"I'll feel very friendly about him if he's dead." But she handed him the cup, with a PTSD shudder. Bug control was the next place she was calling. She envisioned the audience entranced, silent, absorbed in a dramatic scene on stage...right before the man in row three leaped up shrieking like a girl and flailing, inciting a panic as he tore off his pants to deal with the spider crawling up his leg.

He'd of course be a reviewer for the most-read local entertainment blog.

It was ludicrous for her to be squeamish, since she often encountered bugs even in the cleanest old theaters. But to her way of thinking, spiders were a whole different classification from the rest of the bug world.

The roofer dumped the spider in the cup, putting the lid over it, the small sip spout too small for escape. Maybe. "I'll put him back out when I go." He extended his other hand. "So I'm Desmond Hayes, your roof guy. Logan said you might want me for some other small jobs, since I'm also licensed for electric and plumbing."

A godsend, though she wasn't surprised. Anyone Logan sent her way was reliable and skilled.

Thinking about how she could use this guy professionally was being derailed by other ways she wanted to use him, though. Which, nice voice and provocative tattoos aside, was puzzling. He'd simply rested the side of his hand against her chest, providing the spider a ledge. From the warm tingling in her skin, it was obvious she'd been without the touch of a lover for too damn long.

"I'm also a rigger," Desmond said. "A rope guy? I don't perform, but I mentor other riggers. Logan thought you might want my expertise for tips on staging a rigging scene, since he said you'll have a couple in your upcoming performance."

She shoved herself back into her theater role. "It's a shame you don't perform. With your voice, you'd do well on stage." His lean, intriguing body would be easy on the eyes as well, but she didn't add that.

"I did it a couple times." He shrugged and hooked a thumb in his jeans pocket, drawing her eye to the undulating Marilyn and the corded forearm she was draped over. "Then someone wanted me to do a suspension under a waterfall. Using blue rope and a bunch of fancy lights. I did it, but it was bullshit and took away from the main point, so I decided that was the end of my stage career. I have a sandwich for lunch. Want to share? I assume it's past your lunchtime, too."

She was able to roll with most topic changes, but that

one was abrupt. "We can talk about your roof while we eat," he added.

When she hesitated, he gave her a bland look. "I'll even share my carrot sticks."

"Carrot sticks?" She snorted. "Did your Mom make your lunch?"

"I like carrots. Don't mock a man's food choices, woman."

She grinned. She *was* hungry, and she really didn't want to waste the time to seek out lunch. "What kind of sandwich?"

Moving to the edge of the stage, he pulled a small pack off his shoulder and set it down. "I have a PB&J with homemade blackberry jelly, a chicken salad, a grilled cheese and one hummus wrap."

"Just a little light lunch then," she said dryly. "Or do you usually pack to share?" She swept her gaze over his slim form, head to toe. "If you tell me that's your normal lunch, I'm going to break you in half like the pretzel stick you are."

"You can try, love." He curled his hand around hers and drew her over to the stage, the gesture so smooth and relaxed there was none of the discomfort she should have felt at having a stranger touch her with such familiarity. Though she did experience an unsettling flutter in her stomach as he set his hands to her waist and boosted her onto the stage.

Her mouth dropped open at the sensation of being weightless, as if he'd picked up a helium balloon. His eyes glinted, registering her reaction, and that little flutter expanded into something else as he lingered between her knees, bracing his hands on the stage on either side of her hips. He was decently tall, so despite the height of the stage, his face was still in her line of sight without a significant dip of her chin.

"I'm way stronger than I look," he said. "Now, which of those sandwiches do you want? Or, since they're quartered, you can pick and choose."

He moved to boost himself on the stage next to her. If he'd lingered between her knees, she would have had to decide if it was in the realm of inappropriate, but instead she was left with a nice little surge of adrenaline that came with harmless flirting. Though harmless might be the wrong word, since Des was obviously very accomplished at it and comfortable with making a woman feel womanly.

Not in a sleazy way, either. The pushy male vibe that said "I want to have sex with you right now," was easy enough to shove away or ignore. No, his danger was he coaxed that reaction from the female recipient of his charms. She could picture having him right here, right now, on the stage. Or him having her.

She was back to being baffled with herself. Yeah, she might be sex-deprived, but he was skinny and...well, a roofer. One who seemed to think what they were doing here was bullshit. Well, she'd get to the bottom of that idiocy, and his answer would break this hormone-induced spell he was spinning over her.

"Why do you have the attitude about erotic performance art?"

"Sorry, didn't mean to come off that way." His flash of chagrin showed he was sincere. "I don't mind people watching what I do, like in a club or dungeon, or doing a demo for them in that environment, but the focus has to be on the connection between me and my sub. I want her to be lost in things, caught up in the power of the restraint, my control of her. Knowing she's safe and yet subject to my desires in all ways. You put too many props into it, fireworks and crap, you lose that music."

His gaze slid to hers. And held.

In the BDSM world, there were differences between a top and a Dom. She'd assumed, incorrectly, he was only a top. A top might enjoy taking the upper hand during BDSM play, and get into the mechanics of it, like the rope work. It didn't mean he was a Dominant, a nature and distinction hard to describe but felt by those who reacted to it. Like her.

The way he held eye contact told her he'd detected the involuntary tells of her body language, the response to his words. That confirmed he was a Dom, as did the shift in his body language, the tone of his voice and the laser look from his eyes.

It flummoxed and intrigued her, because up until recently, her primary experience with a Dom, and therefore her mental picture of one, was Marcus. A nun who'd been in a convent since the age of six and didn't know what sex was, let alone BDSM, would still recognize Marcus as a Master. His Dom-ness was that out front.

Desmond Hayes, on the other hand... As crazy as it sounded, it was as if he'd sent her an exclusive message. A message delivered to a place inside she'd only recently opened up to find what secrets she'd been keeping from herself, too busy dealing with the regular pitfalls of her unoriginally tragic love life.

Or maybe that was why that door had remained closed. To keep the treasures hidden in those chambers from being spoiled by her other failures. It was best that something special never be taken out and used, if the alternative was it becoming the same ruined, stinking mess as the rest.

Wow. She needed a rope to pull her out of that pig wallow of self-pity. Fortunately, she was sitting next to a rigger. She hid a smile as she tuned back in to the feast he'd been laying out before her.

The sandwiches, all quartered, sat on neatly unwrapped squares of waxed paper. A generous tub of carrot sticks was open next to them with a squat jar of peanut butter. He was loosening the tops on two bottles of water and placing one by her.

"Hummus, chicken salad, PB&J and grilled cheese." He pointed to each. "Help yourself." Pulling a small palm-sized device like a stopwatch out of the pack, he fitted it with a slim needle, swabbed his finger with a postage-sized alcohol wipe and did a quick stick, glancing at the screen. Appearing satisfied with the number, he detached the needle, put it in a container and tucked those things back into the pack.

She had Type II diabetic friends who checked their blood sugar in such a matter-of-fact way before meals. Seeing him do it was another surprise, since most of her friends who were Type II had weight problems and an aversion to strenuous exercise, but she expected every condition had exceptions.

The efficient, swift way he did it and put it away again without comment told her it was routine enough that he barely thought about doing it in front of a stranger. But his lack of comment also suggested he wasn't inviting questions. Fair enough. A ten-minute acquaintance hardly opened the door to personal health inquiries, so she sat on her natural curiosity. For now.

As she picked up a square of the chicken salad sandwich, she noticed he went for the PB&J first. Biting into her sandwich, she was surprised at the taste and freshness. "This is excellent. What deli did you get this from? I'm still new in town. I'll have to stock up."

"I made it. I make most my food from scratch. Ingredients come from the farmers' market near me." He bit into a carrot stick and gestured at her with the other half, his heels drumming lightly against the stage front as he shifted. "If you're not into cooking, there are ladies who bring home cooked meals for sale. You can stock up and reheat them. They have the market once a week during the seasonal months. I'll take you to it sometime if you like and introduce you to the folks who bring the best stuff."

"Oh. Well...hmm."

"We won't call it a date. Just being neighborly, since you said you're new in town." He winked. "If we end up getting naked after, that'll be because of my irresistible charisma. Like dinner and sex, only we'll do farmers' market and sex."

She laughed and he grinned. He leaned in and touched the corner of her mouth with his thumb, taking off a bit of the chicken salad. She reached self-consciously for her napkin, but noticed he put the tiny piece of salad to his lips, licking it away, which made her mouth tingle as if he'd done it to hers. Suddenly she remembered that weeks-ago fantasy of rubbing chocolate off her lover's lips, only to have him grasp her wrist and taste it from her fingertips himself.

"I'd love to see you in my rope and nothing else," he said thoughtfully. "Have you done any scening in the local group yet? Or did you have a regular Dom or hangout in New York? Logan said you'd come from there. What's your situation?"

She'd blanched at the forwardness of the first statement, but as he continued, she put it together. "Oh no. I'm just a theater manager. I'm just... I don't... I mean, I'm flattered, but I haven't..." She stopped and shot him a narrow look. "You're laughing at me."

"No. I'm pleased with you. You're flustered. Which heightens my interest in ways you can't even imagine." He'd drawn up one knee and had his work shoe propped on the edge of the stage, balancing that way with his elbow on his knee as he chewed his sandwich and studied her. Thanks to the short sleeves of the T-shirt, she noticed he had well-developed biceps.

She should be holding her own better in this conversation, using amusement and her tart tongue to put him in his place. Except he didn't seem to be joking, just considering his own reaction to her. He acted like someone who spent a good amount of time in his own head, which she supposed he probably did as a roofer. However, he didn't seem introverted, quite comfortable in the company of a stranger.

"I don't pigeon hole people to get them to fit my fantasies," he said. "But I'm getting the vibe that you are interested in all of this. Personally. Yet you haven't explored it a whole lot, have you?"

No, she hadn't. Having Marcus and Thomas show her around the scene in New York hadn't appealed to her. Ironic, since one long ago significant event with them had been the trigger to her dormant interests, but she'd felt self-conscious pursuing it further in their company. She'd done a lot of online looking, though. Followed by and integrated with some serious fantasizing, which she'd assumed ever since would be like most of her relationships: better as vibrator material than reality.

After the initial meetings with the cast members, Julie had done more specific Internet research on what she'd learned from them. Suspension, fire, liquid nitrogen, whips, knives, rope. Role play—everything from interrogation and Victorian drawing room scenes, to puppy and pony play. It kicked off her own personal and professional imaginings, though she kept the former firmly channeled into the latter.

"Logan's great at mentoring people who are curious," Desmond suggested. "If it's easier for you to take those first steps by calling it work, he'd do it under the guise of supporting what you're doing here."

"Don't do that." Her tone sharpened. "Passive aggressive jabs annoy me."

The genuine surprise in his face reassured and shamed her at once. "Easy, New York," he said. "It wasn't a judgment. Plenty of people interested in this like to approach it in a more detached way at first. It's a smart way of playing it safe, keeping it a little arm's length. Only an idiot jumps into the deep end without being able to swim. Or even knowing if they're going to like swimming."

"Yeah. True. Sorry. Weird trigger."

He picked up the tub and offered her some carrot sticks, taking a handful himself. "Let me guess. You had a boyfriend who liked to do that patronizing, 'I'm only telling you this for your own good, even though it suits my purpose to emotionally manipulate you the way I want you to be' thing. In the meantime, he made you feel like what wasn't working for your relationship was all your fault."

His wry humor made it difficult to hold onto offense at being so accurately read. She cocked her head, more sure of her footing, especially when he smiled at her. It went deep into his eyes and made a woman feel special. *Danger, Will Robinson.*

"So are you the reformed asshole who did the manipulating, or the recipient of the female version of it?" she asked. "Is that how you recognize the signs?"

"If I tell you that, I'll ruin the fog of sexual mystery that clings to me."

"I think you're safe. It's the carrot sticks that are keeping me enthralled." She smiled and his own broadened.

At a buzz, she looked for her phone, but he'd already shifted onto one hip and reached behind him to withdraw his own.

"Hold on, my butt's vibrating." He glanced at the message and grimaced. "Well, shit. Gotta get back to another job." He slid off the stage to face her. "I did go up on the roof before I came in. I can do you a decent patch job that will buy you another year until you get the theater up and earning some income. After that, Madison'll want to do the full replacement it needed five years ago."

He lifted his gaze to the ceiling. "You've had leaks in here during the recent rains, haven't you?"

"Yes. And two or three in the back rooms."

He nodded, unsurprised. "You'll want that patch job before we have any hard summer showers. I can do it next week, as long as weather cooperates. Sound good?"

He fished out a card and handed it over, his fingers brushing hers. His hands were callused, knuckles chapped and nails painfully short, cuticles predictably ragged. A working man's hands, the skin brown as oak bark. She found herself wanting to hold onto one of them, turn it over and explore his fingers, the lines on his palms. He smelled like male sweat and cinnamon gum, since he'd taken out a piece and was chewing it. He offered her a piece, which she took for later.

"The patch job will cost about a thousand," he added. "Logan's done some work for me, so I can cut Madison a discount and drop that amount off the full price when it's time to do the replacement. I'm going to tell her all that, but I figure she'll be asking you what you think."

Madison would be pleased to get the break. A stage and auditorium had already been part of the building, a big selling point when Madison was considering her options. The private school had built it for student performances. But it had no backstage, so a wall had to be removed and the classrooms behind the auditorium renovated to become the backstage area. Other rooms had been converted into a dressing area and storage. The auditorium had stepped seating in a crescent around the stage, and they expanded that, knocking out additional walls so it could now seat a highly optimistic four hundred. Until the theater provided itself with ticket sales, further major expenses were out of the question.

Des had packed up the remaining sandwiches as he spoke, though he left one block of wax paper holding the remaining square of the chicken salad sandwich and two squares of PB&J, as well as three carrot sticks. "You kept looking at the PB&J," he said with a wink, "so I figured you might want those two for dessert."

The PB&J was what she'd really wanted to eat, but had thought she might look childish for liking it.

"Finish the chicken salad and carrots before dessert," he said, as if reading her mind. "Be a good girl."

She stuck her tongue out at him and he tsked. Shouldering his pack, he offered his hand. "It'll be a pleasure working with you, Miss Ramirez."

"Julie is fine."

"Yes, she is. In every way." His exaggerated ogle had her stifling a laugh, unsuccessfully.

"You're a terrible flirt."

"Actually, I'm very good at it. Your eyes are dancing, you're smiling and you look less tired and stressed now." His smile morphed into something else. "Seriously, don't hesitate to give me a call about the rigging. I'm sure Logan will have recommended good people for your cast members, but there are a lot of good guys out there who dabble in rope, and don't get enough training before taking it to more advanced levels. It's important to me that people do what I do safely."

Now his expression was as uncompromising as a police officer, which gave her all sorts of distracting fantasies. He was a fascinating mix. She'd taken his hand, and he was still holding it in a firm grip. As she met his penetrating look, she let the warmth that his hand spread through her take her a step away from sanity. "I've researched some of it online," she said with forced casualness, "but I don't have a real grasp of what it's like. From the inside, so to speak. Would you be willing to show me what you do? Using me as a subject, I mean?"

She was astounded she'd said such a thing. Maybe it was being immersed in this environment that had propelled her to a tentative readiness to dip her toe into a submissive experience. Or maybe it was Des. He was the first Dom she'd met, in person or online, who'd made her feel she could take that step.

Yes, she'd met him only a few moments ago, so it should be ludicrous, but she didn't feel that way toward the other performers, with whom she'd been working for several weeks now. It wasn't that they gave her the creeps. Far from it. They'd been recommended by Logan and Madison, and, as Des had said, their choices emitted nothing but good vibes. A couple weren't as experienced as the others, but they still had the right stuff for what they needed in this production.

Beginning and end of story, she felt like she could trust Des. His personality complemented hers, and she could double check things with Logan and back out if she was wrong. But she was already fairly certain Des was a pro at what he did. She was used to being around performers, and knew the real deal when she met them. He exuded a quiet confidence in his abilities. The overabundance of honest charm also didn't hurt.

Since he wasn't going to be in the production, there was no real conflict of interest. It also didn't have to be personal. A lot of people did the Dom/sub stuff as friends or BDSM club arrangements, sans the minefields that came with a relationship. That was a big thumbs-up for her. Exploring it from that safe paradigm would make it all the more fun for her. Right?

As he'd pointed out, such explorations would increase her understanding for the productions. Despite her defensiveness, he was correct. Keeping it professionally motivated would allow her to explore her personal interests in a safe way.

Though admittedly, his reaction to her request made those professional walls seem a little thin. His hand held hers with more than a hint of the strength he'd warned her about. It was evidence of a man's interest and desire, and she was far from immune to it.

When he stepped closer, his abdomen brushed her kneecaps where she sat on the stage. She had to fight a ridiculously powerful compulsion to spread her knees and invite him closer. He gave her another of those sweeping glances that made her aware of every curve she had.

"Use you as my subject to teach you about rigging?" He

repeated her question. "I'd say that's a meeting I won't miss."

She covered her unsettled response with a sniff. "You really are a flirt."

"No, I'm not." He braced his free hand on the stage, the heel of his palm brushing the outside of her thigh. Betty's lush body, her helpless tied state, the pleasure in her eyes and parted lips, were distracting for more empathetic reasons now.

Though his jaw and mouth were relaxed, friendly and non-intimidating, that impression vanished when she met his eyes. "I just know what I like when I see it," he said. "I already like you. Not only because you're willing to let me tie you up, though I admit that just vaulted you from Miss America to Miss Universe."

She snorted. "They're far under my weight class."

His smile disappeared, and he stepped closer, somehow parting her knees and standing between them. Or had they simply given way before his obvious intent? Rough palms curved over her thighs. She'd been a New Yorker for most her life. People did not get up in her face like this. She'd shove them back in a heartbeat, tell them to piss off, demand *what the fuck* or...something.

Maybe it was because she was sitting on the stage, and she had always experienced a shift there, as if she'd stepped into a world where the dramatic and unexpected were more acceptable. She inhabited a world of quirky people who could be infected with that same virus when they were close to a stage. Things that would seem over the top and out of place outside the theater were just the standard within it.

Or maybe there was an entirely different reason he'd caught her off guard.

Her pulse thudded against her throat as his gaze held hers. If she'd doubted the Dom thing before, she didn't now. His captivating voice was a low croon, close to a growl, a thrumming note that her body answered with a hard quiver, coming from those chambers that were suddenly wide open to him.

"Sometimes women get self-conscious about the way

their bodies look when they're tied up," he said in a deceptively conversational way. "Like when I tie an ankle to a thigh, and they think the thigh looks too spread out, or the flesh of their stomach is squeezed between two wraps."

His hands slid along her thighs, back toward her knees, a short, intimate stroke. "The things I could do with these thighs," he murmured. He lifted his gaze to hers, and she discovered his eyes could look like a new penny caught in the rain. "When we first meet one another, we're shells. The shell might be pretty, but what I learn about you when I bind you will take me to what's deep beneath that. I suspect your eyes will look like heated molasses when you're aroused."

His gaze slid down. "Your nice breasts would become a pillow, where I'd rest my head and listen to your heartbeat, because when I tie you up, your submissive nature will rise. You'll want to give me that gift, lie still to serve my needs and desires, because I think your instinct is toward care and compassion, serving a Master's needs beyond his cock or orgasm."

His gaze slid back up. "When I uncover that instinct, that's when the shell completely vanishes and I'll know just how beautiful you are."

"You don't really see someone until you see their soul," she said, surprised she could even form words, let alone try to sound like she was reacting to his words as if he were giving her an instructional lecture, not a personal mandate.

"Exactly. That matters way more than what I see in a two-dimensional way. It's the best way for you to get to know me better, too." He moved back, though his hand whispered along her knee, a hint of how he could touch her. Maybe would touch her. "Like just now. When I was talking about tying you in rope, and things were all quiet and intense, were you seeing the skinny guy with questionable taste in second hand clothes, or did you feel the touch of a broad-shouldered god hung like a moose?"

She burst out laughing, as she was sure he'd intended, for his eyes sparkled with humor. The laughter brought a rush of good feeling, that sense of ease again, which had a peculiar reaction with things that weren't at ease at all, but on full, anticipatory alert around him. "Maybe something in between. Damn, you're good."

"I'm good because I'm honest." She saw that flash of sincerity, the hint of dead seriousness, the gleam in his eyes that said he would do all of that and more to her if she opened the door. What's more, he'd proven he could do it in less than a blink. The realization stole her smile and her breath at once, leaving her reeling.

"You have my contact info," he said, shouldering his pack again. "Ball's in your court, Julie. But I'll be ready to hold onto it when you send it back. All right?"

The look he had upon her now expected—maybe demanded—an answer.

Though an innate part of him, Marcus's Dom qualities always had a deliberate, calculated quality to them that was overwhelming. In contrast, this seemed second nature to Desmond Hayes, something he wasn't conscious he was doing. Remarkably, it made him even more potent to her.

"All right," she said. Was her voice breathless?

As he nodded and turned away, she had a feeling he'd registered it. The same way she'd recognized the answering heat in his eyes.

Good Lord, who was *this guy?*

Chapter Two

"Okay, who the hell is this roofing guy? Desmond Hayes," Julie added at Madison's blank look.

"Spiderman," Logan supplied. Madison's expression cleared in a blink.

"Oh, Des! Sorry. I've been dealing with so many contractors." Madison leaned back in the span of Logan's long arm. The couple were on the front porch swing at Logan's house, where the three of them were sharing an after work drink. Julie was sitting on a facing chair, shoes off and toes curled over the edge as she drew her knees up to her chest. Through the screen that protected them from the ever-present mosquitoes, she could see the manmade pond Logan had on the large rural property. The acres of surrounding open fields and forest formed a cozy cushion for the clapboard farmhouse he'd renovated.

"Des is a 360 degree experience, isn't he?" Madison asked with a chuckle. "First you just see this grungy handyman, a little on the skinny side, though those eyes are as deep as moon craters. Then he gets to talking in that voice like...it's hard to describe."

"Keep trying and you'll find yourself in all kinds of trouble," Logan advised.

Madison dimpled at him. They'd only been married a few months, and so they still had that newlywed miasma around them that could be as wondrous as it was annoying. But since Madison was the only person Julie knew who'd had a worse dating record than herself, it was hard for her to be annoyed or resentful. Just wistful.

"That's all right," Julie interjected. "I'll say it. His voice already falls into the 'drop my panties and take me now' range. Look into those brown eyes, and it's a done deal. It's a bit disconcerting. The rest of the image doesn't fit."

"Well, at first you think so. But if you ever see him do his rope work, or the way he relates to a sub, you change your mind about that."

An understatement. Julie had recalled that moment on stage a million times. Des so inappropriately close to her for a guy she'd just met, her sitting so still and captured by whatever mojo he emanated. He was like some kind of freakish Dom wizard. Who did roofing on the side.

"Earth to Julie?"

Julie snapped back to real time when Madison touched her bottle to Julie's. "Want another?"

"Yeah, maybe just one more."

Logan gripped Madison's thigh as she started to rise. "I'll go get them. You've had a long day."

"Hey, aren't Doms supposed to order their subs to wait on them?" Julie asked. "And beat them when they don't?"

Logan's brown eyes glinted. "Only if that's what turns on both Dom and sub. I only beat her when I think she needs some smacking around."

"How very redneck of you."

"Well, Doms, rednecks. It's a fine line." He kissed his wife's forehead, his large hand loosely curled in her hair, then straightened and headed back into the house.

Madison's interest in creating her theater hadn't been driven solely by her store's focus. Since meeting Logan, she'd embraced a submissive orientation that had simmered within her for years. Logan radiated Dom enough that Julie easily added him into her shadowy night fantasies. While she didn't tell Madison that, Julie rationalized her friend had no right to be mad about it, since she went to bed with the real thing every night. No need to be greedy.

Julie had nursed submissive feelings of her own for some time. Being around Marcus and Thomas, another Master and sub pairing, had only increased her fascination. Yet if she couldn't get any traction with a vanilla relationship, there was no way she'd wade into the far more complex waters of the BDSM world. But now she had a way to explore it beyond the Internet without risking herself, and combine it with her love of theater productions.

As Madison's gaze followed her husband, Julie couldn't help doing the same. The man's shoulders and ass filled out a shirt and a pair of jeans just right. Anyone who thought a guy in his forties was past the prime years of his life hadn't seen Logan. For some men, middle age was when they reached their personal best. John Schneider, Robert Downey, Jr... She wondered how old Des was. It was hard to tell, he was so sunbaked and...something. He looked in his mid-twenties, and she'd never been the type of woman who wanted a man that much younger than her. Yet he'd acted with the maturity of a man closer to her own age.

Madison glanced her way, catching her in the act. "Don't be eyeing my man, ho."

"Hey, he's made from head to toe to be an eyeful. You were doing it, too, bitch."

"I'm allowed."

"Yes, you are. He may have a great ass, but what makes me like him is what he's done for my friend." Julie sobered. "Cheers to finding the unicorn."

She'd intended to keep the comment light, but Madison caught the edge she couldn't keep out of it. Her friend's expression became kind and concerned, but Julie didn't want to go down the road of her own relationship discontent. She was working really hard on the 'suck it up and snap out of it' philosophy of life but, beyond that, she loved her friend too much to feel anything but happiness for her, and didn't want to rain on that parade.

Before she had to scramble for a distracting subject, Logan's heavy tread heralded his return with two beers for him and Madison, and an Angry Orchard hard cider for Julie.

"So how did you and Madison meet?" he asked, settling back next to his wife on the swing. He braced his long legs, keeping it in an easy rocking motion as she settled in the span of his arm again. When he asked the question, he glanced pointedly at Julie's hands. Julie shot a glare at Madison, who feigned innocence.

"Great. You told him," Julie accused. "Another marriage based on total honesty. Sister code out the window."

"She said she couldn't do it justice and that I needed to hear you tell it," Logan defended his spouse.

"They adored her at Children's Story Hour at the local branch of the Boston library," Madison supplied. "She may work behind the stage, but she could just as easily perform on it."

"Buttering me up will not save you from my ire," Julie said ominously. "Okay, I'll tell it, but if I decide to paint you as the villain, it's your own fault."

"I accept the consequences." Madison beamed at her. Julie heaved an exaggerated, put-upon sigh.

"Fine. I was getting a community theater on its feet in Boston. We met when I asked her if I could share her table in a crowded Starbuck's. She was on her laptop doing complicated financial things." Julie gave Logan a devilish look. "She looked all trim, neat and severe in her suit and heels, deceptively Dommish with her mouth tight and cheekbones all drawn in. You should have her role play it sometime."

Julie sucked in her own cheeks to demonstrate, and laughed as Madison tried to shove her with her bare foot. She was thwarted by Logan, who still controlled the back and forth motion of the swing with the pressure of his big feet on the porch boards.

"So she was on her laptop," Julie continued. "I was on my earpiece with an actor who was stomping on my last nerve. I mean, Christ on a Triscuit, it's community theater, not Broadway. When he wasn't playing our lead, he was a plumber and coaching his kid's Little League team. Anyhow, as you not-so-subtly implied," she threw another aggrieved look at Madison, "I was getting so annoyed with Pain-in-My-Ass Wannabe-Olivier that my hands were entering the conversation. I hit a home run."

She assumed a public service announcer's drone. "Using a hands free ear piece in your car is a good idea. Using it in a crowded Starbuck's is not." She shook her head. "Whacked her iced latte with enough force the cap came loose and the cup did a half gainer over her computer. It dowsed the keyboard, sprayed coffee all over her suit, her perfectly coiffed hair and her lovely face. Before landing in her lap."

Julie gazed at her friend fondly. "The funny thing was, when I first sat down, I thought she was one of the unhappiest people I'd ever seen. Mouth set in a permanent frown, her eyes kind of detached. I knew she was probably awesome at her job, but I thought she didn't really feel anything about it. Hadn't felt anything in a while, maybe."

Madison's gaze met hers as Logan's arm tightened around her shoulders. Yeah, he knew that about Madison's past. He'd helped make it better. As a result, Julie would be as fiercely loyal to him as Lassie, now and forever.

"I expected her to tear me a new one. Everyone around us sucked up all the oxygen, a horrified collective breath. I'm sure they were expecting her to freak out, just like I was. I seriously thought about throwing my card down on the table, blurting out, 'send me the bill' and bolting.

"But the most peculiar look came over her face." Julie cocked her head, studying Madison's fine features. Looking at her now, dizzily in love, it was obvious she was a pretty woman. That day, Julie wouldn't have said so, because of all the discontent within her friend. Until she'd had coffee all over her and done what she'd done next. Which made Julie think of what Des had said about shells and souls.

Stop invading my mind, freakish Dom wizard.

"I think the horror of it was so off the charts, there was no response big enough to cover it. So she went the opposite direction. She blinked three times and said in this measured, precise way: 'you missed my blueberry muffin.' Then she smiled. That's when I thought, 'Damn, she and I are going to be awesome friends.'"

And they had been. Madison had first called her about her theater plans eight months ago, while Julie was still in New York. During the six months before Julie accepted her offer to be her managing director, she'd walked Madison through all the steps of being a production manager. Madison had met the challenge and exceeded all expectations.

In hindsight, it hadn't really surprised Julie. Madison

had been a finance wizard in Boston before she came to North Carolina to take over her sister's erotic boutique, Naughty Bits. She'd made the shop hers, profiting enough that she'd decided to diversify into erotic theater. She'd also fallen in love with Logan, who was the hardware store owner next door, an astute businessman in his own right, and one with deep and vital ties in the BDSM community.

Madison had handled the capitalization of the first show, an astronomical accomplishment. She'd had an initial fundraising event at a rental space in downtown Matthews that targeted BDSM lifestylers specifically, rousing their interest. As such, when Julie arrived, Madison had a volunteer list of performers and stage hands from their ranks. Lucrative donors from the BDSM community had become the angels that brought Wonder to life. Their generous checks were a confidence vote in Madison and Logan's ability to turn the theater into something that would educate audiences on what BDSM was and wasn't, while offering a satisfying and entertaining view of that dynamic.

Julie was used to having to handle the production manager end of things, in addition to a bunch of other hats, including managing director, so it was refreshing not to have to dedicate so much of her energy to fundraising. For once, she could focus on the fun part, the theater and show development, except when Madison needed her guidance on the producer's end.

Julie returned her attention to the story she'd just told of their fated meeting. Logan curled a loose lock of Madison's long hair behind her ear, leaving his fingers there to caress her neck. "She didn't tell me all that."

"You notice so much when you look at people, Julie," Madison said quietly. "You have a gift that way."

Julie shook a finger at her. "No mushy maudlin stuff. We're drinking, so we're already in the danger zone. Next thing you know we'll be crying and watching *Beaches* together."

"I can hold my liquor," Logan informed her.

"You'll be singing 'Baby Mine' and sobbing. I guarantee it. Anyway, to finish up the story," she said over their chuckles, "the staff brought us towels to clean up, and a bucket so we could turn the computer over and let it drain in the hopes it could be dried out and salvaged. She very politely asked if I would buy her another cup of coffee. As I was apologizing, I told her this was just the type of spastic behavior Loser Boyfriend Number Three had hated about me. She said she was up to Loser Boyfriend Number Five and, since she could tell she was younger than me, I was behind. I called her a bitch, she laughed, and that was that. We spent an hour talking about how many relationships we'd screwed up, splurged on a chocolate muffin we split, and we've been friends ever since."

"It was worth the ruined computer. Though maybe not the ruined suit. I loved that outfit." This time Madison was able to poke Julie's knee with her toe since Logan had her on the upswing. Julie swatted at her bare sole with tickling fingers.

"Yeah, but you get to wear even cooler stuff at Naughty Bits." Madison still wore today's choice, a lavender gauze tunic with a lace black camisole beneath, over form-fitting leggings. She'd found an artistic side to balance her considerable business acumen. It was a good look for her.

"Our friendship gave me the chance to see what I'm seeing now," Julie told her. "You've gone from the unhappy but amazing person I met that day, to this obviously happy woman actualizing herself in so many ways." Julie spread out her hands as Madison flushed. "You have this incredible store, you're starting a theater, you're married to a great guy... You won. You give me hope that the Loser trail can lead to this."

As Madison's gaze softened again, Julie told herself to stop drinking. She steered them out of dangerous *Beaches* water by giving Logan a lecherous look. "You know, a little Internet research is a dangerous thing. I've been looking at the polyamory sites. Any chance you're into that?"

"No, he's not," Madison said decisively.

Logan laughed. "If the two of you want to have a girl-girl scene to change my mind, I'll give it fair consideration before I say no."

Julie's phone started to ring. "Let's put a pin in that,"

she said with a snort. She didn't recognize the number, but considering all the contractors, crew and cast communications she was juggling right now, she wasn't going to ignore it. "Hello?"

"Do you like orchids?"

"It depends. Who is this?" But she already knew, because that little tingle went up her spine at his voice. Logan and Madison were doing the intimate newlywed bubble, complete with brushing lips, murmured words and light touches, so Julie rose and moved to the rail.

"Why would who's on the phone change whether or not you like orchids?" he asked.

"It's irrelevant to my like or dislike of flowers. It's what strings are attached to a yes or no answer."

He chuckled. "Cynical. Hey, Julie. This is Des. I assume you know that, though."

"I can neither confirm nor deny. If I confirm, it suggests you made enough of an impression on me that I recognized your voice."

"And if you deny?"

"I only had a clever retort for Option A. For 'deny', I've got nothing."

"Let's focus on confirming then. Come with me to the Daniel Stowe Botanical Garden tomorrow morning. I like walking through the orchid garden in the Conservatory. We can do that, hang out, get a snack at their café. I'd have you back to your theater by noon. Harris said you work there 24/7, so I figure morning's as good as any other time."

"I have an internal leak. I'll have to plug that."

"Go easy on him. I overcame his resistance with carrot sticks."

Julie leaned against a post. She had a lot to do, but tomorrow's schedule wasn't dependent on anyone but herself, so she could work into the evening hours. Madison had been admonishing her to take a day off every once in a while. "I'll meet you there. That way if I do have to get back sooner than later, I won't cut your trip short. Okay?"

"I promise I'm not a serial killer."

"How disappointing. I've always wanted to meet one. From a safe distance, of course, and the public area of a garden would qualify."

"If I find one willing to come with me tomorrow, I'll bring him along. So that's a yes, then?"

Julie waffled, then chided herself for being a coward. "Okay, but only if you understand it means nothing. I'm really not into relationships anymore."

"That's interesting. I'll look forward to hearing why. Eight o'clock too early?"

"I'll be there."

She clicked off and turned to face her friends. "Des," she said in response to Madison's quizzical expression. "He wants me to meet him at a place called Daniel Stowe Gardens tomorrow."

"Oh, that's a nice spot. You made an impression."

Julie saw her friend's mind turning with possibilities and shook her head. "He knows I'm learning about the BDSM stuff. He offered to give me more information on the rope end of things. I guess he figures it's a good setting to talk about it."

"That was either a poorly executed lie or a badly thought out rationalization."

"I'll let you decide. But...um, while I'm on the subject, I told him I might be interested in letting him do some rope stuff on me. Purely to increase my understanding of the dynamics we'll be bringing to life on stage. I can trust him for that, right? No caveats?"

Madison straightened, her speculation going to full wattage, but it was Logan's instantly sharpened gaze that caught Julie's attention in a heartbeat. Yep, he and Marcus were right there together in uber-Dom land. Julie told herself she was not going to fidget like some school kid under a taskmaster's hawk-like scrutiny. And didn't that thought just spur the fantasy train about Madison's husband to full throttle?

But that was the interesting thing. She had a rich fantasy library on Marcus, and could add volumes with someone like Logan, but it was Des who'd been the first to make her want to cross the reality threshold. She didn't think it was because he was less overwhelming in that role or more manageable. She felt safe and not safe with him, both in the right ways. It was like finding a kid on the playground with whom you clicked for reasons you couldn't explain. Past life regression worked as well as any other idea. She and Des must have been BFFs in a foxhole in WWII together, or some such nonsense.

"Yes. You can trust him," Logan said, relieving her by not asking her anything she might not be able to rationalize without stammering. "We call him Spiderman because he has a relationship with rope like a spider does its web. Very intuitive, though that intuition has been built through years of practice. And he puts his sub first, always. You'll be totally safe with him. Safe as you want to be."

"Good." Julie ignored that last comment, and the gleam in Logan's eye, because she was sure he knew that last statement had caused a somersault of reaction. Damn Doms.

"Julie." Logan had stilled the swing as if by some kind of marital telepathy, so Madison could reach forward and touch her hand. "I agree with Logan, but when you decide to do this, if you'd feel more comfortable having an unobtrusive third party there, I'd be happy to do it. With a Dom like Des, you might find yourself going pretty deep into yourself. I know what you said, but I'm thinking you're feeling an attraction to him, and..."

"No need for any warnings," Julie said quickly. "I told him I don't do relationships. Remember, the Loser race is over. You got married and I retired from the sport. This is strictly for research. I'm not denying there's a personal component, but it's taking a backseat to the professional. That's the way I want it."

She diverted them onto a new topic. While she was sure she didn't fool them into thinking there was nothing else to talk about there, they were considerate enough to leave it be. The concern in Madison's caring eyes that met and held Julie's for an extra moment, told Julie her friend understood.

All well and good, because the sinking feeling in the pit of her stomach reminded Julie of the common belief she and Madison had shared about their failed relationships. At least until Madison met Logan and left Julie alone with the feeling.

That belief was that the real loser in all her past relationships—and why they'd all failed—was herself.

§

The Daniel Stowe Botanical Garden was in Belmont, another one of the satellite towns that perched on the edges of Charlotte's urban sprawl. Julie enjoyed the pastoral scenery as she drove the rural route to get there. After traversing the winding driveway to the garden's parking area, she parked next to a bed of brightly colored tulips interspersed with other flowers she didn't recognize.

She'd been born with two black thumbs and a lack of passion toward adding to the green world, but she liked flowers and greenery as much as the next person, and possessed a cheerful gratitude toward those who created such places. The flowers edged the walkway up to a large hexagon-shaped building with a cupola on top, both created with lots of sparkling glass.

Des was waiting at the door. Despite the small handfuls of people walking in and out of the building, and all the sights of a new place to see, he stood out to her the second her eyes passed over him. She was struck again by his singularity. Yesterday he hadn't fit her image of a Dom or roofing contractor, yet had conveyed his capabilities in both roles without doubt. Today he didn't fit the manicured entryway, against the backdrop of a building she was sure was a pricey wedding venue. The contrast only enhanced his appeal. A man of mystery, yet one with an open, inviting personality.

He'd seen her and was walking to meet her. His hair fluttered over his shoulders, thick and all the more touchable for having been brushed to a silken sheen. He was wearing a black button-down shirt loose over blue jeans that, unlike yesterday's, weren't faded or stained with his builder's trade. It gave her the pleasing sense he'd dressed up for her. She admitted she'd chosen her outfit with more care, though she refused to assign any significance to it, since for the past few weeks torn jeans and old T-shirts had been her uniform.

When he came closer, she noticed from the rolled-up sleeves that Betty and Marilyn were gone, the temporaries scrubbed clean. She inhaled coffee and French vanilla from the cup he was carrying. That enticing scent would linger on his lips. She'd left her mug in the car, but evidently they each needed a caffeine kick start.

"Good morning," he said.

She could strike up conversations with total strangers on the subway. Success in her business was all about networking, and she'd made plenty of useful contacts due to her social skills. People fascinated her as a general rule, and genuine interest in another human being was a great way to make friends. Des seemed to possess a similar knack, his self-assurance making her curious about how he'd acquired those qualities. When they'd met yesterday, she'd let that curiosity lead her, but now she felt defensive, closed.

She recognized it, and it baffled her, but she didn't seem able to turn it off. His proximity turned it up even higher.

"Good morning." Retrieving the file folder she was carrying under her arm, she waved it before he reached her, like a sword keeping him outside her personal space. "I have a favor to ask before we get started, if you don't mind. It'll only take a minute."

It was a legitimate request, but she'd brought it to reinforce the message that she didn't want this to move too far from a professional relationship. Should she have come at all?

Why did she always second guess herself like this? Every fucking time she found herself edging toward a relationship with a guy, all the confidence she possessed to excel in every other aspect of her life deserted her like rats from a sinking ship.

"Sure," he said, appearing far more casual about it than she felt.

She sidled to his left side, opening the file to let him see. Thank goodness her head was dipped, so when she closed her eyes briefly to inhale his scent, he didn't notice. But he touched her back between her shoulder blades and slid down, a reassuring stroke. Opening her eyes, she glanced up at him. He was looking at her, not the folder, and his brown eyes were thoughtful.

"You okay?" he asked. "You seem a little tense. I promise this will be fun. No stress. Unless you have a flower phobia."

She forced a laugh. "I'm fine. I guess I'm stuck in work mode. These past few weeks have been crazy."

"Okay. Let's take care of it, and then put it away for the next couple hours. All right?"

There it was, that tone of voice, the direct look, a subtle, enticing taking-of-control that put a nervous twitch in her hand. It made the folder shudder like a trapped butterfly. His gaze shifted to it and she forced herself to stillness.

"Yeah, okay." She looked down at the folder contents as if she'd just affably agreed to something far more innocent. His hand remained on her back as he pressed closer to her to share her view. The heat of the full palm contact penetrated her thin, silky blouse, a jewel blue color. She'd kept her hair up in a ponytail, though she'd taken more care with it, arranging short wisps around her face. The thick tail had an abundance of curls that wouldn't turn to frizz until the day gained more humidity, so for now it was looking good. She'd refused to shellac it with hairspray. He might want to touch her hair, bury his fingers in it, tip her head back to put his mouth on her throat...

So much for the pretense that this was an arm's length, friendly exchange of information. For one thing, she was standing well within his arm span.

His fingers played with the end of the ponytail, making her think he was wrapping short curls over his knuckles as she showed him what she'd brought. She'd never let anyone touch her so intimately, so casually, so fast. She needed to tell him to stop, to reinforce what she'd told him on the phone. She hated being one of those women who said one thing but acted just the opposite, whose words were a smokescreen to cover what she really wanted.

Long and short of it, she didn't want to get hurt one more time. She was done with the slide along the rainbow that always dumped her into a pot of ice cold sludge.

That reminder recalled her to sanity. She sidled away from him, breaking the contact, and thrust the folder at him so he had to take it from her. There. If she had to get more direct about it, she would. Hands off. Her mind approved of her self-control even as her skin registered severe annoyance at the loss of his touch.

"I know New York prices. I don't know Charlotte's," she said. "These bids I collected for Madison on other work seem low to me, but would you mind taking a look before I turn them over to her? I don't want to waste her investors' money."

Des slid the small pack he was carrying on his shoulder to the ground and handed her his coffee. He paged through the folder, skimming the data on the thin sheets of yellow and pink paper, tear-offs from estimate pads. She curved both hands around the cup.

He closed the folder, took his coffee back and handed her the paperwork. "All of those are good, with the exception of Bolton. That bid is way over the top. Derrick does great work, but for that price, Jesus *and* Joseph better be your carpenters. It should be about thirty percent cheaper. My guess is he heard your Yankee accent and figured he could squeeze more out of you because he's from Jersey himself. He knows how high prices are there. I'll give him hell for that next time I see him."

"Oh no. Don't you dare deprive me of the pleasure." She wrote down the percentage, tucked the pen into the folder and walked with him back to her car as she spoke. "I've negotiated at Hell's Kitchen flea market. When I'm done, he'll be paying me for the work."

Desmond's eyes warmed in appreciation. "I believe it. Now put the work away. The world can spare you for a couple hours."

"Okay, but if the zombie apocalypse breaks loose by lunchtime, it will be your fault for distracting me."

"I'll accept full responsibility for that. And fight at your side against the undead to the very end."

"What if one of them bites me, turns me into a zombie?"

"I will pick up your parts as they fall off and duct tape them onto your sexy, rotting torso."

She chuckled and put the folder in the car. His teasing helped reduce the uneasy sense that she was giving up her armor before entering a battlefield. Locking the vehicle, she pivoted toward him. "Okay, I'm ready. Let's go look at pretty flowers."

"All right." As they walked companionably side by side toward the entrance again, he cocked a brow at her. "I don't usually use this as a lead-in, but I'm guessing it's why you're so jumpy. You said no relationships. Care to explain that?"

She couldn't claim he was being too personal, since she'd brought up the subject, right? "I know I said that, and I hate it when people bring up something that's an obvious discussion point and then say they don't want to talk about it, but I'd prefer not to go into it. I just don't want to give you the wrong idea about why I'm here today. You're interesting and fun, and I wanted to spend more time with you and learn about the rope part. Is it okay to leave it at that?"

"Absolutely. But I'm going to hold your hand, because you look like you need it."

She should object, but his grip was strong, and she didn't feel caught. She felt like a bird who'd been cupped in his very safe palm.

He released her to toss his coffee in the trash and hold open the front door. Inside the lobby, he approached a large horseshoe reception desk and handed the lady a ticket he must have bought before Julie had arrived. When she offered to pay her fair share, he shook his head. "I have a season pass here, and I get guest tickets at a discount. I'll treat."

"I'll buy lunch."

"No need. I rarely have a date outside a rope session, so paying your way gives me the chance to feel manly. Come on. There's so much beautiful stuff here, you'll fit right in."

He bumped her body at the compliment, a gentle flirtation. He was trying to help her relax. She was impressed by his non-pushy intuition, and annoyed at herself for being in need of it. It really had been a while since she'd tread in these waters, and she hadn't expected to be so weighed down by the millstones of the past. She could call this not a date all she wanted. They both knew what it was. The heated energy between their two bodies, the sure clasp of his hand on hers, and the little dance inside her when he implied she was beautiful, were all proof of it.

He'd also caught her attention with the rare date comment. Another common ground for them, though she wondered what his reasons were for not dating, when he was so wonderfully, despicably good at it.

"How about before we go to the orchid area, I show you around the park some? I assume you haven't been here before. It's also probably smart to scope the terrain so when those zombies come, we'll know the best defendable ground."

"A man who plans for the worst. I appreciate that." Her hand involuntarily—so she told herself—tightened on his and he gave her that smile that made her feel like she'd be okay with him. He was going to be kind.

Kindness had become the quality she valued most in a relationship, one that was far too rare. Though she was well aware of the conflict in her nature that craved a passion that wasn't always kind, that would be edgy and demanding, she knew wanting both was like pissing in the wind. When the choice had to be made, kind was the better option. She'd learned that lesson.

For the next hour, he gave her an unhurried tour of the outdoor garden areas that he seemed to enjoy as much as she did, despite his familiarity with them. The Canal Garden was a long, rectangular koi pond with a fountain display where sparkling arches of water ran all the way along its length. The Lost Hollow, the children's garden, enchanted her. It included what Des dubbed the Troll Cave, a stone hollow underneath a wooden bridge with square rock seats where the kids could sit and enjoy the coolness. With a little stooping, it worked for adults, too, so she sat with him under there. Des amused her by singing high note choruses from Air Supply songs to demonstrate the acoustics.

They visited the Serpentine and Ribbon Gardens, then

looped back to the White Garden, a sheltered courtyard decorated with beds of white flowers. Tall, slender-stemmed dancing flowers, thick ground covers and medium-sized clusters were interspersed with the variegated greenery.

Throughout his tour, they talked about different topics. Initially about their surroundings, then what gardens she'd visited up in the New York area, and the tomato plants she'd attempted to grow on her tiny window balcony in New York. If she hadn't forgotten to water them, and the cat upstairs hadn't discovered them and used them for a litter box while she was caught up in her long theater hours, she was sure the poor things could have supplied the metropolis with tomatoes.

He asked her about hobbies and she confirmed the theater was her main passion. She found out he didn't watch much TV and preferred music, which launched a discussion of favorite songs, bands and music periods.

During all that, he kept holding her hand. He'd drop it periodically to illustrate a point, or change hands as they shifted around one another on the garden paths, but inevitably, their bodies would bump and the hands would relink. She began to wonder if it was him doing it, or both of them, because it seemed so natural to let her hand find his and their fingers intertwine. As he spoke to her, he kept leaning in, brushing her shoulder and body with his hip, a casual intimacy that heightened her awareness of his proximity in an unsettling way, while simultaneously making her more comfortable with his touch.

It was when they were in the White Garden, surrounded by the lacy purity of those flowers, that she realized she was reclaiming her sense of herself. She was also feeling lighter, no longer carrying around the past relationship worries she'd had in the parking lot.

"So how old are you?" she asked. "You look like you're twenty-five, but you're more mature than any twenty-five year old I've ever met."

"I'm old enough to drink, though I don't."

"Does that have to do with why you check your blood sugar? I assumed you have Type II diabetes."

"Type I, but yeah. Most diabetics can drink, at least in moderation. I'm just not one of them." He sat down on one of the benches and looked up at her. "But I don't really like to talk about that. Not just for the sake of curiosity."

"Oh." That stung a little, but since he said it so matter-of-factly, she told herself not to take it as a personal jab. She was surprised to hear he was Type I, but it explained why he didn't fit the expected profile for a Type II diabetic. She wanted to respect his feelings, but she hoped he'd let her have one follow up. "Is it okay if I ask why you feel that way?"

"Sure." His casual shrug relaxed her again. "I was diagnosed at six years old, after a near fatal case of DKA. Diabetic ketoacidosis," he added. "It wasn't the only health problem I had, so a lot of other shit went along with that. For too long I wasn't a person. I was symptoms and medications and what did I eat today, and have you tested your blood sugar, and endless lectures. 'Des, experimenting with drugs or alcohol could kill you.' And they didn't mean it like you say it to normal kids. It was: 'A couple drinks or try that pill, and kaput. End of you.' Blah blah blah."

He shook his head. "I didn't ever care about being in the drug scene or getting drunk, but the endless hyperawareness was like being a specimen in a jar, no matter where I was or who I was with."

"Wow." She sat down next to him. "That would suck for anyone, but especially for a kid. I get it. I'd never want to talk about that again. I'm surprised you don't carry a sign that says, 'You can ask me about my diabetes if I can twist off your left nipple.'"

He laughed. "I hadn't thought of that. I'll get a few T-shirts made up." He considered her, then he shifted to lift the tail of his black shirt. On his belt he had a wallet holding something that looked like a pager. However, a tube, thin as pencil lead, was connected to it, the other end inserted into his abdomen several inches above his belt. The tube was held in place by a round piece of adhesive tape. Despite her curiosity about the set-up, she couldn't help noticing he had a very well-defined abdomen.

"When you want to touch me"—his gaze met hers— "I

didn't want this to startle you. It's an insulin pump." He tapped the pager-looking device. "You don't have to worry about dislodging the cannula just by bumping it. The cannula's the tube part. The adhesive over the injection site is so strong I have to have prescription wipes to remove it."

He was suggesting he anticipated her touching him, something she rather anticipated herself, despite any pointless admonitions to the contrary. She wanted to trace the muscles of his abdomen now, brush her fingertips over the arrow of silky hair between them.

"So you can shower in it and everything?"

"Shower, sweat like a roofer. It's not moving." He flashed her a smile. "Though I sometimes remove the pump when I do roof work because I burn through so many calories I don't have to worry about insulin. I can use other pieces of tape to hold the connector to my body, unless it's a day when I'm moving the injection site, and then I just remove it all together and check my numbers more often."

He'd made the decision to tell her, but she could tell he was ready to move on, so she glanced up at him through her lashes. "If I asked to touch it as an excuse to fondle those awesome abs of yours, would you be okay with that?"

"Well, I told you about it because I wanted to avoid a clinical discussion during a passionate moment. It sounds like you're right on board with my unsubtle plan to get you to touch me as much as possible."

His tone was teasing, but mild, as if he anticipated her flipping back to gun-shy again. She was sure he could feel the chemistry between them as strongly as she could. The only way that chemistry wasn't going to trigger something between them was if she bolted.

The look in his eyes as his attention dropped to her mouth and slid down over her torso to her hands wasn't conducive to that move, because his expression was no longer kind. He'd mixed his gentle tone with the gleaming edge she craved, and she was losing ground fast.

Her clever wit deserted her and, when his hand closed over hers, she was tense. He didn't pull her hand toward him. Instead, he shifted his grip to her wrist, holding her as his fingers slid over her pulse, stroked her forearm. She kept her gaze on his throat as he brought his other hand to her face, caressing her cheek. His thumb moved over her lips to her chin, exploring her. She closed her eyes, absorbing his touch.

The breeze wafted through the courtyard, the sun a mild heat on a partially cloudy day. The flowers offered a mixed musk of light fragrance, deep earth, nourishing fertilizer.

At last he drew her hand to him, sliding it up under his shirt. She touched the tube and round adhesive lightly, his grip still guiding her, and then she caressed his abdomen on her own as his hand loosened and he let her do as she wished. He returned to his absorption with her face, fingertips gliding over her cheekbone, back down over her lips, around the back of her neck to thread through her ponytail as she dipped her head, brushing her ear and cheek against his hand.

His abdomen was muscular, but not so overly pumped that it was more rock than flesh. He was a manual laborer, and she liked the way that translated into layers of muscle and warm skin. She pressed her fingertips into it like she would firm, damp clay. As she did that, she also felt small hard lumps beneath the skin.

"Scar tissue," he told her, as her fingers quested. "Over time, the pump causes that. They don't hurt."

His grip returned to her wrist, and he drew her touch away from him, holding their fingers loosely linked on his knee. She opened her eyes, and he glanced toward the entrance to the garden, a subtle pointing. A group of chatting Red Hat ladies were wandering into the White Garden.

"Thirsty?" Des asked as she took in the delightful array of purple and red hat designs, embellished with velvet, feathers and sparkling brooches. "We could grab a drink from the café before we walk over to the Conservatory."

"That sounds great."

They rose and he escorted her through the main lobby to the café to get them both a drink, her a soda and him a flavored water. Finding an outdoor table with a peaceful overview of the Four Seasons garden, they settled in. They sat across from one another, and Des slid his long legs out so his calves bracketed one of hers, rubbing companionably against it.

She locked her fingers around her soda. Neither of them had said a word about what they'd just done, what it meant. He seemed as comfortable now as he'd been before they'd entered the White Garden. She didn't want to be the idiot who had to put a label on it, dress it up, make it anything beyond...feeling. Words ruined things. It had felt sexy, stirring, comforting. Time had stopped and things had balanced, while all the right things somersaulted and tilted. Maybe this was all part of him acclimating her to a future rope session together. That would make sense, right? No need to make more of it than that.

"You know," she said. "You've totally ruined my chance to talk about my traumatic adolescent experiences. Training bra woes, dealing with the cattiness of Paula Winfield and her letter girl squad. Pimples. All that sounds so trivial compared to facing death at six years old."

His eyes sparkled. He had thick, dark lashes, and his eyebrows were ebony thickets she wanted to trace and smooth. "You're right, it was selfish of me to bring it up," he said. "But you can still tell me. I'll make sympathetic noises. And if you and the letter girls had a fight in the locker room where everyone was half naked, I will listen very attentively. So what was wrong with Paula? Was she too pretty?"

"It wasn't that. It was what was under the melts-in-your-mouth, not-your-hand, candy coating. That wasn't pretty at all. "

Des took a sip of his water and nudged a Ziploc bag of snack mix he'd pulled out of his pack toward her. It appeared to be a combination of pretzels, cereal and nuts.

"I've never heard a woman compared to a peanut M&M."

"Women are plain M&M's." She took a handful of the mix. "Men are peanut ones. For obvious reasons. Did you make this, too?"

"Yeah. It's pretty easy." He crossed his arms on the table, leaning forward, his lips quirked at her M&M observation, she was sure. She realized she was in a similar position toward him, creating an intimate triangle of body language.

She drew back and cleared her throat. "All right, I promise I'm not obsessing about work, but I'm too curious not to ask some questions about the Dom thing. Is that okay?"

He cocked his head, his lips unsmiling and eyes intent upon her, capable of waking up every part of her body. She wasn't usually this easy of a mark. He was a roofer who dressed like a homeless surfer, and, and, and...

"It's okay to ask." He interrupted her internal redundant babbling, thank God.

"From the stuff I've read, each Dom and sub seem to have a sense of who they are, deeper layers of meaning. The more I understand those layers, the better scenes I can help create. So tell me what kind of Dom you are. "

Unfolding an arm, he slid his fingers through her ponytail again, bringing it forward over her shoulder. He had an obvious liking for her hair, and she had a vision of him wrapping his hands in it, pulling hard as he pushed her down to all fours and...

Seriously? Julie, rein it in.

"I'm hearing your professional interest," he said. "How about the personal one?"

"I meant what I said about having relationships, or talking about mine." She stiffened when she detected a mild flash of impatience in his expression, gone in a blink. She couldn't blame him for feeling that way, which just irritated her with herself. "I know that's stupid, after what we did a few minutes ago, but...is the way you're acting toward me just to make me comfortable with the rope stuff?"

"You're interested, I'm interested. If you were really as relationship-shy as you claim, you wouldn't be here," he said, not answering her question. He wasn't helping her bullshit herself. She didn't want him stepping inside the boundaries of her personal dysfunction, so she bristled.

"I don't need to be told what I am or am not."

"Am I wrong, New York?" He tapped her hand, a reproof and caress at once.

He wasn't. She sighed. "I'm okay with flirting, but you're kind of intense, Des. It's easier for me to wade in the shallows on the rope stuff, but it feels like you want to go deep sea diving. I don't want to make a fool of myself over someone, and I don't play the games well."

He touched her face before she could close down entirely. "Let's go with straight honesty, then. I'd prefer you be interested in the Dom/sub stuff for yourself, first. Because you interest me that way. And it works better that way, however you use the information."

Well, that was direct and reasonable. The sliding touch of his hand on her face was something she wanted to follow. She wanted to reach out and thread her fingers through the strands of dark hair on his shoulder. She shivered, drew back.

"You've said your main relationship outlet happens in the BDSM world. I like the sub angle, but I haven't really explored it much. It may end up being purely academic for me. I don't know about what kind of Dom you are. We may be entirely incompatible..."

"A lot of maybes, and only a couple ways to answer those questions, love. There's a fine line between staying away from the games and drawing a complete map that leaves no room to explore." He curved his hand over her shoulder, thumb pressing into her collar bone in a distracting way. "Breathe for me. The nice thing about Dom and sub interaction is you can negotiate the lines and boundaries with no censure on either side. I may be intense when I want something, but I'm not pushy and I'm not going to ever make you feel like crap because you want to move at your own pace and define your own finish line. All right?"

She believed him. It was part of his dangerous appeal. She knew the bulk of this unpleasant feeling was coming from her own worries.

"Why don't I just answer the question?" he suggested. "For you, not the theater manager."

"I've forgotten what the question was," she said.

He smiled. "About what kind of Dom I am. I'll answer the question in the Conservatory. How about some more snack mix?"

"Why not?" She rolled her eyes and scooped up another handful. She'd noticed everything he made seemed to be both healthy and tasty, even his PB&J sandwich. Another eerily wonderful thing about him. Maybe he was an alien.

"So do you know why I asked you to meet me here, instead of at the theater?" he asked, turning them to a different subject. She latched onto it gratefully.

"Because you wanted to win points by inviting a woman somewhere she'd enjoy, instead of to a monster truck rally or gun show?"

"You strike me as the type of woman who'd enjoy a gun show. But there wasn't one in town this weekend."

"Damn. I wanted to add to my assault rifle arsenal." She sighed. "Another weekend maybe."

"See? You're already contemplating another date with me. Progress." He rose. "I'll answer both questions in the Conservatory."

§

It was a short, sunlit stroll to the glass building where the orchids were. As he opened the door for her, the moist, close air enveloped her skin, the smell of growing things saturating the senses.

"Oh, look at all the different shapes and colors." Moving along the concrete path, she stopped to gaze at orchids in shades of orange, purple, pink, red, white, magenta...countless colors. They weren't planted like daisies in a field that grew thick together and formed a carpet. They were spaced to display their assets in a jungle-like environment, surrounded by rock formations and water fountains. They looked like jewels in carefully designed settings, so the delicate twists and shapes of the petals could be examined from all angles. Some grew out of tree trunks. Others twined like vines over branches. Still others grew on their own stems, nodding from the wind generated by the fans mounted throughout the building.

"So why do you come here?" she asked. "What do you like about it, beyond the obvious that it's amazing?"

He'd stopped before a trio of white orchids. As he shifted his weight to one hip, he drew her over. "Notice the shape of the petals. When I look at them, I imagine transforming the female form into the same shapes, using rope. I get a lot of ideas from gardens, particularly orchids."

She shifted her gaze to the white orchid in the middle. He traced the air before it. "Imagine that's her thigh, lifted, bound to her ankle. Her back arched, arms behind her so her breasts form this curve here... I'd suspend her, but I'd also twist a rope beneath her, so it would become the stem of the flower and anchor her."

As he described it, she could see it. "Why does it give you such a charge? It's not just about tying a woman up so you can do whatever you want to her, or is it?"

He gave her a quick, very male smirk. "That's a very important perk. But yes, there are other reasons. I explore a lot of rope disciplines, and one of my personal favorites is *semenawa*, torture rope. Not as scary as it sounds. It's about contrasting stimuli."

They moved in front of another display, this one of lavender orchids grouped around a stone pool with a trickling fountain. He shifted behind her. "Pull all your hair over your right shoulder."

He could say things in a manner that wasn't saying them at all, as much as commanding them. What made it so intoxicating was that he pulled it off in such an unexpected moment. As Madison had said, Des didn't appear the commanding sort...at first glance. Yet he could compel a woman's attention with his unwavering gaze, the set of his jaw and an energy that emitted from him even when he was saying nothing at all. Some people were a fulcrum around which people unconsciously kept their radar attuned. When he was in this mode, he was one of those fulcrums.

"The other right shoulder." His voice held heat with humor, acknowledging the reason for her distraction. When he shifted closer, his breath stirred the fine hairs on her exposed neck. His body didn't touch hers, but a dense aura stroked her, a cushion of magnetism between two closely aligned bodies, the strength of his interest in her, his desire.

Curving his hand over her hip, he put his lips over the pounding pulse in her throat. A small breath escaped her, a shudder swaying her into a light brush against him. He moved in, and his lips parted, tongue teasing her.

"See how the top part of the orchid is slightly twisted?"

She nodded, her eyes fixed on it. His grip left her hip and cupped her hand, her knuckles nested in his palm. His thumb came over them to press into the flesh at the base of her fingers while his other fingers constricted, capturing her hand fully. Slowly, as his mouth stimulated a thousand nerve endings in her throat, he began to turn her wrist. Not a lot, but his hold and the angle made her gradually aware of pressure and his strength, discomfort edging toward pain. Just when she thought she was going to have to ask him to stop, he did, holding her hand at that unnerving stress point.

His lips created a lot of mad swirling between her chest and the folds of her sex. His inflexible restraint on her hand sent a bolt straight to her core just as powerful. The mix of sexual stimuli had her reaching for his hand on her other hip to steady her, even as things became far less steady.

"Imagine I can tie you in the shape of that flower," he said, lifting his mouth a fraction from her skin. "I can. You'll struggle between pain and ecstasy, and I'll use both to break you into a world of your mind you can't imagine, where every reaction you have belongs to me. I have full command of your senses, your body. You're not even sure if your soul belongs to you anymore. You're stretched to your physical limits, but you're aroused, too, not wanting the tension to end."

He turned her around to face him, though his hands remained on her hips, holding her. "You asked what kind of Dom I am. Spanking's not my thing, or putting a woman in a collar."

"Oh."

He rubbed his jaw against her cheek, his eyes close to her face. "You're sounding disappointed," he teased her in a husky voice.

She pushed half-heartedly at him and he drew back,

taking her hand once more, continuing their stroll. Julie wondered if she was as flushed on the outside as she felt on the inside. "Running a theater, bringing a production together, that's your thing, right?" he asked.

"Yeah. Yes."

He stopped, showing her a tiny cluster of orange orchids, none bigger than her thumb. "The mice of the orchid world," he observed before continuing. "You understand theater in and out. It's your passion, your heart. It's become your bible, in the sense that you can use it to center yourself, to interpret all sorts of things in your life. Rope is my passion for the same reasons."

He touched her neck, brown eyes turning rust and gold from the sunlight coming through the glass ceiling. "I can tie you up in ways that will leave marks on your skin for days. I can put you in a harness that keeps your hands and arms free, that you can wear under your clothes, but while you have it on, you'll feel completely restrained, captured. I can make it real clear I'm in control. When you're in my ropes, with a little twitch or tug, I can take you to orgasm. Or I can make you feel the burn, the pain. You'll be begging for forgiveness the way you would in a spanking...all while being wet and hot and wondering if I'll let you go before I fuck you, or if I'll take you while you're bound like that."

When he stroked her mouth, making her lips part, he was reminding her to breathe. She'd stopped.

"Hypothetically speaking, that is," he added, straightening. "I wasn't directing that at you specifically...unless you want me to do so."

Her hands had dropped to his hips as he slid his palms slowly up and down her upper arms. She would have punched him for picking at her, but he wasn't unaffected by her reaction. He was logging and absorbing it. Wanting to drive it, just as he'd described.

"And if I do?" She dared to ask the question.

He shot her a look that stilled her racing thoughts. Everything around them had gone behind a curtain, leaving them center stage.

"Then that opens a whole different dialogue between us," he said.

She started walking again, feeling the need for some space, some sense of control. She wanted to make sure she could walk without his direction. He could take her over so easily. It was terrifying as a drug. "You do really unique small talk," she said as he caught up to her, walked at her side.

"Well, these things keep a conversation lubricated. Only thing worse than a dry fuck is small talk."

She choked on a laugh at the crudity. He took her hand again, squeezed it. "Let's ease back some and I'll tell you stories about the origins of these orchids. The depth of botanical trivia I know will send you into a coma of boredom."

"I did all sorts of menial labor to get a foothold in the theater world. Your flower trivia would be amateur hour."

"Well, since you've given me a challenge..."

He was as good as his word. Not the boredom part of course. He could read the phone book and she'd hang onto every word. But he kept things relaxed and friendly, the intensity of those earlier moments gone like they'd never existed, except they felt imprinted on every inch of her body and her lightly throbbing wrist.

She was still reeling from it, even after they concluded their tour, had soup and a sandwich from the café, and he was walking her back to her car. Stopping by her door, he turned her to face him.

"Did I answer your question about what kind of Dom I am?"

"You did." She wasn't sure if 'thank you' was the appropriate response. She was wondering if he was going to kiss her, like at the end of a normal date. Nothing about this felt normal, and she meant that in the best way.

"You said when we met yesterday you'd be interested in letting me demonstrate my rope technique on you," he reminded her.

"I think you may have just done that. I'm sold. If ever you change your mind about performing, you have a slot. As far as the consulting you offered, if you give me your email, I can send you the specifics on who will be doing what for the show. You'll want to—"

"Stop." Des touched her shoulder. She realized she'd placed a hand on his chest when she'd turned toward him, and was worrying the button of his shirt. He closed his hand over hers, glancing down at it. "Julie, I want to come see you later this week. I want you to experience what I do. I want to see you decorated in my rope. Is that what you want? Yes or no."

"I don't know." She drew her hand away, stepped back. "Yes. Or rather, I'd say yes if I knew it could stay manageable. If it won't be another great experience that will end up crashing and burning."

His gaze softened. "Your honesty is heartbreaking, love. Okay, let's do it this way. It's a session, like you'd experience in a club environment. We'll set ground rules. Helping you understand what will be happening on your stage is the biggest part of it. All right?"

So you're going along with my farce to get your foot in the door. We'll both fake it and pretend it doesn't mean anything, because we both know I can work with that.

Snarling at herself for being a smart ass, she tilted her head in a stiff nod. "Okay. Uh...what should I wear?"

"That will be up to you. If you want to do clothes, wear something that's not loose, like leggings and a sports bra. If you're okay with no clothes, I can incorporate more things into the experience. Like candle wax."

"Got it. Um, anything else?"

"Yeah." He brushed her face with his knuckles. "Bring someone with you, like Madison. It's important to be safe, and it will help you keep the control you need right now. You don't really know me as a rigger and, while I have a good reputation and you're not going to be hurt under my care, you've only got my word on that."

"So it will be rope, maybe some candles, and Madison there. No sex."

"No sex. Not that night. And not just because of Madison's presence." He had his back to the sun, so his eyes were dark. He had a very straight nose, a firm chin. Nice features upon which she tried to focus so she wasn't caught in his deep, rich earth eyes. She should be saying no to this. A big hell no. But she'd suggested it, hadn't she?

"This is your first scene, isn't it?"

She warred with embarrassment, even as she knew it was stupid to feel it. It wasn't like saying she was a virgin. He snapped her attention back to him as he wrapped her hair fully around his hand, used it and the pressure on the base of her neck to bring her closer to him. Her hand fell on his chest again.

"Answer me, Julie," he said quietly.

How did he do that? "Outside of my really vivid imagination, yes. This is my first scene." She pretended she didn't sound breathless.

"That's what I thought. And why I'll save my vast seduction techniques for another night."

She was fairly sure he'd already seduced her in the Conservatory. It sounded like a game of Clue. Mr. Hayes, in the Conservatory, with that intriguing pain-pleasure grip on her hand. It had made her nervous, her knees weak and her whole body stimulated. But he was trying to make her smile now. When she couldn't summon one, he touched her face, his own expression sobering.

"I'll come at six o'clock, day after tomorrow. You have my number, Julie. If you have to cancel, cancel. But I hope you won't. I've enjoyed spending time with you today." He straightened, making a show of surveying the parking lot. "And look. No zombies."

"Yet," she said ominously. "They would attack urban centers and then fan out, right?"

"You are a fascinating, weird woman." Giving her a friendly look, he left her side, headed for a battered green Ford pickup she expected was his. "I look forward to seeing you soon."

55

Chapter Three

For the first production, Julie and the stage manager were doing double duty as co-directors, and Julie already considered Harris a gift from the gods. He was an obese thirty-something with sharp pale blue eyes, a golden beard and silky blond hair he kept in a long tail down his back. He looked like the first mate on a pirate ship. He'd done stage manager work in dinner theater out on the West Coast, and was in a position to volunteer fulltime to help Julie.

Like most of the cast and crew, he was part of the BDSM scene, a submissive who served and lived with two Mistresses, also lovers. Though Julie had yet to meet them, his adoration for Millie and Tiana was obvious.

Over the past few weeks, he'd shared long hours here with Julie, and his eyes had glowed as brightly as hers as they took each step toward turning the building into a playhouse and bringing the production together. He had the marvelous and terrible passion that afflicted all those dedicated to the theater, whether in front of the curtain or behind it.

Madison had recruited theater students from the area community colleges to provide technical skills. On Julie's recommendation, she'd shamelessly used Julie's resume to attract their interest. Whereas actors could look for work through the trade papers, those interested in a career in backstage work had to build themselves from the ground up, not only volunteering in high school and college productions, but doing heavy networking to get experience that might lead to paying jobs. Julie had worked in almost every backstage capacity in her twenty years in theater, including paid work on Broadway and Off-Broadway shows, before deciding to move to community theater work. Working under her would look good on a theater student's resume.

Harris's ability to organize the students freed Julie up to focus on the other million details a managing director had to handle. Like today, when he was at the theater handling some technical direction, while she was signing off on the scene pieces the set design students were finalizing in Logan's barn.

Unfortunately, once she took pictures and measurements for Harris, she was still later than she'd intended to be. Tonight was the night she was supposed to meet Des at the theater, and being late only spun up her nerves further. Rush hour traffic had her pulling back up to the building at 6:20.

Harris was already gone, but he'd received her text to let Des in before he and the others took off, because Des's old truck was out front without Des in it. She'd texted Des as well, filling him in on the delay.

As she walked past the Ford, she glanced in the open bed. Tar paper, shingle bundles, several coils of twine. A cut piece of PVC pipe, an empty gas can, a scattering of fresh clumps of dry red clay and dried leaves. A crumpled coffee cup was wedged beneath the shingle bundles. She wondered if he'd tucked it there to throw away later, because except for it and the natural debris, everything in the truck was organized and secured with twine.

The bindings on the shingles seemed more thorough and far more elaborate than she suspected was the norm. Had it been an idle pastime on breaks between jobs, practicing his skills?

She hadn't let herself think about what was going to happen tonight, though it had been in the back of her mind simmering like a witch's cauldron ever since she'd somewhat agreed to it. The parameters he'd set had helped her rationalize away the multiple flares of panic. It was just a session. That was all. It didn't have to be anything outside of that. Inside of it, it could be incredible and intense, as

Madison had warned. Yet when it was over, it was over. No fallout. That was what she wanted. As long as she held onto that, she could fully enjoy the experience.

She hadn't had a second thought about Des being in her theater without anyone else there. Out of all the worries she had about Des, trusting him here wasn't one of them. That feeling was reinforced when she found him sitting on the edge of the stage.

He had his hair pulled back more sleekly tonight, accommodating the jaunty black plaid fedora he wore. He wore a dark blue button down over stonewashed jeans. Several brightly-colored woven bracelets were on his right arm and he had a small knife sheath threaded onto his belt. The untucked shirt crumpled high enough up on his hip in his seated position to see it, and the curve of his ass pressed to her stage. His biceps rippled in an appealing manner as he sipped from a bottle of his preferred flavored water, black cherry. When her footsteps made him twist around to find her with his russet eyes, he smiled.

He could lasso a woman with that smile as easily as with any rope he could call to hand. It was the real deal, a gift of the gods. Not artificial charm, not the luster of the sun reflected off a fortunate surface, but the sun itself, a limitless energy source.

If she was composing flowery narrative, she was in trouble. He screwed the top back on the bottle and set it to the side as she crossed the stage. The curtains were drawn, leaving a several foot wide apron of the stage visible. A ghostlight was on to illuminate the theater area. In theater lore, it was kept burning throughout the night for friendly spirits. It also kept unfriendly ones away, supposedly. She mused it must be working, since all she saw was Des.

"Hey there. What are you doing?" She took a seat next to him. It felt natural to sit close enough to brush his shoulder, particularly when he flipped open the cooler next to him and twisted the top off an Angry Orchard to hand it to her. It was crisp apple flavor, her leisure time drink of choice. He'd talked to Madison.

"Listening." He leaned back on both palms, his side touching hers. He smelled like heat, tar, smoke, wind. "You must do this all the time. Sit and listen to it."

"I do." Though she was surprised he guessed that. When Julie had arrived, she'd given up her room at the Extended Stay as soon as she'd set up a cot in the dressing room. Madison had already achieved so much, but Julie would require some insanely long hours to get the theater, staff and first performance, already being promoted, ready on time.

That was just an excuse, though. She liked exploring the silent building in the middle of the night, imagining the performances that would happen here, the responses of the audience.

"What do you hear?" he asked.

"All of it. Every performance, the characters laughing, crying, talking. The audience responding. The thumps as they rush across the stage. The audience gasping." She gestured, sweeping her arms wide. "And I won't have to imagine it much longer. Once we start doing performances, the theater stores it away. Then you can hear all that even more clearly in the silence. I think it's the way a theater breathes."

Initially, Madison had hoped to start the theater in the building she'd used for her earlier benefit, but the cost and city regulations were too prohibitive. The rural zoning had been essential, since permitting for an erotic theater might have met greater opposition in the city limits. It might have even in the county, but Logan's personal friendship with two of the county commissioners had helped, as he'd been able to assure them this would be avant-garde theater, not a sleazy strip club that attracted criminal elements.

One of the donors had offered Madison a great lease-to-own deal on a long-vacant tax write-off property outside Matthews. The picturesque town where Madison ran Naughty Bits butted up against the edge of Charlotte.

Inhaling the energy of this building, an infant theater about to be born, Julie knew this was where it had meant to be all the time.

She took a thoughtful sip of her cider. "You're like a character come to life yourself. Far too colorful to be real."

"Most people are colorful, if you shine the right light on

them." He studied the darkened rows of seats before them. "I'd like to be a pirate stepping out from the curtains, loud and dangerous." He straightened, puffing out his chest in parody. "I'd pick the most spirited woman out of the audience, tie her to my main mast and bring out all her inner fire."

"That would be great for a scene. Oh..." She drew in a breath, grabbing onto the idea and his arm at the same time. "You come out dressed as a pirate. Your partner, she's in the audience, an aisle seat. When you head in her direction, she tries to run away, but you cut her off, like you're kidnapping her. You toss her over your shoulder, carry her to the stage... While you have her over your shoulder, you could bellow at the man nearest you: 'If you're thinking of rescuing her, mate, my cutlass is far bigger than yours... Wanna see?'"

She made her voice boom, echo off the walls, causing his eyes to widen and a grin cross his face. She knew her gaze was sparkling, filled with the idea, because his reaction seemed as much for that as for her unexpected vocalization.

"Okay, but how do you transition that to the intensity of the rope scene?" he asked. "You don't want that part to be comedy."

"No, definitely. Even the audience part shouldn't be entirely farce. Except for that one joke, you would be serious, romantic, dashing. Very large, powerful and dominant, making every sub's pulse flutter. Or that part of each person that can imagine being a sub, even if we aren't actually that way all the time, or identify as that."

Des pursed his lips. "I could pull off romantic and dashing, but you'd need to pad my shoulders to make 'large' work."

She nudged him. "I've felt your grip. You can pull it off. The pirate bit would inject humor, pageantry, a hint of the sexual excitement to come. Your outfit could be piratical in the audience, but on stage, you strip down to black trousers, returning us to the contemporary, and a more serious note. We could apply some sexy tattoos on you, like your ladies. Do you have any real ones? Can I see?"

The lines alongside his eyes were still creased with amusement at her enthusiasm. "Yes, but I have to take my shirt off to show you."

"How horrible. I'll suffer through it. Off, off, off."

He shook his head. "Don't get pushy with me wench. I'll tie you to my mainmast."

"Is that a hugely optimistic double entendre?"

She shrieked as he reached out and grabbed her thigh above the knee, a ticklish spot. "Remember, this is hypothetical," he warned. "I'm not one of your performers."

"No, but roll with it. I might be able to make it work for another rigger. Seeing you shirtless will help the creative process."

He snorted but complied with her hopeful request. He took off the hat and playfully put it on her own head. As she adjusted it to a cocky angle and gave him an expectant look, he removed the shirt. He did it in a functional way, telling her he was neither overly proud of his physique nor self-conscious about it. Slipping several buttons of the garment, he pulled the whole thing over his head rather than unbuttoning it all the way, and put it down next to him.

He was lean and hard all over, as her glimpse of his abdomen at the garden had suggested. He wasn't wearing the insulin pump or cannula tonight. It must be a day he was changing out the injection site. She saw some nicks and scars on his torso, probably the result of his very physical job. The light mat of dark hair on his chest funneled to that silky arrow of hair she still wanted to touch. To prevent herself from being too forward, she focused on the reason she'd asked him to remove his shirt.

A tattoo of a black dragon coiled around his biceps. It started as a spiral of rope and became a serpentine version of the mythical creature. The other arm had a black inked rope wrapped around his biceps, intertwined with a vine of thorns.

"One more on my back." He twisted around to show her the design, a sunburst between his shoulder blades in blazing colors of orange, gold and red, the orb outlined in another twist of rope.

"I'm sensing a theme," she observed.

"Yeah, rope's kind of my thing."

She reached out to the dragon on his biceps. It was lovely work, but it was merely an excuse to touch him. He was incredibly resilient, his muscles even at rest as evident as an anatomical drawing. She wanted to explore that terrain further, but when his gaze dropped to the contact, she withdrew.

"I'm sorry. If you're a Dom, and I'm here to see how a session works, I guess I should have asked you if it was okay to touch you first."

"Not a problem for me. You touch what you want to touch, love. When I want you to keep your hands to yourself, that's what my rope is for." He tilted his head to watch her trail her fingertips over the length of the dragon's tail. "You've an easy way about you, earthy. Did you get that from your family?"

She'd been nervous about tonight, but his lack of urgency about getting to anything fast helped to relax her. She suspected he was doing it intentionally. She probably wasn't the first nervous sub he'd had to help calm down. The realization didn't thrill her, since she wanted to think of herself as unique, an entirely unrealistic expectation. She squelched the negative reaction.

"Most people down here think I'm too direct and brassy, too New York. And God, no. My family...they're Upper East Side, old money. Well, my father is. All of them polished and contained, clear markers. No personality ooze overflow. Don't get me wrong. I love them and they're family. I'd go after anyone who hurt them with a tank, but...you know how Mowgli was raised by wolves?"

"*The Jungle Book*? I thought it was Baloo and Bagheera that raised him?"

"You get serious points for remembering their names, but it was wolves that found and raised him. Bagheera and Baloo were his friends. I'm not sure if that was the book or the Disney movie, or a little bit of both. It's been a while." She ignored the amused sparkle in his eye. "Anyhow, back to my point. Humans and wolves are both predators. They think in a lot of the same ways, so Mowgli wasn't a bad fit for them."

She sighed. "My family and me, it's more like they're rabbits, all snug in the same warren, and I'm a turtle with fin feet. Can you imagine anything more different? Turtles are happy swimming along in our shells, our home on our backs. We're not trying to be cute or fuzzy. Our shell is shiny when it's wet and we're kind of wrinkly, but there's something so damn cool and unclassifiable about us. Just don't turn us over, because it ruins everything."

His brow creased. "Are you babbling?"

"Yeah, a little. It's the manly chest, the lack of recent sex, and I'm nervous about what we're going to do tonight."

He removed the hat from her head, stroking a tendril of hair away from her cheek, an oddly tender gesture. "I'm flattered by the chest comment. I don't get that too often. When's Madison getting here?"

"I decided against that."

His expression shifted into disapproval, the first time he'd looked less than affable. It made things tighten in her belly, adding to her reaction to his bare upper torso, and that was doing a good job at unsettling her all on its own. She figured he didn't get the compliment that often because he didn't take his shirt off much in mixed company. From what she was looking at, manly covered it. Who knew he'd have such distracting shoulders and pecs?

"It's not just about you trusting me, Julie. It's about safety."

"I know that. I'm not an idiot." She made a face. "I checked with Logan and he vouched for you 100%. If you make a liar out of him, he'll remove one of your lungs with a garden spade. Right?"

When he continued to give her that look, she shook her head. "I really would rather get into the moment and feel it as a sub would feel it. I don't want an audience making me self-conscious about that. I just want to feel. I trust you to stop if I say stop, or change anything that scares me or makes me uncomfortable. Am I wrong about that?"

"Not at all. But you should never just take the word of some bastard you don't really know on that."

That was the problem, wasn't it? She felt like she did

know him. But at least it appeared he'd decided to accept her judgment. He stood, giving her a hand up to face him on the stage. He captured her other hand, too, closing the connection between them. His gaze slid over her tunic top, belted over a mid-length skirt. "Did you bring an outfit like I described, leggings and sports bra?"

She shifted her gaze to his throat. Her shyness was silly, she knew, but it didn't change it. "I want you to be able to do the candle thing you mentioned. So I figured I'd just undress. On one condition. That you leave your shirt off."

His lips curved. "Quid pro quo?"

"Well, if I'm going to be fully without, asking you to leave a shirt off seems reasonable."

"It does. The jeans okay?"

She nodded. His were loose enough at the waist that she saw a hint of hip bone, and when he'd turned to get up, she'd glimpsed the rise of his buttocks, telling her he wasn't wearing underwear. That look would work for her just fine. Especially since the stretch of the denim in the groin area suggested she'd already successfully engaged his attention.

"All right." He touched her chin, drawing her eyes back up to his. "I need to be sure we're on the same page. This isn't a performance. And even if a Dom and sub are doing a session in front of an audience, it's not a magic show. It's real, or it doesn't work."

"I get it. Sometimes even when actors are just rehearsing, they get caught up in the characters. But when the scene is over, it's over."

"Yes. But the best performance happens when you become the character. When this kind of session is done right, the two people involved are open to one another during it. When it ends, something has changed in each of them. It's a gift they can carry, that binds them, even if they're not in a relationship. If a scene is done right, you're completely naked."

"I said I was okay with that. I've been in theater forever. Costume changes sometimes happen barely out of range of the wings."

"I said naked. Not undressed. They're different." His voice was calm, rhythmic like waves, but what was beneath it was deep enough to pull her under in tropical, wet waters.

Though her knees were quivering, she used the grip of his hands to counter that. "I told you I want to do this. It feels like you're trying to scare me out of it."

"No. I just want you to understand what it is and isn't. I can't let you stay detached, Julie." He increased his hold on her. "You have way too much going on beneath the surface for me to deny myself the pleasure of diving in."

Her pulse jumped at the sudden shift in his expression, a glimpse of something hungry. "But you can say stop at any time," he continued. "And if you feel uncomfortable or afraid, you tell me. Okay?"

Yep, she had all the control. Control of a bag of wild cats, all of whom were wanting to tear loose, make her act in inexplicable ways.

Des let go of one hand and picked up his shirt. He kept a firm clasp on her other hand, leading her through the slit in the curtain to the stage beyond it.

He'd prepared for her arrival. A table held neatly coiled figure eights of black rope and a glittering pile of silver carabiner clips. Next to them were a half dozen pale ivory candles and a lighter. A backpack was on the floor, leaning against the table leg.

Several ropes were hanging from the support beams above the stage, with hooks attached to the ends of the lines. Maybe she should have brought Madison. What did she really know about Desmond? What was he going to do with those hooks?

He stopped, perhaps feeling her hesitation. "Anything you want to talk about, we can," he said. "If you change your mind about having someone here, we can do it another night when you can give Madison some advance warning. We can go get a pizza or something."

She swallowed. "No. I think I made the right decision. What I need... I need your help feeling right about it."

At his quizzical expression, she colored. "It's going to sound stupid, but when we were looking at the orchids, you had this way of tapping into what I am... I mean, what I felt. It made it okay. I think I would have let you do anything to me right then."

His jaw muscles flexed, suggesting her bald admission had elicited a primal response, barely held back. She felt it in the strength of his grip on her hand, but he only said, "Okay."

Pressing his shirt in her hands, he tilted his head down so they both looked at the cloth bunched in her grip. "At the end of our session tonight, I'm going to put my shirt on you."

The worn cloth was soft, and she resisted the female urge to lift it to her nose to smell. Hard and strong he was. Broad chested, not so much. She glanced down at her D-cup breasts. "I don't think this is going to fit."

"We'll button what we can. I think the effect will be interesting."

He took the shirt from her, walked it over to the table and left it draped over the pack. Moving to the side stage, he drew back the curtains. As they retracted, he revealed the darkened theater, the empty chairs.

He returned to her, a masculine figure moving through alternating shadows and shafts of light. Any words she'd planned to say dried up. He didn't tell her to be quiet; his expression and body language did.

Turning her to face the front of the stage, he put his hands on her shoulders. "Close your eyes. Feel the theater breathing like you talked about. Imagine there are a few hundred people out there, all silent and waiting, watching. Each of them imagining themselves in either your shoes or mine, or both, bringing their own personal stories to life in a million different ways. We inspire their imaginations, but we're also oblivious to them, because that's the point."

His lips brushed her ear, making her shiver. "There's being a story and telling one, and this is being a story. If the crowd stirs, even just a little, I'll silence them with a look, a raised hand. I won't permit anything to distract you or intrude on your experience. That's part of my job, part of what you can trust me to do."

It had been years since she'd performed on a stage, so it was peculiar to feel a bit of stage fright as he created an imaginary audience watching them.

"Everyone is quiet. Now it's just us."

His captivating voice, too deep for his frame, too compelling for an individual who looked like a roadie and who might be too young for her, held her in place. Through the touch of his hand, the stroke of his voice, he evolved into the Dominant she'd felt on their first meeting and in that unforgettable moment at the orchid garden.

She told herself it was just performance. He possessed that incredible charisma that incited crushes from so many actresses for their leading man, even when he was a total dick outside the role he played onstage. She didn't have that risk of being crushed by reality. They'd set the boundaries. She could be swept up in her own character, enjoy it without losing perspective.

But he'd said he couldn't let her hold herself apart. This wasn't a performance with a review write-up tomorrow. This was intended to be an experience.

He swept his hands down her arms and back up to her shoulders, his fingers caressing her throat. She swayed and he closed the gap between them.

"When I do a scene, my submissive is the center. She's everything."

He removed the barrette from her hair so it spilled over his hands. He combed through the thick locks, tugging harder with each pass, scraping it all together as if he was going to create a ponytail. Only instead he loosened his grip, spread her hair back on her shoulders, then did it all over again, digging into her nape, her scalp, mixing force with the tug. Her eyes had closed again and she was swaying with his motions, a spiral of reaction inside and out.

"I'm going to undress you, Julie," he whispered. "I want you to feel my hands on you, get you used to me touching you, taking control. All right?"

As she'd said, there was little modesty in theater. She didn't see her body as a glowing treasure that had to be hidden until some presto moment where she'd reveal it to an awestruck lover. It was just a body. They were all sizes and shapes, and fit society's definition of beauty at different levels, but in the end, a body was a body.

Everyone had one.

On the other hand, her body had never been unwrapped as if it *was* a treasure. A far different experience from matter-of-factly stripping off outer garb while cast and crew members passed by like orbiting planets.

"When I tell you I'm undressing you, I'm demanding a paradigm shift in your head. Answer me, love."

She moistened her lips. "Yes. Okay."

His fingers curved around her waist, slid around and plucked open the tunic's sash. "Lift your arms."

When she did, he pulled the tunic off of her. He did it slowly, so the silken fabric caressed her skin as he drew it away from her. He didn't remove her bra or skirt yet. He wrapped his fingers over her waist again, fanned them out so they were caressing her ribs, his smallest finger below her waist band and tracing her hip bone. He rubbed her lower back with his thumbs, loosening the muscles there. His chin remained against her pulse, just below her ear, so his breath stroked sensitive nerve endings. She unconsciously tilted her body up toward that stimulation. Her breasts wanted his strong hands cupping and caressing them, and her nipples ached at the thought of him capturing them in his fingertips to pinch and play.

The shift rubbed her backside against him, and he made an approving noise. "I love a naturally sensual sub," he said. "No calculation from the mind, just following your own desires. Move anyway you wish, love. It's like the orchids when the wind or sun touches them. They lift and bend and, even caught on their stems, they can't help straining toward what they want."

He unzipped her skirt, so it slipped to the floor. When he drew back, she suspected he was examining her underwear. She'd chosen black lace for both bra and panties, and the panties were the boy short style. His palm slid over one cheek, rubbing the lace against her flesh, then he slid a finger beneath, drawing the fabric up further to expose the curve.

"Gorgeous ass," he murmured. "When we're done tonight, my rope will be marking it. I'll leave that language printed all over you."

Unclasping the bra, he slid it off her arms. He didn't cup her breasts as she hoped and expected. He took off her underwear so she was naked, and moved to face her.

She wasn't expecting that, him mostly dressed and examining her from head to toe. He'd let her hair drop back on her shoulders, so some of the strands had fallen forward onto her right breast, others spread over or behind her shoulders.

"Put your hands behind your back."

When she did, it straightened her posture and she realized she'd been hunching. His eyes glowed and he cupped one breast, giving it a light stroke. She was trembling.

"Cold, love?"

She shook her head, and he nodded in satisfaction, as if he'd anticipated that answer. "Do you have any old injuries that could affect your joints, your back?"

She shook her head. "Nothing more than the usual aches and pains of middle age."

"Yeah, they catch up with you. I'm going to be gentle with you tonight, but I like to ask. From here forward, you move only as I tell you to move. If you need something you tell me. Yes?"

"Yes."

He left her to go back to the table. In the corner of her eye, she saw him light three pillar candles on the table and pick up a couple coils of rope, a handful of clips. He must have activated a music player, because the opening strains to "Ever After" by Marianas Trench filled the air.

"Like a candlelit dinner without the candlelight."

"Mmm. Hush now. Don't move also means don't speak. Just experience this, love."

She noticed one of the coils of rope was smaller in width than the others. It felt like he used that one first, binding her wrists together but not stopping there. He created an intricate looping between fingers, knuckles and wrist. When he was done, her hands were drawn into balled fists she couldn't open.

"It's different, when you can't use or move your fingers. Every part I immobilize can open another level of consciousness for you, if you let it. You'll be bound but you'll also start to fly."

Moving in front of her, he shook out the thicker rope and looped it over her neck. He didn't rush, but he didn't hesitate, tying the first knots as fluidly as if he was a spider spinning its web. Hence the Spiderman nickname, she assumed.

She was glad he didn't tell her to close her eyes, because she could watch the movement of his hands and arms, the shifts of his body, the concentrated expression. His gaze flicked up to hers periodically, a touch of flame that made her lips part, her body quiver harder and her brain cut loose to drift in a lust-filled haze. She'd expected something dramatic to propel her into this state. She hadn't realized all it required was him taking control, and her feeling the first brush of the rope. With every binding and loop, she was sinking deeper into an edgy, needy bliss.

If it hadn't had that effect, or if he'd allowed her to talk, she might have asked him more about what he was doing. She liked learning the 'hows' from her artists, but she understood the point of his earlier instruction. He wanted her immersed in it, not learning like a student sitting behind a desk.

With every knot he tied, every diamond shape he created between the knots, putting her body from throat to pussy in a net, heat spread through her. His nimble fingers caressed and manipulated her body so it melded with his work.

The high notes in "Ever After" heightened her reactions. On one drawn out note, she felt a spasm between her legs as if the range had plucked at her clit like a guitar string. Before creating the diamond shapes, Des had drawn the double strands of rope between her legs, split them around her labia and pulled that line up between her buttocks. As he created the net, the compression increased, so her bound sex throbbed. She dropped her head back as the lead singer screamed to fight for something. To face the music... Her knees quivered, but Des had her.

He was touching her incidentally, the sides of his hands, his fingertips, his knuckles, brushing her breasts, her nipples, her pussy. The casual stimulation was maddening, all the more because a glance down showed a steel bar of response against his jeans. Those flickers of eye contact between them were more weighted. When she licked her lips, his gaze followed the motion. He slid his fingertips over her hip as he bent and kissed her shoulder.

"You are fucking unforgettable, love. Time to make use of the hooks." He unbound her wrists, but left the hands in their closed state. Moving around her to retrieve one of the lines from the ceiling, he hooked it to the knot between her breasts, then hooked another down at her waist, and a third above her pubis. He left all three suspension lines slack. "Put your arm around my neck for this next part."

She did and he lifted her right leg, bending the knee and securing it so she was standing on one leg. Grasping her arm, he lifted it over her head, attaching it to a loop at the upper part of the rope that he'd secured between her breasts. He restrained the other hand to her upper thigh.

"You're safe, Julie. You can't fall. I have you at four points. When I go to the wall, I'm going to draw the ropes taut, let them lift you off the ground. I need you to completely relax. Just let the ropes take you. Don't fight them."

He reinforced the command with a caress of her hip as he moved away. She focused on doing as he'd commanded and, when the ropes slowly began to tighten, she let her body go limp. The rope holding her leg lifted her first, and she drew the other off the ground as she found herself tilted so she was at a forty-five degree angle to the stage, her hair spilling down toward it because her head was tipped back. That felt a little uncomfortable, because she couldn't figure out if she needed to strain to keep it lifted or let it drop back.

He was back in a blink, his hand cradling her skull as he wrapped rope over her forehead and nape, knotting and weaving them with the lines at her back, shoulders and breasts so that when he tied off the ends to the suspension rope above her breasts, her head was supported, no unbearable strain on her neck.

Yet there was enough discomfort left over to make her

feel...excited. At the orchid garden, he'd told her he liked contrasting stimuli, but he'd proven that was a two-way street.

"That a girl. You're a goddess, love. You feel it, you look it." He put both hands in her hair, fingers stroking again, combing deep, the sensation feathering over her scalp. Twisting her hair in a tight corkscrew, he bound the hair in a wrap of rope. He cupped her chin and loosened but didn't release the other ropes. Easing her head back, keeping tension in the binding on her hair, he knotted it in the back of the breast harness so she was looking at the ceiling lights, the two opposing tensions supporting her head and holding it in place, increasing her sense of helplessness. His hand slid from her jaw to stroke her windpipe.

She was suspended in the air, her head back, one arm lifted above her and knee bent as if she were a fairy who had suddenly decided to turn over and face the sky, fly that way.

Her pussy was wet and her limbs were shuddering, her stomach a mass of hopping frogs. She was spread open, vulnerable, and she realized she was no longer silent. Little sounds were caught in her throat, a pleading noise.

"Still with me, love?"

She nodded.

"I need to hear your voice."

"Yes." She was breathing hard. He stroked her torso, a soothing and stimulating gesture at once. She was suspended at waist height to him and he took advantage of it, curling his fingers around her breasts to knead them in their rope bindings. The pleasure of it had her writhing. Bending, he put his mouth over one, and indulged a long, slow suckle of her nipple. She gasped at the sensation, those pleading noises now unmistakably moans. His fingers slipped down between her open legs to probe, caress and find her slick.

He'd said no sex. At this tilted angle, he would have had to be a lot taller for sex to happen, but his touch was a vivid reminder there were plenty of over the top sexual experiences that didn't involve fucking.

Moving back to the table, he changed the music from

Marianas Trench's now mournful "Porcelain" to "Henny and Gingerale" by Mayer Hawthorne. The twisting, provocative notes, the rocking tone of 'I can't get enough', slid through her like his fingers through her hair. If he kept her his prisoner like this forever, she thought he'd never use a brush, preferring to comb it with his own hands.

She was spinning in romantic imaginings. He'd put her in a fantasy world.

He returned and dropped to his heels, fingers templing on the floor to brace himself a few feet from her. In her peripheral vision, she could see him studying her. She could hear her heart pounding, feel her breath clogging in her throat. She was naked, and spread open. Her arms and hands bound, breasts framed in more rope, a snug but not too tight harness that displayed them. His stillness was a tranquil, arousing, living thing. Even if he'd told her it was okay to talk, she couldn't. She was in the center of his web, which made her think of what he'd said, that his sub was the center—was everything—during his sessions.

He stayed motionless and watching her until the song ended, replaced with Mandy Moore's compelling "Have A Little Faith in Me." How was it that every tune he played had that strong under beat that kept need pumping through her like an answering chorus? She felt alive, wild, tied up, at his mercy, but so vibrant, like the sun. When he rose, bending over her to put his mouth on her throat, she wanted to meet him with eager demand, tangle her tongue with his, bite his bottom lip. He denied her that, her heated, erratic breath a whisper of sound between them.

"Desmond." She felt so incredibly exposed, caught on an edge of euphoria, mixed with panic and unbelievably strong desire. She would come with only a whisper of contact, but she didn't want to leave this state. She wanted to ride the edge between euphoria and tranquility. Her heartbeat vibrated in her throat.

"You're a work of art, love. Let's put the finishing touch on this masterpiece."

Retrieving a clear folded tarp from under the table, he spread it out underneath her. When he brought the taper candles to her and stretched up to position one above her, she noticed he was also carrying small lengths of rope to anchor the tapers to the thicker lines. He positioned one candle over her breasts, one over her abdomen, one over her open legs. Once he had them seated, he lit them with a silver lighter.

"Now we watch, and wait, for each drop to fall..." He stood back as panic fluttered through her, wondering how much it would burn.

The one over her abdomen struck first, the drip a momentary intense heat that melted away into sensation near her navel. Then another fell. Drips from the one over her breasts hit the areola of her right nipple, making her buck in her bindings, just as several fell onto her pubic mound. He grasped one of the suspension lines and slowly began to rock her so he could direct where the drips fell, within an inch forward or back, side to side, the rhythm unexpected.

"Oh..." She couldn't move much, but she made the most of what she had, her body creating friction with the roughness of the rope. The psychological effect was the strongest stimulant of all. She was completely helpless, and yet she felt so safe, as if she could trust him to care for her. Was it the first time she'd ever believed that, with any man who'd interested her as a lover? She thought it was, and it terrified her, the enormity of it, how wonderful this all felt. This was supposed to be just a scene, a way for her to understand her performers. She'd known that for a lie, but she hadn't realized how big of a lie it would end up being.

The smoke from the candles, the smell of the wax, mixed with her own intimate scent. He was stroking her body with his free hand and he bent to press kisses to her upper thighs.

"I brought a vibrator, but that's too damn impersonal. I'm going to use my fingers, love." He doused the candles and dropped to his heels between her legs, his hand on her knee. When he rolled his fingertips lightly over her clit, she jerked, her tissues already engorged. He tapped, stroked back and forth. She began to gasp, then cry out, sounds that increased when he shifted around her to stroke her breasts, play with her nipples. He slid his hand back between her legs to torment her.

"You're dripping, love, you're so excited. I can't tell you what it does to me, seeing your cunt cream like that for me."

"Des..." The urgency was all powerful, too demanding.

"No," he said in a low voice. "I'm not here. This is all about you, love. You're floating on a cloud, about to explode like a star, scattering your light over the universe. I'll feel the beauty of it, but you are far above and beyond me. You're what I worship."

"Ah...God...help..." Her cries went to screams as he stroked her clit and an even stronger response surged through her core.

His words should have seemed ridiculous, fantastic. But with the way he'd tied her, the rolling waves of sensation he sent through her, she did feel disembodied, a celestial body set to go super nova. She was powerful, beautiful, detached and yet connected to all. Because she was helpless to him.

"Are you ready, love?"

She could barely speak, body straining, breath rasping, body on fire, pussy spasming. "Yes. Please, God, Des..."

He rubbed her pussy slow, torturously. "Work yourself against me. Show me how fucking hot you are. How you want to rock my world."

She managed three jerky rotations of her hips, then she exploded like that star he'd described. The climax pulled from her inner thighs, ripped through her cunt and into her womb. Her back bowed up farther and the cry that came from her throat was a sound she didn't recognize. A primal scream, a wail in an unbroken firmament. Before anything had ever been created, this was what was there.

It echoed through the theater and came back to her. She was rocking so hard she should have wrenched something out of joint, but now she understood why he'd tied her so securely. He carried her to paradise and back safely, while taking her to a dangerous edge that could destroy her sanity.

When the orgasm at last ebbed away, everything was too bright. She shut her eyes as he rose and dimmed the ghostlight even more, registering her discomfort. He returned to untie her, supporting her so she had no worry about falling as he freed and carried her away from the tarp. He had a piece of carpet behind the table, a blanket spread out on it. Keeping her in his arms until she was laid out on it, he dropped to one knee beside her.

The sheath at his belt held both a knife and a pair of what looked like medical snips that EMTs carried. He flicked open the knife and left the snips. As she watched, he used the flat blade to scrape the wax off her smooth skin in curled, vanilla scented-petals. He followed the movement with his fingers, soothing chafed skin.

All she had the power to do was breathe and stare at him, watch everything he did. It was as if taking her eyes away would break the spell he'd created between them.

After he removed the wax and set it aside in a small pile, he reached for his shirt and threaded her arms through it, lifting her up enough to get the shirt to lie smooth beneath her. Because of the musculature in his shoulders and arms, the sleeves and back were no problem. However, as she'd predicted, the front was problematic, but it didn't faze Des. He buttoned the shirt up to just below her breasts, so the straining fabric above framed them, her nipples and curves exposed. The tails of the shirt split over the juncture between her thighs, leaving her pussy bare to him as well. "Arms above your head, love."

She was like a noodle, with no strength of her own. She raised her trembling arms, but he helped her take them to the position he wanted. He held them there, his fingers curled over her wrists as he bent and brushed his lips along her throat, the top of her breast. When he lifted his head, she could tell he was enthralled by how the shirt barely contained her ample bosom, framing it in such a provocative way.

Normally she would have made some weak joke about how easy men were in their fascination with breasts, but all she could do was shake beneath the weight of his absorption.

"Keep your hands where I put them."

He released her wrists, leaving her arms above her head. He molded his hands over her curves, then buttoned the buttons of his shirt over them, pulling the fabric together as needed to make it work. It was a tight enough hold to create an additional sense of restraint, one she craved. She wanted to be back in the ropes, wanted that feeling again.

With a savage look of lustful pleasure, he ruined his own shirt, tearing it open with one powerful jerk so her breasts spilled forth with a generous bob of reaction. He bent to put his mouth on her again. Suckling, nipping. Despite his initial roughness, now he was gentle. She was spiraling up again as if she hadn't just climaxed, rolling and lifting under his hands. As he moved his way down her body, the fabric of his shirt slid against her back, cloaking her on one side as he cloaked her on her front. When he put his mouth between her legs, she cried out, the sensitive tissues meeting the stubble on his cheeks and jaw. He rubbed it deliberately against her again and nipped at her clit, dragging his tongue over her labia.

She was lost. He was insatiable, and she had no will to stop him. She wanted to tell him to fuck her, take her, drive into her until there was nothing left, but the fear, the tiniest voice in this raw wilderness, kept her silent. Until he sent her over another peak, a level she didn't think she could reach so fast, so hard, clawing at his bare shoulders, a strangled scream burning her throat

"Enough," she gasped as she came down from that. "Enough. You'll kill me."

"It's never enough, love. Not with a gorgeous spirit like yours."

He straightened and drew her into his arms. When he cradled her on his lap, it was clear how very hard he was. She didn't have the strength to sit up on her own, let alone do anything else, but she wasn't a selfish lover. "If you want me to..."

"Sssh. I'll tell you when I want something from you. Rest. Just rest, love. Let me hold you. This was all to give you your first sub experience. It doesn't need to be anything more than that."

Apparently shattering her universe was more than enough for one night. She closed her eyes, her arms creeping around his back and waist to hold onto him. She tried not to think beyond this moment or resurrect the ludicrous idea she could keep herself detached from this. If she'd had any doubts about her dormant submissive side, he'd just chased them all away. And brought it to full, vibrant life.

She craved surrender. She craved the trust that went with it, this feeling of safety and flying. The feel of being in the arms of a man who knew how to command her heart and soul while cherishing both.

She'd had plenty of loser dates and boyfriends. Yes, they'd hurt her, but she'd recovered, found herself again. Yet she was suddenly, terrifyingly sure she'd met the man capable of breaking her past repair. This was supposed to be a research exercise. Not even a real date.

She was in deep trouble.

Chapter Four

"You know how, when you go to see something like the Grand Canyon, you get this sense of a once-in-a-lifetime experience?" Julie frowned. "You're really grateful for it and everything, but if you look at it from the Grand Canyon's perspective, it probably doesn't see the big deal. It's awesome all the time."

Madison lifted her head from her perusal of a catalog. "Why do adult toy manufacturers put the most hooker-ish looking porn star possible on their packaging?" she asked. "I'm selling these things to women. They want beauty and sensuality, not someone who looks like she just sucked off an entire NFL team. Look at this. Her botoxed lips are stuck in a fish mouth shape."

Julie looked and nodded sagely. "The Grand Canyon's self-introspection and fish-lipped porn stars on vibrator packaging. We should find the overlap. What's that horrible math thing that involves the interlocking circles? Is that trig?"

"You're using a cryptic analogy to avoid talking about what's really bugging you. I'm waiting for you to work your way to the real problem. Maybe they figure men are buying the vibrators for women." Madison continued her musings. "Get your wife this vibrator and she'll turn into a porn star who will want to blow you every hour of the day, except during football."

"She'll do it at half time," Julie suggested. "Which will make you feel awesome, like the Grand Canyon. Or turn your pecker into one of those big rock pilings in the Grand Canyon. See, overlap."

Madison snorted and set aside the catalog. "I want to go shopping. Let's go buy Christmas decorations for the theater."

"It's not Christmas yet. Your theater may flop and be closed by then, and the decorations will make you sad."

"Wow, thanks for the optimism. I want to go to that new year-round Christmas store on Harris Boulevard." Madison offered a plate of scones. "We both need a break. We've been laying out the program, figuring out front-of-house staff, estimating ticket sales against future theater improvements, et cetera, et cetera, for the past three hours. Enough work for a Sunday already. You've been doing nothing but working since you got here. Well, except for that Conservatory date that wasn't a date."

Julie took a scone. "If you keep feeding me like this, I am going to become a very round theater manager."

Madison cocked a brow. "Okay, that time you cut your eyes away from me. You did something with Des other than the orchid date that wasn't a date, didn't you? Did you do the rope session with him?" When Julie refused to say, focused on chewing, Madison hmphed. "Hence the Grand Canyon question. And the type of math you mentioned is the area of union of two intersecting circles. Geometry."

"Do not practice your mathematical wiles on me. Let's ask Troy to come over and model some underwear." Julie looked toward one of the wall displays in Madison's shop. "Ooh, or that harness thing. We could test body oils on him."

"Shale put a halt to any experimentation on Troy. I'm only allowed to do that if she or Logan is present. Spoilsport bitch."

"Which one of them, Logan or Shale?" Julie grinned. "And she only put the kibosh on you. I can say it's a skit idea for the upcoming show."

Troy was Logan's hardware store employee, as well as a submissive for the stunning and intimidating Mistress Shale. Shale and Troy were part of the *Consent* cast, so Julie had had the pleasure of getting to know both of them better, enough to enjoy teasing them in absentia, like now.

Madison's shop was closed today, the front drapes drawn so they weren't disturbed by the sidewalk traffic. One of their reasons for meeting here had been to go over things in the erotica boutique they would be using as props in the upcoming show.

"In your dreams, girl. I'd advise you to keep your greedy paws off Troy's body. I've seen what Shale can do with a whip." Madison sobered, reaching across her glass display counter to touch Julie's hand. "Seriously, what's going on? You look a little miserable. Was Des unkind? Does Logan need to break his legs?"

"No. Far from it. He's amazing. Too much, really." Julie put down her scone.

Madison's friendly openness, the kind expression on her face, were a welcome invitation to open up about the chaos of feelings Julie had been experiencing since what had happened with Des. She hadn't seen him in several days, though it wasn't because he'd dropped her like a hot potato. He'd left her a couple of messages and inquiring texts, gentle leads to give her space but welcome her communications.

She'd responded generally but she guessed she'd done a good job at indicating she needed a little space, because he hadn't pushed. Though she wondered if that was because it didn't matter to him what the sub whose world he'd rocked was doing. She was just one of many subs with whom he'd done scenes. It was stupid of her to resent that, since she'd stated up front that was what she'd intended their session to be. Just a session. But she hadn't expected it to feel...the way it had. World rocking. She hadn't expected to feel this way about *him*.

She hated this insecure side of herself, but Madison was in a position to understand it better than anyone. Julie didn't know if that made things better or worse.

She started with halting sentences before pouring it all out in her usual circular, free flow way that could tie a listener's brain in knots. Fortunately, Madison kept pace with her. Her road with Logan had been zigzag, double-back and upside down, too, though he'd helped her find her way forward again.

Was that something that all Doms had, or just the really good ones? The ability to steady a submissive soul? And did they also always leave that soul so flipped out and feeling out of control once the session was done?

"Yeah, at first," Madison said. "In session, you have this mind-shattering experience. Outside it, you have to wrap your mind around what happened, what it all means, how it will impact your world, and what does this guy really want from me, blah, blah, blah."

"That sums it up," Julie said glumly. "But that's the thing, Madison. It was incredible, it really was, but it happened so fast and so smoothly, I can't tell if it's like a doctor's office. The doctor knows his role, and steps into it with all this authority, and we understand our role as patient. But when we leave, here comes another patient. I don't know if I can handle that this guy can give me this incredible experience, and yet I'm just one of many incredible experiences he hands out like ice cream from the back of a truck on a summer day."

"Have you asked him to clarify?"

"Uh, no. I have no desire to be the woman who says 'Hey, I know we met about a minute ago, but I'm just wondering. That mind shattering orgasmic experience you gave me? Was that headed on the road to permanent commitment, a shared apartment and adopting a dog together, or was it more in the hippie category of a great LSD trip, aka let's do it again when we're both in the mood, sometime, maybe?' I am so done with being the clingy, strangle a commitment out of somebody, kind of girl."

She stood up. "I said I wasn't going to get into any more goddamn, freaking relationships, so why am I thinking about him like this?"

She shook her head, holding up a hand before Madison could answer. "I have a hard enough time with vanilla relationships and not screwing them up. I don't have the strength for this. I should just let it go. I can't become part of his harem."

Madison tapped her fingers on the glass counter. "Okay and fine, if he did take you at your word and it was just a session for him. But what if he's genuinely interested in you?"

The leap in her chest at the idea was far too immediate and schoolgirl crush crazy. "Why would he be?" Julie retorted. "It's far more likely he just wants to encourage me to do more sessions with him, so I can be another fascinating submissive experience. He'd walk away after a few more times, and I'd be blown away by it. Quite literally, with me looking for the pieces for the next five years. But that's not what I'm looking for."

"What are you looking for then?"

"Nothing," Julie said bluntly. "Nothing anymore. Let's go shopping."

§

On Monday, she'd decided she should reinforce her point by oh-so-casually telling Des she'd really enjoyed their time together, but that was all she needed in terms of firsthand experience on rigging. Closure, end of story. Over the weekend, by firmly blocking any memory of his touch, voice, scent or otherwise overwhelmingly masculine attributes, she'd been able to regain perspective, and she knew what she'd told Madison was right. She just had to hold on to that. He wasn't interested in her like that, and she wasn't interested in thinking otherwise.

Okay, yeah, she was, but what had captured her was the first, exciting, wonderful, lighter-than-air feelings that happened with infatuation. She wasn't interested in the soul-sucking crash and burn that always happened afterward. If the cookie was poisoned, say no to the cookie. The two couldn't be separated.

Regardless, there was no time to deal with it today. The lights and sound equipment had arrived, along with a few of the scenery pieces and larger props. The theater was overrun with students setting up the technical elements, as well as carpenters, electricians and a few cast members providing extra hands. Tomorrow the full cast would start doing the run-throughs in the theater with the sound and lighting in place. Prior to this, they'd been meeting at

Harris's house as a temporary rehearsal studio, since his Mistresses had a large basement for both home dungeon and rec room.

Like her, her stage manager was a tornado of energy today. He was making constant updates to his production book, which he maintained on his tablet and file shared with her and the volunteers who would be in charge of light, sound and scenery cues during the performances.

"Hey, Julie." He buzzed her on the radio, since she was in the lobby with the house manager. "We've almost got Pablo's frame set up and Des texted me. He's going to come by shortly to review the rigging stuff with Pablo like you wanted."

"Was Myers able to make it?"

"No, his kid had soccer practice, but he said he and Des could meet one-on-one. He'll take care of the arrangements."

"I love a self-sufficient cast member. Thanks."

Okay, so good then. She'd tell Des her feelings when he arrived, all quick and casual like, and catch two birds with one net. Or let them go, because their wing beats against the inside of her stomach and chest were making her want to fly to pieces. She didn't have time for this shit.

"Honey-chile, you are going like a freight train today. Or like a freight train's chasing you."

The sultry voice, a masculine Lauren Bacall, wreathed her face in a smile. Billie Dee-Lite was a professional drag queen popular in clubs across the Carolinas and in Virginia. He and Logan were friends, so the she-male, as Billie liked to call himself, had agreed to lend his emcee talents to *Consent*. Good transitions were essential to maintaining and transforming the mood between the erotic skits, and Billie would provide that very effectively.

Technically, he didn't have to be here today, but he was in town and had offered to pitch in. To do that, the drag queen was wearing jeans that made the most of his high, taut ass, and a pair of square-heeled boots. The only nod to his profession was his expertly applied makeup and the Moulin Rouge T-shirt he wore with a spray of sequins across it. It was a provocative look, Julie admitted, the makeup and entrenched female movements of Billie's body coupled to the obviously well-developed masculine torso and biceps.

The world of alternative sexuality was filled with fascinating contrasts and contradictions that, on closer inspection, didn't contradict as much as she'd expected. Everything about Billie fit who Billie was. When he'd offered to help with the grunt work, she'd liked him immediately. He could earn over five thousand dollars a night in gigs in other venues, and yet there was nothing diva-ish about this diva, even though she could call up the diva side in a moment. He, Julie corrected herself, though she expected it wouldn't be the first time she made that stumble. She had a feeling it was fine with Billie to call him by either gender, regardless.

"Yeah, freight train is right." Julie blew out a breath. "This is the back stretch, with a million things happening and the 'oh-my-god is this going to work or fail miserably' terror grip."

Billie pursed his full burgundy lips. "I've heard about your rep in Boston, Philly and the Apple, honey-chile. I don't think that's what's got you all spun up. Some troublesome man put a thorn in your ass, didn't he?"

It was an apt description, but before she could indulge or shut down Billie's fishing for gossip, Pablo came through the double doors that led to the auditorium.

Pablo was one of the few cast members Logan hadn't seen perform himself, but Pablo was a member of a reputable South Carolina BDSM group. Logan had spoken to some of his contacts there, who indicated Pablo was a young up-and-comer in the rope scene and they didn't have any significant flags or concerns about him other than his experience level.

Pablo had met Madison at a trade show, since he was in retail himself. He'd been so enthusiastic about helping her out with her theater endeavor, Logan told him to submit a video file. The rigger integrated wax, fire play, role play and modern dance into his offerings. The session had been dramatic and flashy, Pablo possessing a raw energy and impulsiveness that Julie knew would translate well to an audience. The submissive in the file was the one who would be working with him on stage.

Logan saw no flags, either, though he'd advised Julie to have Des go over Pablo's show with the performing rigger. "Rope at that skill level isn't my main area of expertise," Madison's Dom had told her. "I'm not seeing anything that says he shouldn't be in the show, but Des can point out any safety issues that might need to be tweaked up."

When she thought about the audition tape now, she compared it to her one experience with Des. She suspected Des would find all of Pablo's flash a distraction, but as Des had said, performance wasn't his focus—his submissive was.

Julie had felt firsthand the pleasure of that singular attention. But she had to think like an artistic director for *Consent* and Pablo's offering would contribute the right mix. She and Madison wanted to cross the reality of the BDSM world with the fantasy, without straying so far outside the boundaries people went home with the wrong conception of it. Since everyone in the performance were real players in the BDSM community, both women felt the touches of dramatic flair wouldn't clash with the overall goal.

"What's up, Pablo?" She noted Harris was with him, with a partially amused and expectant look on his face.

"I need a stand-in sub for the lighting guys to check something. I was going to get Sandy to help, because she's done rope bunny work before, but she had to take off for an afternoon class. You're about her size and build. Could I borrow you for a few minutes? I saw Madison over the weekend and she said you've worked with Des some."

While Julie hadn't given her friend many details about her and Des's experience, Madison had apparently picked up enough that she thought Julie was interested in learning more about being a 'rope bunny.' Though that wasn't entirely untrue, Julie thought her interest might be connected more to the man who'd put rope on her than the rope itself.

"I notice you're not asking this fine queen standing right in front of you," Billie said with mock accusation. Pablo grimaced good-naturedly.

"I already know you're a Dom, Miss Dee-Lite. I try to truss you up, you'll have me hog-tied faster than I can blink."

"Such a wise boy." Billie tilted his head toward Julie. "And I suspect Miss Julie here is the type of pretty little sub who likes to help a top out."

"Who says I'm a sub?" Julie demanded.

Billie rolled his eyes and twitched a hip in her direction. "See how fine this ass is? It's an indisputable fact, one anyone can verify by simply using their eyes. That's the answer to your question."

"He has a radar for submissives," Harris said dryly. "Or those he'd like to be submissive."

That set off some trash talk back and forth where Billie threatened to take a switch to Harris's fine white marshmallow backside. During the exchange, Julie looked at Pablo, who threw in his own opinion to keep the one-liners rolling. He was funny and she was comfortable around him, yet she found herself hesitating.

Was it the powerful, erotic nature of what she had experienced with Des making her unsure? Did she want to recall that memory in front of a theater full of milling crew and performers? Then her professional side kicked her in the butt. Pablo wasn't planning to have her strip down and take her to orgasm. He needed to demonstrate something for the technical direction. *Get a grip, Julie.*

"I just need a similar body type to position in the way I'll be doing for the show," he said. His detection of her concern should have reassured her, and she told herself it did. He elbowed her. "Unless you want to get naked for all of us. We're a very open group, you know."

"Totally open," Harris said with an innocent blink. "I'll get naked, too, to make you feel better about it."

Julie chuckled. Billie was right. That thorn was being a pain in her ass and interfering with a simple request. "Yeah, yeah. I've noticed most people in the BDSM world are happy to see anyone get naked I think we'll all keep our clothes on, especially if we're going to get any work done today."

"Wanting to see naked folk isn't a kink thing, honey-chile." Billie snorted. "That's anywhere there's a human with a pulse. Rabbits got nothing on us."

"Okay." Julie made her decision. "We're talking what, about ten minutes?"

"Maybe twenty. I've got to get you set up..." Pablo launched into some rope intricacies that mostly went over her head.

She remembered Des's hands moving over her, his fingers and the rope moving together like an erotic dance on her skin. Today she'd worn a long T-shirt over leggings, with a sports bra beneath, so it would be easy enough to strip the T-shirt off and fit the parameters of what Des had suggested as proper "rope bunny" wear if she'd not wanted to remove all her clothes.

What was it about men, that they liked terminology that melded rabbits and women? Badge bunny, rope bunny, Playboy bunny... Well, rabbits were soft and furry. Who didn't like rabbits?

As she followed Pablo back to the stage, Billie and Harris following, she took off the long T-shirt. She told herself not to be self-conscious. As Pablo had said, she and Sandy were the same body type, about twenty pounds over what Hollywood thought was ideal for women.

Well, these days they did. She remembered the temporary tattoos on Des's arms, the lush Marilyn and Betty. She recalled Des standing between her spread legs, heated palms sliding up them. *What I could do with these thighs...*

Had she really let him do that on their very first meeting? It had to be the carrot sticks. It was a subliminal message, the carrot stick to get a mule moving forward.

She snorted at herself as she joined Pablo on center stage. The collapsible frame he used had been set up, locked down on tracks. At his direction, she moved inside of it and lifted her arms to her sides.

Within a few moments, it was clear Pablo was not as confident and smooth as Des, which suggested why his video had started with his sub already suspended. At the time, she'd thought it was because he'd wanted to emphasize the non-rigging aspects of his performance.

However, he shook out his lines and had her in a decent harness fairly quickly, handling the positioning around and over her breasts in a functional and not inappropriate way. He worked other lines in an intricate net over shoulders, head and beneath her thighs as he prepared to suspend her. He was talking to Harris and the lighting guys at the same time, explaining his intent in a roundabout way. Some of the students and other stage hands had paused to watch him, probably intrigued seeing the managing director as his subject. She thought he seemed rushed, nervous at having to do all this on the fly in front of them. Or maybe he was nervous about using her, too, and didn't want her getting impatient. Hoping to relax him, she stayed quiet and gave him reassuring looks as he did what he needed to do.

Yet she also found herself counting the minutes until he was done. The rope was putting uncomfortable pressure on the inside of her thigh, enough that she'd decided to tell him that when he turned and hoisted her off her feet. He did it while still talking to Harris and the other crew, not giving her warning, so it jerked her off her feet precipitously.

She could have adjusted to that, but something wasn't right. As she was dipped backward, the discomfort went to pain almost immediately, and the binding around her arm pulled her shoulder at an odd angle. Things felt unbalanced.

The frame was steel and one of the larger props they would be using for the show, but when he hoisted her, it shuddered. As she tried to adjust and began to speak, the scaffold swayed alarmingly. With a sharp pop and plink, two pins fell out of metal joining pieces.

"Oh, *shit.*" Pablo cursed and dove for that section of the frame, just as the scaffold started to go over.

Up until that moment, Julie hadn't felt fear, just irritation, but suddenly everything was going wrong. More screws pulling loose, a screech of metal as the legs gave way. She suddenly realized how helpless she was. She had no way to protect herself as the rope in which he had bound her rolled, pinching her in several places. Her leg was throbbing painfully. But it wasn't that which catapulted her from fear into gut wrenching terror.

The harness he'd worked around her shoulders shifted. A loop of rope constricted around her windpipe. As the structure began to collapse, her head was jerked back in a harrowing snap.

She had a blink to think—*my head's going to hit the stage*—but she had no air to cry out at the certainty she was about to be seriously hurt.

Her body did land hard, metal jabbing into her back, but her head didn't bounce off the stage floor. It was caught in a very capable and unexpectedly familiar palm. She was staring up into Desmond's face, which would have been a very welcome visage to see, except she couldn't breathe. Her head was starting to swim and her leg and shoulder hurt, blood damming up with nowhere to go.

Des was snapping out orders and people were scrambling, pulling at the broken frame, but someone stepped on something that jabbed one of those fallen metal pieces into her leg. When she choked on another painful cry, his snarl sent them all skittering back like a startled flock of birds. He yanked out a knife sheathed at his belt, something that looked much sharper than what he'd used to scrape wax off of her. The flicked out blade flashed like a prop in West Side Story.

"Sorry for this, love."

He forced his fingers roughly under the noose at her throat, slid the flat of the blade in the space and cut through it. A light burning sensation told her he'd had to make a shallow cut in her skin, but she had no complaints because she could breathe again, a relief so overwhelming she hyperventilated, trying to pull in too much breath at once.

Billie was at her head, kneeling, saying things in a soothing voice, stroking her shoulders as Des sliced the rest of her rope off her. As he moved her off the wreckage and to the floor next to it, putting her on a folded blanket someone had produced to cushion her, he rubbed her inner thigh briskly. It eased the sudden painful rush of blood and re-established its flow.

He checked her arm, which was tender but had full mobility. She hadn't dislocated it. "Easy," Des said. His touch was so gentle. Since she was shaking like a reed in a typhoon—the aftereffect of realizing she'd just had a damn close call—she needed it. When someone tried to approach he held up a warning hand, backing everyone out of her line of sight but him. She was glad for it. Though she wasn't having fuzzy feelings for Pablo right now, she liked these people. Some of them, like Billie, she liked immensely. However, while she tried to pull herself together, she just wanted Des, not a bunch of people staring at her.

He had come from a job, because he was wearing his stained dark jeans and a T-shirt frayed at the collar. A bill cap was pulled down over his brow, his hair bound back in a short tail. He had dirt in the creases of his neck and elbow, and the combination of sweat, shingles and other construction odors was stronger than that first day, but it was all welcome. He was giving her a more thorough examination now, his penetrating eyes covering every inch of her face and body, his fingertips performing the same thorough appraisal. She was able to move or rotate everything he asked her to do, which relieved her as much as it seemed to do him.

"You might have some nasty bruises here," he said, hands settling on her throat, stroking her as if he was also monitoring her pulse. She lifted her chin, needing to feel his touch there, his hold. His eyes darkened, as if she'd said something meaningful to him with the gesture, and she supposed she had.

"We're getting you to an urgent care. You need to be checked out."

She shook her head. She was fine, she was sure of it. Bruised and battered maybe, but nothing broken. She gripped his arm, indicating she wanted to sit up. He didn't deny her, thankfully, lifting her into a sitting position and adjusting so she was leaning against his kneeling body, her back against his one propped leg.

"Are you able to draw a deep breath? Get air in and out of your throat okay?"

"Yeah," she rasped. "Now that the rope's off, I can breathe just fine. I promise."

"Okay then. Okay." He ran a hand down her back, gripped her hand. "Billie?"

The drag queen appeared. Harris was hovering as close, his eyes hard with worry and mouth set, an echo of the look Des had, but only an echo. She wasn't sure anyone could look the way Des did right now. His voice was strangely even as he spoke to Billie. "Stay with her." He glanced down at Julie. "It's okay. Just relax here a minute. I'll be right back."

He rose and moved across the stage. Pablo was standing by the ruined frame, staring at it. Julie wondered if he was in shock himself, because his gaze was locked on it as if he were in a trance.

He saw Des approaching, though, because he lifted his head and cleared his throat. "Man, this is going to take a while to put back together," he said awkwardly.

"Oh, you poor dumbass," Billie murmured.

Julie wasn't sure what he meant, but the others had registered Billie's dismay, if the frozen looks and indrawn breaths meant anything. Though no one moved, it was as if everyone else's energy drew back and away from the young rigger, clearing out of Des's path.

Des nodded in a neutral manner and picked up one of the broken metal rods. In a movement too fast for Julie to follow, he grabbed Pablo by the shirt front. Despite the man having more mass and height, Des dragged him down the three stairs off the stage and slammed him against the wall. He had the bar against his throat. Pablo's eyes bugged out and he struggled, but Julie wasn't the only one discovering how strong Des was.

"Feel that?" Des hissed at him. "Notice how you can't breathe? I'm putting no more pressure on your windpipe than it takes to dent a soda can. You suspended her from a frame that wasn't properly balanced or anchored. I'll bet you didn't even test it with your own weight first. Your ties were sloppy. You didn't isolate the sections to prevent tension in other areas. They slipped, forming a noose around her neck. You could have snapped it. Her larynx could have fractured. You were cutting off her femoral artery."

Pablo choked and Des apparently eased his hold, but not by much, because when Pablo's lips parted only a wheeze came out.

"Shut up," Des said anyway. "You're not talking now. I am. You were so busy thinking how to make it pretty, you didn't make it safe, which is the only fucking bloody thing that matters, ever. This is why this performance shit causes problems. It's more about impressing a fucking audience than taking care of your bottom."

Menace rolled off Des in waves. Billie's fingers pressed into Julie's shoulders. A bleary look up at the drag queen's face showed it set in a serious mask, a rare but impressively intimidating look for him. The rest of the people watching were motionless, held by Des's fury.

With a sound of disgust, Des took a step back and tossed the metal bar aside, though his body language was looming enough to keep Pablo where he was.

"You're going to make mistakes," Des said, staring at the rigger who'd paled under his brown skin. "Everyone does. That's why you *always* make sure you're ready for it. You reacted to the damn scaffold and dove for that first, when your first reaction should have been to protect her with whatever superhero adrenaline shit is necessary. Where were your fucking snips?"

Pablo's mouth worked, but nothing came out. Des nailed him with a look that could drill holes. "Let me guess. They're in your pack, which was somewhere backstage. If you tell me they're in your car, I'll fucking kill you, so keep it to yourself."

Des took a turn around the pit, as if calming himself, then he pivoted toward Pablo, freezing him in his sights again. "If you have a sub tied up, your cutting tool is on your body or no more than arm's length away. Because when she's in your hands, she's in *your hands*. She's got nothing but you and luck, and luck has the attention span of a fucking squirrel."

Pablo had finally recovered enough that he started to look belligerent. "Oh no, boy," Billie muttered. "You know what's good for you, you just stand there pissing yourself and listening."

Looking at Des's face, Julie didn't disagree. She struggled to a more upright position, lifting her hand to draw his attention. It wasn't necessary. As soon as she moved, his gaze snapped to her. Even now she was his focus. She swallowed, not quite prepared for an additional sweeping off her feet, even if it was a far better one than the kind she'd just experienced.

"Des, I'm okay."

Talking wasn't such a good idea, since she croaked like a frog. A second later she also realized it wasn't a great idea to shed light on her role in this. Billie's dubious look seemed to concur, though the message came too late.

Des gave her a glare no less wilting than he'd given Pablo. "And what the hell were you thinking? You do *not* put yourself in the hands of an inexperienced rigger if there's no mentor standing by spotting him. Not for any reason."

"Hey." Pablo rallied. "I'm not that inexperienced."

Julie gasped as Des turned and punched him in the jaw, knocking him on his ass and making his eyes damn near roll back in his head. At another time, she would have been impressed by the force of the blow, but she was too fragile to do more than cringe.

"Saw that one coming," Billie said, stroking her back, a calming gesture. "Easy, honey-chile. Just let him work it out. I love to hear your voice, but right now it's best you just focus on breathing."

The punch had Harris and a couple other male members of the staff coming down the stairs to intervene, but Des backed off, both hands raised. As they helped Pablo up, though, he stabbed a finger toward him.

"You're too stupid to know when to shut your mouth and listen," Des snapped. "You've been doing this for six months. Your basics are shit. Learn those, or you're going to fucking kill someone."

Julie's inevitable reaction to a fright—once she had enough distance from it—was anger. She'd had enough of being handled. Though Des had pretty much just saved her life, she wouldn't have him treating her like a child. ""I'm not an idiot, Des," she rasped, managing to get to her feet, though Billie had to rise to keep her upright. "It was just a mistake. Risk Aware Consensual Kink, remember?"

"Can't keep you babies from touching a hot stove," Billie said under his breath. She pretended like she hadn't heard him.

Des left Pablo's vicinity, thankfully, to march up the stairs and square off a few feet from her. He took off his cap and shoved it in his belt. "A few days surfing the Internet learning buzz words doesn't make you an expert, either," he said. "That fucking mistake could have ended up with you in a coma or dead. And him carrying that around on his dumbass soul for the rest of his life. What do you think this would do for Madison's hopes of having a place that helps people understand what BDSM is and isn't? It'd all be gone, and if your family decided to bring a lawsuit against her, she could be wiped out."

She opened her mouth to argue, but then she thought of her family. Their lack of comprehension about her theater life and what kind of person she was, coupled to their obvious yet clueless love for her, didn't rule out such a senseless decision. But that wasn't the point. None of those things had happened.

"Des," Billie said. His low tone was pointed enough that Des's gaze flickered at the quiet rebuke, then shifted to Julie's hands, trembling on Billie's forearm wrapped around her waist. The look that crossed his face made her wonder if he was going to snatch her out of Billie's arms to hold her himself or go pound on Pablo some more.

Instead, he pivoted to glare at all the cast and crew. "The next one of you who touches her with a rope answers to me. You clear it with me first, then her."

"Hell, man. I'm sorry. I didn't know you were her Dom." Pablo coughed it out as he tried to stand on his own two feet, though he was still wobbling between Harris and one of the men who'd been building the pipe structure to suspend the lighting equipment.

"He's not," Julie interjected hotly. She pushed away from Billie this time, though her balance was likely as precarious as Pablo's. "He's angry and has lost his mind. You don't have the right to impose that condition on them. This is my theater. My rules."

Des shot her a look and closed the distance between them with two solid steps. She told herself it was her recent trauma, not his imposing demeanor, that had her giving way a step, bumping into the solid bulk of Billie. Christ, he had a buff torso.

She almost drowned in the turmoil of emotions she saw in Des's face. It forced her back to what had nearly happened to her, something she wasn't prepared to handle while she was still so unsteady on her feet.

Maybe he saw that. His jaw relaxed a fraction and he glanced at Billie. "If you don't mind watching after her, I need to get out of here a few minutes. If he says one more stupid thing, I'm going to break his fucking neck."

"Go, honey-chile. She's safe here. I'll watch over her like a mother hen."

Des gave Julie another searching look. This one was less angry, but held enough other messages to dry up any other fumbling defenses she could launch. He left the stage, but not before he gave every person around them another fierce stare. "You all heard what I said."

The slamming of the stage door rocked the theater. A moment of silence prevailed, then Billie touched her arm with one finger, making a sizzling sound through his teeth.

"What are you doing?" Julie asked, twitching away.

"That was a branding, honey-chile. Sure as my finely tuned nose detects a prime piece of beef."

§

Pablo cleaned up his mess and cleared out without saying much of anything to anyone, and nothing to her. Billie told her to expect a text from the young rigger, backing out of the show. "He's embarrassed, and he figures you're going to fire him anyway. But if he's a decent human being, and I think that silly boy is, he'll take to heart what Des told him. Once he sets his ego aside and spends more time learning his basics instead of showing off."

Well and good, but it left a hole in her program.

Once she'd assured Billie she could leave his side without a major critical care incident, Julie went into the bathroom and gratefully closed the door. A renewed wave of shaking took her down to the floor on her backside, and stress tears spilled out. Before it became outright sobbing, she pulled herself together, struggled to her feet and took stock of the damage in the mirror. Des was right. She was going to have some bruising along her neck, a major hickey. From the increasing soreness throughout the rest of her body, she was sure she'd be groaning when she got out of bed tomorrow morning.

As she stood there staring at herself in the mirror, instead of reflective glass, she saw it all happening again and quaked. It could have been so much worse.

Which was why Des had been so enraged. He'd turned caveman on her, bigtime. During their two brief connections, she'd recognized his protective instincts, a genuine caring for another living being. He also took what he did damn seriously, and now she understood why. Risk Aware Consensual Kink, indeed.

None of that was wrong, but something more personal was going on in his reaction to the situation. No. She told herself not to go there. She'd fooled herself about a man's feelings toward her before. She wasn't going to jump into that pool again. Hadn't she told herself only an hour ago that she wasn't even interested in that?

She washed her face, combed her hair, and left the bathroom. Hesitating backstage, she realized she wasn't ready to go back up front and watch them repair things or resume the day's work. Instead, after some waffling, she went out the stage door to get some fresh air. And to find Des.

She'd been almost certain he wouldn't leave the premises until he checked on her again, and she felt an odd tilt in her chest to find she was right. He was sitting on the bay of their one loading dock, eating peanut butter pretzel pillows and sipping from a bottle of water.

He tucked it away in his pack as she sat down next to him, a careful buffer of space between them. He detailed her physical and mental state with one look, and his gaze flared with anger again as it passed over her throat where the abrasions were already showing.

She wanted to apologize, and she steeled herself against that, knowing it was a kneejerk reaction. It might also set him off again and she'd lash back. Normally she'd summon her usual sass and tell him to stop being a dick, but she couldn't say that to the guy who'd made sure she hadn't ended up in an oxygen-deprived coma.

"Are you okay?" he asked. It was his normal voice, which helped settle her nerves.

"Yeah."

"Good. Madison's on her way. She's taking you to the urgent care, since you won't go with me."

So much for relaxing. Her back went up again. "I won't go with anyone. I told you—"

"Julie." His sharp look made her bite back the words, but he tempered it with a brief touch on the top of her hand. "I'm not being a jerk. I told Logan what happened and the first words out of his mouth were why you weren't already on your way to one. I told him it's your call, and it is, but hear me out. I know you're rattled and it's natural to try and regain control by saying you're fine. But if you trust my expertise, believe me when I say there's damage that can occur that you can't feel and I can't see. You don't fuck with injuries like this just to save face. Go for the people who care about you. It's a few hours of your life."

She stared out into the parking lot, refusing to look at him. He might be right, but she wanted to bristle and spit. Which was probably part of wanting to regain control, too.

She turned her face back toward him. She knew she looked mutinous, but she didn't want to be stupid. She just had too much crap happening right now. When he reached out to touch her cheek, his expression softening, she drew back. It was instinct, not planned, but a clear telegraph she was still feeling too fragile. He dropped the hand back to his side. "I'm not going to yell," he said. "I'm not going to say anything. I'm just going to listen. Tell me what's going on in your head."

"I'm not okay," she said after a protracted silence. "I'm

freaked out by what could have happened. I'm embarrassed it happened in front of everyone. I'm wondering if I should have known better and I just proved to them I know less than nothing about this stuff. I'm mad at you for yelling at me in front of them. I'm also really, really glad you came when you did."

She blinked back traitorous tears and looked away, her fingers gripping the edge of the loading dock. The others had experience in BDSM play, but she remembered the chaos of those first vital seconds. She wasn't sure if any of them would have been level-headed enough to know to do what Des had done. None of the others were riggers.

His hand settled alongside hers. Not covering it, just pressed against it, their smallest fingers aligned with one another.

"I'm glad I did, too."

"I don't know any of this stuff, Des," she said, tracing cracks in the parking lot with her gaze. "That first time with you, you made me feel so safe. I guess it didn't occur to me it could be different, that Pablo wouldn't know what he was doing. Like you said, I was being stupid."

"Hey." When he touched her face this time, she didn't draw away. His expression was serious. "I never said you were stupid, and I never would. You weren't being stupid. I was."

It was then she saw the component of his rage she'd missed—guilt. Her lips parted on a protest, but he held up a hand so she'd let him finish.

"Because it did work so naturally with you, I focused on that and not on your lack of experience. I didn't think about how you'd be exposed to other performers here. Since you're so proactive, I should have realized you might offer to help them in a situation like that, thinking that what happened with us was the way it always goes."

"That's a lot of things to anticipate. If you'd put all that together, you'd be God. No one can anticipate everything. Even a Dom."

"There are eastern philosophies that postulate all of us are God. That the collective unconscious is the true source of Divinity."

She made a face, but she was glad they'd both recovered enough to tease. "How about this? Let's go Dutch on the guilt. I'll take half and you take half, because ultimately we're all responsible for ourselves. Though I didn't care for the way you made your point—patronizing and assholish—you weren't entirely wrong. I should have thought it through."

"And I shouldn't have been so caught up in how well things worked between us last time that I didn't give you a safety lecture afterwards."

"That would have been a buzzkill," she pointed out practically. "Plus I'm not sure I had the brain cells to process anything afterwards."

"Nice ego stroke, but I would have made it really easy. Tarzan breakdown. 'Des great at this. Everyone else sucks. Only let Des do this to you.'"

She elbowed him, then decided to stay leaning against him. Putting his arm around her, he kissed her forehead.

"You scared me, love. Scared the shit out of me. Are you okay, really?"

"Yeah, I really am. Promise. Pablo might be a dumbass, but he wasn't some mean person intending me harm. I think the deal is he's always performed in a club environment, and this is the first time he's really been on stage. He got a little distracted and self-conscious."

"I'm not excusing him," she said as Des's expression became ominous. "I'm just saying it wasn't much different from the tech guys almost braining me with a boom. I've learned to be nimble and duck when needed. But it's hard to duck when you're tied up."

"Yeah." He stroked her hair, held her close with both arms, squeezing her hard. "Don't do that again, all right?"

"I promise to never again let someone tie me to a frame that's going to fall over and make me a theater ghost."

"Smartass. Say the Tarzan thing. Make me happy."

"Des great at this. Everyone else sucks. Only let Des do this to you." She chuckled into his shirt front. "And Des needs shower."

"Yeah." He sniffed himself ruefully. "It was a particularly nasty job today. I was going to do a quick clean up in the back bathroom and change my shirt before I came to find you, but I wanted a quick glimpse of you first. Fortunate timing."

"That's an understatement." She dropped her head back to give him a speculative look. "So, you become a rage monster when you're pissed."

"Pretty much. Might as well put that down on the con side of things about having a relationship with me."

"I don't know, I better hold off. I don't want that side to outweigh the pros too quick."

"Ouch." He winced. "What else have I done?"

"You've left a gap in my program, for one thing." She held up her phone. "Pablo texted me that he's pulling out, just as Billie predicted. So can you recommend any riggers to me that could come up to speed yesterday? I don't want just anyone. You owe me someone who will absolutely wow my audience. Someone who can compete with Billie for top billing."

"Nobody can compete with Billie."

"So you know him? Her."

"Yeah. Billie's a hell of an interesting Dom. Or Dominatrix. Depending on his or her mood."

"You have the same problem I do."

"Billie's told me never to consider pronouns a problem. She likes being flexible."

"That's the feeling I've gotten from him, too. And no dodging. I want a fabulous rigger."

He lifted a brow. "I think you've already got someone in mind."

"I'm looking at him." She poked him in the chest. "Billie had some footage of the sessions you've done at shibari conferences. He said you let him record it."

"Under the mandate that it was only for his private use. He wanted to learn about rope bondage."

"We privately viewed it together," she assured him. "We're not posting it on the Internet. Unless you turn me down. I'm not above blackmail."

"Julie..." He grimaced and she held up a hand.

"I get why you don't like to do it as a performance. But you're creative with it, you like to explore all the possibilities and, if the energy you conveyed to me one-on-one translates to an audience, I think they'd learn a lot from watching you. And be totally mesmerized while doing so."

"Or be put to sleep, because I get so into it with the sub I forget they exist." He put his bill cap back on, and she tapped the brim, dipping her head to look at him beneath its shade. It gave him a more mysterious look and emphasized the curve of his mouth, the glitter of his gaze under the bill's shadowing. All of which confirmed she was dead on right about this. The audience would be enthralled by her Dom-wizard.

"Madison wants people to see how beautiful the mutual give and take we *all* crave is, and put it in a BDSM context. Show the overlap, that people who are Doms and subs aren't freaks. That does a hundred times more good than beating people with lectures about alternate sexuality and tolerating diversity."

He pressed those fine lips together and leaned back on his palms, a look that stretched his T-shirt across his chest and made her want to trace the sun-warmed denim on his thigh. She was apparently having an *I'm alive and I need to jump someone to confirm it* moment.

"You know, all of us are freaks," he pointed out. "Vanilla or kink."

"Duh. Most people with any sense know that." She tapped the bill of his hat again and he caught her wrist, tugging her toward him. She resisted, but only to gain capitulation. "Will you do it? If you really don't feel comfortable with it, I'll lay off with a minimal amount of pouting, but I think you'd be brilliant."

He cocked his head. "Show me your best pout. Give me something to fantasize about with those soft lips of yours."

She shifted so she was leaning over him, and transformed her face into a sad, longing look, complete with full pursed mouth that she moistened with a sultry pucker.

"Damn." His brown eyes sparked. "You sure you don't perform?"

"I was a drama major, but I was a mediocre actress at

best. I discovered I loved the production end more."

He'd released her wrist to slide his hand under her hair and caress the sensitive point at the base of her neck. She took advantage of her position to put her palm on his chest, fingertips sliding across the T-shirt. Des studied her.

"Okay. I'll do it. But not because you're exercising feminine wiles on me."

She straightened abruptly, eyes widening. "I was doing no such thing."

"Either I'm so irresistible you couldn't keep yourself from touching me, or you were trying to use feminine wiles. Which is it?"

She tucked her tongue in her cheek and examined her nails. "If you put it that way, it was totally feminine wiles."

"Liar. I told you I was irresistible."

"Whatever helps you sleep at night, Mr. Need to Get Over Yourself." She relented, though, slanting a glance at him and smiling. "Thanks, truly. So who will you get to do it with you?"

"Well, if you're not volunteering..."

"No way. First off, I'm Harris's troubleshooter that night. Second, I couldn't do stuff like that in front of people."

"I told you I don't perform on stage, and see where that landed me." But he waved a hand, telling her he understood and wasn't going to push it, though she appreciated being asked. "There's a sub at Logan's club, Missive, who enjoys rope play. She's a knockout, too, a good-looking twenty-something blonde, but she's the real deal, not a poser, so she'll make a good impression on an audience."

In her professional capacity, Julie was pleased to hear it. As the woman sitting next to him, not so much. But she'd just told him she couldn't do it and, beyond that, it was a performance, like watching male and female leads do a love scene, even if their spouses were sitting in the audience.

Only Des didn't have a spouse, or girlfriend. No firm commitments. She wasn't looking for one herself. Hadn't she planned to have a talk about that with him? *Don't be stupid. You and he have barely even started...whatever this is. And you haven't even decided in your mind you want to start anything.*

Could she be more wishy-washy? She was being a coward and she knew it. She also had never asked him if he was involved with someone, but she was pretty sure he would have been up front about that, or Logan or Madison would have told her.

She rubbed her hand over her throat again unconsciously. He saw it, that ominous flash going through his gaze as he touched her hand there. She drew back, though, and hopped down off the dock, in time to see Madison pulling in. Great. A couple hours of being poked and prodded. She'd do it, but she wouldn't like it.

"There's Madison. Thanks for being willing to fill in for Pablo, okay?"

"Yeah." He was studying her. "You okay?"

"Totally. Touch base with Missive and let Harris know if you guys are a go. He'll coordinate everything with you and pull me in as needed. Tell Madison I'm just going in to grab my purse."

"Julie..."

But she pretended not to hear and went back into the building, letting the door close and trap her in shadows in the back hallway of the theater. *You cannot afford this shit,* she told herself. Time to do the hopefully unnecessary medical check, then get a hot shower to head off the worst of the aches and pains. The physical ones at least.

Maybe afterward she'd use a vibrator until she lost consciousness, so she wouldn't be having nightmares about or dwelling on her near-death experience. No, instead she'd be fantasizing about Desmond Hayes. She'd like to lie to herself and say she could ban him from any masturbation montage, but he was right.

She found him irresistible.

Her phone buzzed and she pulled it out. "Speak of the devil," she muttered.

Text me and tell me you're okay after your appointment. Madison says you're staying with her tonight and she's making you take a half day tomorrow. Unless you'd rather sleep in, I'll pick you up at nine to go to a farmers' market. A friendly non-date.

No. Definitely no. They were handling her. She didn't appreciate that.

There's a woman who makes a better-than-sex broccoli casserole.

There will be peanut butter cookies.

And homemade wine.

A WWII vet makes airplanes out of beer cans.

In the time she sat there staring at the phone and wrestling with her own responses, he sent her a list of twenty perks associated with the farmers' market. She was smiling and near tears both. *I can't afford you, Des. I just can't.*

She wanted to type that, but she was struggling between cowardice and desire. He made her feel good, he made her laugh. As a Dom, he made her tremble and ache in all the right ways. So what if he could do the same thing for a million other women? Didn't make it less true for her, did it?

Don't make me use the 'I saved your life' card.

She snorted. *Do you have no shame?*

Let me check all my pockets. Nope, none here.

That did make her laugh. She leaned against the wall, beat her head against it and groaned. Pressed the phone to her forehead until it buzzed with one more text.

Please, Julie.

"You just never learn, do you?" she demanded of herself in the darkened hallway. Yet even as she loathed her weakness, she was typing.

Okay. Nine o'clock. But pick me up here. She'd have Logan drop her off on the way to the hardware store, which opened early. She wanted to be back in her own space before she saw Des again. No matter how unsteady he made her feel, she wasn't going to forget how to stand on her own two feet.

Chapter Five

"This is me, take it or leave it. My own girl, better believe it..."

She was pleasantly off tune, with feminine pride and gusto. Des grinned as he followed the sound of her voice through the theater to her makeshift dressing room apartment, where she appeared to be sorting laundry and shaking her very fine booty to the beat of the Mindy McCready song.

He watched her dance to the music through her earbuds, arms and hips gyrating, her glossy thick brown hair swinging with her movements, her breasts bouncing. He knew she thought herself too heavy by about fifteen to twenty pounds. Most women weren't happy with their bodies, and women with generous curves like hers, almost always. It baffled him, though he expected it was because they saw themselves the way women did, not men. It was one of the many reasons he loved tying up a woman and topping her. He could show her how she looked through his eyes with no white noise, everything driven out of her mind but honest, pure reaction.

He loved Julie's energy, her quirky nature, her responsiveness. She brought out protective instincts in him, more than his usual response to a woman who'd given him the privilege of adorning her in his rope. He noted she did have some residual bruising on her throat, but it wasn't as severe as he'd feared it would be, and her loose hipped dancing said she'd taken some good pain meds. It still made him want to choke the life out of Pablo with a prickly coconut twine.

He shouldn't be pursuing this. He'd spent his life knowing down to the minutiae what was good and bad for him. Sometimes the lines were fuzzy, yet when it came to getting close to other people, there was no mistaking the boundaries. He had no desire to hurt anyone.

But God, look at her. Her life. Her joy. She embraced everything around her. People, new experiences. From the things she tried so hard not to say but ended up stumbling over, he knew she'd been hurt too often. Those clueless bastards' loss was his gain. At least for as long as he could keep this inside the box he always kept his relationships.

You're already outside the box, asshole. Don't be the next one to break her heart.

He wasn't going to do that. They were both adults. They could have fun. He could help her learn more about BDSM. She was here only temporarily, anyway. She wasn't looking to set up house.

Wow, feeding yourself a major line of bullshit there, buddy.

He wanted to slide up behind her, take off the earbuds and ravish her neck with lips, tongue and teeth. He wanted to hold her heart-shaped ass against his cock and grind. He wanted to hear her laugh, gasp and whisper, feel her tremble, all because of what he could do to her.

Proving he had restraint, he leaned in the doorframe, giving himself a private moment to enjoy. He'd met women who put effort into an eccentric persona. Goth, off center, social justice warrior, name your role or emotional costume. That didn't bug him. They weren't pretentious. They were merely donning the clothes that best helped them handle their world, same as everyone did. Yet his favorite gift to his Dom side was stripping the physical and emotional clothes off each woman and finding out who she really was. In return, he learned more about himself. It was a two way street of pleasure and emotional satisfaction.

Julie was his first experience where the inner core of the woman was open, dazzling to see in all its honesty. Nothing proved it more than her reaction when she discovered she wasn't alone.

She'd executed an enthusiastic spin, fist pumped the air,

and saw him watching her. She gave a surprised yelp, but recovered fast, as he somehow knew she would. She did another shimmy and shake for him, belted out the last chorus with impressive lip synching skill, and finished on another spin. When she popped out the earbuds, she fixed an accusing look on him. "You're an hour early."

"I brought coffee." He lifted the flat from behind the door, in the hallway where he'd stashed it. "And flowers."

The bouquet of yellow daisies had looked playful and bright, like her. "I'm a traditional guy."

She took the flowers just as he'd expected and hoped she would, with clear delight, but as she sniffed the flowers, she tossed him a mild glare.

"Didn't you say this was a non-date?"

"I lied about that. Figured after you had time to think about it, you'd realize a date would be much nicer."

She smiled, but he saw wariness in her eyes, a woman who didn't trust herself, whose heart was fragile from past wounds. It took an unusual grip on him.

She's different, you idiot. Back away from this.

We're just going to a farmers' market. Not running away to Vegas.

There was no harm in enjoying her company and using his skills to help her trust again. He'd done it with other women, the lines of care and affection clean.

You're going to the farmers' market to prove to her she's different, because she thinks she's just another rope bunny to you. How is that not crossing the line into relationship territory? Lying asshole.

His conscience was a persistent bastard. It didn't help that every moment they stood in what was essentially her bedroom, he wanted to grab her around the waist, press her luscious body against the wall and kiss her until she was writhing against him in that nice, cock-hardening way she did.

This might be a date, but it couldn't be that kind of date. She was skittish, relationship-shy. Even if he had to rubber band his dick in a choke hold, he was going to make sure she felt less skittish around him. Then maybe he'd reward his tremendous restraint by tying her up on that cot and fucking her brains out.

"Want to help me fold some towels?" she asked. "That way we can get out of here even sooner."

"It'd be my pleasure." He'd do his best not to think about how folding towels would clear the mattress. She was right. The sooner they got out of here, the better.

§

"Those are the biggest chocolate chip cookies I've ever seen," Julie said, pointing to a stall.

"Yeah. They're hard as rocks and taste like crap. The lady you want is over here." He drew her over to a table where the cookies were much smaller but wrapped a half dozen to a pack, brightly colored curly ribbon tied around cellophane. "Trust me, they're worth every cent of your $3." He bought her a couple of them and dropped them in the tote she'd brought. He gave the bedazzled Tinkerbell design a bemused look.

"Everyone loves sparkly things," she told him. "Even if they don't admit it."

"I'd bedazzle all my jeans if it wouldn't blind the roofing crew and cause accidents," he agreed.

"Safety first." She chuckled and glanced back at his truck in the parking lot. "Weren't you going to bring your cooler for the meats?"

"I buy perishables at the end. No fun lugging around a cooler when you're looking at other things. This is all I need right now." He gripped the strap of the pack he seemed to always have with him, now on his shoulder. Then he squeezed her hand. "And this."

"Being a roofer must pay pretty well if you can buy food like this regularly," she observed, covering the absurd desire to dimple like a teenager. They'd moved into the stalls where the organic, humanely raised meats were advertised.

"Well, yes and no. Subcontractors often get paid crap, but I've run my own roofing business for some time now. I hire the crews that work with me and pay them fair, and it works out well for all of us. Plus, meats are higher priced, yeah, but I don't buy a lot of it. It's a small part of my diet. And a lot of stuff here isn't as expensive as you'd expect, like the fresh fruits and vegetables." He shrugged. "I don't carry any debt. I rent a small place on my landlady's property and she doesn't charge much because I help her take care of her horses."

He cocked his head. "So, if you think about ratios of income to expenses, I'm doing a lot better than most millionaires. Keep that in mind if you're looking to be a kept woman. As long as your needs are small."

"It has ever been my goal in life to be a kept woman. I did offer myself as a sex slave to a very wealthy gay man and his partner, but they didn't go for it. Even though they agreed keep me anyway, as a friend, I didn't want to be a charity case. I wanted the sex slave job."

"Well, that's good news. I can offer you a sex slave position immediately. I have a current opening. I just didn't want to scare you off."

Julie made a face at him, then her attention was caught by something else. "Oh, look at all the colors."

While she wandered into another stall, Des gestured. "I'm going to double back and tell the meat guy what to hold for me. I won't be far."

"Okay. Ask him to set aside a pack of the burgers for me. I'll pay you for them."

His noncommittal gesture as he walked away told Julie she'd probably have to stuff some money in his truck console when he wasn't looking. She wasn't going to let him pay for everything today. Especially since they'd walked through ten stalls and she'd already seen twenty things she'd love to have. A bunch of them were in front of her now.

The colorful kites, windsocks and chimes made a delightful symphony of rustling fabric and striking metal as she ambled through them. The proprietress, a stocky woman with brush cut hair and a giant tattoo of Snoopy on her biceps, was more than willing to talk to her about how she created her wares.

"Do you have a bunch of these where you sleep?" Julie asked at length, turning around in a circle. "I'd keep a fan running so they could make music all night."

The vendor laughed. "It would be a little much every night, but I do have a hammock in my workshop to take naps there. I open up the windows in the fall for just that reason." She winked. "There's a ceiling fan for winter."

Julie trailed her fingers through a field of filmy wind socks that looked like snakes, dragons and rainbows, and left the stall as more customers entered it. She found Des sitting under a tree, knees bent and head against the trunk as he watched her. His expression suggested she pleased him merely by giving him the opportunity to watch her, which brought back that silly teenage dimpling urge again.

"Tired you out already?" she asked, sitting down next to him.

"Just enjoying you," he said. "I spend so much time on rooftops, I forget how nice the view is at eye level."

"Hmm." She linked her fingers over his bent knee and considered him. "I'd like to ask you a question. Conceptual, not personal."

He cast her an intrigued look. "Okay."

"If your dog was trapped in a burning house, and a little boy you didn't know ran out into a busy street, who would you try to save?"

"My dog," he said.

"Really? Why?"

Des ticked off the points on his fingers. "A kid runs into the street, cars will wreck to avoid hitting him, and other pedestrians will run after him to help. Very few might run into a burning house to save my dog, but lots will run into the street to save the child."

"Do you think you'd think it through that fast?"

"My dog only has me," he observed, "and I'm his person. By adopting him, I made a covenant to care for and protect him. He's the most helpless one in that situation, so instinct would take me toward him." He studied her. "Why did you ask me that?"

"It tells me whether you give expected answers, or if you give it straight from the heart."

"Why else?"

"I like being surprised. You manage to impress a girl by

not trying to impress her."

"I've fooled you, because everything I'm doing is about impressing you. My turn. What's your biggest fear?"

She tilted her head up to look into his face. "About relationships or life in general?"

"Your choice."

"Typical stuff. Death, getting older, being alone. Normal for hitting the forty year range." She shifted uncomfortably. He touched her hand.

"Why death?"

"It's the ultimate unknown, the biggest loss of control we face."

"So how do you deal with it?"

Her gaze lifted back to his face. She'd been worried he'd zero in on the "alone" part, yet it was the death part that interested him. His expression was neutral, but she wondered how he'd dealt with it through his formative years. Death was a specter that usually grew in size as one aged. As a child, it was a barely understood concept; as a teen, a fly brushed away, inconsequential to their misguided sense of immortality. Yet he'd had to live under its shadow in a way different from a healthy child, teen or adult with typical fears about the ephemeral nature of life.

"I think about Skye Bartusick and James Garner."

"Excuse me?"

She grinned. "It's rare to see a clueless look on your face. It's cute."

"Annoying woman." He snorted and flicked her fingers, still linked over his bent knee. "Who is Skye Bartusick?"

"She was in the movie *The Patriot* with Mel Gibson. She played his youngest daughter, Sara. The actress died at twenty-one, complications related to seizures, or something like that. When I saw a picture of her on the Internet, she still had that sweet little girl's face she had in the movie. It upset me, thinking how panicked she might be, how afraid, when she wasn't expecting death to happen so suddenly. Then I found out that James Garner died on the same day."

Julie paused as a man walked by with a trio of Australian shepherds. She went to her knees to pet the enthusiastic threesome, and asked the man for their names. When she settled back, she was feeling a little foolish about her complicated answer and was going to drop it, but she saw Des was waiting for her to continue, his expectant look asking for more.

"James Garner was so reassuring and fatherly in a lot of the roles he played later in his life. I saw the two of them arriving at the gates of Heaven together, this little girl from *The Patriot* and James Garner, maybe like in his older *Maverick* reprise role, also with Mel Gibson. Seven degrees of separation, right?" She plucked at a couple blades of grass, wondering if Des was thinking she was nuts, but she was going to finish the story, because he'd asked.

"When you get to Heaven I think you can be any age you need or want to be, so I could see James deciding to step into that reassuring fatherly role for Skye one more time. He'd hold her hand so she wouldn't be scared. Even if he was looking forward to being young again in Heaven, and knew she had nothing to fear now, he'd want her to feel safe, and nothing does that like holding someone's hand."

"Hmm." He was looking at her, but his eyes weren't focused, as if he was thinking about her words. So she finished her thought.

"I thought, if the Powers That Be took them on the same day, there has to be something making sure we're all okay, right? No matter how dumbass a theory it is, it makes me feel better."

"It's a good theory." He stroked her hair away from her cheek. "I like it. I like you."

Suddenly nervous, she rose to her feet and offered him her hand. "I like you, too. Want to go walk by the lake?"

He grasped her hand but used his own strength to pull himself up. He retained his grip on her, though. Holding hands. "Sure."

"My turn again," she said, seeking to fill in the silence. "Your most embarrassing moment?"

"Why would you want to know that?"

"Because I want to know you're not perfect."

Des laughed. "I've never been called or considered perfect in my entire life." He stopped and put his hands on her face in a caress, but like he was removing glasses.

"What are you doing?"

"I'm removing those rose colored lenses I must have accidentally put on you."

She gave him an amused look. "You did tell me once if you touched me a certain way I would see an irresistible guy hung like a moose. Maybe the enchantment hasn't worn off yet."

"Even after I yelled at you about Pablo?"

"Oh, well see, I'd forgotten that. Enchantment blown. And you still haven't answered the question. Most embarrassing moment."

He didn't let her pull away, bringing her back to his side. "Just the stereotypical shit. In middle school I was the self-conscious skinny guy. I was always getting called out of class to handle stuff related to my diabetes and other health crap. The weak get targeted; it's the law of nature. A bunch of guys stripped me down in the locker room at PE and shoved me into the girls' area."

As she winced, he grimaced. "That wasn't nearly as bad as the epileptic seizure I had because of the stress. They all bolted, except this one girl, who called the coach and put one of her books in my mouth so I wouldn't bite through my tongue. She had an epileptic brother. She was also one of the prettiest girls in the ninth grade."

"Oh, Des."

He shook her head. "That wasn't the most embarrassing thing. Every time she saw me after that, she was really kind to me. Probably because she knew how her brother had to deal with the same thing, but I was a stupid seventh grader. The other guys would pat me on the head after she talked to me, mocking me, making me feel like she pitied me. One of them told me I was her little pet. When I denied it, he dared me to steal her bra out of the locker room and hang it over the school entrance with her name written on it."

Julie stopped. "You didn't."

He gave her a pained look. "I did. I'll never forget her face when she knew it was me. That was the most shameful, embarrassing moment of my life, because I'd repaid her kindness with being a shit, just because I wanted not to feel like a special needs kid. Which is exactly what I was, of course. I'd like to say I've improved since then, but I still don't really like getting a lot of attention over it, as you already know. But at least I've evolved. I don't retaliate with underwear theft."

"Progress." She linked arms with him. "Did you apologize to her?"

"I did. She didn't forgive me, understandably, but I've always hoped when she became an adult, she understood better why I did what I did and realized I was just a dumbass kid who didn't know better."

"Or she morally disintegrated from your unkindness and now grifts old ladies out of their social security. Which she spends on heroin instead of caring for the three kids she's had from all different fathers."

"Oh, thanks for that. Come here."

She shrieked and dodged as he made a grab for her, setting off an impromptu chase to the edge of the manmade lake. He caught her there as she tried to feint around him and he took her down to the ground, albeit gently, as if knowing she might still be sore from her Pablo experience. Julie had loaded up on ibuprofen, though, so she wouldn't mind if he was a little rough. Des handed out a far more pleasurable kind of pain.

Her reaction probably showed when he pinned her wrists. She quieted as his hands closed around them, holding her arms to either side as he bent over her.

"I like how you get when I hold you like this," he said. "Quiet, like a bird cupped beneath my hands. Waiting."

Her breath went somewhere else at his intent look. But either he realized they were in a too-public venue for such intimate play, or he recalled they were supposed to keep this casual, because he eased off, though his fingers caressed her wrists.

"Want a snack?" He pulled out one of the sandwiches from his pack and offered her half. As they chewed in companionable silence, they shared a bottle of water while sitting on the grass shoulder to shoulder. He posed the next question.

"Worst moment of your life?"

"It'd be hard to top the one you just described."

"That was the most embarrassing. Nowhere near the worst. My childhood is one big tragedy." He winked at her. "It's why I'm so warped now. You're avoiding."

"A little bit. I don't really want to go there. Okay?"

"All right. But you can tell me sometime, Julie. It'd be okay."

She met his gaze, and believed him. "What about you? Can you answer the question?"

He found a napkin in the tote and used it, offering her half. "I don't really think of my life that way. During a bad moment, I think of what's going to happen next, or what good I can get out of the bad, because there's usually something. I just don't think about things being a worst moment."

"I like that." She ate most of her sandwich, but gave some crusts to the hopeful mallards and sharp-eyed imperious Canadian geese gathering around them.

"I always imagine them as a biker gang." She looked toward the geese. "Their wings like leather jackets, cigarettes dangling from their bills. I told Thomas that once, and he did a sketch of it for me."

"Who's Thomas?"

"One of my two best friends."

"Ah. The ones whose approval any potential suitors have to have." He had his arm propped behind her so she could lean on it as he ate his sandwich. When he looked toward her, their faces were distractingly close. "I know how women are about their BFFs liking their boyfriends," he said. "Are they very intimidating? Just asking hypothetically, since this isn't a date."

She stuck her tongue out at him. "They're...well, a picture makes more sense." She called up the photo she had on her phone. It had been snapped at a nightclub where Marcus and Thomas had taken her dancing. When Des glanced at it, his expression became far more speculative, giving her stomach a nice roll.

"You have two male BFFs?"

"Yep, that's Marcus and Thomas. They're the gay couple I mentioned earlier."

"Hmm." Des studied the photo more critically. "What I see is you in a sexy red dress, between two men whose body language makes it clear they think you're amazing. And this one, he's angled in front of both of you, saying he's the alpha and he'll fuck up anyone who messes with either of you."

"That's Marcus. You're good," she said. "Thomas can do good old boy Southern macho in a heartbeat when he's riled, but otherwise he's the lake. Marcus is the crashing ocean. Thomas's storms come out mostly in his paintings. He's an artist and Marcus represents his work. He's also a gallery owner in New York. They keep a second house in North Carolina, because that's where Thomas's family is. You might get to meet them."

She studied the picture fondly before tucking her phone back in her pocket. "They're married. To each other, in case your superpowers didn't pick up that they're wearing wedding rings."

He made a face at her. "It's a small picture."

"You got all that other stuff off of it."

"That's body language, easier to translate even in reduced size." He shifted, his side pressing into hers, and bent his head to trail his lips along the tender flesh beneath her ear. Julie drew in a breath at the sensation and was glad she'd pulled her hair up.

"So explain one thing to me," he said. "Why does Marcus have Dom vibing off of him, and the body language between the three of you suggests they've seen you naked?"

He caught her off guard. She prized her honest nature, but sometimes she wished she had a poker face, where she could avoid certain subjects without a single ripple on her countenance. Instead, she tripped over her own tongue or hesitated, like she did now, making it obvious there was something to tell.

She was an adult. She didn't have to say anything. She could say, "I don't want to talk about it."

Yet he was looking at her in that way he had, and it was like truth serum. It was also making her ridiculously flustered, because his gaze was pinned on her like he was...jealous? No, not jealous. That was a negative emotion she didn't think was a positive in any relationship. But possessiveness came with a kick she felt all the way to her vitals. He wanted to know what his competition was, and he wasn't going to be patient about it.

"It's not like that," she hedged.

"You said I was your first Dom/sub experience."

"Yes and no. Yes, in all the really important ways." She grabbed for her dignity, though it was going to be fleeting. "It's...I want to say it's embarrassing to talk about, and it is, but up until the time I met you, it was one of the most special sex memories I had."

She looked down at her hands. "Which would normally sound like the 'oh, it was the best sex I ever had until you', ego stroke, but it's not. It's...sad, in a way, and that's the embarrassing part. But..."

When he put his hand over hers, she saw his expression had softened. "Hey. Sorry. I didn't mean to back you into a corner, love. Not about something that's special to you." He cleared his throat. "Sounds to me like whichever one of them had the privilege was the damn lucky one."

"Oh, well...thank you." She shifted. "It was both, actually."

His brows lifted and she would have laughed if she wasn't so nervous. "It wasn't like that. I'm going to do this with my eyes closed and get it over with. No chance you'll let go of my hand so I can bolt?"

"Not a chance."

"Figures." Closing her eyes, she drew in a deep breath so she could get it out in one rush. "For my birthday one year, Marcus orchestrated a scene where Thomas used a vibrator on me and Marcus took control, did the Dom thing. Then they slept in my bed on either side of me. Well, eventually. They were worked up by the situation, which happens when they barely think about one another, let alone orchestrate a birthday sex party. They had sex in my bed while I watched them. After that, they held me through the whole night and made me pancakes for breakfast."

"The pancakes were included."

She cracked open an eye, relieved to see he was trying to alleviate her tension with dry humor. His hand was still curled firmly around hers.

"Absolutely. Their pancakes are to die for. Almost as good as an orgasm. Before you, I might have even said they were better than. You don't look horrified. Or amused in the wrong way, like you're laughing at me."

"I would never do that." He leaned back on his arms again, their sides still touching. "Was it then you realized you had submissive cravings?"

"I suspected before then, but that sort of stirred the pot. I can't believe I'm telling you all this."

"I can. You're a very open person." His expression still held an intriguing, simmering testosterone current, but he'd dialed it back, his tone matter-of-fact. "I can handle your honesty, love. I prefer it. And when honesty moves into nervous babbling because you're worried about losing control or being perceived in a way you think is wrong, which is bullshit, then I know how to deal with that."

"How is that?"

"A gag."

She pushed at him and he caught her hands, grinning. Rising, he helped her up and they continued their stroll along the water. As she did some idle people watching, she came up with a far less emotional question, a transition she thought they might need.

"Why do you see so many skinny men with larger women? Or large men with petite women?"

"Maybe petite women make bigger men feel more masculine, and a skinny guy loves the idea of being surrounded by a lot of woman, an earth mother thing. I like those netsukes, how they twist and twine the characters together. It makes me think of all the ways you can manipulate soft flesh with rope. Particularly a woman who's got an hourglass shape, with the right amount of nice curves."

His gaze slid over her, telling her which woman he was thinking about. "You know," he mused. "I haven't kissed you yet. Not a real kiss."

She blinked. "That was quite a segue."

"Only if you weren't paying attention." Then he turned thought into action.

Drawing her over to a large tree, he put her against the trunk, keeping her there with the press of his body and his hands caressing her jaw, her face.

She was done insisting this was just a casual date, and not merely because her body was telling her to shut the hell up. She couldn't find words with him so close, his eyes on hers. She'd backpedal later.

He put his mouth on hers and she swam in that feeling, the heat, his hands gripping her, kneading the sensitive skin at the waistband of her jeans since he'd found his way beneath her shirt. The breeze ruffled against her cheek, and she inhaled him, her arms sliding up his back to hold on. When he lifted his head, she was lying in his arms in a standing position, her head propped on his biceps.

"You know trust is the foundation of every relationship," she whispered. "You *did* lie about this being a not-date."

"I can't think of you just as a friend, Julie."

"Why not?" She moistened her lips.

"Because I don't want to."

He wasn't being flippant. His eyes and mouth were serious.

"Oh. Okay. Good reason."

He allowed himself a tight smile but eased back, though he kept her inside the frame of his body. Brushing her hair back from her temple, she scrambled for distraction again.

"Look, a toy sailboat." She pointed to it. It had drifted to the center of the lake and appeared to be caught alongside the turtle platform.

"I think they prefer to call them models." Des turned to look with her.

"Pfft. Boys and their toys. An actual one this time." She nodded to a boy standing on the edge of the water. From his working of the controls and his distressed look, it appeared he couldn't untangle the boat from what was holding it to the platform. "It's stuck."

"It may also be out of signal range," Des mused as they moved down the slope of grass.

The boy had turned to speak to an adult male sitting under a nearby tree. Surmising it was his father, Julie watched as the boy appealed to him. The man responded with impatience, not taking his eyes off the phone he was scrolling. As they drew closer, she heard what he was saying.

"I told you that you were going to lose it if you didn't keep it close to shore. There's no swimming in the lake. If it doesn't drift loose before we go, you'll just have to leave it. I told you to be more careful."

The boy bit his lip and looked back out at the boat. "But Dan gave it to me."

"Well, it's not Dan's day with you, is it?" The sudden blast of irritation brought the man's head up. "I'm your father. Why'd you bring one of his expensive toys with you? Just to rub my face in it?" The boy flinched.

"Asshole," Julie muttered. She was already starting forward, not sure what she planned to do, but Des stopped her. Winking at her, he stripped off his shirt and started to unbuckle his belt.

Her brows lifted. "It was a nice kiss, but I'm not sure it overwhelmed my aversion to public sex and subsequent jail time."

"I'll have to work on that." Handing her his shirt, he detached the connector between the insulin pump on his belt and the cannula. Putting the pump in his pack, he pulled out a small cap that went on the now open end of the cannula. Then he secured the tube and connector end against his body with a couple pieces of medical tape.

"Wow. That pack of yours is like the bottomless bag Hermione had in the Harry Potter books."

He winked at her again. When he removed the jeans, he revealed a pair of dark blue and green plaid boxers. "Good thing I didn't wear my leopard print thong today. It would scare the ducks."

She realized he intended to use the boxers as a modest swimsuit. Well, they'd be modest until they were soaking wet. She was looking forward to seeing that, even as she glanced at the water, concerned. There were a lot of no swimming signs posted, but Des seemed unconcerned about the reasons behind that. The pond had fish, ducks and geese, so she surmised dubiously the water might not be too toxic.

He put his shoes back on without the socks. "Are you sure the water's safe?" she asked.

"I'm Spiderman. I've already been bitten by a radioactive spider." He kissed her lightly and then waded into the water without hesitation, though the ripple of gooseflesh across his arms and back suggested the morning sun hadn't yet warmed it to a comfortable temp. Some of the geese plopped into the water, paddling companionably after him. When he reached the point he couldn't touch, Des began to do a breast stroke, headed toward the boat.

At the sight of Des, the boy had sidled back down along the shoreline. His father was absorbed in his phone again, oblivious to the rescue effort. The boy plucked at the switches on the remote control box and looked at Julie. "He's not going to steal my boat, is he?"

"Oh, honey. Heavens no. He's going to get it loose for you."

"Oh." He brightened and, with a boy's typical relish, he foretold gore and doom for Des. "My friend Buddy says there's giant snapping turtles in there that can bite off your leg. And the most venomous snakes in the whole world."

"I think those are in Australia, not here." Though Julie saw several sizeable turtles on the platform, ponderously climbing over one another to avoid the dip of the boat's mast in its caught position. She hoped Buddy was a big fibber. She liked all of Des's parts, and didn't want any to fall prey to snapping turtles.

He'd reached the sailboat and seemed to be having trouble determining what had captured it. He sank below the surface. The ducks and geese circled, quacking among themselves at the oddity of a human swimming in their midst. Julie felt a trickle of unease. *Damn it, Des.* If he didn't emerge, and she had to go rescue him, she'd kill him.

"It's loose," the boy said excitedly as the boat started drifting their way. The remote also started to function again. As the child operated the controls, Julie heard a healthy purring noise from it, not the earlier futile tick-tick.

Des broke the water's surface a few feet away and started back to shore, his expression cheerful as he saw the boy navigating the craft in the same direction. Man and ship arrived at almost the same time.

As he trudged out of the water, he slicked his hair back, an effect that sharpened the planes of his face and made even more of his deep set eyes and moist lips. She'd been right about that plastering effect. Thank goodness the shorts were a dark fabric, else others at a greater distance would be enjoying the well-defined view she was getting.

"Hey, you said this isn't a date situation," he teased her. "No ogling. And no comments about cold water."

"A fine, male form is worth ogling, whether it belongs to a friend or more than a friend," she informed him. "I suppose you don't look at female strangers with nice racks."

"Of course not. That would be treating them like sex objects, and—" Whatever else he was about to say was muffled as she tossed his T-shirt over his face. He removed it, eyes twinkling, and used it to dry off before putting his feet back in his jeans and working them back up his still damp thighs.

She chuckled as he grimaced but managed it with an intriguing flexing of muscles. "It's like taking off one of those Chinese finger puzzles, in reverse," he complained.

"Hmm." She'd automatically put out a hand to balance him, but as he straightened, her touch drifted across his chest, over the short hairs glittering with water droplets. From there, she slid her fingertips up to his throat and along the strands of wet hair on his head. His eyes stilled at her caress and she almost drew her hand back, but she couldn't bring herself to do so. He tilted his head to brush his jaw along her wrist, but lifted a brow at her bemused expression. "What?"

"I like this look. Very...Tarzan."

"You can see all of it in the shower. If you agree that friends help friends scrub noxious water off one another."

She dimpled, but uncertainty nixed her overwhelming desire to agree. She stepped back. "Ahem. I think someone wants to talk to you."

Des turned. The boy had pulled out the boat and was walking over to them. "That was really cool," he said, sticking out one adolescent hand. "Thanks, man. I'm

Lawrence."

"You're welcome, Lawrence." Des shook the outstretched paw. "Tell me about your boat."

The boy launched into an enthusiastic enumeration of the boat's specs that went far over Julie's head, but Des seemed to take it in stride.

"Hey, your rigging snapped here. Let's get that fixed. Do you know how to do a bowline?"

The boy didn't. He brought the boat's stand over so he and Des could prop the vessel up and go over the finer points of rigging knots. In the meantime, Julie noticed Lawrence's father had finally stopped checking his messages and realized his son was talking to a wet stranger.

"Dad, Des got my boat loose," Lawrence said as the man approached with an expression caught between fixed politeness and a scowl.

"Yeah. Thanks. Time to go. I'll pick you up some McD's on the way back to your mother's. Let's go."

As he strode past them with a grudging flicker of acknowledgement to Des and Julie, Julie wished she had a Taser handy. The boy bit his lip, but he saw Julie's look. "It's okay," he told her in a low voice. "He's kind of a jerk. I like Dan, my stepdad, much better. And my mom's really cool. But he's my dad, so..."

"He's your dad." Des shook the boy's hand once more. "You're pretty cool yourself, Lawrence. You take care of yourself."

"I will. Thanks again, man."

Des and Julie watched the kid go, trailing after his father.

"Thank God for Dan," Julie said hotly. "Else I was about to kidnap that kid and take him home."

"He'd like Betty's horses," Des agreed. He looked at himself and sighed. "Guess this calls it a morning for us, love. I should wash off before I start to glow. I'll drop you back off at the theater. Unless you're interested in that shower offer...?"

"I'm sticking to the friendship idea. Until after opening night," she allowed.

"Really?" He shifted closer. "That's new. What

changed?"

"Your heroism impressed me."

"All part of my diabolical plan," he said, but he touched her cheek, his expression serious. "Julie."

She pressed into the contact briefly, then stepped back and took his hand. She liked holding his hand, for practical purposes as much as other reasons. She could somewhat control him touching her elsewhere, because she didn't think clearly when he was doing that.

"Let's keep it as friends, until I know how I feel about what you do with other subs. That just feels right to me. I don't want to talk about it, because we've talked about it enough. This is something I have to figure out from the heart. Does that make sense?"

"Yeah. So does this."

Okay, so maybe she couldn't keep him from touching her whenever, however he wanted. When he bent and put cold, damp lips on hers, she knew she couldn't get close to him without getting wet herself, but after two seconds she didn't care. She curled one set of fingertips over his bare shoulder, the other hooking into the waistband of his jeans and the elastic of the wet boxers. His hipbone pressed against her knuckles.

As he kissed her, the sunshine warmed her body outside as he warmed her inside. He cupped her face, fingers tunneling in her hair below her barrette. He drew it over her shoulder to stroke.

When he lifted his head, she stared into his eyes. What she saw there made her wonder if she wasn't the only one rocked by what happened between the two of them whenever they did that. He kept his tone light, though, as if he knew how easily spooked she could be.

"Until opening night, then," he said.

Chapter Six

Despite staying insanely busy for the next few days and avoiding Des the couple times he came to the theater to go over his scene with Harris, it preyed on her mind. She wasn't going to be able to wait until opening night to resolve it. Or maybe she just wanted to get the letdown over sooner rather than later.

When he tied up another submissive, touched her, and became aroused by her responses the way he had with Julie, she wouldn't be able to handle that. No matter what she'd rationalized, she knew it was far different from watching two actors kiss during a play.

She really wasn't amused by the term rope bunny anymore.

Despite Billie Dee-Lite's taunt about that "branding," she couldn't trust herself to believe Des's possessiveness that day was anything more than his natural protectiveness and pride in the integrity of his craft. He'd have reacted the same way if another of his submissives was the one who'd been nearly lynched.

And she was so certain of that because of the damned intuition that Madison had praised. Des was funny, kind and sexy, and made her feel wonderful. But there was a wall inside him. A wall that suggested his only interest was exploring her submission and enjoying some friendly pleasure together.

She wasn't wired that way. She wished to God she was, because it was obvious Des was more than capable of giving a girl a great time. But if she was going to have sex without love, she'd have it with her vibrator, not with a living human being who could fuck with her head in the worst ways.

She wasn't going to make it awkward for him. She'd summon up the courage and figure out a way to confirm her suspicions without sounding like she was asking for more than he wanted to give. Then she could walk away with her dignity intact. Sure. Piece of cake.

She should do it by phone, because it was impossible when she was with him. But each time she picked up the phone, she'd remember him standing behind her at the Conservatory, his breath on her throat. Or him bringing her to orgasm on the stage, his gaze riveted upon her. The aftercare he'd done, wrapping a blanket and himself around her, holding her, calling her *love*. Him swimming in a polluted pond to rescue a boy's boat, his pleased expression when he saw the boat free and the boy's relief. His hair slicked back on his head and body shivering slightly in the cool air.

"You do not seem like the Taylor Swift type to me."

"Hmm? What?" She broke out of her absorption to see Harris studying her with a peculiar look on his face.

"You're humming 'Today Was A Fairytale.'" Light dawned in his expression. "You're thinking about Des, aren't you? Spiderman. His subs always seem to get that starry-eyed look when they have sessions planned with him."

What a perfect way to underscore a point, like a dull edged knife sawing through her middle. "Des and I aren't like that," she said with forced casualness. "He showed me some rope stuff once, so I'd understand it better here. I'm just happy we're on schedule and things are unfolding so well for the performance."

Harris gave her a dubious look but moved off the topic and back to the dry tech run they had coming up tonight, when their student stage hands finished their classes for the day.

She had no one to blame but herself for his or anyone else's doubts, including her own. But that was the final straw. She'd visit Des at his work. He couldn't do anything to overwhelm her defenses at work, right?

It was time to get to the bottom of this in whatever convoluted, awkward way was needed. God help her, and poor Des. He'd be glad she was walking away. The thought only made things worse, but also confirmed what she kept telling herself. Her heart could refuse to listen, but her brain knew the truth.

She needed to abstain from romantic relationships of any kind. Period. Otherwise this hamster wheel of redundant emotion would drive her to insanity.

§

Julie pulled up to the job site. Harris had fortunately known where Des was working today so she hadn't had to alert him with a text. While she told herself she wasn't going to lose her resolve, now that she was here, faced with the actual task of having the discussion, it seemed more daunting. And ludicrous. She'd had an overreaction fueled by too much thinking and her dysfunctional and overly dramatic personality.

Being confronted with an army of men working on the new construction site didn't help. Their pickups and vans clustered around the house like a drive-in movie. Hammering, sawing, power tools and men's voices created a drone like bees around a hive.

She noticed a half dozen children of varying ages gathered on the sidewalk, watching. Two straddled bicycles, one held a skateboard and another was on roller skates. The remaining two were on foot. The myriad transportation options available to the young. She idly imagined skateboarding to work if she eventually found a small place near the theater.

Which she would do if she was planning on a long term stay in Matthews, which she wasn't. The thought wouldn't have occurred to her, if not for a couple over-the-top experiences with a skinny, young roofer who didn't seem that skinny or young when his strong arms were holding her, or he had her captured in his ropes.

Which was exactly why she was here and needed to go through with this, even if she had to have the discussion in front of a battalion of wide-eyed grade schoolers and sweaty men in tool belts.

She'd parked near the kids. Since she had the windows down, she heard several of them call out. "Do the Slinky. Slinky!"

As she glanced back at the house, she discovered the roofing crew coming down the ladders. They must be taking a scheduled break. She took it as a sign, one that made her feel better and worse about the chances for her private conversation that couldn't wait.

She looked to see if Des was one of the men coming down and didn't locate him. Then she lifted her gaze to the roof and did.

He was by himself, standing straight and tall as if he wasn't on a steep incline that looked miles above the ground. When he raised a hand to acknowledge the kids, they whooped in response.

His hair was tied back under a bill cap, and he wore a gray T-shirt with some kind of logo on it over his jeans. Standing on one leg and then the other, demonstrating the balance of a flamingo, he removed his work shoes and socks. Putting the socks in the shoes, he tossed them off the roof, letting them thud to the ground.

"What is he..." She'd left the car and was a few feet from the knot of children. None of them noticed her, their eyes all on Des. A blink later, she understood why. Her heart jumped into her throat.

Up on the spine of the roof, he levered himself into a nimble handstand, his back to his audience. He held the pose for several beats, then slowly let his feet come over his head, down toward the roof's slope. It seemed like an impossible angle for anyone's spine, but then everything speeded up. His feet came down to complete the full backbend, and he used the propulsion to catapult him swiftly to his feet and forward into another handstand, but this time he didn't pause. Julie bit back a cry.

As he kept going, building speed, he did look like a Slinky going down a set of stairs. Three times, and he was at the edge of the roof. He somehow slowed his forward progress enough to hold himself up in a handstand again.

He twisted around and his body swung toward the house like a trapeze artist, his toes finding purchase against the siding. He hung there for a second, then pumped his feet out and he let go, dropping two stories to the ground, light as a cat. As the kids cheered, he did a standing somersault and took a bow in their direction.

Julie noticed some of the other contractors chuckling and waving at him, that gesture that communicated *yeah, you're a crazy bastard*. This was apparently all routine. Since the kids had called for "the Slinky", she guessed it was.

As the children moved off, the show over, she saw Des's attention shift and find her. His brown eyes lit with pleasure, which made her want to ignore all the warning signs of a crushed heart. That was why they called it a crush, right? Because the heart could be frozen, pulverized and served up like a snow cone.

He put his shoes and socks back on, and said something to a couple of the guys. A few wolf whistles followed him across the street, which he answered with a quick flipped bird and a comment she didn't catch but they did, laughing him off. She heard them using the same name for him the kids had.

"Slinky?" she said as he approached with that relaxed, sinuous walk he had.

"Yeah, it kind of stuck. I actually thought about it as a scene name, the Kinky Slinky, but it was too campy. And I'm not really into scene names. I like just Des."

"Good decision. What else did they say?" She nodded toward the men.

"The usual. Tell her when she wants a real man, they'll be here waiting. And that you're way too hot for me, which that part is true."

She flushed, even as she felt silly for the unsophisticated reaction. "What did you say back?"

"To the real man thing? That you didn't have any use for a guy choking on his own broken teeth. What are you doing here? Just couldn't wait one more day to see me covered in work filth?"

"Oh, you're nothing next to the homeless guy behind the

theater. He hasn't bathed since Y2K."

"I'm surprised you could keep your hands off him." He smiled, but his brown eyes were suddenly far more focused on her. "I'm going to get you dirty, so you'll just have to deal. You've been avoiding me, and you're the best looking thing I've seen all day."

"Um...since you're working with a bunch of equally grungy men, I think I'm insulted."

"Come here." Ignoring that, he slid an arm around her waist and pulled her to him with that effortless overwhelming strength that didn't give her breath for refusal before he was kissing her. Yes, he was dirty, but beneath it, he was Des. She pressed her body against him, reveling in his hands pushing into her hair, taking control, possessing her from head to toe.

When he lifted his head, she blinked and blurted it out. Desperately. "I can't do this anymore."

He drew back and studied her expression. "Do what?"

"Let you overwhelm me with the Dom thing and the rope thing and these kinds of kisses that only happen in *The Princess Bride*. And how old are you anyway? For real? You won't even tell me that, because this doesn't mean anything to you."

As his brow furrowed, she bit her lip and revised. "I didn't mean it to sound like that. Of course it means something to you. It's your art, like a religion, and I'm like a canvas or an altar. I should be grateful for any moment I get like that, because how many women get the chance to be worshipped? To totally be the center of a man's attention to that depth and intensity, ever. It's an incredible gift, like going on a once in a lifetime trip or doing something on your bucket list."

She shook her head fiercely, denying herself. "But I don't want the once in a lifetime trip. I want the whole lifetime. I want eggs for breakfast, or pancakes or cereal. I want those kinds of decisions with someone I love, not jumping out of an airplane or saving baby seals in Alaska, though I don't want seals hurt. What I'm trying to say is that, for me, quiet moments are just as breathtaking as adrenaline shit is to other people."

His lips parted to speak, but she rushed on. "Yet in those intense moments, you invite me into your soul, which is a huge *wow* factor. But I don't know if you want me to stay. And next week, next performance, next session, it will be someone else, another woman you take to the same level of ecstasy. Some part of me says to ignore it, to ride the same train, refuse to allow it to be more than that, but see, that's where I always fuck up. I can't settle. I want more, and I'm afraid you're not a 'more.'

"You're a drug masquerading as a 'more,' and I'll get addicted to it. Every man has a shoe drop factor, when you realize they're too good to be true. Your problem is you *are* too good to be true. I'll be in your soul watching other females go through like a revolving door. I'll wither and die there."

She closed her eyes, stepped back from him. "I'm a private person, a possessive person. When I decide I'm falling in love with someone, I don't want to share the house with anyone else. I'm not that friendly. Yet everything you're doing to me, it's so incredible, and so I wonder if I'm letting the decisions I've arrived at after so much careful thought derail the chance for something incredible, even if it is temporal. I'm not strong enough to handle my heart getting crushed, Des. I'm not. And everything about you says you're capable of crushing my heart. You're too much, too amazing, too...beyond anything I ever expected to be able to call mine, so I know it can't be right or real..."

She took a breath. "And all of this is why I shouldn't be doing a relationship with anyone, let alone you."

She'd finally run out of words before those fathomless brown eyes. This was the part where he could tell insane, babbling woman it was okay, they could just be friends. And that would be that. Or maybe she'd learn she hadn't done it in time and her heart would be crushed anyway.

"Thirty-five," he said. "Thirty-six in three months. That's how old I am."

She stared at him. He was somehow holding her hand, his thumb rubbing her palm, her rabbiting pulse. "No way," she said. "You're in your twenties."

"Thought you were getting a much younger man, did you?" His lips curved but there was no humor in his eyes. Her words had made an impact and she realized his touch was as much firm hold as caress. "I've always looked about ten years younger than I actually am. Arrested development. It was a bitch when I was seven. Must be why the kids in the class nicknamed me Fetus."

"Great. Like most men don't already have the advantage in aging; you got the extra helping."

"Most gifts like that come with strings attached." He tipped up her chin before she could pursue the faint bitterness she heard in his tone. She was too worked up anyhow. She realized she was shaking and so did he.

"Hey," he said, dropping his hands to run them up and down her arms in a soothing manner. "It's okay."

She shook her head. "I really liked what happened on stage that night. I wanted more of it. But I don't want to become whatever the term is for someone who's strung out on sub experiences. And I don't want to go down a road with someone whose interest in me... It's like the 'everyone is special' argument. If everyone is special, no one really is, according to the literal definition. I want to be special to someone. I want to see a look in their eyes that says I'm the person that makes their day better. I'm the one who lights up the room for them, even if it's just a sixty watt bulb. Actually, I prefer it that way. I don't want to be this grand explosion of light and passion that happens for one rope session or for a short, unforgettable relationship."

She curled her fingers in his shirt. "I want to be the person who will always keep the porch light on for the other person, and he knows that, he can count on it. I'll put a night light in the bedroom so he can find his way to me without stumbling in the dark."

She didn't want to blind her soulmate. She just wanted him to know he'd always be able to find her heart, because the light they shared would be soft, steady and strong, like love itself. And why was she telling this to Des, when she knew he wasn't willing to go that far with her? Was she using him like some kind of bizarre confessor?

"Take a breath," he said, drawing her attention from the

whirl of her thoughts to his serious face. "You've been spun up over this for a while now."

"Yeah. Since...well, it's been building since the orchids, really. You have a really bizarre effect on me. I wasn't going to get involved with anyone ever again. That was the promise I made myself."

"That's a shitty promise," he observed. "Like promising to shut your hand in a car door once a week."

"Not if falling in love feels ten times worse than that. The car door would be preferable."

"Good point. I've never let myself fall in love. Never thought I could afford it. Turns out, we're not given much choice about that, are we?"

Her gaze flicked up to his face, not sure what he meant and not getting any further clues from his neutral expression, because he changed the topic. Somewhat.

"When I came in to meet with Harris this week, I watched you. Doing something right is in the details, and, more than that, in loving those details, the subtle ways they add to a scene. You have that. That's how you'll make the show come alive and become something memorable. It's not about pyrotechnics or the big flash. I like that about you." He stroked her hair over her shoulder, ran his thumb along her collarbone. The sleeveless knit tank she was wearing allowed him to slide his thumb beneath it, tease her bra strap.

"There's very little about you I don't like or find pretty terrific, except your absence. Seeing you here today was like a birthday three times over."

"See, you're doing it again," she accused. "Making me feel so special, like you—"

"Hey." He tightened his grip, commanding her full attention. "You *are* special to me, Julie. You're giving me a lot of good information, but you're not listening. Or rather, I think you are listening, but there's so much static from your past relationships, my message isn't getting through."

She wanted to get her back up at his impatient tone, but he wasn't done. "Sounds to me like you're saying you need a guy to court you, not just stumble into it. You don't want him leaving himself a clear path of retreat by never openly declaring his intentions."

"I guess that's asking too much of the average guy," she said bitterly, thinking he was mocking her.

"It is. There's nothing average about you, Julie. You should be demanding something exceptional. You want subtle but you also want sincerity. Courage."

He cradled her jaw so she had to meet his eyes. "Say it. Honestly, from the gut."

He was doing that Dom thing, drawing her into his gaze, holding open that door inside her soul that couldn't lie to him. That couldn't lie at all.

"Yes," she said quietly. "I'm done with anything less."

He nodded. "That's a hell of a lot different from giving up on love. If you're going to have your guts torn out, it should be for a guy who's worth it, not a loser who doesn't know how to appreciate the gift of love."

He returned to the light stroking of her collarbone and bra strap. He didn't say anything further, either to deny he was that guy, or confirm he wanted to be in the running. Probably because of that wall she sensed within him before and could feel rising now. Only this time, from his words and expressions, she suspected he was struggling with it. Which didn't make her as eager to throw up her own defenses. What an idiot she was.

"At one time, the first step in courtship was asking permission to write to the person who interested your affections," she ventured. "Then you moved to carriage rides and walks in the park. It was more balanced."

He considered that. "So, in a way, dating services where you meet online and get to know one another through email first are connecting to a historic tradition."

One of the things she liked about him—among many things—was that he could shift topics with her, all while retaining the original motive driving the conversation. His gaze flickered with heat now, proving it.

"If I kissed you again, would things be better balanced?"

"It might. You're a decent kisser." She adopted a nonchalant look rather than that of an eagerly panting puppy, though it took an effort. His dark eyes gleamed and he slid an arm around her.

"Liar. I'm a hell of a kisser, love. I can make your knees weak."

"If my knees wobble, it's because I haven't had lunch. Just for the record, I'm not trying to be pathetic or clingy. It would really piss me off if you thought that. I'm trying to be rational and calm, except I don't really do rational and calm. I'm just—"

"Shut up a moment."

Her attention flicked up from the hole she was staring into his throat, and his mouth was on hers again. Slow, exploratory, deep. She was still worked up enough she tried to wrench away, thrust at him, but he clamped a hand on the side of her throat, the other at her waist, and held her fast, refusing to let her throw him off.

It was the blade he knew how to draw at the right instant, more instinctive than calculated, which made it far more powerful, galvanizing her own instincts. Her body softened against his, despite all her internal warnings that he still hadn't provided an answer that could make this turn out okay. Her fingers slid up to his neck and tangled in his sweat-dampened hair. She was vaguely aware of whistling across the street, but she couldn't be embarrassed or care, not when Des didn't seem to be paying attention to anything but taking her will and her heart in one soul-penetrating kiss.

When he lifted his head this time, his eyes bored into hers. "I don't kiss them, Julie," he said, low. "Not like that."

She blinked, uncertain of his meaning, and he let her lean against the bumper of her car, keeping himself pressed against her knees, his hands at her waist.

"My turn to talk. Okay?" He brushed a finger over her swollen lips. "I love the way you look after I kiss you. Makes me want to have you right here on the hood of your car like some kind of animal."

When she quivered and closed her eyes, everything too fragile to look at him, that same protest rising to her lips to protect her, he brushed his knuckles against her face. She opened her eyes again.

"I do sessions with submissives who love rope. I care about each of those women and, in the session, you're right, we can get fairly intense and intimate. But there's a beginning and an end. It's a lot like a stage play where the actors lose themselves and become those characters. But when the curtains come down, the spell is lifted.

"When the session is over, I do whatever aftercare they need, kiss their forehead, light kisses on the mouth. I stroke them, give them an orgasm if they need it to decompress. And yeah, if she's the kind of sub who doesn't feel complete unless she's given her top release, and that's within her boundaries, I might make her go down on me. Sometimes there's sex, because, hell, I get worked up too. Until now, I've never thought about having someone who'd be that outlet for me afterward."

He moved his hands to her shoulders, caressing the round shape of them revealed by her sleeveless tank. She'd become more rigid at the discussion, but she didn't look away. She understood he was trying to tell her something that would answer her question, even though she wasn't really thrilled about the route he was taking toward it.

"After it's over, I help them dress and I make sure they're okay. Then we go our separate ways. If we see each other socially, it's at the club BBQs or hanging out at play parties, talking about what other Doms and subs are doing. I don't kiss them like I just kissed you. When I kiss you, it's different and new."

She twitched under his hands and he nodded. "Yeah, sounds like that load of manure you always hear, 'It was just sex, baby. It didn't mean anything.' But those sessions do mean something, Julie. I don't deny that. When I'm that connected to a sub, the sex can be out of this world, but it is sex, not love. I have affection and care for every woman I've ever tied up, because I'm never going to treat her like an object or an instrument.

"I move in and out of a world where there are very distinct lines between session play and a relationship that's outside a session. Doesn't always work out that clean or neat, but up until now, I've made sure it is for me, because as I said, that's what I thought I could afford. You're changing that viewpoint."

Humor glittered against the taut set of his mouth. "You

said the quiet moments, like choosing breakfast, are just as special to you as the passionate stuff. In only a few days, you've made me very interested in figuring out breakfast with you."

She lifted her chin. "But it's still there, Des. A wall. You're bullshitting me without bullshitting me."

"What do you mean?" He frowned. "I'm being straight with you."

"Yeah. You're being straight with me, telling me incredibly personal things and yet somehow weirdly holding me at arm's length. It's like we're in a classroom and you're standing up front, relaying info about yourself without giving me any of yourself. I can't really figure it out, but I can feel it. I bullshitted myself, thinking I could come out here and say 'hey that rope session was nifty, thanks and bye.' I want more, no matter how scared I am. But I will not go out on that ledge by myself one more time. I just can't. Just please...tell me now. Am I ridiculous to think I already feel something so strong for you that we've fallen into a relationship without any warning, or am I on that ledge by myself?"

"No. No you're not." His hands were on her shoulders, and his expression was frustrated. She saw a flash of aching need so powerful it both frightened and reassured her in a way a million charming words couldn't. "I don't want you scared, love. Of anything. And particularly not of me."

"So tell me." Taking a page out of his own book, the way he could use wry humor to make her feel okay about saying anything, she took both his hands. "What's your issue? Daddy, Mommy, fear of love, of commitment? Spill, then it's out of the way and in the open. Treat it like a Tweet. One sentence or less, because the rest is window dressing, justification, caviling, explaining. I just want to hear the basic problem."

He brushed his fingers through her hair, giving it a little tug. "I've been really careful not to let anyone be too close, Julie. Not that I've closed myself off, but I make sure they don't get so deep they get hurt."

"Okay. We're getting closer, but we're still not there. Don't invite me in but leave me in the front room. Don't use protecting me as an excuse to protect yourself."

She'd struck home. For a moment she saw something angry in his eyes, but he reined it back.

"Fair enough," he said. "But first tell me why you stopped dating. You've given me some of it, but I'd like to know the other part of it. It's something beyond what they've done to you, isn't it?"

She bit her lip. Well, it was no worse than what she'd already dumped on him, but if he didn't have something comparably fucked up to share, she was going to be pissed. "I got tired of relationships kick-starting the same emotional shit. Can I trust him? When will he hurt me? It's the typical clichéd romance conflict crap that happens in everyone's story, and I got tired of being in the same play. But you...I can't predict anything about you, so it doesn't make me tired. Just scared."

"What are you scared of?" His hand settled on her shoulder again, fingertips tracing patterns. He really didn't like hearing she was afraid, and she was just weak enough to respond to the light in his eyes, the closer shift of his body, that said he wanted to fix that.

"That I'm still in the same play. I just don't recognize the set."

He digested that. "Okay, but I'll be the first guy you've dated who can give you something different."

"What's that?"

He grimaced and met her gaze. "I'll be dead before I can tear your heart out and stomp on it."

§

At first she thought he was saying something over-the-top romantic, like he'd die before he'd ever hurt her. But as he kept holding her with his piercing stare, it sank in. Her hands reflexively gripped his. "What?" she said faintly.

He swore under his breath. "I didn't mean to say it that way. You're a pushy woman, love. Let me take you out to lunch where we can talk. There's a Bob Evans about a mile up that way. I'll meet you there."

From his closed expression, she supposed he wanted to

take separate cars so that she had an escape route. She didn't know what she'd want. She was torn between his hints of wanting to share pancakes with her, or not having a choice about falling in love, and the implication he was...

No, she wasn't going to say it in her head. She was too confused. She focused on the other things he'd said that she could process.

He was right. The upfront things, like how he felt with a sub in session, smacked of every lame excuse for infidelity she'd heard. Yet she'd already known about his sessions, had experienced one herself first hand, and she'd been immersed in the BDSM world these past couple months, witnessing the interactions between those who practiced it.

She thought her whole information dump upon him had been too much, too soon. She and he hadn't come far enough in a relationship where infidelity could be a crime committed against it. They hadn't even actually had sex yet.

But he'd taken her outpouring in stride, as if he felt strongly enough for her that he'd welcomed hearing every worry she had. Maybe that was also due to the BDSM dynamic. As he'd said, boundaries and structure were set quickly, to keep things safe and protect feelings. Only where was the line between letting love happen spontaneously and trying to control everything? She thought she'd obliterated that line a couple failed relationships ago, and now she was out to sea with him, trying to figure out how this was going to work or if she could walk away. And he'd just thrown a new wrench into it. A pretty damn significant one.

As they were taken to a booth and handed menus, he touched her hand. "Why don't we keep it casual for a few minutes before we launch into anything?"

From the strained look around his mouth, she figured that was more for him than herself, but she was okay with giving him that breathing space. He'd implied she'd pushed him into a corner, and she guessed she had. But Des didn't seem the type to let himself be pushed around, so she held onto the hope that he was willingly having this conversation with her.

As she glanced at the menu, he pulled out his monitor

and fitted it with a lancet. At her glance, he passed it to her. "Want to try it? Test your blood sugar?"

"Oh, God, I'd pass out. I could never stick myself."

"Do me then." He held out his hand. "Just hold it against my finger tip, then press that button."

She did, a quick click. He captured the tiny drop of blood on a test strip. At a beep from the monitor, he glanced at the resulting number and put it all away. Removing his pump from his pack, he slid it on under his clothes, connecting it to the injection site cannula by feel, his hand moving under the shirt.

"You've been doing this a long time."

"A very long time." He checked something on the pump screen, made an adjustment, then tucked the device back into the wallet he hooked over his belt. He flipped his shirt back down over it and picked up the menu as the waitress returned.

They ordered, and when the waitress asked if it would be one check, Des nodded. "I'll be taking it," he said. "My treat."

"I should have ordered the Belgian waffles to go."

"You still have time." Whatever he saw in her face had him reaching across the table and gripping her hand. "I'm sorry I've caused you any sadness or doubts, Julie. I really enjoy being with you."

"I love being with you." She gave him a weak smile. "That's kind of the problem. Sorry. I guess it's impossible to get someone without baggage once they pass thirty."

"I bet my baggage outweighs your baggage."

"Oh really?" She fished in her purse, pulled out a dollar and set it on the table. "I'll bet a dollar it's not. You seem totally together."

"I'm a Dom. We're all about the illusion of total control." He winked, but set his own crumpled dollar next to hers. He sipped his unsweetened tea then, as if gathering his thoughts. He'd let go of her hand and she curled both in her lap, feeling adrift until he pressed his foot against hers under the table, connecting them.

"Just tell me, Des. Please. I poured my guts out to you. Quid pro quo."

His lips quirked, but he set down the tea and nodded, crossing his arms on the table. "I don't have any interest in in-depth discussions about this. But I owe you what's behind the curtain if we're going any farther. So I'm going to tell you what I need to tell you and, when this meal is over, there's no need to talk about it further. I'm not a disease."

The sudden fierceness in his tone, the set of his jaw, alerted her to the maelstrom of emotions going on beneath the surface. She might lose that dollar. He wasn't as together over this as he'd first appeared.

"Doesn't matter what you tell me. I could never think of you that way, Des."

He glanced over the dining room absently, as if he'd rather be anywhere else than talking about this. She shifted her foot so her toe pressed on his and he brought his gaze back to her. He had some kind of glitter on his shoulder, maybe from the shingles he'd been handling. When she reached toward it to brush it off, he caught her hand.

"It's probably fiberglass. The splinters are nasty." He held onto her hand, resting it on the table, playing with her fingers and studying them.

"I told you I had a bunch of health issues when I was a kid. I was a preemie, and my mom split as soon as they discharged her. They said I wouldn't survive a week, because she was a prescription drug addict and that affected my development. When I made it to age five, I started having seizures. They said I'd be dead before I was ten. Then the diabetes started. So on and so forth."

Her heart skipped a beat as he lifted his gaze to her face. "About the time I hit twenty-five, the damn doctor stopped giving me the doom-and-gloom, 'You won't live past so-n-so.' Probably because I told him next time he said it, I'd feed him his stethoscope through his anus. But there are a couple things I can't beat. I'm insulin-resistant and my kidneys are wearing out. I don't need dialysis yet, but it will come sooner than later. Renal failure. That's the track toward the end, love. I'm not a good transplant candidate because of my medical history."

The waitress brought their food. As she placed the plates

on the table and asked them if they needed anything else, Julie watched Des switch gears. His usual genuine charm and humor made the waitress smile and Julie's chest ache. She'd poured open her heart to him, all her worries about pursuing a relationship, and he was giving her the same. Quid pro quo could be a bitch.

"Hey." He drew her out of her head. The waitress was gone. "Don't look like that, love. Nobody knows when it's going to end."

He took a breath. "But that said, I'm not in denial, either. That's why I'm telling you. I have no way of explaining to you, other than this, that you're different to me. I've gotten involved with plenty of women in session. None outside of it. Yet when you look at me the way you do...I like it. I want to spend time with you, in every way I can. But I'm not going to let you get any deeper without knowing what might happen. I wouldn't want to do that to you."

She swallowed and he narrowed his eyes, making a threatening gesture with his fork. "You get teary on me, I'll take your pancakes and eat them myself."

She blinked the tears back. "That's just mean."

"I'm not always nice." He made a stab at her plate and she fended him off with her fork, making him smile and things unknot a bit in her gut. He sobered though, probably because she couldn't entirely mask her reaction.

"Will I have a much shorter lifespan than you?" he said. "Pretty likely, unless you die in a car crash, though I'd be severely pissed if you did."

"I'll keep that in mind."

"You do that." He reached across the table and tapped her hand. "But I'm not going to be gone tomorrow. In the meantime, we can keep going as we're going, figure out where we'll end up together. Or you decide we're friends from here forward, and that's the end of it. Ball's back in your court, love."

His tone, his direct look, said he was ready to be done with the subject. She sensed a withdrawal in him, a closing down, the wall coming back up. He'd put himself out there for her, to let her know, but he must be anticipating rejection, pity, sympathy or her withdrawal. Whereas she'd dealt with her build-up of feeling with an outpouring that made her feel drained, he dealt with the same kind of stress by containing it.

He genuinely didn't like talking about this. But he had, for her. Because he wanted more from her. He wanted to see where this would go.

He'd given her the answer she'd sought, mostly, and now the question was whether she was willing to risk taking this road one more time. Up until the other day, with Pablo, she hadn't given a lot of thought to her mortality. Des dealt with his on a daily basis. Could she really be so chickenshit as to back away from a relationship with a guy she really liked for fear he might hurt her with his death? If nothing else, it was the first time she'd had *that* risk in a relationship.

"Ball's back in my court, hmm? Thought you said once you had the ball back you wouldn't give it up."

"I did say Doms were all about the illusion of total control. You have to give me the control, love. Every time."

She wasn't sure that was entirely true. When he was exercising his will upon her, she couldn't find her own with both hands. But this was a different kind of moment.

She picked up her fork. "Can you pass me the maple syrup?"

He obliged. "You're not going to tell me which way you're going to go on this?"

"Not until I eat. I don't make any decisions on an empty stomach."

"All right, but just keep this in mind. If I do tear your heart out like those other losers, you'll get the satisfaction of dancing on my grave while you're still young enough to do it without a walker. How many guys can offer a girl a perk like that?"

She paused in mid-pour, blinking at him, and then a laugh bubbled out of her, she couldn't help it. He looked so earnest, only a little twinkle in his eye. She set down the syrup. "I'm sorry. Oh God, it's awful of me to be laughing at that."

"Actually, it's the most beautiful thing I've ever heard."

She stopped, seeing the truth of it in his gaze. He was looking at her as if he'd like to see her laugh every day of their lives. She cleared her throat, feeling heat in her cheeks.

"So this is why you haven't had many relationships outside of a scene."

"Yeah. It's my big skeleton in the closet. So do I get the dollar?"

"I'll think about it. Not sure if your mortality really measures up to my wretched dating life. Maybe we'll just leave both dollars as part of our tip."

His lips curved, and though her stomach tilted at the gesture, she covered it with a noncommittal noise. "Honestly, I feel kind of dumb for unloading all that other stuff on you now. It would be nice to turn back time, to undo every stupid thing I've ever done."

"Then you wouldn't be who those moments taught you to be, right?"

"Why can't we learn lessons from being brilliant and perfect?"

Des smirked. "Because the Powers That Be are sadists." He touched her fork with his, a small tinny noise. "You shouldn't be embarrassed. I'm very glad you trusted me enough to share all that."

"If that's your kind of show, anytime you want a front row seat to my insecurities, I'll give you a free ticket."

"Don't do that, Julie." He spoke sharply enough her surprised gaze flickered up to his face. "Anything you share with me so honestly is a gift. That's part of what drew me into rope and working with subs. During a session, if everything goes the way it should, all we feel is so out front, no hidden motives or things unsaid, left to fester and infect the relationship." He pressed the toe of his work shoe down on her canvas sneaker, enough she felt his weight upon her toes. It was an intentional discomfort that focused her attention and sharpened other things inside of her. He saw it, his expression whetting with a Dom's interest, but he wasn't letting it go. "Okay?"

"I'll try. Okay." She wet her lips. "Why is that so important to you?"

"Because the world is full of so much crap we tell ourselves and each other that doesn't really mean anything. That's one of the things I liked about you from the beginning. You're clever and funny as hell, but there's not a dishonest bone in your body."

"Hmm." She returned her attention to her food, wanting to conceal how unsettling his words were. To be praised for the things she'd begun to think were flaws...it annoyed her, the clear evidence that she'd let those who tore her down define her. She should know better than that.

He'd ordered a giant vegetable omelet with a side of dry wheat toast, and she stole a sliced grape tomato that fell out the end of the omelet. In turn, he took a bite of her pancake, soaked with syrup. Fair was fair.

"When you tied me up, I noticed you touched my hands a lot. I liked it. Why do you do that?"

"Any blackberry jelly on your side?"

She checked the condiment container, and handed it over, their fingertips brushing. He briefly held onto them, giving her a warm look.

"It connects us emotionally, making sure we're still taking the journey together. The practical side is I'm testing your circulation. If your hands are cold, I know I need to adjust the form or release you to avoid damage."

"Hmm." That was how it had made her feel. Connected to him, not objectified or separate, the subject of an experiment, no matter how sensual. "You know, you're kind of a hypocrite. You'll do a dangerous stunt on a steep roof, but you freak out if I have a rope mishap."

"That's different. One's about me being in charge of me, where I can be as much of a dumbass as I want. The other is wanting to take care of you."

"I can't feel that way about you?"

"You don't need to feel that way about me."

She screwed up her face and crossed her eyes at him. "You know that's crazy thinking, right? Being in a relationship is caring about each other. It's not one-sided. That's part of you trusting me."

He rolled that over in his mind, obvious from the

introspection, the slight gold glint to his irises when he was giving something real thought. His jaw had a light layer of afternoon stubble on it and she reached across the table to trail her fingertips over the sandpaper feel, just because she wanted to do so. He had told her she could be open and honest about all her feelings, and she hoped that included when she wanted to touch him.

"That idea will take me a little time," he said, closing his fingers around her wrist and pressing his lips to the heel of her hand. She liked the feel of that, especially as he gave her that look that said he liked knowing he had her caught.

"Okay," she said. She feigned indifference, despite her pulse speeding up against his hold. "But it's kind of Relationship 101."

"A lot of things are Relationship 101. Doesn't mean they're easy skills to master."

"Isn't that the definition of 101? Entry level, beginner stuff?"

"Eat your food, woman." He released her with a smile. "Else you'll find out how we Southern boys handle mouthy females."

Chapter Seven

He was drawing her away from more serious topics, and she took the hint. She caught him up to speed on what was happening with *Consent*, the successes and setbacks, routine for a theater's first production.

"I'm grateful to Madison for being so hands-off and yet so accessible at once. Sometimes a producer can really get underfoot, but in all fairness that usually happens when there's a clash between budget and art and the producer has to remind the directors they can only work within the resources they have. She and I don't have that problem. I've done enough of the fundraising side I know you have to squeeze the most out of every dime. And she loves and appreciates the creative process. She's worked with any changes I've suggested to help the show and the theater succeed. She's a managing and artistic director's dream."

"So you're both?"

"I'll wear a lot of hats for this first performance. We already have great volunteers. They just don't have the expertise a paid staff would be expected to have, so I'm doing a lot of teaching. Thank God Harris has a strong background in technical direction, and the students Madison recruited have been a godsend."

They continued their meal with more conversation along the same lines. She appreciated how keenly Des listened, and the useful insights he offered, but she couldn't forget the weight of that kiss by her car, the words they'd exchanged here. Or the question she hadn't yet answered for him.

She watched his hand, tapping the table to make specific

points, and how his fingers spread out loosely when he was listening. Like a resting spider. Yet there was a waiting tension to them.

He finished his meal first and when the waitress took his plate away, he took the salt and pepper shakers out of their holders and absently twisted them around one another.

"I wasn't entirely honest the other day, about why I was so pissed with myself about Pablo," he said. "Or rather, I was, but since then I realized there was another reason. Maybe the main reason. It went back to the first rope session I did with you."

Making the salt and pepper shakers the pillars on either side, he started stacking the jelly packs into a brick wall. "I give *every* sub I work with the safety lecture, to make sure she knows how to take care of herself when it comes to rope bondage."

When his gaze flickered up to hers, Julie was caught by the russet shades, the golds, rusts and browns in his vivid irises. "I didn't do that with you. I didn't want to think about you seeking out similar experiences with other Doms. I figured your next rope session, if you had one, would be with me."

"Oh." That night, her first sub situation, she'd thought what had happened had only happened to her. She'd thought it was nothing unusual for him. Yes, it could be special and hot, as he'd said, but it was like cake. Cake was always wonderful, but a man could have lots of different pieces of cake.

"Can you say right out what you're saying?" she asked slowly. "I have a bad habit of assuming feelings that aren't there."

"I didn't want you doing that with anyone else," he said bluntly, making her heart jump. "That was a new feeling for me, so I didn't really get it until I walked in and saw you in the middle of another rigger's set up. So I'm sorry that my testosterone surge was what kept me from protecting you better."

"Ironic." She attempted to keep her tone nonchalant. "Testosterone is what usually triggers the 'get behind me and I'll take the hail of bullets' vibe."

"Yeah, but it's not known for triggering brain cells at the same time. Just for the record, I'd find us both a place to hide from a hail of bullets."

"Smart and sensible." She put the grape jelly at the apex of his structure of jelly packs. "I have some marmalade left over here. Who likes marmalade? The name doesn't even sound appetizing."

"It's okay." He kept his hand still as she curved hers over it, tracing his chapped knuckles. Beneath the table, their feet still touched, pressed, stroked.

There wasn't as much noise in her head as there'd been earlier. Hearing that Des was interested in more with her had shut down her litany of defenses. *The lady doth protest too much, methinks.* That damn Will Shakespeare.

"Give me another bite of your pancakes." He reached to pinch off a piece. She fended him off with her fork.

"Rude man. Don't even say please."

"You're supposed to get hot and bothered by my commanding tone, not criticize my manners."

"That sounded more like a whine. Madison warned me there's a fine line between a Dom and a guy being obnoxious. Or avoiding household chores."

"Who said there has to be a line at all?" He gave her a look of triumph when she cut off another hunk of pancake and passed it to him. She hadn't put syrup on this one, so he ate it like a piece of bread, then sat back. He pulled the band from his hair to let the thick strands fall on his shoulders and rumpled his hand briefly through it, as if to ease the pull on his scalp. He slid the band around his wrist.

She'd put down her fork, having eaten the last bite, and he gestured to her. "Come over here."

She complied, scooching into the booth next to him. He stretched his arm out behind her and turned her so she hooked her leg over his knee.

"So, the other day, the James Garner thing," he said. "If you could—without guilt—request anyone to die with you so you'd have them for company on that journey, who would it be? First person who jumps into your head."

"Will you tell me yours if I tell you mine?"

"Maybe."

She sniffed and pretended she was going back to her side of the table, but he put a hand on her knee, keeping her still. He played with her ponytail, twining his fingers in it. "So spill. Who would it be?"

"I guess it would be Marcus and Thomas. If something isn't right, Marcus steps in and makes it right." She deepened her voice and imitated her friend. "'Hey, what the hell is this Pearly Gates shit? Heaven's a gated community? Really? Who's in charge here?' Thomas would calm him down and be the pure soul that gets Marcus and me in despite all our flaws." Who would your person be? Or persons?"

His expression was thoughtful, but his eyes dwelled upon her in a way that held her still. Like a bird in his hand, as he'd described at the lake.

"I'll tell you another day," he said.

Since he didn't say anything further and seemed lost in thought, she chose to remain quiet. Thinking he'd want to put his hair back up before he returned to the job site, she took the band from his wrist and scooted closer to comb her fingers through his hair and pull it back from his face, working the band over the thick tail in a double wrap. He dipped his head down to accommodate her and, when she finished, she let her fingers linger on his rough jaw.

He looked up, their faces close. "You've eaten, so there's another answer you owe me."

The increase in tension in his fingers on her shoulder, in his leg beneath hers, told her the answer mattered. She wanted to give him the answer he wanted, but it was how much she wanted to give him that answer that worried her. But he'd said this took courage, didn't it? She was far less courageous than he thought, but maybe, just this one last time...

"You've told me what I need to know, Des. If you mean it, I want to keep going forward. I want to be with you, keep figuring things out with you. I think we've already passed the point where I'd choose anything different, anyway. But watching you do a session with another woman...that's going to be a tough one for me. I'm a traditional girl, all in all, and this world is new to me. I'm going to have some out of sync moments about it."

His fingers dropped to stroke the valley of her spine beneath her shirt. Her answer had changed his eyes to that copper intensity. If there'd been room in the booth, she suspected he would have pulled her onto his lap then and there. She wondered how late he could be back to work and if either of their vehicles would accommodate two grappling adults. Were there any isolated parks nearby?

Fortunately—or not so fortunately—he helped distract her. "Maybe when you see me perform with Missive, it will help. And you can ask me anything you want about that, before or after."

"Not during?"

"Well, Miss Director, I have no problem with you walking out on stage and making it a Q&A, but I think your audience might." He became more serious, hand returning to her leg, gliding up and down her thigh. "It does get intense. So if you do end up feeling unhappy about it, promise me something. Don't walk away. Let's talk it out. I think it will be easier to talk about it afterward, after you've watched it first, rather than trying to hash out all your possible reactions beforehand. Okay?"

"Okay."

"Hey." He tapped her forearm. "In case I haven't stated it clearly enough, if we're walking this path together, I'm not planning on having sex with someone else in a session. Or out."

It was reassuring to hear, though a BDSM scene was sexual by nature, whether actual sex happened or not. But it was something. She wasn't going to be a baby about it or quiz him about particulars. Not right now. It was like he'd said. They'd just wait and see how she reacted to his stage performance.

She closed her hands around his on her thigh. "All right. Is it okay if we keep it kind of light until opening night? That still feels like a turning point to me, a starting line, if that makes sense."

He didn't say anything for a few moments, studying her as if he was considering variables beyond her comprehension. When she was about to shift uncomfortably, he spoke.

"I think you might be right. I'll plan accordingly."

He didn't explain that further, shifting topics. "But I want to see you between now and then, Julie, and not just when I come in to do my part for the performance. How about a couple normal dates, when you can fit it in?"

"That sounds good." Perversely, she was caught between happiness that he wanted to keep pursuing this like a real relationship and disappointment he wasn't overriding her caution and taking her to a dungeon lair where he could shatter her mind.

He muttered something under his breath and leaned in to speak against her ear, teasing it with his mouth and his tongue as he did so.

"You don't have a poker face at all, love." The suggestion he subsequently planted in her mind was enough to push away any worries and send erotic shivers through her body. Her fingers tightened around his hand, the one that had been inching up her thigh. As he drew back enough to stare into her eyes, she realized Des could be pushed beyond civilized behavior, even in a public place.

"When will *that* date be?" she managed in a breathy voice.

"Sometime after that starting line. Sooner rather than later." His voice dropped to a whisper, sending shivers down the side of her throat and tingling through her body. "Though it may happen sooner than that. All sorts of things can happen on a 'normal' date."

His eyes glowed with the promise of it.

§

Despite sexual frustration and what she'd decided to dub sub-anxiety, a state where a submissive personality wanted more, more, more, now, now, now, she was in a good mood when she returned to the theater. She was ready to sing some more Taylor Swift. She ignored Harris's snicker and finished out the rest of the day with a million thoughts in her head.

When he and the scattering of stage hands went for a dinner break before the dry tech run, and she had the theater mostly to herself for the next half hour, she knew it was at last time to make a call. She'd done the texting thing the last few weeks as promised, and Marcus and Thomas had both responded regularly. They'd also emailed and posted things on social media to let her know they were no farther away than she needed them to be.

She felt guilty she'd pushed them away as she sorted things out for herself, but they were the type of friends who would understand. Well, Thomas would, and he would help Marcus to understand. Marcus just liked to control everything. She grinned and took a seat on the empty stage, punching the button on her phone that would connect her to Marcus.

It wasn't purely a social call. She needed to understand a few things that only Marcus could explain from the Dom, aka Des, perspective. What he couldn't, Thomas would, but she generally went to Marcus first. Must be the sub in her.

She smiled again, the gesture broadening at Marcus's opening line.

"She *did* remember how to dial a phone. I was beginning to think being beneath the Mason Dixon line had made you forget about technology all together."

Thomas had once said that Marcus had Lucifer's voice, a purring masculine timbre that could bring the deadest libido to life, male or female. She wasn't immune, but she'd been exposed to it enough not to become brain dead from its influence. She sniffed.

"Typical Northerner. Assuming anyone in the South is an ignorant hick."

"Hey, I married one of those hicks. I should know."

She laughed. "He'd punch you in the gut for that."

"Fortunately I have abs of steel."

"To match your head of solid rock. How are you guys?"

"Ah, how I've missed your lovely ego strokes." He chuckled, another weapon in his seduction arsenal he could wield with intent. Yet it was far more devastating when used as it was now, with such unconscious awareness. He picked up on her desire for a casual opening easily enough, giving her the highlights of a reassuringly normal day-to-day on their end of things. Gallery showings, temperamental artists, the latest happenings in the New York social scene, the parties Thomas hated to attend but were necessary to help promote his ever more popular work.

"He's still charmingly thrilled every time someone gushes over his art, which is why he does so well at the parties, despite hating the attention." Marcus didn't bother to conceal his tender fondness for his spouse. "He's like the kid watching the adult Christmas party, hiding in the shadows at the top of the stairs. He wants to listen to what people are saying about his pieces without having to be in the midst of the social scene."

"Well, he's a shy farm boy and always will be." Julie used the term with affection, since Marcus often called Thomas 'farm boy.'

"True. Every morning he marks the calendar with a big red X, one day closer to heading back to his little rustic corner of the world."

"I can't wait for that myself. When?"

"Not long. Linda will handle my gallery like she normally does, because I've promised Thomas we can stay in North Carolina several weeks. I can always take a quick flight back up for a day or so if I have to. He needs some uninterrupted time to work on new material. He does fine here, but his best stuff happens when he's surrounded by farm animals and his mother. Which might be an unnecessary distinction."

"Ooh, I'm going to tell Elaine you said that. She'll whack you with one of her wooden spoons."

"It's our form of familial affection. How long do I have to make idle conversation before you tell me what's up?"

"You can feel the vibes?"

"Like a New York symphony overture. Not that I don't enjoy our casual banter immensely, but you called for a reason. Tell me."

"I met someone. I think he's...different. I wasn't going to ever get involved with anyone again. You know that, I told you that."

"A decision I knew was misguided, but I held my tongue because I'm a good friend who waits for the right moment to say 'neener, neener, neener, I told you so.'"

"Something I really appreciate about you." She paused. "He's different, Marcus. Terrifying, brilliant, special. I'm scared, because I'm so gone over him, so fast."

"How is he different?" His voice had sharpened, reminding her Marcus had a very protective side when it came to those he considered his family.

"He's...well, he's a Dom. A rigger. He does rope. He's going to be performing in our opener. I hope you guys can come to at least one of the four shows."

"Hmm." Marcus didn't say anything for a second, making her wonder what he was thinking about Des. His next question told her he was mulling. "That's a short run, isn't it?"

"We're on a limited budget right now, and it's not really that kind of show. But if it does well with the audience and in reviews, the buzz should improve demand for longer running productions."

"Good marketing move. So he's a Dom and a rigger. Does he know what he's doing? Who do you have to vouch for him?"

"Logan. He almost didn't need the references. When I'm with him, I get a really safe feeling. But he's also cruel in the right ways, if that makes sense. Cruel might not be the best word. Ruthless?"

"That edge you crave without it cutting you to pieces. You've been down that road before, looking for it with the wrong guys. Not your fault," Marcus added, drawing out the sting. "The world's full of assholes and you have the biggest heart of any one I know, except Thomas."

She stayed silent a few beats. "Marcus, will you and Thomas meet him?"

"Try to keep us from it, baby."

Love flooded her. "I really do adore you guys."

"Oh sure, you just say that because we once gave you the best orgasm of your life and made you pancakes."

"It's no longer the orgasm against which I measure all others. And he just took me out for pancakes." She examined her nails, in the mood to be playful. Marcus didn't disappoint.

"Oh, really?" he drawled. "Lucky for you, we won't consider it a competition."

"Would you if I asked? I'm happy to be a test subject. First Des could try, then you guys could try. We could do a six out of a ten thing. Okay, maybe three out of five. Six times at once might kill me, but what a marvelous way to expire."

"You twisted, sick woman. So this guy is into sharing?"

She sobered, remembering the questions she'd intended but hadn't really wanted to ask. "Yes. No. I don't know."

"You're not a polyamory type of girl," Marcus said.

"Does that make me old-fashioned? Stupid?"

"I would remove the left lung of any man who made a move on Thomas," Marcus said without a change of inflection. "And twist his nuts off. Does that answer your question?"

Julie sighed. "Des is really good at the rigging stuff. He's considered an artist in the BDSM community here, and so he's popular with subs who want to experience it under his hands. Who am I to argue? Hell, I've been there and it's out of this world."

She rocked back and forth on the edge of the stage. "He says he's not going to have sex with any of them while he's with me, and I'm glad for that, but I know the whole thing is sexual in nature. So will I get more comfortable with that as I go along, or am I just not wired this way and it's doomed before we start? He kissed me and told me he doesn't kiss them that way. I'm not sure if I'm okay with him kissing them any kind of way. And didn't I say I wasn't going to do a relationship again? I just freaking met this guy."

"Stop. You're panicking yourself and doing your run-on, redundant babbling thing."

"Oh, this is amateur stuff. I did a filibuster on him at his job site earlier today."

"He didn't cut and run?"

"No. He took me out for pancakes. Christ, I don't know why any guy hangs around me."

"Hey." The sharpness of Marcus's tone reminded her of Des, so much so that her stomach did that quick pretzel knot cinch of sexual awareness. "We've talked about this. You are a fucking amazing woman. You don't let some asshole who can't figure that out drag you down."

"I know. I know." She drew herself up, made herself believe it. Hadn't she just castigated herself for letting the poor opinions of others tear her down? The joy of dysfunction: no memory retention. "I'm nice, and fun, and interesting, and I just want someone to love me for me. And it feels like...this guy might be able to do that, Marcus. I'm fucking scared to death. I got used to handling rejection and failure. It became familiar ground. Talk about being twisted. And this has all happened in a blink. I care about him. I *want* to be in love with this guy."

"Easy." Marcus's tone gentled, picking up on the break in hers. "There was more to this conversation, wasn't there?"

"Yeah. A lot of stuff I haven't processed yet. I think focusing on this is the easier part, to tell the truth. So can we stick with it for the time being?"

"All right." She heard a noise and a click and realized he'd switched from his hands free to the phone so she'd have his full attention. "So, say you and this guy keep on this road together. Would he stop doing sessions with other subs to keep you?"

"I couldn't ask him to do that. He is *really* good at this. I saw video. Even when I was six years old and had cartilage like a rubber band, I couldn't bend the ways he ties some of these women. I think as long as I can keep it separate in my head like any other stage production, I can manage my feelings about it."

She wished they could video chat. She imagined Marcus in his New York penthouse, putting together a salad for dinner while Thomas finished something in their home studio. If they did video chat, he'd have the hands free tucked in his ear so he could toss the salad with his fine-boned hands, wield the chopping knife, and caress the supple skin of a beefsteak tomato. Watching Marcus do anything was a feast for female senses. She'd observed him from a corner at his gallery, directing his assistant manager with silent signals as he spoke on the phone or tapped on his laptop. Unlike most men, he was an impressive multi-tasker.

"But you'll talk to him if it becomes a problem."

"Maybe. I don't want to change who he is just because I'm insecure and have had a couple of boyfriends who thought monogamy was a high school virus."

"It's good to know your triggers," Marcus said evenly. "But no matter who or what he is, you do what's best for your physical and emotional wellbeing. If you don't, I'll kick your ass, and so will Thomas. The same thing you'd do for us—and have done for us—when we were trying to figure out how to make our relationship work."

She laid back on the stage to stare up at the ceiling. They'd had no leaks since Des had patched the roof. "I'm being a dumbass about this, I know. Oh, Marcus, what have I done? He makes me feel so incredible, so special and wonderful. When I see him, I ache inside. I said I wasn't going to do this to myself again."

"And as I said, we indulged your delusion. You want to be in love, Julie. You have so much love to give. Don't deny yourself that opportunity just because the road has dead ended so many times."

"I don't think I can handle another selfish jerk."

"All of us can be selfish jerks. It's the human condition. The question is whether it's his predominant super power or a balanced part of a whole pool of traits that makes you want to dive right in." He paused and murmured something.

"What?"

"Thomas just emerged from his studio and called me Superman. I was obliged to flip him the bird and threaten his life."

Julie smirked, but her mind was still caught up in the conversation. "I think I'm already in the water, close to being over my head."

"You have friends who can pull you out if needed." Marcus's voice was a stroking reassurance. "Julie, we love you. We both hope this is your guy, the one you've deserved for so long. Don't be looking for ways to shoot him down arbitrarily. How you talk about him is new for you, and I'm going to take that as a good sign. Here. I'm going to hand you over to Thomas so he can do that nurturing crap he's so good at."

"You're actually not so bad at it yourself, no matter the hard-ass routine."

"I am a hard-ass. Just ask anyone. If this guy doesn't treat you right, he'll find out first hand."

§

Hard work gave the subconscious mind a chance to work out the tangles of life's more complicated issues. Over the next few days, the end run toward opening night took up most of her waking hours. She and Harris were neck deep in production details, while at the other end of the burning candle she and Madison pursued the endless ways to market the event.

Promoting a BDSM erotic event in the mainstream community was a delicate tap dance, but with Madison's passion for her theater's mission and Julie's marketing savvy, their efforts started to bear fruit. Ticket sales that had started initially as a harrowing trickle became a solid flow when they stepped up the social media campaign and secured radio and TV spots. Madison's loyal customer base, Logan's wide network of BDSM club members and the students helping with the production proved invaluable at spreading the word.

On the production side, there were run-throughs to review scenery, light and sound cues. The cast run-throughs were different from formal rehearsals, much heavier on the technical end and blocking than on running lines, because this first offering was intended to be a glimpse through the looking glass at the BDSM world. The show was billed as unscripted, organic, unfolding on stage according to the direction of Dom to sub, which helped increase buzz about it.

Avant-garde theater typically didn't command large audiences, the players doing it more for love of the medium than an expectation of big ticket sales. However, Wonder was offering an inside glimpse at a world that fascinated the mainstream. When they'd sold two hundred and fifty of their four hundred ticket capacity, Madison was ecstatic.

Julie was happy, because she could turn her attention back toward the production itself. She and Harris focused on improving the stage elements for each performer so their presentation would be even more dramatic, without messing with the integrity of the scene itself. She also made sure each of the initial run-throughs or any significant changes were reviewed by Des, Logan or whatever expert they recommended to double check safety matters. All the stage hands and cast members were required to sit in on a comprehensive safety discussion with her, Logan and Des.

"We're all responsible for the safety of our performers," Logan told them. "A Dom can get stage fright like anyone else and miss details he or she wouldn't normally. So if we all watch out for one another, we have a good show on every level."

"It's fun, it's play, it's intense in all the right ways," Des had added. "And it only stays that way if we watch out for one another every fucking minute."

Julie had concluded the talk with a reminder. "During the show, if there's anything that worries you about what's happening on, behind or around stage, you bring it to Harris's or my attention immediately. We want this to be a resounding success, but we won't hesitate to stop a scene right in the middle if someone is at risk. We want people to learn about the beauty and reality of BDSM, and keeping people safe is a very real, true part of it."

Des had been sitting in the back during her little speech, but when she'd said that, her eyes had shifted to him, held. His lips curved and he gave her a slight nod. Knowing his concerns about "performing" BDSM scenes, she was bolstered by his approval.

She had met Missive and spoken with her a few times as part of the show prep. She was everything Des had said she was. Slim, blonde, young and beautiful. She was also pleasant and smart, so helpful and service-oriented that Harris had suggested they lure her back as crew for future productions.

Desmond had told her a lot about Missive. She had no permanent attachments in the scene, and possessed an adventurous submissive nature that enjoyed a wide variety of experiences. Yes, she and Des had done quite a few rope scenes together, but she'd also volunteered as Logan's sub for his whip instruction classes at his club. At least three other Masters and Mistresses in the cast had had the pleasure of doing scenes with her for violet wands, fire and role play.

Outside the scene, she was an engineering student with a busy lifestyle. Des suspected she might have a vanilla relationship in that world, but Missive preferred to keep that part of her life private.

Knowing all of that should have made it easier for Julie, and spending some one-on-one time with Des did help. As promised, he'd taken Julie on a two low-pressure, no-sex dates in the little spare time she'd had. The first had been dinner at Mac's Speed Shop, a popular pseudo-biker and BBQ hang out that had to-die-for mac-and-cheese and brisket. They'd listened to a great live band, Des's arm stretched over the back of the booth behind her, her leaning into his side, tapping her fingers to the music on his thigh. The noise made conversation a lips right against the ear requirement, and they kept one another laughing with the conversations they shared, and half aroused from their close proximity.

She was a hypocrite, because the casual, safe atmosphere unleashed her inner tease. She'd pressed up against him when she spoke in his ear, and he acknowledged it with a snug arm around her waist, fingers sliding intimately into the back pocket of her jeans. Light kisses exchanged became deeper, more lingering, his eyes heating on her face when they broke apart, but he hadn't taken it further than that. When he dropped her off that night, he'd given her a kiss that had left her vibrating, but he hadn't asked to come in. She'd told herself she wouldn't offer, and then spent the rest of the night aching from her own stupidity.

Not until after the performance. Take it slow. No one

has ever died of sexual frustration. Yet.

Whenever he came to the theater, whether it involved meeting with Harris about his own scene or helping out some of the carpentry guys, he always came to see her first. He'd kiss her, then wrap his arms around her, letting her tuck her head beneath his chin as he held her for a lingering few seconds in an embrace that conveyed romance, affection and sexual interest all at once. It was the best part of her day.

Once when he came to do that, she was in the pit with Shale, where they were discussing her scene needs. The Mistress was doing a provocative cage scene with her sub, Troy, the handsome blond male who worked with Logan at his hardware store. Shale was a nurse but always reminded Julie of a cross between a tall, slim fairy and a biker chick with her snug jeans, heavy metal rock T-shirts and her love of motorcycles.

"Des," Shale said fondly, giving him a hug and brushing her lips along his cheek. Julie had decided the man was known and loved by everyone in the BDSM community. "I never thought I'd have the pleasure of seeing you up on a stage again. It's made us all love Julie even more. I suppose you'll be doing something suspension related?"

"Yeah." Des borrowed Julie's water and took a swig, handing it back. Julie noted Shale's speculative look at the casually intimate gesture. She maintained a look of bland innocence, though she really wanted to succumb to a cocky and far too premature *yeah, that's right, he's my man* smugness. The amusement that touched Shale's features made Julie wonder if she'd detected that. Des did say she had a rotten poker face.

"He's a circus performer, Julie. Don't let him hide his gifts from you. He can do it all. Rope, fire, electric, roleplay, whip, wax, impact...name your freak."

Des made a noncommittal noise. "I'll always learn new stuff, but I'm a rigger at heart."

"Yes you are," Shale agreed, and elbowed Julie. "His suspension will be a crowd favorite, but he prefers the quiet stuff. That's where his heart is."

Des shrugged. "Give me a few coils of rope, and a nice

quiet outdoor place with a stream, a big tree...that's the best."

He lowered the bottle, wiping his lips with the back of his arm as he put Julie squarely in his view and considered her with frank and thorough interest. "A tree with a branch thick enough to hold us both. I'd stretch you out on it, tie you face down. Then I'd slowly fuck you while the tree sways with the wind." A thoughtful look crossed his face. "I'll have to work on finding the perfect tree for that."

The carpentry team called to him, pulling him out of whatever setting he'd placed her in his obviously busy imagination. Handing her back the bottle, he swiped a cool, damp kiss over her stunned lips, then strode back toward the wings.

Shale nudged her wrist, reminding Julie she was holding a bottle of water for her suddenly dry throat.

"He goes from casual and friendly to intense like that in a blink. It's hard for a woman's heart not to be tipped by it, isn't it?"

"Yeah." But instead of feeling good about that, Julie thought of Missive, the face she now put on every sub he'd ever had or would have, before and after her. She took a swallow of the water.

"He's always been careful to maintain boundaries, though," Shale mused. "I've never known him to date a sub, and we've been in the same circles for about five years. There's obviously something a little different with you. He's more engaged, and his eyes have a harder gleam." Shale fluttered her fingers toward her own long-lashed ones. "More predatory, in the right ways. But I suspect you know that, since you just took another swig of water at the thought."

Julie snorted, but she was feeling better. "Should I be afraid or happy, or send him packing?"

Shale smiled with a Domme's feral pleasure. "That's always the question, isn't it? Good luck with that."

As Shale left her, Julie watched Des. Though he was involved in a scenery issue, she had a feeling he was as aware of her as she was of him, particularly after dropping that distracting visual.

Their second date had occurred in her little room at the theater. The day had ended at nearly midnight, after the *Consent* version of a dress rehearsal. After Harris left, and it was just her and Des, he'd taken her to her room, pushed her onto her bed and given her a foot massage that had her moaning with pleasure. He turned her on her stomach and also gave her a full body massage that had her vibrating but limp as yarn, the day's exhaustion covering her like a blanket.

When he'd pressed a kiss to her cheek, she knew he was getting ready to leave her. She found his hand with her eyes closed and held it. "Stay a while," she mumbled. "Watch TV or something."

He'd obliged, stretching out on the cot with her. She'd adjusted so she was sprawled against him, cheek pillowed on his chest, arm wrapped over him as he brushed his lips against her temple and she made a contented noise. He channel-surfed her small TV while she fell into a heavy doze.

Nothing had marred her opinion of him. His sense of humor was as uncensored and outrageous as hers. Their intellects were well matched. While she wanted to see how his performance with Missive made her feel, and she was determined not to move beyond flirting and simple enjoyment of his company until then, sometimes she wondered who she was fooling. Even the most casual interactions with him had a way of making her feel like she was falling deeper into a sweet abyss.

Then there was the other side of things. She read up on Type I in her spare time and, the more she liked him, the more she worried, because what he'd said at Bob Evans told her he wasn't a typical Type I patient. But except for that discussion, he'd made that subject off limits. Would that change after opening night, if she was still okay with their relationship?

Truth, she didn't want to wait until after opening night. Maybe some part of her worried that what she saw would ruin everything, and it would be over before it had barely started. Maybe if she had something more to solidify their relationship before then, it would help her perspective, help her weather whatever that night would bring.

No, she wouldn't try to control fate that way. She was going to trust her instincts. Opening night was going to be the start or finish line, and that was that.

Chapter Eight

Opening night. No matter the show, opening night was always special, infused with a tremendous energy and excitement. And nervousness, because no amount of run-throughs or rehearsals were ever enough, especially in community theater, where they were limited because of day jobs, school and other scheduling factors for a volunteer cast and crew. From cast choice to opening night, they'd had six weeks to prepare for the show that could make or break Wonder.

Jitters were to be expected, but Julie had been down this road before. She embraced and transformed them into an ebullient excitement, letting that flow of positive energy ground her cast and stage crew. She created an infectious "we're going to totally rock this" feeling. Hell, things could always go wrong and they would, because that was the nature of the business. Part of the fun was figuring out how to make it work so the audience thought everything went exactly as planned.

Tonight, though, she had a niggling barb in that rainbow-and-unicorns flow of energy. When Des was with Missive tonight, it would be for a performance, she told herself fiercely. Yes, Sand Kilroy, one of the actors she'd dated, had screwed his leading lady. A couple of them. He hadn't limited himself to the theater manager. But he wasn't Des. Des made her feel extraordinary, a way no other man had made her feel.

Tonight she'd have to watch him do the same thing for another woman. For the past week, she'd been unable to tune out her cast members, raving about her "coup" in convincing Des to join the line-up.

"He takes subs on an indescribable journey," Tony, one of the Masters, had told her. "It's spectacular to watch, even for a Dom. He may not like performance, but when he's in the zone, it's like he was meant to be on a stage."

Des had told her that she was different. What did he have to do to prove it? Why the hell should he have to? She knew why she was back to square one on this crap. For the past several days, as her insecurities mounted, there'd been no more time to spend together. This was why, in romance novels, the hero was a gazillionaire who ran his empire on two languorous hours a day, and the heroine always had a mega-important altruistic job that never seemed to take up any of her romance time. A job that in real life would have denied her a social life of any kind or even regular showers.

Yep, she was doing the panicking thing, just like Marcus said. She was back to thinking she shouldn't do this with anyone, ever again. The stage was her lover, the one that had never let her down. She didn't need the rest of this. She was already composing a text to Des in her head.

REALLY REALLY REALLY can't do this. You're too perfect, and I can't handle that. Please don't talk to me again. Consider this a restraining order, one on the honor system. You don't want me and I can't want you. I am too fucking fragile.

"Stop it." She slapped herself, earning a startled look from one of the lighting guys rushing by. It was all right. He'd just figure it was some pre-performance superstition. She ignored him and slapped the other cheek.

She wasn't doing this. She had a performance to run. She had to be on her A+++ game. Fortunately, the muses sent Madison as a reminder. The theater owner appeared at her elbow like a serial killer popping out of a closet, making Julie yelp.

"Hey. You okay? You look so pale. Did you eat anything today?" Pulling out a pack of peanut butter crackers, Madison put it on the podium where Julie would be posted in the wings. Harris would be in position on the other side. Tonight was really all his show, because on performance nights, the stage manager was the hub of the wheel. She was just here for troubleshooting support and to see how the show unfolded so they could evaluate and adjust afterward to make the next one even better.

Madison handed her a bottle of water. "I think you lost ten pounds rushing around these last few days, and I gained it through nervous eating. It's filling up out there. We sold out, Julie. Can you believe it? You said that almost never happens. Tell me not to be terrified."

Thank God. Just like that, Julie clicked back into the role she knew, finding her footing and her joy again. *Damn man.*

"Totally be terrified," she said, giving Madison a maniacal grin. "That's the fun part. Over the next two hours, you get to slide from terror into handspring happiness when the audience abandons their reserve and gets fully into the show."

"What if they don't?"

"There is no don't. There is only doo. Which is why I carry doggy poop bags." Julie did her best Yoda imitation and chuckled as the joke visibly derailed Madison from her one-track catastrophe scenario.

"You idiot." Madison poked her. "Anything I can do to help?"

"No, we're good right now. Harris and his trusty production book are in charge of it all. Look at him over there. He looks like Napoleon ready to launch a full scale invasion of Europe. He's a god and he doesn't even know it."

"I think he threw up in the bathroom a little while ago."

"It's his little ritual. Don't worry about it. It's going to be fun, because it's so unscripted. That's exactly why it's going to be magic." Putting an arm around Madison, she gave her a squeeze. "Your man is there in the front row looking for you. Just go enjoy. You paid me the big bucks to be here and handle this."

"Oh yeah," Madison said dryly. "I traded on our friendship and gave you enough to cover your weekly groceries, and you took that only because I insisted. You lived in the theater these past few weeks."

"Because I wanted to. It's the place I feel most at home."

In ways that weren't always healthy, but her self-actualizing side could just shut the hell up and go eat a pint of ice cream. "Now scram. Nervous owners are bad luck backstage on performance night. Just be ready to accept all the congratulations at intermission."

Or do damage control, but Julie held that thought to herself. The worst would come if it came. No sense in wasting energy on it.

"I think you made that up, but I'm going." Madison hugged her impulsively and then disappeared, heading down the side steps to return to the audience. Julie could hear the crowd building, but it was one of many details she absorbed right now. She watched the lighting and sound guys taking their places, making final tweaks. She heard the radio through her headphones on the podium beep and crackle, Harris doing last minute checks. Performers moved through the shadows on her periphery.

One of them was standing silently, waiting nearby yet out of the path of the stage hands. Mistress Lilith apparently had her own ritual for getting her and her sub into the proper mindset. As she threaded a whip through her fingertips meditatively, her sub knelt at her feet, his head down as she stroked the bright red hair at his nape. He had a tattoo of a snake down his spine, visible since he wore only a pair of jeans. Lilith was in a silver catsuit. Neither of them looked nervous.

Doing this in front of a rapt audience, particularly if they were hidden in the shadows behind the lights, might not seem that different from their normal club environments. Even if it was, she thought of what Des had told her. When done right, it was just the Dom and sub. No one else.

Energy kicked up inside and all around her as the house lights blinked, the five minute warning. Experience shoved everything else out except making this the best damn experience the audience had ever had.

Cast for the opening scene were forming a line to her right. Six women dressed in filmy flowing robes dusted with glitter to catch the stage lights. The Mistresses would wield violet wands with artistic and erotic effect, sorceresses performing magic on a bound virgin on a sacrificial altar.

Julie did a quick scan of the scenery and stage props to ensure all was in place, even knowing Harris would be doing the same. An altar was on a raised dais against a mountain scene—painted muslin wrapped over thin board—that would be illuminated by lightning. Putting on her headset and adjusting the volume from the controls at her belt, she heard the sound guys cued for the Loreena McKennitt score, which opened with a rumble of distant thunder. She sent Harris a thumbs up.

Showtime.

As the lights started to darken, she touched the arm of the sorceress Domme closest to her, a black-haired woman who went by the name of Lady Myst. "Break a leg," Julie whispered, and earned a wink. As well as a mildly inappropriate but appreciated brief fondling of her ass with elegant nails before the Mistress headed out on stage. Her female acolytes followed, tugging along the male sub stripped down to nothing but chains and a loin cloth.

"Some Dominants can't help themselves. They detect sub and it's like a dog lover keeping their hands off a puppy."

She choked on a laugh at Billie's remark, and his own inappropriate gesture. The drag queen had arrived at her side and delivered the whispered comment deadpan, all while having his hand clamped on her left butt cheek.

He'd start his emcee duties right after the dramatic opening scene, providing transition between acts. And apparently butt patting support when necessary. "This is going to fucking kick ass," she whispered back.

"You bet your sweet patootie it will. By the way, your man is looking extra fine tonight. Think you're having a good effect on him."

Billie wandered off before she could respond to the assumption that she was the reason Des looked good, but she liked the sound of "your man." Des had been in and out of the wings like a shadow himself, no time to do more than throw her a smile. But he was here.

She let the fierce certainty of success at all levels fill her and then reined it all in. She centered on the details and the big picture simultaneously, an edge she would ride with consummate skill for the next couple of hours without a single falter. This is what she knew better than anything, including the vagaries of her own heart.

§

The violet wand performance went off without a hitch. As the chained male bucked under the attentions of the priestesses, "lightning" flashed against the mountain background, enhancing the cracking electricity of their wands. They sketched the air with lines of blue, purple and green.

Madison's budget had allowed a modest lighting set up, so Julie was deeply impressed by what the students had accomplished with what they had. Drama and pageantry did the rest.

The male sub's groans of pleasure as one of the acolytes straddled him and shared the electrical current with him, captivated everyone watching, including the crew. If every act was this intense, they'd all need to be zapped with wands to avoid missing their cues.

Billie Dee-Lite picked up on that vibe when the scene concluded and he sauntered out onto stage in his silver sequined mini-dress and stiletto thigh-high boots. The silken red tresses of his expensive wig gleamed from the stage lights and framed his dark eyes, enhanced with glittering silver lashes. "What a way to start a show," he purred. "This is what erotic performance is all about. Bringing our deepest desires to the surface and giving them a fantasy flourish.

"If you enjoyed that, boys and girls, you are in for a treat, because every scene tonight will showcase the beauty and power of Domination and submission. The things it can call out of our hearts, minds and souls, whether you are vanilla, or like to walk on the wilder side... Or somewhere in between you don't tell your Momma about. When you leave here tonight, you will be changed in delightful ways. You will want more."

He drew himself up into a dramatic pose and pointed at

the audience with a glistening, sharp nail. "You will go home and you will 'like' this theater on all your social media sites. You will book your online tickets for the next showing so the poor people who run this theater don't have to resort to cannibalism to survive. And you will tell all your friends."

He put his hand on his hip and affected an even more effeminate tone. "'Oh, Gladys, it was amazing, even though you know I'm not into all that kinky shit. Hush now, Pastor Brian is beginning his Sunday sermon. But did you know his wife was there? No telling what kind of freaky shit happened when she got home. She looked like she was ready for Pastor Brian to pull out his staff and part the Red Sea...'"

He strolled across the stage as the laughter settled. "Sexual expression is limitless, babies. It can make us laugh or cry, it can lift us up to the heavens or take us to hell...and have us booking another roundtrip ticket."

He stopped and pinned them with a look. "If done right, it's when we feel closest to our best selves and those we love, the person you'd tear your heart out to have standing at your side for all your life. If that person is not by your side tonight in this audience, you need to bring them back so you can take this journey with him or her. But for now, let's all take this journey together.

"And one last thing, my babies. You'll see astonishing things tonight, but no applause except when the curtain closes at the end of each scene. Trust me, your performers will give you more than you expect if you don't distract them...or yourselves."

Billie moved into the shadows as the lights came down. Julie's heart ached a little in the rapt silence he'd created. Either Billie was speaking from experience or he was a damn good performer, but either way, he'd skillfully brought the audience from laughter back to the right mood for the next scene. Julie blessed Logan's connections that had won them the skills of the talented diva. When Billie sauntered back into the wings, she high-fived him and didn't even mind him slapping her ass hard enough to make it wobble. She took it as a go-team kind of gesture, and returned to her own responsibilities with a grin.

A haunted flute melody opened the next performance, a snake dancing scene. A Master in slashed silken pantaloons sat cross-legged, playing the short wooden flute as the open weave basket in which his sub was contained began to rock to the music. Her hands came out the openings, moving in a sinuous pattern. She was twisting her torso, trying to escape the narrow basket, and Julie suspected she became too immersed in her snake persona. She overbalanced and the basket toppled.

The edge of the stage was too close to where it fell and started to roll. Fortunately, one of the crew positioned in a crouch on the side steps as a spotter began to move, doing his job, but the Master was quicker. In one fluid leap, he was on his feet and brought the basket to a stop by planting his foot in front of it. He did it so smoothly, it looked as if it was part of the performance. His sub played right into it, her hands coming out of the top opening to caress his calf, wander up his leg.

He piped a shrill, commanding note, as if admonishing her for the unsolicited caress. She froze. He backed away when her hands flattened on the floor, stabilizing the basket. While he resumed the sensuous melody, she came out just as a snake would, in writhing movements along the floor, her body undulating in ways that Julie's advanced yoga instructor would envy.

"Hell, we can go get a burger, Julie. They don't need us."

She smiled at Harris's comment in her headphones. Des had said a good Dom was ready for things to go wrong, that the protection of the sub was the most important thing. This Master had heightened the intensity of the scene by injecting a powerful additive to it. Protection. Either they'd all taken the admonitions about safety to heart, or they already knew the importance of it themselves. Either way, she was impressed and reassured.

The sub was covered in spotted body paint intended to make her look like a sleek cobra. A harness over her shoulders and around her waist held the folds of dark cloth that became a "hood" when she lifted her arms in strike pose toward her Dom, advancing upon him and then falling back. The notes of the pipe, his focus upon her, made the shift between power and control clear. When the scene concluded, she was coiled around his feet, arms twined around his calf, head resting on his knee. Generous applause echoed through the theater as the curtain closed.

The next two scenes were also well-received and smoothly executed. With an ever more impressive costume each time, Billie returned to cover each break as props and scenery were changed out. Julie registered the responses of the audience to his discourse, but she was busy, pitching in with an extra set of hands a dresser needed for a costume adjustment, then helping with a large scenery piece that had cracked a support when adjusted. The stage hands put in a quick fix and the next group of performers went out only ten seconds late.

Billie covered the delay by sticking her head back out of the curtains, gathering them around her as if protecting her modesty in the shower.

"I know you were looking at my ass, you bad boy," she chided, pointing to Logan in the front row. "This next scene is a public service warning about what happens to those who don't mind their manners around Miss Billie Dee-Lite."

Laughter rippled through the audience. Logan grinned wolfishly at Billie as the lights rose. This performance was closer to a real-life BDSM scene. A female submissive was strapped to a St. Andrew's cross, prepared to experience several forms of impact play. As her Dom extolled her various infractions and what her punishments would be, the sub's impish excuses flavored the scene with humor. She wore a cute school girl uniform, the Dom in the dour suit of a schoolmaster.

The whimsical note put the more vanilla audience members at ease about what was about to happen, as intended. As the scene progressed and became more edgy, Julie kept a weather eye on the rows she could see. While some of the audience looked vaguely uncomfortable, the role play appeared to have drawn them into the scene.

She and Madison had decided to purposely scatter more realistic scenes throughout the lineup, knowing those were the ones the mainstream attendees might have more trouble handling. They could have left them out entirely, but Madison had wanted them to have something to think about that couldn't be dismissed as mere fantasy.

The next scene would be the fire players. They had a dramatic show planned, like a Cirque du Soleil offering. They'd bring the comfort level of the audience back to an even keel. After that would be a simple Victorian man-and-his-maid scene that would take place on the stage apron so Des could set up behind the curtain, since his performance would happen after that. He'd indicated he'd need about ten minutes to get Missive in place.

Julie wondered in which direction Des's performance would fall, reality or fantasy.

"Miss Ramirez?"

Missive preferred to use surnames and honorifics. She called Logan Mr. Scott. Julie had noticed she called Des by his first name, a curiosity because she didn't do that for anyone else.

"Yes, Missive?" While surprised at finding the young woman at her elbow, Julie masked it. She hoped she looked friendly and professional, rather than like a cat about to scratch someone's eyes out. However, she purposefully kept the touch of "Remember, I'm pretty damn busy right now" in her voice to discourage chitchat. Though Harris and his crew didn't need her right now, that could change. It didn't have anything to do with her wanting to minimize her exposure to the girl. So she told herself.

Regardless of her motive, her effort was wasted. Missive didn't seem to notice the brusque tone. Since the fire players were taking the stage, she could speak in a low voice instead of a whisper, because their scene was accompanied by the unfortunately named but thrilling "Night on Disco Mountain."

"You know, people think I chose my scene name as a shortened form of the word submissive. It did work out kind of awesomely that way, but my real name is Ivy."

Julie blinked. "That's interesting, but…"

"When I was in middle school," Missive continued, placing a light hand on her arm, "I had this very stern history teacher who would call me Miss Ivy. I had so many fantasies about him. I think he was my first Dom, though he never knew that. So though people say Missive the way it's supposed to be pronounced, often in my head I hear Miss Ive, short for Ivy."

Missive had been a big help throughout the week, always saying and doing the appropriate thing, so Julie wasn't sure what her ill-timed conversation now was intended to accomplish. She kept a weather eye on the fire scene, but it was going fine. Nothing susceptible to sparks was close to the action. This scene had received more run-throughs than any others, due to safety concerns.

She could simply tell the girl she had to focus on the stage, that she couldn't talk right now, but she wasn't doing that. She didn't know why. But she did feel she should point out the oddity of the conversation.

"Have you taken an excess of medications today, Miss Ive?"

The young woman laughed softly, and it sounded like chimes in a garden. If she had to be subjected to one more lovely thing about her, Julie would conk her over the head with a blunt object and bury her under the stage. Oblivious to that hazard, Missive put her hand on Julie's arm again. "Des said you have a great sense of humor. He told me to come and tell you something personal about myself, something I've never told anyone in the scene."

Ah, the light dawns. "Why would he want you to do that?" Though even as Julie asked the question, she knew. The damn man was too damn intuitive. She wanted to be mad at him, but the tactic actually worked a little bit. She was seeing Missive as more of a human than the object of her inner torment. But it didn't change anything. She was doing that honorary restraining order text to that long-haired roofer as soon as this was over.

While their conversation had been happening, the fire scene had concluded. The man-and-the-maid scene didn't require Billie's transition. The curtain had closed, a dramatic silence descending after the applause for the fire players.

Since the curtain was closed, Julie could no longer see

the scene, but she could imagine it from the run-throughs. The Dom in Victorian gentleman's wear would be walking onto the stage, a follow spot covering him as he brought a single chair with him and a riding crop. His sub, dressed in frilly black and white maid wear, would be working her way over to him, looking like she was dusting invisible drawing room furniture with her feather duster.

Missive was too friendly to prop up Julie's snarly feelings. "He didn't say why I should tell you that," she whispered, "and I wouldn't presume, but if you're okay with an educated guess, I'd say he's centered on you." At Julie's quizzical look, she lifted a pale shoulder, her silk robe having slipped away from it. Along the base of her collarbone was a tiny chain of tattooed flowers. Julie figured it had hurt like a son of a bitch, since there was little flesh there to absorb the sting of the needle, but it was a delicate piece of work.

"Centered is my word for when a Dom or sub finds someone they want as their hub, no matter what other scening they do with others. It's kind of lovely to see it happen for him."

This was not fitting where Julie wanted her mind to go right now, but she didn't think it was appropriate for her to tell Missive the same thing she'd told her self-actualizing and self-conscious sides. *Shut up you perfect, impossible not to like bitch.*

"I'm sure you already know all this stuff about him," Missive said in a confidential tone, "but what gives me a charge is watching him scene with subs who think he's only a top. Soon as he opens up his Dom side, there's no mistaking him for anything else. It pulls the carpet right out from under them."

Missive gave her a mischievous wink. "He completely takes control, and his instincts are so good... He's taken me places I couldn't have imagined, and I don't mean in the rope sense, though he's astounding there. I mean inside myself. And he choreographs on the fly. He'll have a concept for tonight, but it will be just the high points. He gets this flow of energy going and you trust him to direct the current."

Hopefully he'd told the lighting guys that and they'd set up his light cues accordingly. Nothing gave a stage manager or director hives like an actor changing blocking so significantly nobody knew where he'd be on stage from moment to moment.

Oh hell, she wasn't worried about that. Harris was thorough and as anticipatory of that shit as she was. Why was Missive telling her this? It made Julie want Des more, even as it reinforced all her earlier insecurities. It made her waffle, and she hated waffling.

Fortunately, her inner need for a primal scream of frustration had to wait. Des slid out from behind the curtain and gave both women his usual warm look, but Julie noticed it was more quick and distracted than she was used to seeing, as if half his mind was already on what he was about to do.

Des ran a hand along Missive's arm and up behind her neck, drawing her to him with that cradling hold.

In a blink, his distracted look was gone. Missive had his full attention, evaluation and appraisal. With that touch, a similar metamorphosis happened to Missive. Her body, her eyes, all her energy, visibly centered on Des. Her lashes lowered and she went quiet and still, as if she and Julie hadn't been in mid-conversation.

Julie wasn't sure if she felt like a third wheel or a reluctantly fascinated spectator. She was all too aware of how it felt to be the focus of the attention Des was giving Missive. "Ready?" he asked quietly.

"Yes," Missive said. "I'm ready."

"Good. Go kneel in front of the display I've set up. Leave on the robe."

The blonde moved obediently past him and disappeared behind the curtain. Julie wondered what she would have done if Des had told Missive to disrobe there. Offer to take the garment and hang it up? She had no frame of reference for this.

Maybe not, but some part of her understood it. Not only from her growing submissive orientation, but from watching rehearsals, going with Logan to his workshops, from talking to Madison. It was a culture, she'd realized, one that overlapped and lived inside, through and around the one she'd always known, giving it a different look.

"Hey."

She looked up to see Des studying her. She wondered if he was about to say something. He didn't.

He drew her to him, planting a hard, heated kiss on her mouth. He took his time with it, too, so her hand latched onto his shirt front and her head swam in a way that would not be conducive to focusing on her job. When he lifted his head, he stroked her hair away from her cheek and helped her straighten her head phones. She was wearing her usual theater performance night attire of black dress slacks and blouse, no jewelry to catch the lights and sparkle in the wings, distracting the audience. "Tell me you're wearing something black and lacy under that," he murmured against her mouth.

"White and lacy. I like contrasts." She drew her head back enough to meet his brown eyes. "And you have to get your narrow ass in gear. That curtain's opening in eleven minutes and the managing director will tear you a new one if you're late. And then Harris will kick your prone body."

He planted another hard kiss on her mouth. "For luck," he told her. "Like Luke and Leia in Star Wars."

"Except I'm not your sister," she retorted, not sure how to feel.

"Hope not. I used some tongue there."

Still smiling at her, he turned and moved back behind the curtain. When Julie shifted, she saw Missive kneeling before a shadowed rope form Julie couldn't make out, because only the blues, or blue light, was on behind the curtain to ensure there were no leaks around it to distract from the Victorian scene.

Missive's silhouette showed her head bowed, her body seemingly relaxed. Yet when Des had shifted her into a submissive state with one key touch, Julie had felt the sizzle of anticipation off the young woman. She thought of how she'd felt when she'd first seen those hanging ropes the other night and understood it better than she wanted to admit.

Des put his hand on Missive's head and stroked her,

speaking words Julie couldn't hear. Then the crew needed Julie to move so they could stage another set piece. Julie registered the thrilling feminine cries of the maid as the Victorian Dom put her over his lap and spanked her with the crop, all while she tried futilely to follow his direction and polish his boots in that awkward position.

After the scene concluded, there were four minutes to go. Billie was doing the transition, and Des and Missive's act would follow him.

Abruptly, Julie noticed she wasn't alone. Some of the other performers were gathering in the shadows, staying out of the way but clearly wanting to get a good view of the upcoming act.

The minutes went by both fast and slow to her. Billie wrapped up his part and returned to her in the wings. He positioned himself right behind her, so she couldn't see him, but she would have recognized him with her nose. He favored Elizabeth Taylor's White Diamonds perfume. When in drag, he always had a light mist of it clinging to him.

She turned to look at him. He now wore a bronze gown with an ebony wig that spilled silk to his waist and over his shoulders. He shifted to link his arm through Julie's.

"What you're about to see, honey-chile, is why we recommended putting him right before intermission," he whispered as the lights went down again. "After his performance, the audience is going to need that wine bar in the lobby."

Julie sighed. "I wasn't sure if I was going to hang around to watch. I haven't figured out how to deal with him doing this to another woman."

"Just watch, baby girl." Billie's arm slipped around her, holding her close with a woman's fragrance and a man's strength. "You'll feel better after."

Or worse, she thought dourly.

In the dark, she heard the hushed conversations and shifting of the audience. She closed her eyes, drinking in that energy. The trundling sound told her the curtain was opening, and the light behind her lids told her the scene had begun. She opened her eyes.

The music cued was a woodwinds piece called "Pan's Melody." As it filled the speakers and poured into the audience, Julie imagined the Fae lord winding through the forest he loved, as much a part of himself as breath, blood and bone.

Light spread over the scenery like a rising silvery moon. The audience inhaled in appreciation, creating a rippling wind sound, echoed by the performers closest to her. While Julie automatically shushed them, she was as engaged as they were.

Des had used light brown jute against a dark brown board suspended about seven feet above the stage. His rope was woven in the shape of a tree against the board, a complicated network of interlaced, spreading branches that twisted into a thick, knotted trunk. As the trunk cleared the board, the rope spread out into a nest of tangled roots, forming a cocoon for the bundle of precious life suspended in their cradle. The rope ends beneath the cocoon anchored it to the stage, more spreading roots.

Missive was in that cocoon, tied in a fetal position. Rope had been wrapped over her eyes, blinding her. Her hands were folded over her breasts, legs drawn up to her stomach. Since she was naked, light played over pale skin.

A cutout looked like the moon shining above. They'd talked about doing an ankle level fog, but Des had nixed that, not wanting anything to obscure his vision. Always taking care of his sub. It was a good aesthetic choice, though. The silvery light added the right touch of ambiance, nothing else needed.

Like Pan walking through the wood in truth, Des appeared out of the shadows of the opposite wing. He was shirtless and wore dark, close-fitting trousers and bare feet. The light played over his tattoos, darkening the sunburst on his back while etching out the dragon on his biceps.

He moved with grace and strength, with intense attention on what lay before him. Julie saw several people in the front rows inch forward in their seats, unconsciously drawn toward him, toward the unspoken messages of the scene, toward all of it. She was very conscious of Billie's firm hold on her waist. She must have leaned forward, and he thought she was about to be drawn out to the stage, enchanted by Pan's allure. She wanted to be amused, but she thought he might be right. She curled her hand around the edge of the podium.

Des circled the cocoon, suspended at eye level. He trailed his fingers along the curve of Missive's shoulder, her flank, and curled his fingers over her ankle. He made a complete rotation around her, shadows dancing and drifting like they would if clouds were wafting over the moon. The effect was spectacular. She was so buying the light designer a keg of her favorite alcoholic beverage.

Des drew a dark rectangular object from his back pocket. A dramatic snap of his wrist revealed and released the blade of the knife, and he swept it across Missive's body. In the same fluid movement, he threw the knife down so it plunged quivering in a rise in the earth, a firmly anchored piece of layered foam board. Des caught her curled body as it unraveled into his arms.

Billie had clutched her at the waist at the same moment Julie had increased her grip on him. Des swayed with the flute piece, turned, turned again, a slow pivot on the ball of one foot. He removed the smaller lengths of ropes from her eyes, around her wrists, casting them away. A new length of rope shook out from his hand on the turn, a silver metallic nylon that reflected the moonlight.

"Now from a static form to *ichinawa*," Myers murmured. He'd drawn closer for a better view. Since he was her other rigger performer, Julie wasn't surprised to see him. At her quizzical look, he explained in a whisper. "It means one rope. For Des, it's kind of a foreplay before he moves into more demanding disciplines."

Des had Missive on her feet but was holding her with one arm. He spun her away from him and the rope was looped on her wrist. He used that hold and his other hand to spin her back to him, the rope now wrapped around her body, holding her elbows to her sides. Then back out again. He turned and twisted with her, bringing one arm over her head and pulling it back so her hand brushed her shoulder blade, elbow pointed up.

Keeping their movements like two dancers, he turned

her and brought her to her knees, her head and back in a convex shape, a position that showed her surrender and his strength. Then he had her down in a turtle-like pose, the rope coming through her legs as he tied it to both ankles and plucked on the line, obviously to stimulate her between the legs. He'd looped the rope over the back of her neck, so when she quivered and shuddered, it emphasized how she was unable to lift her head or move out of the compact position.

Des knelt over her, slid an arm under her waist and then flipped her, loosening the rope in several graceful movements and drawing them both back to their feet. Missive was a bending willow in the circle of his arms.

Another rope was lowered. Des picked her up, did that slow turning dance again to bring them to it. As he put her feet on the ground, he attached Missive's bound wrists to the hook at the end of the rope.

"Now the *semenawa*," Myers whispered to her. "Torture rope, mixed in with other styles. He's like watching a sidewalk painter with no formal training, but endless raw talent. You never know what he's going to do or combine, but it's always a work of art."

Strings had joined the woodwinds, interjecting a note of danger, like a flight through the woods. Des had Missive netted in a matter of breathless moments, taking her off her feet and then tying ankles to thighs, bending her body back in a far more extreme curve than he'd done with Julie. He'd turned Missive into a pale crescent, straining from all the emotions gripping her. The audience could hear her gasps, sounds that revealed both her excitement and the stress the torturous position was putting on her body. At this angle and this close, Julie could see her reaction glistening on her thighs, and Des rewarded it by bending and pressing his lips reverently over one damp streak.

The moon above was the same crescent, as if he'd put her in that position to honor its light. He tied Missive's hands in a marionette's supplicating pose, reaching up to the moon, but as he continued to craft and shape her, she became a fairy dancing in air, contorting in a way only a fairy could. Des drew a pair of wings from the side stage and added those to the knots of rope beneath her shoulder blades. The wings looked like a moth's, a pale silver green color.

Once he had them on her, a discreet and deft movement of his hand made it appear as if flame had leapt from his palm, rather than the lighter he had concealed there. He set the tips on fire and backed up, sending her spinning so the flame fanned out, eating through the paper that formed the wings. A blink before the fire would have gotten too close, he whipped them off of her and doused it.

Some of those in the audience began to applaud, but Julie noted they were quickly shushed by those around them who'd remembered the rules. While she hoped the firm admonishment hadn't alienated new patrons, she understood it now better than she ever had before. No distractions could be permitted between a Dom and sub, not even for adulation.

When Missive stopped spinning, she was moaning, incoherent pleas. The theater was so still, Julie was certain even the back rows could hear. Des raised a finger and the music stopped. One second, two seconds. He did that deliberate circling of Missive, his gaze taking in everything about her state, and her eyes followed him as if she would do anything he asked her. When he reached her legs, he settled his fingers on her cunt, and lightly stroked.

Once, twice...perhaps a half dozen times, and then she began to come, her cries and the jerking in her bonds the only sounds in the theater. Julie couldn't look away, caught in something she couldn't explain. It was both pain and arousal, fear and longing. Then Des's gaze lifted and locked with hers.

Need replaced everything else. A need for him to be telling her the truth when he said he wanted to be with her. If he'd told her to come to him right then, she might have. She might have knelt on stage, laid her head on his leg and stayed that way. It didn't make sense. What she was seeing should cause her to retreat, should have her doubting his intentions even more. But what she saw in his eyes was a different message.

This is what I love to do. And I want to do it with you,

in a way I won't do it with anyone else. Was she crazy for translating all that out of one look? She just didn't know. She didn't know what it would take to make her fully believe him, but she knew she wanted to do so, with every aching, pounding, throbbing inch of her body and soul.

Des's attention returned to Missive as he made sure he gave her a full climax, wresting another cry from her lips as he slid several fingers inside her and removed them to paint her response on her lips. He lifted a hand and the music started again.

After he pushed her back into a slow spin, he retrieved his knife. With the same sweeping movement as before he cut the line, caught her in his arms once more. He rocked her, brought her to the ground, stretched over her as if he might take her then and there, except he still wore the dark trousers. Her legs wrapped around his hips, her arms splayed out on either side of her in complete surrender.

Rising on his knees, he held her that way as he rose to his feet, the muscles in arms and back rippling though he did it without any other obvious effort. He rocked her again, spun and brought them back down to the ground by him dropping to one knee and cradling her head so it didn't hit the stage. This time he bent and buried his head in her bosom, a supplication. She wrapped her arms around him, over his head, her lips brushing his crown. Then they rolled and he was back in control. He came to his feet with her still wrapped around him. Taking them on a gliding waltz back through the forest, he returned to the tree.

Des rebound Missive in the roots, a different pose this time, not quite as tight a fetal curl. He left one slim leg and delicate foot dangling. When he was done, he sank to one knee by it and pressed his lips to the arch, holding that pose as the curtain closed.

The audience exploded in applause. At the calls of *bravo*, Julie knew Madison would be feeling what Julie had promised—and hoped—she'd experience.

"I think that was all for you and your show, baby girl," Billie said. "He does performance-worthy sessions, but I've never seen him put that much pizazz into it before. Holy God, I wish he'd do it more often."

The audience seemed to agree, because they were still applauding, as if they wanted a callback right now. Julie experienced an adrenaline surge that was a mix of nerves and ebullience, reflecting her muddle of feelings about all of it.

"Julie." Harris barked through the radio, disrupting that. "We've got a problem. The act we have scheduled right after intermission is going to have to move to the end."

"What? Why?"

"Come on back to dressing room three. I'll explain there."

"Okay. Crap." She cut the mic then pressed it again. She trusted Harris's judgment like her own, and they had fifteen minutes to do damage control, which superseded her need for explanation. "Forget that. I'll see if Shale and Troy can go on right after intermission and tell everyone else we're moving up one scene for the second act."

"Got it. And I'll piss off the crew by making them adjust everything mid-show." There was laughter in Harris's voice, because humor was the best defense against hysteria.

Julie clicked off. "Billie, can you hold the fort here?"

"Do what you got to do, honey-chile. Though tell Harris it's been my experience boys will forgive anything for a good blowjob. Girls too, though sometimes chocolate works."

"He and I may be on our knees for every one of them by the end of the night," Julie muttered, dashing away. She ignored Billie's bark of raucous laughter.

§

After a panic attack she concealed so masterfully she was sure she gave herself an instant ulcer, she and Harris had everyone on the same page and Shale and Troy cued up to start right after intermission.

Madison had invited some of the local newspaper and blogger critics to this opening, sending them free tickets. While Julie didn't know if they'd accepted, and amateur theater was usually given some latitude, not expected to be up to the standards of a professional production, that wasn't the bar she set for herself. She wanted Wonder's opening performance to blow those critics away.

Master Tony and his sub Charlotte, the couple performing the scene they'd had to move to the end, were doing a combination of role play, liquid nitrogen, knives and fire. While it might not have the same tone as the scene they'd intended to wind up the show, it would end the event with an exciting flair that would dovetail well into the post-event reception.

She hadn't been in the wings to congratulate Des after his performance, which gave her a twinge of guilt, but a quick check with Billie said he'd been involved in aftercare for Missive. After that, he'd gone to help Tony and Charlotte. Apparently, Charlotte had epilepsy and, though she hadn't seemed nervous during rehearsals, being faced with the reality of an audience had brought on an attack of nerves. Which had led to her worrying about having a seizure on stage, which had then turned into a self-fulfilling prophecy, though the seizure had happened backstage instead of on it, thankfully.

Charlotte had assured Harris that she'd be recovered enough to do the performance shortly. Tony firmly indicated she would need an hour of recuperation. Des had seconded that opinion once he arrived at the dressing room.

Julie learned all that through Billie, since Des had pitched in to help the crew with the set rearrangement. She caught only brief glances of him, still in the dark trousers and no shirt. A welcome distraction she couldn't indulge, because the change had all of them scrambling.

As the curtain opened after intermission and the performance resumed, she couldn't have been prouder of everyone. The cast and crew managed the change with only a handful of minor glitches. While she didn't disagree with Billie's assessment of what would best reward them, she figured she could offer copious amounts of alcohol in lieu of a marathon of oral sex. And she'd personally tell Harris's Mistresses he deserved the most explosive orgasm of his life...after he had a good night's sleep.

When it was time for the final scene of the second act, no major disasters had occurred. She refused to let herself relax yet, though. Not until it was all over.

"I am so, so sorry." Charlotte slid up next to her. While shorter than Julie, Charlotte was much heavier, carrying about sixty extra pounds. But she carried those pounds with an air of Mother Earth sensuality that went well with her long golden hair and brilliant green eyes. Eyes that were filled with chagrin. Julie linked arms with her.

"Nothing at all to be sorry about, Char. These things happen. You've given the crew a chance to feel so proud of themselves they'll be puffed up like roosters at the after party. Are you sure you're okay?" Julie gave her a critical look. She looked a little pale and drained. "Because if you and Tony have to pull out, it's okay. Your health is way more important than this."

"No. It wasn't a bad one. I really think I could have gone on sooner, but Tony wouldn't budge on that." Her cheeks flushed. "He doesn't usually go all Master-like on me in our day-to-day life, but he did this time. I was too weak to jump him for being overbearing."

"Well, he loves you."

"Yes, he does." Charlotte dimpled.

"Silly woman in love. There he is, out there waiting for you." As the cue for the final act came, Julie nudged Charlotte forward. She was glad to see the woman move onto the stage with no apparent nervousness, dressed in nothing but a burlap smock she would soon be shedding.

The first time Charlotte had stripped for a run through, she'd had no self-consciousness at all. Julie had remarked on it that day to her, how she admired a woman with no self-consciousness about her size. While Julie immediately worried she might have offended Charlotte with the implication of her weight, Charlotte had offered her friendly reassurance to the contrary.

"I wasn't always that way. I was focused on being model thin, not on understanding why I was mistreating my body, making it harder for it to take care of me. I've been unable to lose weight most of my life. Yet since I became part of the lifestyle and collared by Tony, I've lost twenty-five pounds. I hope to lose about fifty more. I'll still be heavier than magazines think I should be, but my lab numbers are going down and my doctor couldn't be happier. Tony showed me that I don't need to lose weight to be lovely. I want to be healthy, not thin."

The woman had smiled, showing even, white teeth and generous, moist lips glossed with a salmon-colored lipstick that complemented her skin tone. Whenever she came to the theater, she wore lovely, well-accessorized outfits that reflected her positive self-image.

"For the first time in my life, I don't care about being the size of a pencil. I just want to be in good health so I can enjoy my life to the fullest. You'll find a lot of that in the BDSM world. Fat, thin, tall, short, big dick, small dick, old, young, it doesn't matter. It's about the give and take, seeing the soul within. Which to my way of thinking is what every relationship should be, vanilla or kinky. Maybe I'm biased, but BDSM seems more open to that idea. At least where and how we enjoy it."

Returning to the present, Julie watched Charlotte's Master crook an imperious finger at her. Tarps were spread out on stage, and a draped table held a vat of misting liquid nitrogen, along with a line-up of knives and fire wands. The music was a dramatic piece that evoked witches dancing around a cauldron. The flickering light against the brick painted scenery suggested a dungeon lit by braziers.

Tony was dressed as an Inquisitor in dark brown robes. The fifty-something nuclear plant engineer with a handsome head of silver hair and a goatee was one of their few cast members with theater experience, having played Arthur in a Raleigh area production of *Camelot*, and Don Quixote in *Man of La Mancha*. His dramatic abilities showed now. "Strip, witch," he commanded in a booming voice that vibrated through the audience.

Charlotte unlaced the neckline of the smock and let it drop. While Tony had more theatrical experience, Charlotte's reactions were natural and un-choreographed, a compelling combination. She sank to her knees as if prepared to plead with the Inquisitor, bending to kiss his foot. His expression stern, he bent and wrapped his hand in her hair. When he yanked her up, preparing to drag her back to her feet, he paused, as if suddenly caught by the picture she made, on her knees to him, her head tipped back and hands loose, offering herself to him.

He traced the curve of her breast and her lips parted, tongue sweeping across them in unscripted reaction. Lifting her to her feet, he brought her to the tarp with a solid black backdrop flanking it on two sides, creating a protected corner. He put her hands on the wooden stake that had been erected on the tarp, as if that was where he might bind and set the witch on fire.

"Do I need to tie you, or do you submit to my will?"

"Don't you mean God's Will, Inquisitor?" Charlotte asked, batting her eyes at him, sending a ripple of laughter through the audience.

Tony picked up a paddle and whacked her generous bottom with it, earning a yelp. "Insolent witch. Answer the question." He spanked her again and she let out a gasp that hinted at something other than discomfort.

"No Master, you don't need to tie me. I submit to your will."

She curled her fingers around the stake and spread her legs. He bound up her hair in a tight knot, pulling on her scalp roughly, and stepped back. He drizzled alcohol on her back and then lit a fire wand. As he passed the bundle of cotton gauze over her flesh, it appeared as if he set her on blue fire, but he doused it with his hands immediately, stroking her that way, over and over.

"The fire does not burn your pale flesh," he said. "You are God's gift to me, witch. You will serve me."

He pressed up behind her to caress her flanks, and between her legs. "You like the idea, I think," he muttered, and she gasped in response.

Charlotte had lost all awareness of the audience as soon as Tony motioned to her from across the stage. Several times tonight, Julie had watched her players experience that transition, insulating themselves in a scene together. When Charlotte gasped at Tony's touch, Julie could tell Tony crossed that threshold himself.

Stepping away from his wife, he picked up the bouquet

of roses that had been left on the draped table with the wands and blades. After he selected one of the blooms, he held it up to the light. Putting his hand on her back, he stroked her silken skin as he considered the silken petals. He lifted the bloom to his nose to inhale the scent, and then ran it between her spread legs and brought it to his nose again. Charlotte kept her forehead pressed to her overlapped hands on the stake, but a visible quiver ran through her as he trailed the rose over her back.

Returning to the table, Tony donned a rubber glove. Dipping the rose in the nitrogen, he pulled the blossom free, pivoted and slapped it hard against her back.

The rose exploded, leaving a red mark on her skin and showering frozen petals around her. Charlotte clung to the post, shuddering from the cold. He rolled another fire wand over her skin. He began to alternate the two stimulus, fire and ice, making it a dance, her body moving in reaction to the two sensations, him moving with her.

Then he brought her to stillness as he jerked her up against him, turning her toward the audience. Producing a short curved blade that looked like a bird's beak, he ran it along her throat, under the curve of her breast, harrowingly close to her nipple... Charlotte was motionless against him, a moan caught in her throat, her eyes glazed.

Julie suspected very few in the audience were still seeing an obese woman or a white-collar man in his fifties, past what most would consider his sexual prime. They were seeing a Master and sub engage in an intimate, fascinating power exchange. The energy of it changed their lenses, let them see the beauty of two souls struggling to connect with one another, taking joy in one another. Charlotte was immersed in everything her Master did to her, and he in turn was ensorcelled by her response.

For the same reasons, Julie knew the moment Desmond was standing behind her. She knew his energy, and didn't know how to explain that, except to know it was true. He gripped one side of her podium, propping himself behind her so he bracketed her body, his other hand caressing her waist. He didn't speak, the two of them watching the scene progress. He was still a little sweaty from helping with the prop and scenery rearrangement. He was also still shirtless.

His hand slid up to cup her breast, cloaked in shadows. Fortunately, no one like Billie was keeping her company now.

"God, I want you," he muttered against her neck. "I'd fuck you right here if I could get away with it. You've been amazing tonight. Watch this next part."

Tony had returned Charlotte to the stake. Picking up another rose, he dipped it. This time he didn't use it like a flogger. He smashed it against Charlotte's ass using his hand, rubbing the coldness in and making her squeal. He picked up a bouquet of daisies, and struck her with them, one by one, after he treated them to the same nitrogen dip. They left more red marks on her, and Des whispered that flowers with thin petals felt like tiny bee stings.

Tony had one rose left. He turned Charlotte around, guiding her to lean back against the stake as he handed her the flower to hold. He coated his hands with alcohol, so he could put fire on his palms and run that flame over her breasts, her arms. Dousing them against her flesh, he retrieved and lit a fire wand. Dropping to his knees before her, he blew its heat between her legs with pursed lips. The flame was inches from her and didn't touch her tender regions, but the rippling effect was clear. She pressed harder against the stake when he exhorted her to stay perfectly still. As he blew that heat against her, over and over again, her cheeks began to redden, her nipples hardening even further. She had the rose clutched hard in both hands.

"Come, witch," Tony ordered, and Charlotte climaxed, her orgasm gushing onto her thighs in small, trickles. Tony never touched her between the legs, merely letting the manipulated fire create the magic. In the aftermath, she was so sensitive that when he pressed his mouth to her cunt, she cried out in erotic agony.

He took the rose from her hand, pressed it between her legs, and kissed it. "A gift from God is what you are, witch," the Inquisitor said. "I will be glad He made you mine for all my days."

She dropped to her knees, pressing her forehead to his boots, ending the skit the way it had begun.

As the curtain closed, there was a harrowing pause, the audience digesting the scene. Then the applause began, continuing and building into a strong response. Julie let out a thready sigh of relief. While the enthusiasm might be heavily salted by the BDSM community members in the audience, Julie predicted the rest had been swept up in the approbation.

Curtain calls began. The first set of performers, the priestesses and their chained sub, took the stage for a bow. As they stepped back and the next cast members entered from the opposite stage wings, Julie's body was matching the audience's fervent response, because Des was paying no attention to anything but her.

"I want you to stay after everyone goes home tonight," Des said against her ear, both hands kneading her breasts in those useful shadows, his pelvis firmly against her ass. "I have something I want to do to you, and I want to do it here, while all this energy is still pouring through the place."

After a performance, she was temporarily euphoric, followed by exhausted. Yet she wanted him with a throbbing fierceness that wouldn't be denied.

"Okay."

"It wasn't a request," her Dom said, nipping her ear and sliding his hand down between her legs behind the podium as the cheering built with each performer. Billie Dee-Lite was doing a sashay and pivot to wild cheers.

"Des..." She caught the edge of the podium, shocked when the tiny, intense orgasm rolled through her from the demand of his fingers. He carried her through it, even as those on stage motioned to the wings, calling his name, wanting him to come out and take a bow. Missive appeared at his side a mere heartbeat after he took his fingers away from Julie. It told her he'd stayed aware of their surroundings and protected her privacy. Though Missive pulled on him with a smile on her face, he held onto Julie an extra second, making sure she was okay on her feet.

"Go on," Julie said. "Take your bow. You deserve it."

Her breathy voice earned her a cocky grin and she snorted. "Not for that, you ass."

"Could have fooled me." He winked, but his eyes conveyed a lot more than casual humor as he slid away. His hands left behind burning needy sensation, not just where they'd touched, but all through her.

Julie heard the cheers swell to a roar comparable to that for Billie. Des had been their unexpected star tonight. Yes, Missive was part of that. But it was the young woman's utter trust in him that had made it all work, and that trust had to be earned.

Was there anything about Des that wasn't going to rock her world, take her by surprise?

Then they were yelling for her to come out, and for Madison to come up on stage. Julie did a quick check to make sure there was nothing inappropriately disheveled about her, though the madness of intermission had probably made a wreck of her hair and outfit. But to hell with it. She trotted out on wobbly legs to meet Madison and waved Harris out of the wings so he could take his well-deserved bow. Madison hugged her, squeezing the life out of her.

"I love you," the Naughty Bits owner said. "You did this."

"We all did it," Julie said. "To many more successes. Long live Wonder."

"Long live Wonder." Madison threw up her free hand and shouted it. The cry was immediately echoed by the performers, and Tony and Billie's booming voices carried it across the audience. In one of those magical, spontaneous moments that only the theater—and love—could provide, the audience answered in a roar.

"Long live Wonder!"

Julie was sure they'd just birthed the closing tradition for their new theater. She loved it.

As she took her bow, she caught Des's eye. The possessive heat, the knowledge that he'd just brought her to climax, was there, but it was mixed with something even more distracting. Maybe she was riding a performance high, but she'd always believed she saw things most clearly in moments like these.

He was genuinely happy for her success. In his countenance, she saw not only desire, but awareness of who she was down through every layer. He wanted everything there. She wanted all of him, just as badly.

The smile died from his face, as if he sensed how overwhelmed she was by those truths. His expression shifted, reflecting the powerful intent she'd felt from him when he'd pressed against her at the podium.

I have something I want to do to you, and I want to do it here, while all this energy is still pouring through the place.

He didn't break eye contact until she and Madison separated to sweep their arms out to encompass all the performers and crew, and offer them another ovation.

Julie made her own silent offering to the stage.

Thank you for giving me this so many times. No matter what happens with him, whatever I'll end up screwing up, or whatever shoe will drop, I am always grateful to have this.

She wished that comforted her as it normally did. But she didn't want a safety net when Desmond Hayes inevitably disappeared from her life.

She wanted him. Now and forever.

Chapter Nine

Julie drew in a deep breath, let it out. It had been a success. *Consent* had worked out better than even Madison and she had anticipated. She grinned, remembering Madison rushing up to her after the reception in the lobby, where they'd served sparkling water and hors d'oeuvres.

"Oh my God, reviewers from the Charlotte and Greensboro papers were both here. The one from *The Charlotte Observer* asked me a bunch of questions and seemed personally excited about what we have coming up. I'm half sick and half exhilarated about what kind of review she'll write. But she didn't act like we were some kind of sleazy sex club. She said..."

Madison paused, closing her eyes to recall it. "'Tonight's performance is evidence of the growth of erotic performance art as a legitimate cultural offering to the mainstream.' Freaking amazing. She sounds like she's already composing her review, right? At least that's what I think, and Logan agreed with me."

While Julie didn't doubt Logan's concurrence with his wife's opinion, she'd be surprised if he'd been able to wedge in more than a nod of agreement. Madison was running wide on all cylinders.

"I reminded her a play is the next thing on our schedule. Monday we have to start planning with Lila. She says her script is all finished..."

That had been several hours ago. Now the theater was quiet, everything put away, the doors locked. The cast and crew had enjoyed a small but enthusiastic after party and then headed home with or to family.

Julie stood on stage. She was elated, content. She spun in a circle, tipping her head back. Nothing brought her the sense of satisfaction a good performance did, the culmination of weeks of hard work, coordination and creative talents coming together. Having shared that with those like Harris, Billie and Madison, who understood the significance, added to the lovely sense of fulfillment.

But tonight there was another component to her happiness, taking it to an even higher level. Des. The single person's mantra that career could fill the hole where a significant other should be was crap. At least for her. Career could be a nice, thick curtain over that empty space and, as long as she hadn't looked behind that curtain, happiness was possible. Some people were eventually able to turn that curtain into a wall, and maybe for them the mantra became truth. But Julie's life was all about what happened when the curtain rose, so she'd never been able to shut down that possibility.

Which was why she'd reached this spot. She'd found someone who awakened the longings inside that empty space, and he'd pulled back the curtain. She remembered watching him walk onto the stage, hand in hand with Missive, and take a bow, the other performers urging him forward for a second ovation, generously acknowledging that his segment had taken the whole show up a notch.

Loving performance art as she did, how could she resent his expression of it with another performer, capable of showcasing his talents as brilliantly as Missive had done?

He was an artist, as much as Thomas was. She wished she could figure out the magic spell necessary to instantly get past all her fears and hang-ups and truly believe Des could distinguish between the art he made with other subs, and what he made with her.

She was getting there, though. As she'd watched him elevate and felt him inspire the audience, she'd known then she was falling in love with him. There was no chance of scrambling back up that slope, because it wasn't the fleeting stage adulation that such brilliance commanded. No, she loved the man who'd offered to share his carrot sticks and who had an aversion to talking about his health because too much of his early life had focused on it.

Except for the day at Bob Evans, he hadn't spoken about not having a family. She'd asked him during that meal if he had any memory of his mother. He'd said no, but he'd had a peculiar look as if that wasn't entirely true. Maybe he had some sense of her, a scent, the sound of her voice, buried in an infant's subconscious.

She wanted to know more of his story. She wanted to be part of his story. It was time to stop fighting it and resign herself to future heart-pulverizing pain when he turned out to be an ass, as they always seemed to be. But he felt so...not like that.

She moved to one of the front row seats, propping her tired feet on a crate she dragged over. As she loosed her hair and ran her fingers through it, she tipped her head back to study the rafters. They still had to repaint the ceiling inside, obliterate the water spots, but that was a chore for another day.

At the creak and rumble of a wheeled something coming out on the stage, she tilted her head down. Des was pushing a rack of long, formal dresses, raising her curiosity. But he wasn't ready to explain them yet.

"I just walked Missive and Billie to their cars," Des informed her. "I told Harris we'd lock up. I also told him the boss lady said they could all take the day off tomorrow."

She smiled. "You walked Billie to his car?"

"Her car. 'She' was still in character, so psyched about the show the only thing she'd changed was her shoes, because she said her arches were killing her. Linked her arm through mine and said if I was giving ladies escorts to their cars, that would include her tonight. The way she was working that dress, I wasn't disputing it. I don't dispute much of anything with her, since she could bench press my truck. Plus, I don't argue with a lady. Unless she's being stubborn."

He winked at her, and she tucked her tongue in her cheek. "You protected yourself pretty well on that one. Clever guy."

"Guy has to be clever around intelligent, attractive women, of any gender variation."

"Hmm. Where did you meet Billie? You never said."

"I first met him at Frolicon, down in Atlanta. Billie's a top who loves to Dom men or women. I'll take you to see him perform in Fayetteville sometime. The military guys there adore him."

"Really?"

"Really. Billie has a remarkable way with a crowd. Well, you saw it tonight when he was doing the emceeing. First time I met him and I remarked on his build, he batted his lashes and told me he'd been born in Belhaven." Des affected Billie's tone and cocked a hip as he propped against the rack of dresses. His deep voice and complete inability to emulate a woman made Julie giggle.

"'Honey-chile, let me tell you something about being gender queer in rural North Carolina, particularly around a bunch of the brothers. White people may have their hang-ups about it, but they're all rainbow flags and 'woohoo to diversity' compared to how most black men react to it.' He said he started pumping iron and learning how to fight as soon as he could lift a barbell and form a fist. 'Which is dreadful for a manicure, by the by.'"

Des sobered. "When his mother kept catching him trying on her dresses and wearing bras under his clothes to school, she bought him a burial plot. He was fourteen years old. He said she didn't know what to do with him and figured it was the only way she could show her love."

"Wow. He didn't try to hide it much, even then."

"Yeah. It's kind of a miracle he survived, and survived to be as cool of a guy as he is. Or woman. Or both."

"You should stay away from a drag queen career, by the way," Julie advised. "You couldn't do female if you tried."

"Well, I am a roofer. Not a lot of room to explore my feminine side around the guys at the job sites."

Her lips curved, but she was thinking about Billie's mom, and Des's. "Do you ever feel sad about your mom? Lonely, from not having a family in the traditional sense?"

He left the rack of dresses and sat on the edge of the stage, swinging his feet. He was back in his jeans and one of his quirky T-shirts. King Kong held a voluptuous Jessica Lange in his palm while he screamed his rage from the

Empire State building. She noticed Des hadn't tied the laces of his thick-soled work shoes.

"I guess I was sad at the beginning," he said. "But I think it's harder to be a kid who knew his family and lost them, rather than one who never had them at all. It's easier to make your own family as you grow up. I'm fairly tight with some of the guys on my crews, and the rigger and BDSM communities are close knit, if you fall in with the right group. Come Christmas or Thanksgiving, I've never lacked an invitation to join someone at their table."

He fell silent, watching her with those brown eyes that contained so many things she wanted to know as much as they scared her. He knew it, too. She felt it, in a waiting, coiled energy from him. It was a different version of a wolf patiently stalking a rabbit, but not one he planned to kill. He simply intended to catch it and never let it go. At least that was what she hoped—and feared—in that perverse conflict she had inside her.

"Did you have girlfriends as a kid? Before you went on your dating dry spell?"

"Some." He left the stage and straddled the crate, picking up her foot to put it in his lap and massage her stockinged toes. She barely swallowed a moan of bliss. "What are you after, love?"

"Loneliness, I guess. It's a powerful word, and I think it affects some people more than others. Maybe becomes an obsession."

"Or a pit they can't climb out of," he said bluntly. "They keep waiting for someone to reach in and pull them out. Yeah, I went there a couple times, before I had a get-over-myself moment. You have to crawl out of that pit yourself. When you do, you realize there are six billion people wandering around, six billion chances to form connections, friendships, shared experiences."

He shrugged. "If you shut yourself away from everyone and say 'I'm lonely', it doesn't make a whole lot of sense, when the rest of the world is waiting outside that door. It doesn't happen instantly, those connections. You've got to be patient, work for them. And that's just normal friendships and family relationships. It's been my experience the soulmate stuff happens when you're not looking for one, when you finally get comfortable with where you're at. When you're a whole person rather than a puzzle piece looking for a matching lock."

He swept his hand around himself, gesturing to the theater. "I know you've been in that pit, but this looks like you're one of the ones who clawed out and found something that works for you."

She lifted her other foot off the floor, twitching it left and right in invitation. He let it replace the one in his lap so he could massage it too.

"Brat."

She didn't deny it. "Is there any time loneliness isn't selfishness? Wanting that one bright line of connection that belongs to you alone? You really think that's just romanticism gone amuck?"

"No, not necessarily. But I think it has the irony of putting blinders on you. Such that when that person's right in front of you, you might miss that they're there because you have this perfect picture in your head of what he or she is supposed to be."

Another silence ensued. As it drew out, it began to have weight. She felt his eyes on her, and shifted. She wanted to tell him to stop looking at her like that, but she didn't really want him to stop. So she straightened, putting her feet on the floor, and gestured to the rack of clothes. "What's that?"

"Glad you asked." He rose from the crate and came to her. When she lifted her face, he bent and slid his arms beneath her, picking her up off the seat. Not expecting to be carried, she caught his shoulders with a little yelp.

"What are you doing?"

"I had a sudden craving to carry you. You're a nice armful."

He carried her up the side steps and let her feet down in front of the rack, her back to the stage curtain. The dresses were in shades of ivory or white. The full skirts and beaded bodices told her they were all wedding dresses.

"I picked these out at secondhand shops. They're in your size, more or less, so they should have a reasonable fit." He gestured. "Show me the dress you'd want to be married in, if these were the choices you had."

She'd had a lot of unexpected experiences with eccentric people. This one took her by surprise, followed by a pressing sense of dismay.

"I'm kind of tired." She stepped back, but he caught her hand.

"Julie."

At his look that could penetrate her so deeply, she couldn't keep herself from saying what was at the forefront of her brain. But when had she ever had a filter?

"I can't do that as a game, Des. I'm a middle-aged woman who's never even gotten close to it, and I'm one of the pathetic saps who really wanted it to happen. It took a long time for me to accept that I'm likely never going to have that, and to figure out how to be happy with my life regardless. It's a can of worms I don't really want to open. Okay? Lot of dysfunctional shit goes with it, and I don't want to feel that with you tonight. I just want..." She swallowed over the ache in her throat, unable to continue.

He drew her against him, his fingertips pressing into her lower back and the upper rise of her buttocks in that firm way that miraculously conveyed just how in control he was. It also reminded her that, while she was exhausted, the exhilaration of the night and the simmering she'd felt ever since he'd kissed her and given her that tiny, intense orgasm were within reach.

Hell, the whole damn night had been an overflowing tub of erotic stimuli. Though she'd been busy doing her job, an important part of her brain had been eagerly drinking in all the pheromones, just like everyone else in the theater. She fully expected a few hundred people had gone home to copulate like rabbits. Some would explore things they'd never thought about, or had carefully buried up until now. Hopefully there'd be no ER visits. That was the kind of publicity they really *didn't* need. Thank goodness they'd put a bunch of "don't try this at home without proper guidance" caveats in the program, as well as had Billie reinforce that mantra in his emceeing.

When he spoke against her cheek, her hand flexed in his

simply from the vibration through her skin. Her internal babblings weren't enough of a buffer against the things he wanted to break open inside of her, force her to release.

"We're back to my earlier reminder, love. This isn't a request. Choose. Trust me to take you somewhere you want to go."

He guided her reluctant hand to close over one handful of rich fabric. "It worked out nicely that you're wearing white lace tonight," he observed, sliding a finger just under the neckline of her black silk blouse to trace the edge of the undergarment. A tingle of sensation shot straight to her nipple.

Shifting behind her, leaving her facing the rack, he reached in front of her to slip the buttons of her blouse. She'd noticed he preferred to remove her clothes himself and, since he combined it with plenty of caressing strokes of his strong fingers, she had no objections.

He'd revealed the lacy cups of her white bra. It was low profile and pushed her up, which won his hum of approval as he slid his touch back over the quivering curves. Her grip tightened on the dress. He moved his hands down her arms, making her release the dress as he drew them back behind her, dropping his grip to her wrists to hold her in that position. His knuckles pressed against her ass as he nudged her hair aside to kiss her throat, tease it with his tongue.

He did that for a while as she swayed in his grip, staring at those dresses, the sparkles and satin. Releasing her wrists, he slipped the button of her slacks and took the zipper down with a quiet tick-tick noise. After he had her step out of them, he looked down at the knee high stockings she was wearing.

"Take those off for me, love. My rough hands will snag them for sure." But he held her as she removed them, leaving her clad only in her filmy underwear.

Her eyes closed. Her head was already tilted for the light kiss he brushed over her lips.

"My gorgeous woman," he murmured, thrilling her. Molding his palm over her buttock, he played with the elastic of her panties for a musing, provocative moment.

Then he stepped back, gesturing to the rack again.

"Choose. I'll be setting up behind you." He stroked her hair, caressing her bare back. "Are you cold?"

She shook her head. "Not right now."

He hadn't addressed her reluctance about the dresses. He didn't try to reassure her about things no amount of words could fix. He refused to turn the light away from the dark chambers of her heart, and she kept stepping into those rooms to risk herself with him.

As he retreated, she looked at the dresses. "Des." Her voice sounded strange to her, strained. "I love you. I mean, I'm falling in love with you. Is that a problem?"

A pause, then she heard his footsteps as he came back to her. She was grateful and wary when he pressed against her back and folded his arms around her, one over her breasts and one around her waist. They constricted almost to the point of taking her breath, and he kissed the sensitive and pulsing spot just beneath her ear.

"Yeah, it's a problem."

She couldn't tell what he meant, not with the mixed message of being in his embrace. He nipped her lobe, dipping a hand to pinch her buttock. "Stop stalling and pick a dress. Don't turn around until I say you can."

"I tell him I'm falling in love with him and I'm stalling," she muttered. But his tone hadn't rejected her feelings. It was just a response she couldn't decipher.

Since she sensed he would work back around to an answer in his own way, she let the statement hang in the air, drift and fill the space with feeling and density that increased as she flipped through the dresses. When she found the one that was right, she knew it, but she still checked out the other half dozen.

"This one." She'd been listening to his rustlings, but she hadn't been able to discern much from them. Not turning around to look was difficult. She was curious by nature, but he knew that. She suspected it was just another way he'd found to torment her.

Before her curiosity overrode his direction, he returned to her. As he reached over her shoulder and unhooked the dress from the rack, he put another of those pleasant kisses at the base of her throat. She leaned into him as he held the dress against her, a crinkling crush of satin, his palm warm on her breast even through the layers of fabric. "Let's get you into this."

The beaded bodice had an off-the-shoulder, scalloped neckline that framed and outlined her breasts, offering a provocative amount of cleavage that pleased him, if the flare in his gaze was an indication. In the back, the dress dipped down below the shoulder blades, leaving a lot of bare flesh to stroke.

He had her raise her arms so he could handle the side zipper. He hooked three small fabric buttons at the lower back that sculpted her upper torso further. When he turned her to him, the dress floated around her, covering her bare feet.

"I think someone a few inches taller than me had this dress."

"That's all right. You look perfect." He ran a hand down her arm, back up to her biceps. Drawing her past the curtain line, she saw the set up was a cushioned mat and a few lengths of rope. So simple, yet it still made her breath shorten.

Taking her to the mat, he used the pressure of his hand and the direction of his gaze to tell her what he wanted. The skirt was yards of soft satin that, when she knelt before him, looked like a rippling lake reflecting an ivory sky.

He guided her arms behind her, adjusting them into a boxed position as he dropped to one knee and held her that way with his hands instead of rope, a flesh and blood restraint.

"A beautiful bride," he said, his voice a low rumble of meaning and emotion in her dark theater, a setting of drama and dreams come to life. Pushing her hair forward, he bared her neck and set his teeth there. She drew in an erratic breath as he kissed her, giving her a hint of his tongue. He held her overlapped arms, keeping her still.

"We're going to get this resolved tonight, Julie, once and for all. So for the next little bit, I'm going to talk and you're going to listen. I want you to listen with your whole heart. Not with your fears. Can you do that?"

She closed her eyes, bowing her head. He knew. Of course he knew. He'd been dropping hints, some subtle and some not-so-subtle, like sending Missive with her confidence about her scene name.

"I can try," she whispered. "I want to."

"Good." He paused, his mouth on her, and then she gasped, arching up against him in involuntary reaction as he closed his teeth on her again. Not gently. A hard, painful clamp. His arm snaked around her waist, holding her against him, his other hand still tight on her overlapped forearms. He increased the pressure of the bite and she whimpered. He wasn't breaking skin, but he was close, and he'd put his mouth over her carotid, so she heard the rush of her blood.

"Hurts," she managed. He made a noise of assent, agreeing with her, but he still didn't release her or change the pressure. The pain was burning through her throat, but the endorphins were swirling in her vitals, her fingers curling and uncurling against his arm around her waist.

He released her arms to slide his fingertips up one and around her throat, stroking her there lightly, a tender contrast to the ruthless lock of his jaw. She kept her hands clasped on her forearms the way he'd put them, because he hadn't given her permission to do otherwise. Everything in that throbbing bite was a command for her attention, and he had all of it.

When he at last eased the hold on her throat and licked the spot he'd offended, the slow swirls of his tongue were met with tingling response. He kissed her throat again, tiny presses of his lips down to her collar bones, and he came to a rest there, nuzzling the pocket between them.

"You asked me if I was lonely," he said, low. "No. Lonely isn't something I've felt, not often. I had an ache, though. In my cock and balls, in my gut. I wanted something I couldn't explain. Haven't ever really been sure what it was. Just knew when and if I ever saw it, it would always be mine and no one else's."

Lifting his head, he touched her jaw, guided her face around so she was staring up at him. He was standing on his knees, leaning over her left shoulder. The position in which he held her head wasn't comfortable, but when he shifted his grip under her jaw, he put enough strain on the tilt of her head that she knew he was reminding her again of that edge he liked. That did crazy things to her insides.

"What I do with rope, the energy I feel when I do it, when I get lost in it, that's all mine. The sub, she's this perfect part enhancing it, an angel giving me the center, the reason to tie, bind, shape, create. But she's never mine. I've never looked at Missive, or any of them, and felt that. Don't move."

He sat back on his heels and stroked her hair. "I want you to look down and to your left. Lifting your chin just a little...like that. Stay in that position."

When she did, he shifted out of her range of vision. She heard a click, like he'd taken a picture with his phone, but when he came back, he had rope in his hands. He let her relax her head and neck in a normal position and began to use her as that center he'd just described.

He was capable of intricate designs, but she intuitively understood the simple one he chose this time was intended to only subtly adorn what he felt was already detailed and intricate enough—herself.

He put rope over her shoulders near the juncture with her neck. He also wrapped it around the points of her shoulders, since the dress design left them bare. Further wraps held her boxed arms to her sides. The ropes passed vertically on the outside of her breasts, and horizontally over and under them. He took all the wraps around her boxed arms, securing them and knotting the ends in a line below her shoulder blades. As he did that, he pulled her boxed arms up, increasing the discomfort. Arousal swirled in her lower belly. It amazed her that he could summon that reaction, when she normally whined over the irritation of a hangnail.

"Enough?" he asked. "Or...here?"

Higher. She drew in a breath. Oh God, it hurt, but something about it felt so good...

He repositioned it at the lower level without waiting for her response. His fingertips passed over her shoulder muscles. "These gave me the answer," he said. "You like the pain, but you're going to be in this position a while. I don't want you experiencing the wrong kind of stress."

She had her head down, her breath shallow, heart doing that heavy, powerful thud it did when he was tying her, capturing her, taking over. It was a language. Someone standing on the outside would only see him doing knots and wraps, but every one of them spoke to her, said something. She was quivering, wet between her legs, soaking the white panties. She felt vulnerable to him, fragile as porcelain.

He shifted back again, and took another couple of pictures from behind her. When he returned, he wrapped his arm around her waist, fingers hooking in the rope wraps below her breasts.

"This is how I would marry you," he said. "We'd say our vows as I was tying you. The dress and the rope would say you're mine." He brought the phone around her so she could see herself on the screen. "This would be the wedding picture I'd carry on my phone."

A woman knelt in a froth of satin, her arms bound behind her, the ropes a tapestry between shoulder and bound arms that enhanced and displayed the beauty of her bare shoulders, her exposed nape, the curl of her fingers around her elbows. Her silken hair was pulled over one shoulder. A submissive, waiting for her Master, devoted and in love with him. Totally his. Pictures didn't lie. At least not that kind of picture.

"You are fucking beautiful, and I mean that literally. I'd mean it when you're eighty. I've never wanted a woman so much in my whole life."

"If you don't mean it...please don't."

He caught her face and drew it up, not gently, forcing her to meet his brown gaze. "Do you think I don't mean it, Julie? Do you think I've gone this long in my life without committing to a woman, only to do it casually now, just to jerk her around?"

She shook her head. "I'm afraid of how I feel. I never get what I want. Not in terms of love."

"Well, I may not be what you want, but I'm what you're getting. Deal with it."

It was an unexpected tease, delivered harshly and gently at once, and she couldn't help hiccupping over a surprised chuckle, though emotions were thick in her throat. His eyes sparked in response, but his touch went to a caress on her face, registering everything happening inside her. She was lost.

"Tell me you want me, Julie," he said. "Tell me you believe me. No matter what other shit I might bring into your life, God help you, promise me you'll never doubt that one thing."

Everything felt taut and too large inside her, no room for anything but the bright, sharp need she showed him. "Yes," she whispered. And though he didn't encourage her to call him that, or seem to believe in that formality, she heard it in her mind clearly enough.

Master.

He nodded, his jaw tight. "I'm going to have you, right now. I'll probably get unspeakable things on that dress. But that will be one more way I'll mark you."

He'd tied the horizontal wraps and her arms tightly. As he passed his fingers over them, she felt the way the rope dug into her skin. He bent and captured her mouth, parting her lips with the pressure of his, sweeping in to take over with tongue and teeth. The faint throbbing of her neck told her he'd already left a mark there with his bite.

He rose and moved to stand before her. He stripped his belt and opened his jeans. He had a practical, efficient way of undressing, as if he wasn't aware of the beauty of his body. At another time, she might ask him to peel each article off slowly, let her savor. But she needed him too much right now, and he seemed driven by the same urgency.

He did take off everything, though, which pleased her. She'd seen most of his lean, tan body the day at the lake, but now she saw his pale, tight buttocks, the thick and tempting erection she'd like to taste, rising above testicles she wanted to cup and stroke.

For the performance, he'd tucked his pump inside the dark trousers, and they'd figured out a way to make the injection site blend, the dressers and makeup students coming up with a flesh-toned gauze bandage that held the cannula against his abdomen and camouflaged it. He still wore it now as he disconnected the pump and set it aside.

When he knelt before her, she wanted to pass her fingers over that gauze and the thin line of the cannula beneath it, over his flesh and muscles. She wanted to feel the full heat of his body against her. Now, now, *now*. All of it was perfect to her. It was all Des.

He didn't free her to do that. Instead, he started to ease her back, slowly, for he didn't allow her to unfold her legs. He supported her head until she was in a full backbend, the point of her skull resting on the mat. She did yoga, she knew he knew that. A couple times during the long days of the last week, she'd done a short session off in the wings to stay limber. She remembered seeing him leaning against the wall, watching her do an *asana* very similar to this position.

She was like his orchids, she realized. He'd observed how she moved in her daily life and was using it here to decide how to shape her for his pleasure.

He nudged her knees farther apart as he lifted the long skirt, folding it up to her waist to expose her panties. He braced himself over her, studying her, a dark ruthless spirit whose hair fell forward to frame his chiseled features and sharp eyes. Those eyes shifted to her.

"If this position gets unbearable, you tell me."

"It's all unbearable. That's why I don't want you to stop." She could barely breathe. The ropes dug into her arms and constricted her breasts, and she lifted her chin, exposing her throat to him. She felt on the verge of a climax that went far beyond the physical.

He hooked the panties in one finger, pushing into her, and she moaned as he passed his thumb over her clit on the outside of the front panel. "Yeah, you're as wet as the ocean, love. Warm and salty and slippery. You want my cock here?"

"Yes. God, yes."

"You know I love the way your voice sounds when you beg. Throaty and female, so sweet and strong. Vulnerable, trusting me." He pulled the panties farther to the side and began to push a couple more fingers inside her. He kept his eyes locked on hers and, though she couldn't deny the power of his touch, it was his demanding gaze that sent her over.

She began to climax before she could stop herself and, once on that ride, she couldn't stop. The orgasm kept peaking and crashing down on her with every slight movement he pushed forward, stretching and penetrating her so deep, fingers stroking and playing, finding sensations she'd never even discovered herself.

Her back and thigh muscles were clenching, her whole body pitted against his restraints. She screamed as the orgasm refused to leave that edge, goaded by the conflict between pleasure and pain. It was as if she was being cut open from stem to stern with excruciating pleasure.

It went on and on, as if she could never get enough, as if she could never climax enough. Then he withdrew his fingers, clasped her around the waist and cradled her head, bringing her back to a quivering, upright position. He'd done it with care, so her muscles and joints had time to accommodate the change in position, but once he had her vertical, he showed his own urgency. His cock was thick and hard, brushing his abdomen, the tip glistening with pre-come. He held her with one arm and reached for the jeans he'd left crumpled close by.

"Do you have to..." Her voice wasn't much more than a whisper but he stopped, tilting his head toward her. He'd told her he'd had sessions that resulted in sex, but if he'd always been safe... "Can you not wear it? If you have to, it's okay, I don't want us to risk anything bad. But...I'm safe."

His gaze was sharp with desire, but now it filled with another emotion. He left the jeans to put both hands on her again, fingers digging into her arms. "The very last thing you are, Julie Ramirez, is safe. But yes, you are safe with me. I've always been careful."

"Okay. Then please...let me feel you."

He lifted her to take her place on the mat, bringing her over his lap to straddle him, her skirt covering his bare legs. She was excruciatingly tight, thanks to the orgasm, but though he was relentless, he was caring, slowly bringing her down on him, watching her face constrict, lips part as he pushed in, inch by inch. She was still wet, and once he was fully seated, he cupped her face, eyes darkening as she turned her head and bit the heel of his hand, hard, conveying her emotional turmoil. He'd given her an orgasm, but she needed an emotional release. She needed that edge. He was finally inside her, and she wanted to feel it like a branding.

"So be it, love." He brought her down fully on him, her clit getting full contact as his cock rammed deep, stretching and invading her vibrating tissues.

"Oh..." She cried out, helpless since he had her arms still bound behind her back, her upper body caught in his rope. Her breasts quivered and bounced at the impact, and his gaze went from there to her throat, to her mouth, and back again. He thrust into her again with that same force and it snapped his own control. As he plunged her into a full bodied immersion of wet, heated joining, she was gasping, making noises of need and encouragement. Harder, deeper. *Please, make it hurt in that way that takes away the pain.*

He gave her that wish and, when he finally shot his release into her, she was caught by the amber fire of his brown eyes, the taut set of his mouth, his arms so tight around her again. She couldn't breathe, didn't ever want to breathe.

Not if the trade-off was that she could feel like this.

He'd told her his feelings. He'd made her say she believed him, because she wanted to believe him so much. But in these moments, she knew no doubts. After all this time, it had come. The relationship that made her pain over the other ones seem ridiculous. That hadn't been heartbreak. Heartbreak was losing someone you truly loved. Someone whose leaving would destroy her.

This was the answer he'd given to her reluctance about the wedding dresses. If she was wrong about him, it would be bad. If she was right, she'd be scared to the core. But when he was holding her now, his face pressed into her throat, her bound body in his arms, she gave her faith to what he'd promised and said it aloud, wondering at it.

"I'm yours, Des," she said.

"Yeah, you are," he said, in that mild way of his that she now knew wasn't mild at all. She dropped her head forward on top of his, inhaled that sunlight smell of him...and let herself be his.

Chapter Ten

After they settled some more, he removed the rope, took off her dress, bra and underwear, and put her in a thick robe. She hoped he hadn't used it for Missive, but all she smelled on it was Des, so she thought he'd brought it with him for *her* aftercare.

Leaving her curled up on the mat, he packed his ropes in his backpack. She was half-asleep when he bent over her. In addition to his pack, he was carrying a small zippered tote she kept in her room, so he'd packed her an overnight bag. He hadn't asked if it was okay to rummage in her clothes, but it didn't occur to her that he needed to do so. It was an unsettling thought, if she was allowing herself any of those. Which she wasn't. Not tonight.

"Did you pack me a bikini top and a mini-skirt to wear tomorrow?"

"Of course. I'm a practical packer."

"No underwear, I expect."

"Why would you want to burden yourself with so many extra clothes?" He kissed the tip of her nose and gathered her up, lifting her in his arms like a child.

"I'm too heavy. You should let me walk. Where are we going?"

"You're not too heavy, I'll tell you when you need to walk, and my place. Time to show you my hovel, princess. Hush and sleep."

He carried her to his truck and she watched him through the windshield, lost in a pleasant, completely energy-less, no-thinking state, as he locked up the theater and set the alarm. He noticed details like that. Despite his joking, she'd bet money she'd find everything she'd need in her tote in the morning, from toiletry items to a comfortable outfit of a favorite shirt and jeans—with underwear. He might choose a snugger fitting T-shirt, but she wouldn't hold that against him. He was male, after all.

When he climbed into the truck, she was turned on her hip, looking at him. He lifted his arm, and she scooted underneath it to be held in its shelter. She helped him put the vehicle in gear, so he wouldn't have to reach across himself with his driving hand. She stayed where she was as he left the parking lot and drove through the night. She had no clue what time it was, or how far away he lived. It didn't matter. They could drive all night like this for all she cared.

She dozed a bit more, waking when he was making short turns that told her they'd entered a neighborhood. She opened her eyes as he turned onto a gravel driveway. It wound through woods, a peculiar transition since the road they'd been on had been lined with the neat, attractive models of a planned development.

When the trees cleared, she saw a large cottage like the gingerbread house in a fairy tale, with blue-grey wood siding. A small guest house with the same architecture was about a hundred yards to the left. Beyond the house and guest house was a barn. She saw the silhouettes of two horses in the open door and the flash of a curious large eye when his headlights passed over the stalls.

"The bigger house is Betty's, my landlady," Des said. He'd realized she was awake, but his low tone let her stay in her dreamlike state. "The horses are hers. You'll like them. One's a big flashy guy, and she used to show him. The other is a little palomino mare with some attitude. I take care of them when she has long shifts. She's a nurse at the hospital."

After helping her shift back toward the passenger seat, he left the truck and came around to open her door.

"I feel like Hansel or Gretel," she observed. "What a magical house to find in the middle of a suburb."

"This place predated the development, and fortunately the previous owners never sold it for subdivision." He stroked her cheek, and she felt absurdly pleased at his obvious enchantment with her sleepy and disheveled state. "Betty may have a touch of witch in her, but she prefers to bake cookies instead of children. She makes some great oatmeal raisin ones. Come on."

Des helped her slide out, and put an arm around her, holding her tote and his pack in the other hand. "Do you want to say hi to the horses before we go in?"

"I'm wearing a robe and no shoes. Yes."

Smiling at the conflicting messages, he put their things on the hood and picked her up, carrying her down the path to the barn. No man had ever carried her this much, and she'd dated a couple men much more physically intimidating than him. Yet she felt secure in his hold and liked the sensation more than she'd expected.

Though the path wasn't well lit, his stride was sure, familiar with the terrain. "Miss Thing," he called out softly. "Come talk to us. We won't wake up Mr. All That," he told Julie. "He likes his beauty sleep and can get a bit nippy when woken up before morning, but Miss Thing is a night owl like me."

He let her feet down outside the open stall door. Julie heard a whicker from the shadows and drew back, startled, as a gold and white head emerged in front of her. However, the liquid brown eyes blinked at her so compellingly she overcame her initial trepidation and petted the horse's forelock and muscled neck. "Oh, she's wonderful."

"Have you ever petted a horse before?" Des had noted her hesitation.

"Rarely," she admitted. "Cop horses in New York, the occasional carriage horse at Christmas. That kind of thing. Never ridden one."

"We'll have to fix that. Miss Thing is a gentle lady."

Julie liked the idea. Still muzzy, she closed her eyes, using Des as a prop as she scratched Miss Thing's forehead and caressed her velvety soft nose. He chuckled indulgently and lifted her again.

"Gotta go to bed, Miss Thing. I wore my baby out." If I plan to take advantage of her again, I have to get her some sleep." He brushed his lips across Julie's forehead. "And I sure as hell plan to do that."

"Don't I get any say in it?"

"Sure. As long as it's an unqualified 'Yes, Des, that's exactly what I want.'"

He took them back up the path, reclaimed the tote and pack from the truck hood and ascended his small porch. He let her stand on her feet again as he fished out his key. She had a brief impression of a potted vegetable garden, tomatoes and some herbs to the left of the door, along with a folding chair and small table. A rusted set of chimes with a faded painted metal butterfly at the top offered a pleasant music.

Des opened his door and gestured her over the threshold. "It's basically a one-room apartment, but I'm fond of it, so be kind."

"I'm living in the back room of a theater. I'm hardly going to judge."

Though she was sleepy, she was curious about where he lived. When he snapped on a lamp, she saw he was right about the cozy size. The main living area space had a futon, easy chair and small flat screen TV. Several bookcases were stacked with magazines, books, notebooks. A file cabinet and a desk were tucked in a corner with a computer. The kitchen, separated from the living area by an L-shaped counter, had a compact set of the expected appliances. A two-seat bistro set was pushed against a pair of windows to the right of the counter, allowing a small passage to squeeze into the kitchen area.

As her gaze drifted back across the living area, she saw a double bed, partially revealed behind a standing wooden screen, hung with a variety of colorful ropes. One door behind the bed led to a small bathroom, because she saw a section of a vanity sink and a blue shower curtain with seagulls printed on it, diving and swooping. There was a second door she assumed was another room or closet, but it was closed.

Unlike most bachelors she knew, Des hadn't hesitated to bring her to his home without notice, but he didn't fit her single guy stereotype in a lot of ways. The living space was inviting, clean and well-ordered, not because he expected guests but because it matched the man's preferences. A brown, black and blue diamond pattern afghan was draped over the sofa, and the fabrics and accents of the living room meshed with that masculine but pleasing color scheme. The bed cover was dark blue with blue and green throw pillows against blue-cased bed pillows. He didn't care for knickknacks, no surprise there, but he had pottery pieces to hold several orchids and a cluster of interesting houseplant choices lined the bookcases. The room smelled faintly of peppermint, making her think of Christmas.

He had few possessions compared to most men his same age, but he had the things a man like him might need. Her gaze went back to the shower curtain. "Everything makes me think of forests but that," she said.

"Yeah. I like seagulls. I like the beach. And if everything matched, you'd figure I bat for the other team."

She considered. "It *is* true that straight single men rarely present such a well-coordinated interior decorating scheme, unless they've enlisted a professional designer to attract women to their lair."

"Yeah, I thought about it, but I already have to beat them off with a stick. I didn't want to cause myself more aggravation. I bought the mismatching shower curtain to thin out the pack."

"Of course." Her snort became a surprised sound as he lifted her again. He wasn't kidding; he really did like carrying her. He took her to the bed, put her on her feet to turn it down and untied her robe, sliding it off her shoulders. She held onto his biceps, blinking up at him as he stroked her hair back from her face and regarded her from head to toe.

"A fine-looking naked woman in my home. And not just any naked woman. You're the only thing my place has been missing."

He had a way of saying things that should sound hokey but made her knees weak. After he settled her in the bed, he seemed like he was going to leave her there, so she held onto his hand until he relented and sat down next to her.

"Where were you going?" she asked.

"Nowhere. I'm going to let you sleep while I do a couple things. I'm a little keyed up."

"Could I help with that?" She dropped her hand to his thigh and caressed him. Yeah, she could barely lift her head, but for the chance to give him more pleasure, she'd find some energy.

He smiled, clasping her seeking hand. "You sure can, but not right now. Not when I've asked so much of you. Sleep first."

"The shower curtain... It's not just because you like seagulls."

He cocked his head. "Even in a post-coital stupor, the girl is sharp."

"Not in a stupor. Get over yourself."

He grinned as she deliberately slurred her words, but as she trailed her fingers up and down his arm and fixed her eyes on him, he became more serious.

"When I was a kid at the boys' home, they took us to North Myrtle Beach one weekend. I was really looking forward to it, but I contracted a high fever and couldn't go. Betty, she was the nurse at the boys' home then. She bought a couple of shower curtains with seagulls on it and hung them around my bed in the infirmary. Bought me a tape of the ocean and played it so I could imagine I was there."

He glanced toward the bathroom. "That's not one of the original curtains, but having one like it reminds me there's something far more important than life not going your way. It's how you and those around you handle that, and knowing you can discover even better things than a beach trip because of it."

"Like friendship, and love. Loyalty." She supplied the unspoken words and thought one more in her mind. *Kindness.* She already loved this Betty, and was intrigued that his landlady was also his childhood nurse. "Did you ever get to the ocean?"

"No. I've never been." A hard-to-read expression crossed his face. "It's a bucket list thing."

Her brows raised. "It's only four hours from here."

"I know. More backstory. Let's not worry about it tonight."

"I need the missing piece before I can sleep, or I won't.

Half a bedtime story just keeps me awake." She let her fingers drift across his chest, moving up to tangle in his loose hair. "You're handsome, you know. Really handsome."

"I'm knotty, like a brown stick with too much hair."

She laughed, as she was sure he intended, but she clung to the front of his T-shirt. "I don't want to make you sad, but I want to know you. Will you finish the story?"

He touched her face. Sighed. "Okay. If you show me your boobs."

"God, men are easy." She tugged the covers down, flashed her bare breasts at him, then her laugh caught in her throat as he gripped her wrist to keep her from pulling the blankets back up. Leaning down, he breathed heated air over one nipple, watching it crinkle under the attention. She quivered as he played the tip of his tongue over the areola, curled around it, then gave it his whole mouth. The deep, easy suckling had her sighing, folding both arms around his shoulders. In her languorous state, the desire unfurling inside of her was like being in a sauna. All of her was so loose and relaxed. When he lifted his head, she tried to keep him close.

"If you joined me under the covers," she whispered, "You'd slide into me like a steam bath. All slick and easy. I don't want you to spare me or let me rest, Des. I want you to have me as often as you want."

His eyes sharpened, as did the planes of his face, telling her the effect her words had on him. He loosened her arms, but his grip on her was urgent. "I want that to build, for both of us," he said. "I used you hard, Julie. Trust your Dom. I know what you need. If I take you now, I won't be gentle about it. Again."

She saw the truth in his eyes, which caused a tiny little shiver in her. "If you think that makes me want you any less, it's the wrong tactic."

His lips twisted ruefully. "I know. It's why you're like a drug. One of the reasons. Go to sleep."

"Finish the story first. Please."

He relented, though she noticed he shifted his gaze back to the shower curtain, as if he wasn't entirely comfortable.

It was something people did when it was easier to pretend they were telling a story, rather than being the story themselves.

"When my mother took off from the hospital, she left behind a postcard of the ocean for me. Cherry Grove, North Myrtle Beach. It had four words on the back. 'Sorry. This is better.' I threw the damn thing away about a million times growing up. Every time, Betty would fish it from the trash and hold onto it until I regretted it and wanted it back. I guess I always counted on that, since I never threw it away where she couldn't get to it. I did tear it into three pieces once, and she taped them back together."

He tilted his head back and forth as if he was releasing tension in his neck. He was sitting up again, so she couldn't reach high enough to massage the area, but she did stroke the leg he had bent on the bed next to her. "Then one day Betty said: 'Maybe instead of focusing on what's on the back, focus on what's on the front. Your mother must have liked the ocean.' That message stuck with me. I could focus on the dark side or the light. Focusing on the dark brought me nothing. When I focused on the light, I found I liked seagulls."

"I like seagulls, too. Maybe we could go to the beach together one weekend. I bet I could make a better sandcastle than you."

"I bet you couldn't."

"You're on. Loser has to paint the other's toenails."

"I prefer passion pink," he said seriously. He tugged the covers up again, with a last gratifying, lingering look at her breasts before he brushed her lips with his. "Go to sleep, crazy, gorgeous woman. So I can fuck you all over again."

§

Julie slowly became aware of her surroundings. It wasn't quite dawn, but thanks to the glow of an outdoor light on the property, she had enough light that the furniture was silhouetted in the living room. Des had eventually come to bed, so they could sleep with comfortably tangled limbs, but he was no longer in the bed with her. He wasn't far away, though. He was bent over her, looping rope around her wrists. Her heart and libido gave a simultaneous leap, making her twitch restlessly. He made a quelling noise, gentle but firm. Then he resumed the humming that had brought her so agreeably back to the surface.

It took a moment to figure out the slow-beat song with his off-tune cadence, but when she did, it gave her heart a little twist. "Oh Girl", by the Chi-Lites. She didn't think Des had chosen it lightly. *Oh girl, I'd be in trouble if you left me now... how I depend on you...*

"Making sure I can't leave?" she said.

She was on her side, her hands curled together like an infant in the womb. When she'd fallen asleep, Des had been flush against her, cradling her body inside the shelter of his, that spooning sensation that was the universally acknowledged best part of having someone in your bed. When the person was special, beginning to mean something, it was almost better than sex. Which with Des was saying something, since sex with him basically realigned her solar system.

She'd experienced just the opposite a few times, having sex with a guy and afterward just wanting him to go away so she could forget the mistake that had led to that decision. Spooning with someone in those circumstances was like being trapped together in a well where the water depth promised death by drowning.

Drowning with Des was a decidedly better experience. With him she became a mermaid, able to breathe underwater and see all the wonders of the deepest levels of the ocean.

My, hadn't she woken in a poetic frame of mind? She was also fast moving toward arousal, thanks to her Master's expert touch. She was still naked, and suddenly even more aware of it with her wrists tied. He was wrapping rope around her thighs, attaching her bound wrists to them with a short length so that her hands had to stay below her navel. Now he'd moved down to execute a loose figure eight wrap around her ankles. He overlapped her feet so her ankle bones weren't rubbing together.

The wrists-to-thigh tether also kept her knees pulled up to waist level, as if she were sitting in a chair, only lying on her side.

"Des."

He lithely moved over her body, settling in behind her, and she drew in a breath when he wrapped a hand in her hair and pulled her head back. Not a yank, but a firm tug that got her attention as he put his mouth over hers. He'd been chewing a piece of the cinnamon gum he favored, which made her self-conscious about morning breath, but he didn't seem put off by it. He curled his tongue around hers, stroking her with cinnamon heat and delving deep, his hand cradling her jaw as he pressed a turgid cock against her bare ass.

"Hate to waste a morning hard-on," he muttered against her mouth. "Especially when I've got a tight, warm pussy for it first thing. Like going down the rabbit hole to pure mind-blowing fucking bliss, all before breakfast."

He made an adjustment, tightening the rope around her thighs, and she made a small noise of discomfort. "More or less?" he asked, his breath along her cheek.

With the constriction had come a throb of need that settled between her legs. How did he do that to her? Or was it already in her, and he'd merely revealed it, opening all the paths not taken but suddenly so appealing? Down the rabbit hole was the perfect way to describe it.

"More," she whispered.

"Good girl," he said, his approval and pleasure obvious. He adjusted it, let the rope bite into her skin. "That'll leave a pretty mark. Now be quiet, because I want to concentrate on fucking you."

He guided his cock into her slow, working his way forward. Though he'd introduced pain into the restraints, he didn't rush or force himself into her tender folds, so as he made his way into the channel his ropes had constricted into an even tighter fit, his penetration was all the more excruciatingly pleasurable. Her cunt contracted on him and she moaned, her wrists flexing in the bonds, forearms jerking against the length of rope holding them to her thighs, a reminder that she had to stay in this position because that was how he'd bound her.

"Fucking heaven," he groaned, gripping her buttock in one strong hand. "Gorgeous round ass, tight pussy, and this..."

Both hands slipped in front of her to cradle her breasts, fingers finding sensitive nipples to pluck, pinch and play. She writhed, crying out in involuntary reaction, the sensations shooting through her like starbursts. "Gorgeous tits. Firm and full and fucking God..."

"Des," she pleaded, though she had no clue for what, since her body was being stormed, invaded, overwhelmed, conquered. All she wanted and needed was more of the same feeling.

"Suck it up, love," he said mercilessly, his voice a caress. "You're taking everything I want to do to you this morning. I want you sore inside and out, hoarse from screaming, and wearing a mile-wide grin thinking of me taking you like this. I'm reinforcing the lesson we went over last night. You're mine. The only woman I want."

He was all the way to the balls now. He dropped his hold to her hips as he began to thrust, making it clear her purpose was to service his need, his thick, pounding need. Her pussy spasmed, but without the clitoral stimulation, the response built and built, holding her on that edge. He was hammering another lesson home. He would let her come when he was good and ready, when she was willing to abandon all dignity and beg for it.

It kept scaring her, the way he did this. She told herself over and over it was the whole hypnotic, addictive power of BDSM dynamics, which could captivate like a siren while meaning nothing. But it didn't feel like nothing. Not in the slightest. And he was telling her in no uncertain terms that it didn't feel like nothing to him, either. He was pulling her so deeply into him, she couldn't, didn't want to say no. To anything.

When he released, she shrieked at the sensation, so near climax but not quite there. He flooded her inside and she felt the seed trickling out around his length and against her labia. Curving himself tight around her, he recaptured her breasts, teeth scraping her neck. She was so needy, ready to beg, but he chose to be merciful.

"Your turn, baby," he said. He lengthened the tether between thighs and wrists and turned her so she was on her elbows, her body still coupled together with rope so her ass was in the air. He steadied her on her bound knees. Wrapping an additional rope around her wrists, he looped it over her neck and cinched it down so her forehead couldn't lift more than an inch or two from her knuckles.

"Des..." She kept speaking his name, and only his name, but each time she uttered it possessed a wealth of different meanings. The climax was so close, but other things as well, a panic roaring up. Trembling had become shaking. She'd been alone for too long, and he took away every shield, every stitch of emotional clothing when he did all of this. She did believe him, she did, but a betrayal by him would literally kill her.

She couldn't put that on him. Things were closing in, she needed to get loose, she needed to stay this way forever, she needed a climax...she needed him, in every definition of the word "need" there was.

"Help..."

"Hey.... Sshh..." He was over her, covering her, his hand cupped over the top of her head, and that gesture alone helped. It said, *I'm here, I've got you. You're under my protection.*

He banded his lean, strong arm around her waist and molded himself against her hips. He was still semi erect, and he reached back to guide himself into her again, her tight fit making it possible to hold him, even when he wasn't at full mast. "See, love? I'm right here. Calm down. Just breathe."

She breathed, pressed her head to her hands and felt his body thrumming with life against and inside her. It was okay. She was okay.

He felt the shift, murmured his approval. Then he was sliding from her, his palm stroking along her spine as he moved behind her, bent and put his mouth on her cunt, framed by her bound thighs. He plunged his tongue in deep to eat her pussy. He attended to it with the same thoroughness with which he kissed her, taking her over, taking his time, tasting her fully. Sucking on the swollen tissues, he lapped at the moist pockets of her thighs, then put his mouth over her clit to massage it with his lips while his tongue darted back into her cunt to lick and play, swirl and stab.

He had his arm banded around her thighs to hold her up, because balance disappeared as the orgasm seized her. It was on the upward rise when the intensity of it wrested the first scream from her, and that cry built into shrieks, a composition of yearning, strident notes as he kept going down on her. He relentlessly took her past sanity, the longest roller coaster she'd ever experienced. She clawed the sheets with her restricted range and sobbed over the screams. Her body shuddered, pulling so the ropes bit into her thighs with a burning ache.

As she was coming down, he slammed his cock into her again, her response obviously having accelerated his recuperation time. He was the best combination of selfishly demanding and generously giving lover she'd ever had. Her cries became animal noises, grunts and guttural whimpers as his hips pounded her ass, testicles slapping her clit. He kept her there until he'd come again, and then he flipped her over, held her knees to her chest with one capable hand on the back of her thighs. He sucked on her clit until he wrested another intense, almost painful orgasm out of her.

At the end of that one, she was a mindless mess. Even the aftershocks had the same intensity as a climax.

He was speaking to her in that calming tone again, though she heard an erratic note that told her he'd been as affected by what had just happened as she was. But he would take control, take care of her, because that was part of what drove him, as much as her surrender to him was driven by her own deepest needs.

He loosened the rope over her neck and removed the tether between her wrists and thighs. When he took off the wraps around her thighs, he soothed the abrasions he'd deliberately put upon her. After wrapping her up in a blanket, he shifted to hold her against him. Both of them reclined on the bed, his head bent over hers, arms sure and strong around her. She clung to his forearms over her chest, twitched and jerked, made little noises he answered with peaceful crooning, holding her even closer. Since her body kept convulsing, she wondered if some of her neurons had shorted out.

"It's all right," he said, many times, in different ways. He spread kisses over her jaw, her throat, her lips. He stroked her body, long, soothing passes that helped bring her back to earth. She realized he'd left her wrists bound, and her fingers were curled in the blanket.

"It helps with the aftercare, to leave at least one restraint on," he said, noticing her awareness. "For some subs in particular, like you."

It spotlighted that this was a normal thing for him, rocking some woman's universe. Stop it, she told herself fiercely. Did she think he'd done his wedding dress routine with every sub? She wasn't going to require him to reassure her over and over again about something he'd made clear. It was her problem to figure out how to trust, how to get past a bunch of baggage from past assholes. She wasn't going to make him responsible for unpacking all that debris and incinerating the suitcases.

"You remember what I told you?" he asked. "That I'm not much into the whole call me Master or Sir thing?"

Had she called him that in her passion? She wouldn't be surprised, but had it bothered him? He squeezed her, dissipating her sudden tension. He untied her wrists but kept one, putting his mouth on her pulse, then her forearm, the crook of her elbow, tickling her biceps with his morning beard, an intimate reminder that he'd spent the night with her in his bed.

When he shifted to her throat, releasing her wrist, she gripped his arm over her chest, holding on as tingles shot through her, up, down, spiraling, somersaulting in her heart, stomach, loins.

He cupped the side of her throat, holding her fast, letting her feel the pressure of his callused palm against her frantic pulse. Then his mouth was against her ear.

"Just because I don't tell you to call me that, doesn't mean that's not what I am. Right?"

"Yes." She breathed it, closed her eyes. "God, yes."

He drew back, caressing her as he did, and pressed another kiss to the top of her head. "You don't have to call me that, either."

She snuffled over a part chuckle, part sob, and hit him with a half-hearted fist. He chided her with a tsking noise, recaptured and kissed it. He sobered, though, touching her cheek and drawing her eyes to his face. "I know you've been hurt, love. I can tell you're having a hard time letting go of the shields, no matter what assurance I give you. I get it. We've known each other what, less than a month?"

She grimaced. "I really want to, but..."

He shook his head, silencing her. "It doesn't have to happen all at once. That's the journey, and what makes it so nice. We can take our time." He rubbed his thumb on her lips, seeming to enjoy their swollen fullness in the aftermath of their passionate kisses.

"This is new for me, too," he said. "I don't want to rush a fucking minute of it. I love the way I feel when I'm with you, though I'm surprised you're not running away screaming."

She tipped back her head. "Why would I?"

His brown eyes took on a leonine golden cast. "Because the more time I spend around you, the more I want. It's a good thing we both work such hellacious hours, else you would have already figured it out." He shifted her so she was on her back and he was leaning over her, his expression even more potent. "I want to devour you, love. Tie you up in a million different ways. I've seen the ways women's bodies, minds and souls respond to what I can do to them with my rope. It never occurred to me I could find a million different experiences with one woman, but when I look at you, I get so many ideas I have to write them down so I don't forget a single one of them."

He gestured to his side table, where a ratty pocket notebook and pen resided. "I carry that with me for the ideas I get. Since I met you, I've filled up twenty pages. There's this patch of woods that I like, far away from anything or anyone. I want to take you there, modify the design I did with Missive. I want to use an actual tree to do it, put you in a cocoon of rope hanging from a branch. Then

I'm going to lie beneath you on the ground and look up at the beauty of your body, stretched and shaped however I tie you, helpless so I can touch and stroke you all the ways I want. I want to do dramatic things like that, but I want to do simple things, too. Share a sandwich, sleep with you in my arms. Ah, love."

She was crying. He let her press her face into his throat and he held her, just held her, the most wonderful thing a man could ever do for a woman when her heart was melting into her tears. He said things to her, some of which she caught and some she didn't, but she absorbed the meaning through his grip.

He was right. It was too soon for her to believe it, too overwhelming, but she'd never responded to a man the way she did to him. Her soul was fighting to believe, to surrender to it, even as her cautious mind and guarded heart were scrambling away from that precipice as hard as they could go, tearing her apart inside. That was why he'd told her not to worry, to take it easy. Just let it happen as it would happen.

"Ssshh....easy, love." He rocked her, pulling the blanket around her. "Enough of that, now. You're all right. I've got you."

§

She took a shower while he made them breakfast. She'd just stepped in under the spray when he ducked into the tiny stall to press her against the wall. He was naked, not even wearing the cannula since he'd removed it when they rose, saying he'd be changing out the injection site this morning.

It meant she could slide her hands over him without any worry of snagging it, though last night when she'd shared that concern with him, he'd told her if she accidentally pulled it out, it was no big deal, that he could fix it in no time. He didn't want her to hesitate to touch him however she wanted, with whatever passion and enthusiasm she desired.

Not a problem this morning. As he fondled and stroked,

she was thinking of all the contortions they'd have to accomplish to have sex in the small space, let alone shower together, but before she could act on those ideas, he'd pulled free and stepped back out.

"Since my job is so dirty, love, I usually shower at the end of the work day. Just wanted a taste of you before I scramble eggs."

When he abandoned her in her simmering state to pull on a pair of jeans and head for the kitchen, she sent a few choice words after him. He threw a warning look over his shoulder.

"I'll remember those insults next time you're tied up."

"Asshole. I want cheese in my eggs."

"My omelets don't come without it. There might even be tomatoes and green peppers if you're good."

"Ugh, no green peppers."

He stopped and surveyed her with leisurely enjoyment. She had her head poked out around the seagull curtain, but a glance down showed a full, wet breast visible and the curve of her hip.

"This relationship is not going to work if you can't appreciate the vitamin properties of a fresh green pepper," he told her, a sparkle in his gaze.

"I appreciate vitamins. When they come in a pill form so I'm not required to eat healthy food to consume them."

"Sad. So very sad. I'm due at a job site later today, but—"

"Oh, well, don't worry about breakfast. I'll just grab something on my way to the theater."

He raised a disapproving brow. "Yeah, a biscuit or some unhealthy thing."

"You ate PB&J for lunch the first day I met you."

"With natural, no sugar added blackberry jelly. On homemade wheat bread chock full of nutrients. And this is breakfast, the most important meal of the day. If you were kind enough to have sex with me, I have time to make you breakfast."

"You're right, it was a sacrifice." She sighed. "Better make that French toast with powdered sugar."

"Just keep it up, smart mouth."

She grinned and ducked behind the shower curtain.

As she washed herself with his pleasant peppermint soap, she discovered the faint aroma in his thick hair came from an inexpensive quart-sized bottle of Suave Deep Clean for men. She took an extra deep whiff, just to revisit the olfactory memory. As she thought of what he'd told her in bed, she knew she felt the same way. She didn't want to be away from him.

Be brave, take a risk. She raised her voice, realizing the benefit of a small, one-room apartment, where everything was in hearing range.

"Um, it's probably going to be a slow day for me. Would you like me to come see you at lunch? I know you usually take your lunch, but I could bring some for both of us, and we could hang out during your break, if you have one. Or not. I mean, you don't have to—" She stopped herself. *Don't be pathetic, Julie.*

She yelped as he reappeared, pulling back the curtain and snaking his arm around her to pull her soapy wet body against his bare chest. As he kissed her deep and thoroughly, his palms molded her curves at waist and hip, sliding around to her ass to take a firm grip. "I would love that," he said against her lips. Then he was pulling her out of the shower, dripping.

"What..."

"Fuck it. I'm a selfish bastard and want this more than I want us to have breakfast first."

It took him less than a second to open his jeans and push them to his thighs. Lifting her against the wall outside the bathroom, he sheathed himself into her willing body. She gasped at the force and demand of it. His eyes were molten as he drove into her, his gaze fastened to her face all the way through to her orgasm.

"All mine," he muttered against her ear as he finished, with thrusts powerful enough to thud their bodies against the sheetrock. Never in her life had a man taken her with such savage need. *I want to devour you,* was what he'd said. Her thundering heart believed it. When he let her down, he was breathing hard and so was she. He touched her face, his eyes so close.

"Don't you fucking doubt me," he told her in a growl. "I

don't care what I said earlier. I want your trust. I need it and I demand it, no matter how unreasonable that makes me."

She managed a nod. Whether or not she had any control over her dysfunctional doubts and insecurities was irrelevant. He was trusting her enough to show her his own raw needs, the irrational level of the soul every person possessed. He had her pinned, her pulse fluttering like captured prey, and his expression required instant, total submission and acquiescence. That alone could work her up again, while leaving her heart a confused, fluttery, fabulous mess.

He broke eye contact to nuzzle her neck, closing a hand over her breast to stroke and play. "Yeah, I'm going to leave you worked up," he said. "Before you leave my place, you're going to lie on my bed, put my pillow between your legs and masturbate to climax. When I come home tonight, the scent of your pussy will be on it and on my sheets, where your sweet body was writhing and gushing. I want you thinking every minute about what I'm going to do to you next."

"Okay," she breathed. He kissed her again, another branding. His gaze swept over her, her flushed, trembling body, her parted lips and feverish eyes. He looked satisfied with his examination.

"That's it. Get back in the shower, love. Meet me in the kitchen."

"I thought you said you had to work?"

"Not until this afternoon. They have a good crew working this morning. You need a ride back to the theater anyway."

"A home cooked breakfast *and* a ride home. This is a first class date." She summoned the will to tease him, to try to act more casual than she felt. Aroused and needy, her foundation shifted.

He touched her face, his eyes softening as if he picked up on all of that, but he stuck with humor, her comfort zone. "What can I say? I spoil my woman."

§

When she emerged from the shower, she found she'd been right about last night. He'd packed her a favorite pair of jeans and her ivory and gold Guggenheim T-shirt. Though he'd never seen her wear it, it was one of her tighter T-shirts, and the bra he'd packed had almost no padding, so the light-colored shirt would give him a nice view of the shape of her nipples. Men must have some kind of radar for that kind of thing, she thought.

While in the shower, she'd resolved to transition back to more lighthearted and casual behavior, to balance the earlier unsettling intensity. However, when she came out of the bathroom and approached the kitchen counter, carrying her brush and hair bands for her unruly mane, that resolve disappeared.

He was putting the finishing touches on two plates of food. While doing that, he was listening to *All Things Considered*, the NPR news show, on a radio that looked twenty years old and was plugged into an outlet by the stove.

It should be silly, to be captivated by the sight of a man making her breakfast, but it was seeing him do it in his home environment, a different picture of who he was, wrapped up with everything that had happened over the past few hours. It took away her ability to play it cool.

She circled behind the counter, slipping her arms around him from behind, brushing her lips over the sunburst between his shoulder blades. He made a pleased noise at her spontaneous affection and dropped the spatula and skillet in the sink so he could turn and put his arms around her, return the hug.

She noticed he'd pulled up the jeans but hadn't fastened the top button. He'd set a new injection site, the pump back on his belt. Reaching down, she buttoned the button for him, her wrists brushing evidence that he was interested in her attentions, despite the two of them having pursued that...how many times in the past few hours? Hell, the past few minutes? It didn't seem to matter.

He watched her, his head tilted, uncombed hair falling over his bare shoulder. Following her desires, she picked up her brush and lifted it to his head. Agreeably, he propped his hips against the cabinets, bringing his height down a few inches. He stretched out his legs on either side of her so she could stand closer and brush his hair back from his face.

He didn't say anything, just watched her, so she indulged herself fully. She brushed through the thick locks, her fingers following her strokes, working until the strands became smooth and gleaming again. As she did it, he stroked her hips, her ass, her breasts, her abdomen. His fingers slid beneath the T-shirt along her navel, exploring and learning even more about her responses. Where she was ticklish, where he could make her tremble, what he could make coil with desire.

When she pulled a band from the several she had on her wrist, her fingers were trembling, but she gathered his hair into a tail and looped the band around it twice. She had to move closer to do it and, as she did, he wrapped both arms around her. When she finished, he was holding her in a full embrace, her head on his shoulder and her arms gripping him as much as he was holding her. He brushed his jaw over her hair.

"I'm in love with you, too, Julie."

She closed her eyes. Later today he would drop her off and go to work. She'd review Harris's stage manager report on the opening night and address a bunch of other details necessary to handle before the next showing. She'd call Madison about some of that, and maybe give herself the post-opening reward of an afternoon nap.

All normal things, and yet he'd just said something to her no man ever had. Not and meant it the way he did.

"What?" He had his strong fingers buried in her hair, stroking her scalp, the two tendons of her neck. His touch was easy, casual, yet made her feel just as he'd reinforced, a couple times now, though she couldn't see herself getting tired of the message. She was the center of his world, his anchor, his tether to what mattered. She also imagined he was even now deciding how he next wanted to tie her up, play with her, because they were still at that point where desire was a constant strong surf washing through all the other emotions. She lifted her head, trying to blink back the tears. She didn't want him to think she was a constantly weepy female.

He wouldn't let her get away with it, though. He cradled her face. "What, love?" he repeated.

She traced the dragon's body on his biceps where it transitioned into rope. "I just thought it would be more difficult. After all this time, the heartache, the waiting, the despairing and giving up, the pure pissed-offness of dealing with near misses..." She blew out a breath. "And there it is. With you, easy as breathing. 'I'm in love with you.' You said it and meant it. It changes the universe, but the way throwing a stone in a pond does. All those ripples. It's...amazing."

She frowned and cocked her head. "There should at least be dramatic music."

"I can retract it if you want. Brood for a while, play commitment paranoia games, alienate you so we break up, sort of, and then I chase you down before you make some monumental decision, like moving back to New York, or signing up for a three year stint in the merchant marines. Then we can have a big makeup scene."

She pursed her lips. "Complete with dramatic music."

"Absolutely. If I could afford it, I'd hire John Williams to come up with the score."

"You'd do all that for me?"

"Hell, no." He snorted, puffing a short, playful breath against her. "I'd tie you up and keep you in my basement until you contracted Stockholm syndrome and couldn't breathe without me."

She tipped her head back, sobering. "Sometimes, it feels like I can't. Crazy, right?"

He put his mouth on hers and took her air in the best kind of way, all while giving it back to her.

"You don't have a basement," she pointed out when he lifted his head. He smiled at her, boyishly appealing, but then sobered.

"We're normal, extraordinary people," he said. "It took us a while, but we always knew what it would look like when it happened. The simplicity of it is what makes it extraordinary. A tadpole gets legs and walks on land, and evolution begins. All in a simple blink, the whole world changes."

Maybe his intuition and articulateness was a Dom thing. Or spending so much time by himself as a boy, something about his history she'd deduced on her own. She thought of the first time she'd seen him. His dark hair fluttering over his shoulder and his loose-hipped stride like a rock star roadie. Something in her had felt and registered all he'd just said then. At an unconscious level, but that didn't make it less true.

God, he was going to destroy her. But maybe for the first time in her life, she'd found a man worth shattering for.

Chapter Eleven

Having a lover again was...well, it was a good feeling. The toe-curling, silly smiles at odd moments kind of good feeling. She told herself to settle down, slow down, but the truth was she couldn't do it. Especially when Des seemed just as eager to be around her. Hell, she'd waited decades to find someone like him. If all his wonderfulness was a precursor to a crash and burn, she had nothing to lose by getting the most out of it now. And if he ended up being the unicorn...well, life was always too short, so the same answer applied.

He'd talked her into not leaving his house at all that day. He'd put in his half day of work and, when he returned, they spent the evening together, doing dinner, surfing TV together, talking, making love. No Dom/sub stuff this time. Just playful, enjoyable sex with lots of exploration and quiet pillow talk. When they both had to go to work the next day, he'd dropped her off at the theater and kissed her like he was going off to war. She had held onto him the same way, feeling as if some magic spell was about to be broken.

Which was why work was a very good thing, a reminder that she was a mature adult. Every mature adult knew that falling-in-love feeling was an illusion. Well, illusion wasn't the right word. It was wonderfully real, but it required pacing oneself. Which kind of contradicted her unicorn versus crash-and-burn theory, but there could be moderation in overindulgence.

She could just imagine Des chuckling at the inconsistencies in that statement, but he'd totally get it. His mind worked as weirdly as hers did.

A few days later she didn't feel as fond about work's balancing properties. Tying up loose ends on the *Consent* opener, getting ready for the showings they'd scheduled the following week, staying on top of social media and other promotional outlets, and working with Harris on planning the next production, the play Madison had mentioned at the reception, took up all her time.

For Des's part, he had several jobs to juggle, and one of them took him a couple hours outside the city limits, requiring him to stay overnight to meet a developer's deadline.

So that going off to war kiss hadn't been misplaced, because after only a day she missed him intensely, though they exchanged some texts. He called her one night at bedtime and, while she loved hearing his voice, she could hear how tired he was and hadn't made him stay on the phone too long.

Her week wasn't as physically grueling, but she worked a lot of late hours. She anticipated seeing him by the weekend, but figured they'd both need a mega-nap like a couple toddlers before attempting more adult activities. Madison, however, had a different plan.

Julie was sitting in on a script review and casting discussion with Harris and Lila, their playwright, when her phone buzzed. Glancing down and seeing Madison's number, Julie excused herself from the table and stepped away.

"My God, I was wondering when I'd hear from you. We haven't talked in over an hour."

"I knew I was running late." Madison chuckled. "Hey, want to have some fun and promote our baby? We've had this fancy BDSM to-do on the calendar for a while and I wasn't sure I was going to go until Logan pointed out it's being sponsored by five of the tri-state area BDSM groups. We could drop off some of our snazzy theater brochures at their vendor table and then enjoy the party ourselves. Logan and I can do it on our own, but I happened to mention it to Des the other day and he said if you'd like to go, he'd take you."

"Oh really? Said it that way, did he?"

There was laughter in Madison's voice. "Just like that. Translation: You're not going without him. I think he's a little taken with my theater manager. Is the feeling mutual?"

"You know the answer to that, ho. Stop picking on me or I'll sabotage this freaking sound system that we just had the electrician rewire and still isn't behaving the way we need it to do. I was tempted to put it through the wall twelve times since yesterday. The only thing that saved it was I didn't pay for it."

"Good thing I wasn't there. I would have done it for you. Nothing frustrates me like technology gremlins. So will you go? It's Friday."

While a part of her longed for a hot bath and an early-to-bed scenario with Des, hearing he was interested in taking her to a party summoned energy reserves. They made her nerves tingle, and not just from excitement about going. If she and Des did this, they'd be pursuing the Dom-sub thing in a public way, even if merely as voyeurs. Those same nerves pushed her to stay in her comfort zone, but...

"Let me call Des and talk to him about it. I'll call you right back."

"Good deal."

He picked up on the third ring. From the lack of background noise, she realized he wasn't at a job site. He sounded as if he'd been asleep.

"Sorry," she said, instantly chagrined. "Didn't mean to wake you."

"No worries, love. You'd enjoy my view right now. Our hotel backs up to a couple farms. You have your choice of watching cows or the wind rippling patterns through young corn stalks. A bunch of the cows have calves, playing like they haven't a care in the world."

"I think I hate you. I've been working like a dog all day." But she brightened at her subsequent thought. "Is your job done and you're sleeping in this morning before you head back?"

"I wish. We've got some more to do, but I'm getting a late start. I'll be heading out soon."

She hesitated. Something sounded off in his voice, but before she could pursue it, he continued. "Once we hit the summer heat, I'll call you out to a job so you can see how I earn my lazy times."

Today was already hinting at those temps. They'd experienced a warm front early in the week, spring temperatures climbing into the eighties. While that didn't sound too hot for normal labor, up on a roof against asphalt shingles and black tar paper, she expected it could be more strenuous.

"All right, I retract my hatred and restore my adoration for your virile self."

"Appreciate it. What's up? Did Madison call you about the party?"

"She did. I understand I have an escort."

"You do. Would you like to go? I know you've had a hellish schedule lately."

"I have. But..."

"But you'd like to go."

"I would," she said. "With you."

Maybe she was getting better at reading his silences, but in his pause she sensed some of the sparks of excitement she herself was experiencing. Knowing he wanted to go to the party with her heated them into flame.

"You take this step forward, I'm probably not going to want to take any more steps back, Julie." His voice was low. "Fair warning. I've missed you."

It was clear what he meant. Her whole body certainly got the message, the reaction swirling in her core. "I've missed you, too. I haven't been to anything like this before. We just watch, right? We don't have to do anything?"

"Absolutely. We play only if that's what you want to do. If you don't, that's completely fine with me. I'm looking forward to getting you alone afterward."

She wasn't a public sex kind of girl, but she could get excited about watching others. And even more excited from the promise she heard in his voice. She imagined what could happen after they were both stimulated by a visual cornucopia of BDSM offerings. It made her wish he was here right now.

Restraint, girl, she admonished herself. "Hey, Marcus and Thomas will be coming into town, week after next. Marcus suggested we do dinner."

"Sounds good. Too bad they're not coming in sooner. They could go to the party with us."

"That's okay. I think I'd be a little embarrassed, you know. In front of them."

"Hmm. I bet I could get you over that hang up." His voice had that deep purr that made her toes curl.

"I bet you could. Which is why I'm hanging up before I'm tempted to have phone sex with you. I have work to do."

"I'm far more interested in keeping you on the line for phone sex."

"Not in front of the cows. That's illegal in most states."

He chuckled, his voice still throaty, sending more tingles through her. "Besides," she added. "I'll bet you already had your morning treats. Milk and cookies before you laid down on your mat for your midmorning nap."

"You can be spanked. Just saying."

"I thought that wasn't your thing."

"I'm rethinking it with you and that mouth of yours."

She grinned, happy to be teasing with him. "Go back to sleep. You're grumpy."

"Only because I've been denied phone sex. And milk and cookies." He paused. A peculiar heat filled that significant silence and surrounded her. "I'll see you in a couple days, love."

"Are you all right?" she asked softly, not sure why she was asking, but there was a great deal in that stillness she wasn't sure about.

"Better than. You've got my attention, love. In every way. Talk to you soon."

When he disconnected, she tapped the phone against her lips thoughtfully. He'd sounded tired, but very pleased to talk to her. He wanted the same thing she did, to be together right now. Maybe it was best she had a million things to do. Otherwise she'd drive two hours to watch cows and corn with him. But anticipation could be a wonderful thing.

She had a meet in a few moments with the volunteer who'd served as their house manager, to go over some front-of-house improvements for the next show. Time enough to text Madison, since Harris and Lila were well on top of the cast and script discussion.

We're going. Any dress code?

Madison's cheerleading emoticons were infectious. Her enthusiasm only stoked those sparks that were still warming Julie's insides. *Inside the party, naked, fetish wear, or club wear is all fine. No T-shirts and jeans. If you wear street clothes, host wants people to dress up. Sets a party mood and reinforces standards of good behavior.*

Julie honestly couldn't picture Des in slacks or a suit, and wondered if she'd be intrigued by the results. She had a sexy little black dress she could wear. Nothing out of the ordinary, but she could razzle-dazzle it up with some accessories.

Touch base with me tomorrow on the marketing end. Look forward to seeing you.

You too. Madison's response was accompanied by a few more cheerleading emojis. Julie pocketed the phone and went back to work. However, a part of her mind remained two hours away, thinking about a lean man stretched out on a bed in a hotel room, dozing and watching calves cavort in the sunshine.

§

The day before the event, she was surprised to get a call directly from Logan.

"Des called and asked if I'd escort you to the party with Madison. He says the job is running behind and isn't going to finish up until early afternoon tomorrow. He doesn't plan to be late, but he said it makes more sense for us to meet him there, since he's going to have to go by his place first to get changed."

"No problem." But she was curious. There was an interesting formality to the call, Logan calling her personally, rather than Des texting her. "I know this sounds strange, but is this an etiquette thing? A Dom calling another Dom to escort...his sub?" She tried to act as if she was talking generally, not specifically about her and Des.

Logan's pause suggested she wasn't altogether successful, but at least he didn't call her on it. "There's no official etiquette written in stone. But a Master or Mistress picks up cues from their sub and responds to them. Or intentionally sends the sub a message to add to what they're building between each other."

She was standing in the middle of the spacious audience area, normally quite cool when not filled with people, but that wasn't the way it felt right now. Message received loud and clear.

"It's so weird. I look at him sometimes and still don't expect him to be like that. But he *so* is."

"We all go through our learning stages before we gain confidence in power exchange and taking the reins," Logan said. "But Des is far past that. I've never seen him handle a sub where I didn't feel he was completely in control of the situation and solidly in tune with her needs. He's a through and through Dom."

"But no one's Master."

"I don't think that's true anymore." Logan's voice held amusement. Julie changed the subject fast.

"Hey, do you know what Madison will be wearing?"

"Whatever I tell her to wear," Logan said pleasantly.

Logan's simple statement, spoken so matter-of-factly, spiked anxiety and thrills through Julie. The reaction was so strong it was a startling reveal of what her subconscious was feeling about this party.

When Logan chuckled at her speechless pause, she narrowed her eyes.

"Okay, it's just mean to tease the newbie sub," she accused. "You're as bad as Marcus."

"But getting a sub worked up is way too tempting to a Dom. You're an easy and very pleasurable target. Are you blushing?"

"Shut up."

He laughed outright, which stroked the nerves up and down her spine. The man was like crack. No wonder

Madison was gone over him. "Seriously, I'm sorry to tease you," he said. "But sometimes a Dom can't help himself. We're sadists, after all."

She thought of the day in the orchid garden, when Des had held her wrist in that peculiar grip. The light in his eyes, the energy gathering around them both as she found the edge of pleasure and pain.

"You are evil and will be destroyed. I'll see you soon."

She heard more chuckling as she cut the line. But it made her think. She guessed she was a newbie sub. She'd been doing a lot of follow-the-leader—or follow-the-Dom—on this. While that was instinctive to both sides of the relationship, she hadn't, until now, had her feet under her enough to start exploring the boundaries of that world as it meshed with her own way of doing things.

Uncoding her phone once more, she decided not to think too much about what she was about to do. She didn't want to worry that he might misinterpret it, or worse, consider it a foolish lead in. Des had said he didn't really care about the more formal Dom/sub rituals, while at the same time proving he could answer those desires for her in a different, entirely satisfying way. Was that because they were so unexpectedly compatible as Dom and sub, or had he recognized that a sub's fantasies could look different in reality?

She typed her text quickly. *Thanks for arranging for Logan to escort me. Second best Master I know to take a girl to a party. Hope the first best won't be too late. What would you like me to wear?* She almost typed "No wrong answer", but that was a way to protect herself, something he'd warned her about. Pocketing the phone, she went back to what she was doing. If he was on a job, it might be an hour before he saw it.

Sure enough, forty-five minutes later, when her meet with the house manager was over and the woman was on her way back to her secretarial day job, the phone chirped.

Something that makes you as hot and bothered when you're wearing it as when I have my mouth between your legs. Something that tells me you want me to do whatever I want to do to you that night.

And people thought *driving* while texting was dangerous. Hell, she shouldn't be standing when reading his. She refused to be worried by his meaning. He wouldn't do anything with her in front of a bunch of people that she wouldn't feel comfortable doing. Of course, if he did certain things to her, she'd forget they were even there. She wasn't sure if that was a bad thing.

She punched in the autodial for Naughty Bits. Could she afford to end her work day a couple hours earlier tomorrow? Yes, she could. She worked 24/7. She'd attend one of her internal workaholic support meetings and make it happen without too much guilt.

Madison was ringing up a customer. She bid them good-bye and "have a wonderful day" before she greeted Julie. They'd talked so much these past few weeks, Julie anticipated it, waiting with a lightly tapping foot. As she looked up, she noted one of the lights on stage appeared to be sagging and made a note to bring it to Harris's attention for the techs.

"Hey, girlfriend." Madison came on the line. "Excited about tomorrow?"

"Your husband was picking on me. You need to keep that man's pheromones in check. Or bottle them to make yourself a millionaire."

"Believe me, I know. But he's been invaluable at increasing our ticket sales. I think he's persuaded every female patron in his hardware store to invite their garden clubs to *Consent*."

"He told them Troy would be out front, handing out programs in a really tiny Speedo, didn't he?"

"No, he didn't. But maybe we should talk to Shale about that." Madison snickered. "Okay, I have a couple more customers coming in. Tell me what you need."

"I need a personal shopper. I'm going to be like Cinderella today and tomorrow, running up to the wire, but here's what I'm looking for. I'm hoping you might have it." She rattled off the specs and grinned at Madison's squeal.

"I have *just* the thing. You are going to look so fabulous. Oh my God, I'll give you the best customer discount. Or you could wear it for free and return it next day." She paused.

"No, nix that. We'll call it a bonus to your already exorbitant salary."

"I can give it back to you. That's not a problem."

"Nope. If he reacts to it the way I bet he will, it will be in tatters. I promise."

The image expanded the ball of lust in her stomach. "You're so demented."

"Which is why you love me. Come over as early as you can manage tomorrow and we'll get you gorgeous. I haven't played dress up with another girl since Alice died." Madison's voice softened as she recalled her sister, the former proprietress of Naughty Bits.

"I'll probably look like Cinderella coming straight from the ashbin, since I'm going to clean out that last classroom so we can start storing things there for Lila's show. You'll have your work cut out for you."

"Isn't a managing director supposed to delegate, direct, represent and stay pristine and professional?"

"Yes, that's what a Broadway theater manager does. The manager of a community theater being built from scratch with a volunteer staff is a whole different ball of wax. I seem to recall the owner down here more than once these past few weeks getting herself covered in paint and sawdust."

"It's more fun that way, isn't it? When it succeeds, it will mean all the more."

"From your mouth to God's ear." And Julie meant it. Succeeding was a matter of professional pride, but with a good friend involved, she wanted to see this theater thrive as much for Madison as for her own sense of satisfaction. "See you soon."

§

She'd escaped the theater and arrived at Madison's all of ninety minutes before they had to leave for the party, but Madison was a miracle worker. She put Julie into a hot, soaking shower, to relax her muscles and do a "paradigm shift", as Madison called it. Sitting her down at the vanity afterward, Madison dried her long hair with a soft towel and did her makeup, chatting with her as if they had all the time in the world. Madison wore a thin robe and had already done her hair and makeup, assuring Julie that all she had left to do was slip on her dress and shoes.

After she did a light blow-dry of Julie's hair and had the curling iron plugged in, Madison showed Julie the outfit and accessories she'd found for her.

"You are the best of personal shoppers," Julie said fervently.

"You made it easy. You chose perfectly for your body type. I can't wait for Des to see you." Madison winked. "It's fun to knock them off balance."

Ninety-two minutes later, they were ready to go. At the sight of both women, Logan put a hand over his heart and staggered, a gratifying response, and then he whisked them into the car and they were on their way.

The dance hall rented for the party had been an old 1920s theater, restored to keep that look for event bookings. Whoever tonight's host was in the BDSM community had deep pockets. Though the party was invitation-only, a nominal cover charge was all that was required from each participant.

Madison had loaned Julie a pair of teetering heels with provocative ankle straps studded with silver eyelets. Fortunately, she knew how to walk in them. The skill had come from her short stint on stage and teaching plenty of other actresses to do it, plus one actor who had to do a transvestite hooker scene.

As they crossed the parking lot and ascended the short set of steps to the entrance, Logan was drawing a lot of attention, and not merely because the man looked devastating.

With her and Madison displayed on his arms, Julie thought the three of them looked like a Bond film. Madison's short red satin dress clung to her slim frame. She wore a black pearl choker and a pair of matching wrap bracelets. Julie had noticed they had a discreet pair of hooks she suspected could be latched to one another if her Master wanted her hands bound behind her back, or at her nape, since the same hook was at the back latch of the choker. Her red high heels had ribbon ties that went up her long legs to just below the knee.

"You look stunning," Julie told her. "You both do."

Logan wore a black suit with a crisp white shirt that made the most of his powerful upper body. A red silk tie coordinated him with his wife's outfit. Julie could imagine Madison untying it at his command before her Master took it from her and used it to blindfold her.

Logan was taking them to the door, but Julie put a hand on his arm and drew the couple's attention to her.

"If you two don't mind, I'd like to wait for Des out here," she said, pointing to a column that flanked the entrance. "By myself."

Logan glanced toward the door. It was monitored by two classy-looking, Secret Service style bouncers, definitely security muscle.

"I'll be fine," Julie further assured him. "You said the party was by invitation, so everyone's been vetted. I won't be getting any rude overtures. And I live in New York, remember? I ride the subway and deal with cabbies." She shot him an impish look. "I want my first impression of this shindig to be with him."

She also wanted him to see she'd waited for him, another of those subtle cues, right?

Logan pulled out his phone and looked at the screen. "He'll be here in about ten minutes."

"So good. See? It all works out." Julie kept her tone casual, though the news sent a little frisson of nerves through her. Both in anticipation of his arrival and from the psychological impact of his continuing direct communication with Logan. Dom to Dom, man to man, watching over the women. Terribly sexist, yes, but she didn't deny in the current circumstances it had a not-unpleasant effect.

Logan pursed his lips and slid his arm around Madison, hand intimately molded over her hip. "We don't mind staying with you until he gets here."

"I know you don't. I just...I'd really like him to see me, and me to see him, on my own. If that's okay."

She hoped they'd understand without her having to

embarrass herself with more explanation. She liked dramatic entrances and exits, portentous meetings with the setting framed the right way. For this, she wanted only two people on the stage, so she could drink in everything about him without embarrassment. All this prep made her feel like Cinderella at the ball in truth.

At Madison's weighted look, Logan relented. "All right. Just promise you'll stay here, where the guys at the door can see you. It's a nice place, but not the nicest area. Sometimes you New York types think you're the only one with violent crime."

"Hey, our muggers can kick your muggers' asses. But since either one could kick my ass, this is where my ass will be staying." She scooched up to the pillar and gave said booty a little shake, eliciting a chuckle from her companions.

"Do that little move when Des first sees you and we won't see you again tonight." Madison winked at Logan. "Don't pretend you didn't notice."

"On the contrary. I'm going to take you inside and see if you'll do the same move for me. Only I'm going to be that lucky column. Double entendre fully intended."

Madison laughed and the two of them went inside, though Julie was amused to notice Logan stop by one of the doormen and point her out. Protective men could be so offensive and sexy at the same time.

Now that her escorts had gone inside, she could put her hand on her stomach and try to hold in the swirl of nerves happening in every area of her body. She was no stranger to embracing drama, but putting on this outfit wasn't about her asserting her flamboyant personality. As such, when she'd looked at herself in the mirror, she'd almost retreated to her little black dress. Then she'd looked at his text again about what she should wear. She thought about it now, and what might happen when he arrived. Would he like what she'd chosen?

Adrenaline was keeping her toasty. She sent one of the bouncers a little wave as he looked in her direction and made eye contact. Madison had said everyone involved in events like this was usually part of the lifestyle, so Julie wondered if he was Dom, sub or switch. His formidable appearance made no difference; she'd learned that much.

The other couples, singles and groups she saw going into the building supported that. Bless a world where racy, barely disguised fetish fashion could pass as club wear. She kept herself occupied by guessing the Dom or sub orientation of the people approaching the door with their invitations. When she went inside, she'd find out if she was wrong or right.

Would the large male with a woman half his size be a sub who liked to kneel and kiss her stiletto clad feet? Would the threesome of two men and one woman tie her up in so many ways she'd be unable to move as they feasted on every part of her body? Protected sex was allowed at this party. Everyone would be what they most desired to be with one another. At least that was how she was picturing it. Maybe the reality would be even more fantastic than that.

She'd chosen her own part for tonight, embraced it for her own pleasure as much as the pleasure of her Dom. Remembering their first meet and the temporary tattoos on Des's arms, as well as his fascination with her curves, she'd catered to those tastes and dressed accordingly.

She was a starlet. A lush, Hollywood starlet, unattainable except by one man. The man who made her knees weak. The one coming across the parking lot toward her.

While he was wearing an outfit far different from anything she'd previously seen him wear, she'd know the way he moved anywhere. Her gaze tracked and lighted on him when he was ten paces away from his parking space.

She'd wondered if he'd look as good in slacks as he did his customary jeans. She'd have to find out another time, because he wasn't wearing slacks. What he had chosen gave her heartrate another nice bump.

He was wearing a black utility kilt, the sporran held in place with a combination of silver chain and sleek black rope that passed over his hip bones. He'd left the ties loose enough at the neckline of his black laced shirt to show a triangle of his chest and the light layer of gleaming dark hair over it. The sleeves were fitted to his taut biceps and rolled up to reveal his forearms, which bore laced black gauntlets. The folds of his sleeves were secured with another short fall of silver chain and held there with silver Celtic knot studs.

He'd donned a black felt fedora with a black braided rope band, his hair sleekly queued back beneath it. His black combat boots had silver buckles with skull heads.

It was Goth meets Scot meets 1950s style meets... Hell, it defied description. It was Des, and it worked on him, from head to toe. She'd take his idea of formal wear over a tux any day.

Then she lost her train of thought, because he saw her. His shift in expression pulled her into a world populated only by the two of them and a lot of passionate, dirty, sacred, sweaty, breathless scenarios of sex, taking, and pure need.

He came to a stop, twenty feet of parking lot between them. Hooking a thumb into his waistband, he cocked a hip to settle in and do an in-depth inventory of her, starting with the four inch heels she wore. The strappy shoes buckled over shimmering stockings that were attached to slim garters. He could tell she was wearing garters, because in her position, leaned against the pillar, the skirt had inched up on the right side enough to show a peek of the ribbon attachment to the stocking.

The dress was ruched sunset-colored gold lace over lighter gold satin that hugged every curve to the mid-thigh hemline. On the sides, from hip to thigh, the satin under layer was absent, so lace covered only skin. The bodice of the dress displayed her breasts like unfrosted cake, the satin straps snug over her shoulders adding to the high, firm, pushed-together and quivering display. While he couldn't see it yet, the straps connected at her nape and one narrow line of satin followed her spine to the back of the dress, scooped well below her shoulder blades. It gave a man's hand plenty of area to caress before he decided to explore how the fabric clung to her round ass.

It was a dress a woman from the age of silver screens would have worn, and in which she would have been immortalized. She felt exactly that way as Des consumed her with his dark eyes.

Shifting away from the pillar, she stepped off the curb. She'd practiced a sultry, hip-swinging walk, intending to add it to the fantasy, but there was no need for calculation. Her body moved the way she felt and how he'd demanded—as the most desirable thing he could ever want.

His attention followed the movement of her body, the quiver of her breasts, and lingered over the fullness of her hips. When he reached her face, she knew the makeup Madison had expertly applied had turned her striking brown eyes into pools in which a man could be lost. She wanted him to dive into her very soul and stay there. She'd take care of his every need, because he would do the same for her.

When she reached him, she didn't say anything. Normally, a hundred things would have come to mind. Sassy, snarky or smartass, words tumbling out from her moist lips to protect herself from being perceived as too over the top, to mitigate self-consciousness, or to let him off the hook before he could say or do something that might disappoint the fantasy. But she chose trust, and stayed quiet, drinking him in with her eyes the way he was doing to her.

His hair was burnished like a bird wing, his eyes as penetrating as she'd ever seen, his lips inviting. *You're beautiful*, she thought, and her hands curled at her hips, wanting to touch. Touch him for her own pleasure, or touch herself for his, and to see if she could feel all the energy his admiration had fueled beneath her skin.

Keeping his eyes on her, he opened the sporran. "Turn around," he said in his compelling voice. With the things moving between them, it was an unmistakable order, sending a quiver through her. She obeyed, cocking her hip to emphasize her ass, and was thrilled at his muttered expletive, a reverence. He stepped close enough his body brushed hers and his arms came around her.

Her heart thudded hard in her chest. He held a strap of thin woven cord, intricately worked with knots and delicate silver links. Tiny charms which had the Celtic design of the studs holding his sleeves sparkled from it. When he fitted the strap around her throat and buckled it, she thought of the times he'd put both hands around her neck. He'd made this for her himself, she was sure of it. The knots pressed into her throat, a mild but stimulating pressure.

"I thought you said collars weren't your thing."

His grip settled on her hips, and he pulled her closer to him in one smooth move, a decisive impact that took her breath and pressed the sporran against her buttocks. "I've never had the urge to make sure other men know the woman I'm with is taken. Often, thoroughly and with extreme prejudice."

The surge of response heated her from head to toe. "Oh...well. Okay." She closed her eyes as he nuzzled her throat, biting it below the hold of his gift. Then he had his fingers in it and twisted, restricting her air so her head tipped back, her fingers lifting to curl around his wrist.

"Feel that?" he whispered, a dangerous rumble. "Your life in my hands, love. Yet you stay so still and trembling, not fighting it, like a wild creature that's given me her trust. Tell me to stop."

She shook her head, fingers tightening on him. He let out another curse beneath his breath, and slowly eased the hold, massaging the constricted area. She kept her eyes closed, absorbing his touch. God, she really had missed him.

"I'd rather just have you to myself right here, right now," he said, echoing her own thoughts. "But we can create a world just for the two of us, no matter how big the crowd. As much as I want to have you alone, I want to watch you react to what you'll see in there."

Stepping to her side, he tucked her hand into the crook of his elbow and touched her chin when she opened her eyes and looked at him. "Want to go watch things far less amazing than you, but still well worth seeing?"

"Smooth talker." Her smile died, because his eyes were too hot, mouth too firm. There was a whole conversation going on beneath the surface, for both of them. A storm of epic proportions. His attention was like a full body wrap around her senses. She wanted him so badly her body felt weighted by it, and she put that need in the clutch of her fingers on him. His answer came through the stroke of his hand on her hip.

"Come on," he said, and led her across the parking lot to the door.

Chapter Twelve

The guys at the door opened it for them, so Des didn't have to let her go. They went through the foyer checkpoint, clustered with people and rich scents of perfumes and colognes. Everyone was dressed for pleasure. Leather, lace, silks, satins and sparkles. She loved noticing the details and maybe she would later, but right now she only had one focus. As Des offered his invitation, she lingered on the way the laced gauntlet defined his arm. He wore no rings on his fingers, no jewelry, but that would make sense, wouldn't it? He wouldn't wear anything that could foul a rope. She was already close to him, but she shifted even closer, inhaling his scent.

Tonight there was something different. Like an exotic blend of masculine spice, possibly the type of aftershave he'd used.

He noted her proximity, his hand curving around her waist, palm resting on her buttock, fingers curved over her hip bone. His gaze slid over her parted lips, down to her throat. While he waited for his hand to be stamped, he bent and kissed the top of her breast, making her drop her head back and shiver at the brush of his jaw on her tender flesh.

Then her hand was stamped and he was escorting her forward to a set of double doors that opened to release the energy and noise of what lay beyond.

In some ways, it was no different from any nightclub she'd ever visited, crowded with people, inundated with music and visual stimuli, though she heartily approved of the current song choice of Bruno Mars' "Moonshine." There was a flashing disco ball, which delighted her, casting a snowstorm of light on the crowded dance floor. Solid spotlights divided the main room into gold, green, blue and red sections and imprinted the party goers with that color, depending on where they wandered.

"A dungeon is usually quiet, focused on building the intensity between Dom and sub," Des said in her ear. "While I prefer that, this will be a fun change. A party can give you a different kind of privacy, thanks to the festive chaos."

She was going to ask him what he meant, but he directed her attention to everything happening around them. And there was plenty to see.

The gold lit section had the disco ball and dance floor. As they moved past that area, she saw suitably sensuous movements that matched the music. Depending on what the participants were or were not wearing, some weren't far off from outright copulation. Correct that. One couple who completed their turn against a wall stopped there, using it as a brace and confirming the undulating hip movements were actual thrusting. During the turn, the woman had had one leg high on her partner's hip, but now, he lifted both legs around him to achieve deeper penetration as she clung to him, fingers digging into his shoulders.

Des let her linger there, watching the many different forms of foreplay and fucking done to a primal under beat, mixed with actual dancing. Couples became trios or more, all sorts of cross touching and stroking going on, one dance rippling together. Her own body rocked with the rhythm of the song, rubbing her against Des's body behind her. When he cupped her breasts, a gentle, foreplay, she had no embarrassment or self-consciousness, sighing with need when he put his mouth to her throat and suckled the pounding artery.

He'd lowered his hands to her waist and she had her fingers wrapped in them when he lifted his head and moved them onward to complete their brief tour of each section.

Fire and electric play happened in the red lit area. Flogging and impact play in the blue, rope work in the green. Except for the fire play, there was overlap in all, restraints with rope combined with paddling or wand play, wax play mixed in with fire. It was an erotic circus, and the flashing light and shadows made all the players look surreal and breathtaking, caught up in a dimension where the world outside of work and worries didn't exist.

She was sure that was a tired description for the marvelousness of it, but circus was what came to mind. Especially when they passed a gold painted woman moving through the crowd, her Mistress guiding her on a leash. The submissive wore an elaborate headdress that gave her a mane like a male lion. She wore an impressive strap-on, the harness of which seemed to be holding her long tail in place over her backside. Julie noticed the "lion's" Mistress had a hand on the base of the tail and was playing with it. The tail was anchored to her body via a dildo sunk deep into her backside.

At Julie's fascinated regard, the Mistress slowed. "My exotic pet wants to play with others tonight, Spiderman. Would you like your sub to be fucked by her? Or feel my pet's claws?"

Before Julie could react to the Mistress's remarkable request, Des slipped his hand around her throat, just under her jaw, fingers hooking the rope and chain collar. A reminder that the question had been directed to him, not her. "Fucking her is my pleasure alone, Mistress, but yes to the claws."

He tipped up Julie's face, an unspoken but clear command to keep her gaze on his. They hadn't discussed what Julie might or might not like, but she trusted Des to suggest things she might like. She also trusted him to honor her and not get out of sorts if she backed away from something he wanted her to do. Frankly, she was less worried about their lack of formal communication than her certainty she might not refuse anything he demanded, not when he was in his full Dom-wizard mode.

The lion sub had glittering metal tips on her fingers she feathered artistically high in the air where Julie could see them before she dragged them down Julie's front. Over the exposed curves of her breasts, to the edge of lace that barely covered her nipples. Before she could worry she'd scrape those, the sub had dropped to her knees and reversed course, talons digging in and scraping up her inner thighs. Des shifted to grip her around the waist, so when Julie instinctively leaned back, her knees loosening to give those talons more access, he held her up. She made a noise of confused arousal and, as he turned her to face him, he adjusted his hand so it was still on her throat, keeping her head tilted up to meet his eyes. His grip was firm, intended to put strain on her neck, to make her feel the pressure of the knots in the collar he'd put upon her, as the Mistress asked a follow up question.

"What a lovely open back this dress has. Would you like my kitten to mark her there?"

Des caressed Julie's throat. "How painful do you want it to be, love?"

"As painful as you want me to feel it."

In a rational moment, could she explain how the flash of approval in his gaze, how pleasing him, made her feel? And how that connected to anything he did to her. It made pain something different, though she was no pain junkie.

"Make it hurt, Mistress Pride," Des said, keeping his attention wholly on his sub. "But don't break her lovely skin."

Julie sucked in a breath when the talons raked her back. They didn't draw blood, but they left stinging scrapes. Whereas the "lion" had been slow and deliberate when marking Julie's front and legs, now her movements were quick slashes, like a whip strike, making Julie bite back a startled cry. Then Des's palm was over the crisscrossing marks, stroking the abrasions. Julie was pressed full against him, straining, needing.

"Thank you, Mistress." He held Julie fast as the woman and her pet moved onward, and Julie dipped her head to his throat, her lips almost touching his collar bone, shallow breaths bathing it.

"Let's go watch some rope work," Des said. He shaped her body against his side, moving her through the ocean of people. Maybe because of where her head was, the noise had become a dull roar, her nerves tingling at the stimulation of nothing more than air movement, the barest brush of bodies against her, the full press of Des's.

She would have felt overwhelmed except he was her boat on these waves. What if he'd told the Mistress he wanted her lion to fuck Julie from behind? What would his expression have said to her, while he kept her chin tipped up to stare at him and that feminine body and thick rubber cock took her over the edge?

Two days ago she'd believed she was a voyeur only. That she had no interest in public sex. They'd been in this room less than twenty minutes and her previous boundaries meant nothing. Only what he wanted.

No. It was because everything he wanted was something she wanted. He was reading her cues and responding to them, just as Logan had said. But knowing it was her response as much as his commands directing her only made it more unsettling.

As they moved forward, other things added to that shaky feeling. At the impact and flogging area, Julie saw Logan and Madison. He'd bound her to a cross and was showing several groups his single tail techniques. He'd shed the coat and had the sleeves of his white dress shirt rolled up.

"Logan's always in demand to teach at these things," Des said in her ear. "He's patient about it, though I expect that's why he likes playing at home alone with Madison the best."

Though Julie was sure Madison agreed with that, her friend didn't look like this spicy public twist on their relationship was bothering her, probably because she still had Logan's full attention. Even as he was teaching, he kept returning to Madison, stroking her, reassuring her, commanding her focus with sudden little flicks from the whip, a sexy, masterful gesture that made Julie's stomach flip flop too.

Madison's glazed expression and the marks already on her said he'd started this some minutes before. He'd removed Madison's dress, leaving her in crimson bra and thong only. When Logan started throwing the whip again, there was a swift continuous fluidity to it. As he struck her buttocks, between the shoulder blades, along the back, the upper thighs, she was jerking in her bonds and making cries that Julie couldn't hear over the music and crowd noise, but could see from the working of her throat and parted lips.

Logan caught the fall of the whip and strode back to her, dropping his head to kiss the red netting of marks between her shoulder blades. His hand slipped between her body and the cross. His own body moved in rhythm with hers, rubbing himself against her backside as he worked his fingers inside her panties. His lips were against her ear.

As her view changed, Julie realized Des had maneuvered her to where she could see Madison's feverish eyes and Logan's concentrated expression, the movement of his lips. She couldn't hear the words, but she didn't need to do so. Everything he was doing showed he was in control, and he was reinforcing that, stimulating her with words to that effect. Julie imagined what those words might be.

"I'm doing what I want to you because I'm your Master. You're hot and wet, because that's the way I want you. You'll let me fuck you, whip you, restrain you, and you'll come for me with the same obedience and desire, because you get lost in this, in serving your Master..."

Whatever he actually said had Madison nodding, her lips stretching back in a plea. Julie remembered her first experience with Des, when it was just them on the stage. He'd painted her such a vision of a full audience she'd almost felt stage fright. Until he'd murmured *it's just us.*

She understood now what Des meant about the anonymity of chaos. Logan might be aware of his audience, those he was teaching, but a very important part of him was in an isolation chamber built through the strokes of a whip, the give and take of power, the love between him and his wife.

Madison came as Des's grip on Julie's hips became bruising. Julie leaned into him, breath shallow and every muscle taut, nerves thrumming as Madison's body bucked between the cross and Logan's protective larger frame. As she came down, he was kissing her shoulder, her throat, and she pressed her face into his palm.

Des moved them forward again. In the fire play area, a

dramatic flogging with a cat o' nine caught her attention. The tips of the flogger had streaks of blue and gold flame as a Mistress wielded it on the back of her female sub. Lit wands were being rolled over naked supplicants stretched out on padded tables. The fire masters followed the wands with quick, intimate strokes of the male and female bodies they were using, reminding her of Tony and Charlotte.

The scent of candle wax touched her nose as she saw two men working on another man, creating a random design on his back, buttocks and legs with shades of purple and green candle drippings.

As she'd seen *Consent* coming together, she'd had a taste of this, how every expression of BDSM could be magnified with color, sound, taste, texture. Here she didn't have to detach and see it through the eyes of a managing director. However, since that was so much a part of her, she couldn't help making a few mental tweaks on the blocking of the *Consent* showings next week, and on Lila's upcoming production. She told Des some of those suggestions as his head bent attentively to her, his lips curving with amusement, probably at her multi-tasking.

When they were back at the dance floor, her Master decided to pull her away from practical thoughts. Des guided her into an impromptu waltz, palm at her waist, other hand firmly clasping hers. She followed his steps, the turns, and he found a path through the dancers that made her feel as if she were gliding. On the far side, he turned her, bringing her back against his body so she could rub against him, making sure she concentrated on his groin area. Though the sporran was in a frustratingly inconvenient spot, she made sure he felt the urgent press of her own body.

"Tease," he muttered.

She was and wasn't. Teasing implied playfulness, some type of planned, intended provocation. She was too mindless for any of that. She wanted him to know how all this was making her feel. Being dressed like this, out with him, as his.

His eyes burned into hers as she faced him. They were still, the music winding around them, the whole world moving. He lifted her hand to his mouth and kissed her palm, working his way to her wrist, around the outside of her hand, over each finger, playing with them with tongue, lips and teeth. Just his attention on that one part of her body, his grip hard on her wrist, made her sway, her other hand clutching his waist.

"Desmond." She breathed his name. She didn't say his full name often, but she wanted to say it now. She wondered if he had a middle name, and she asked him, in that same whisper. It was too loud, so she thought he wouldn't hear her, but somehow he did.

He held her close to answer. "Desmond Arthurius Hayes."

Humor penetrated her haze of lust, reflected in the twinkle of his brown eyes. In the mix of shadows and light, the irises were molasses-colored with flecks of gold. "Betty named me after her uncle. He died a month before I arrived. She said I had his smile."

So his mother had refused to even give him a name. The thought gripped Julie with a fierce anger and protectiveness that, combined with her arousal, almost made her dizzy. Curving her fingers over his hold on her, she lifted onto her toes to press a kiss, soft and urgent at once, against his lips. *She may not have wanted you, but I do. I want you more than I've ever wanted anything.*

The kiss said all that and more. His expression flickered as if he heard the message, his jaw flexing and eyes briefly flashing with emotions just as strong.

Taking her elbow, he drew them to a section of wall flanking the rigging area. The green light spotlighted the different forms being tied on naked flesh, the intense concentration of the riggers. There were different colored ropes and clips. Some of the Doms used frames to suspend their subjects. Others used hooks dropped from the ceiling beams. Others worked entirely on mats on the floor or on chairs or against poles.

The lighting allowed a lot of shadows in the corners. Des maneuvered her into one, so the only thing in her vision was him, with some ambient glimpses of bound and suspended subs twisting in the background. He slid his fingers under her skirt and she grabbed his shoulders as he pushed past her barely-there thong and thrust two fingers into her soaked cunt.

"Just what I thought," he said softly. "Wet enough to satisfy a parched throat. You want to come, love."

She nodded and he thrust a little deeper. "Wasn't a question. Beg for it, in that sexy, pleading voice you have when you're hot and wet."

"Yes...please."

His eyes glittered with pleasure as she sounded as he'd predicted, a shiver of longing through her words.

"Hmm. We'll see." He idly rubbed his thumb over her clit and she jerked up off the wall like he'd touched her with electrical current. "I like to see you suffer like this," he said ruthlessly. "I bet you'd give me one hell of a blowjob right now. Enough to convince me you deserve to come."

She remembered he liked her to use her words. "Yes, please. Let me do that."

His brown eyes were firelight. "No. It's enough to know that you would drop to your knees and suck me off without question if I told you to do it. I want to see you come. Now."

He was rubbing her again, and the climax came at his command, her hips working against his touch. He caught her nape and jerked her to him to kiss her hard and deep as she cried out her release in his mouth. Tears spilled out, that surfeit of emotion that always surged from her subconscious when he commanded her body in new and unexpected ways. It was a painful, perfect edge between ecstasy and heartbreak, between getting everything she'd ever wanted and knowing she was giving him the power to take it all away.

He worked her through the full range of sensation, until she was sensitive and his fingertips were barely brushing her, yet still she convulsed against him, her weak fingers over his wrist. She didn't pull him away, but pressed closer, and he understood, adjusting so his palm cupped her cunt, sealing in aftershocks that coursed through her like rippling water.

He massaged her, taking her down easy. He didn't

neglect aftercare, wrapping his arms around her shoulders and back, letting her burrow against him. He kissed her hair, her ears, soothing her as she shook in his arms. She imagined how it must look, his body sheltering hers in the corner. Surrounded by the whole world but alone together. In what real-world place could they have done what they'd just done without interruption, without censure or judgment? Those around them wouldn't cross into their personal space until they were ready to rejoin the world again.

"Know where I'm going to take you when we leave tonight?" His voice was a vibrating bass through her ear, where she rested her face against his chest and shoulder.

"Anywhere you want. Frequently."

He paused. "I'll remind you of that when we're on the I-85 overpass. I'm going to take you to Steak 'n Shake for a milkshake. They have great ones."

"Okay," she said, smiling into his shirt front even as she blotted her tears there. "But, um, can I do something for you first?"

"You'll take care of that later." He tipped her chin up to meet his gaze. "When we're alone."

"But it was okay to do this to me in front of the masses? A dominance, 'this bitch is mine' kind of thing?"

His teeth flashed. "If you like, love." He kissed her, cradling her face, devastatingly tender where he'd been demanding a heartbeat earlier.

"I would have done what you were just implying here and now," she said, "but I kind of knew you'd want to wait. So I was asking for something else."

"Oh. Typical thickheaded Dom, assuming I know every damn thing." He gave her a lopsided smile. "What is it you want, Julie? Ask me."

He could chastise himself as he'd just done, be self-deprecating, and in the same breath hold onto the reins. He meant it; he wanted her to request permission to do whatever it was she wanted to do for him. It sent another hot little thrill through her. Despite his claim that he preferred private one-on-one time with subs, a public venue brought out a side to him she liked.

"May I touch you? Just touch you."

In answer, he gripped her hand and guided it under the kilt. It was only him beneath. She closed her fingers over a cock that was thick and impressively hard. She stroked him lightly, running her thumb over the slit to gather the pre-come on the pad. "Are you sure about waiting?"

She wanted to take him in her mouth. She didn't care who saw, even though she still wasn't into public sex. This didn't feel like that to her.

"Yes. And no." He gave her a wry look as he removed her hand from around his cock and beneath the kilt, giving her a reproving squeeze. "The way you just licked your pretty lips tempts me beyond description. But I want to watch you get all spun up again. Then I'm going to take you to Steak 'n Shake and home. Once it's just the two of us, I'll use you so hard you'll need a walker tomorrow. Fair enough?"

"Fair enough." She needed the teasing, because things were pulsing between her legs, telling her that her normal recovery time was going to get a serious upgrade tonight, thanks to Des's skills.

As they turned their focus back to the rope area, she found Logan wasn't the only one whose skills were in demand. Once some of the riggers realized he was watching, they called out to Des to come out on the floor and give them a demonstration of his skills. She was moved when he declined politely with the simple explanation, "I'm here for Julie tonight."

What she liked as much as that was the others let it go immediately, respecting his decision. She didn't want to see his hands on another sub tonight, and she wasn't comfortable with being tied up in front of a bunch of people.

Or so she thought.

The experienced riggers did everything so smoothly their subs went into a bound trance almost effortlessly, bodies sculpted into graceful shapes from the knots and wraps of the rope. Yet the less experienced riggers could still tap into that magic, building a similar connection with murmured communication and reverent strokes of their fingertips along a rapt submissive's face, tracing parted, eager lips.

The key seemed to be the connection between each pair. Julie was particularly pulled into the devotion and intensity between committed couples. She could tell which ones were scene hookups and those in a long term relationship. In the latter, the sub was telegraphing *I trust my Master or Mistress. I love him/her. I want to be seen as theirs.* This was a place where it was safe to make that declaration, where it would be respected, appreciated. Understood and validated.

She glanced up at Des. He'd been explaining things to her when needed, soliciting her reaction and opinions, making sure she wasn't getting tired of it and wanting to look at other things. On the contrary. They'd been here for the past thirty minutes, so they'd decided to sit on the floor at the edge of the action. She was turned on her hip, curled up against him, his arms around her and her cheek on his chest as they watched.

"Des." She put her hand on his arm to draw his full attention to her.

"Hmm?" He stroked a wisp of hair off her face, thumb caressing her bottom lip. His thick tail of hair was draped over his right shoulder and she combed her fingers through it, feeling the hard straightness of his collar bone beneath.

"If you wanted to do something, I think I'd like that."

"Yeah?"

"Yeah."

His look could x-ray stone, but whatever he saw satisfied him, because he lifted her off of him to help her to her feet. "All right. Stay right here. I'll be back in a second."

She liked that he didn't question her decision. He'd convinced her that he genuinely wanted her own feelings to lead her wherever she wanted to go. As such, he was respecting her understanding of her own desires. Even as she was sure he'd pay close attention to any indication she was getting cold feet.

He could exert an unyielding will that melted her every reservation into full surrender. He also possessed a sensitivity to her needs that surpassed her own understanding of them at times. Maybe that was what

Logan meant about an experienced Dom. If so, God bless them. And wow. What a freaking miracle of nature. Her freaking Dom-wizard. She chuckled inside, wondering if she'd ever share the nickname with him.

As he disappeared in the crowd, the thought was replaced with some anxiety. The enchantment that made her want him to bind her in his rope was strongest with his proximity. Yet, the main reason she wanted him to do it wasn't sexual, though the idea of it was certainly tempting. She wanted him to do it because it was a critical part of what made Des himself. She wanted to be part of that identity. She wanted to be what was caught in Spiderman's web.

She wasn't bothered by anyone. Those watching were as absorbed by the rigging as she'd been. Then Des was back, his rigger's duffle bag in hand. "Still sure?" he asked.

His thorough look said it wouldn't be what came out of her mouth that made up his mind. She slipped her hand into his free one.

"Yes. I'm glad you're not one of those Doms who's a stickler about not being touched unless the sub asks permission."

"You wouldn't find that arousing?"

She shook her head. "It would make me feel alone."

He kissed her forehead. "I like the feel of your body, your hands, your lips. As I said from the beginning, love, when I need you to keep your hands to yourself, I'll just tie you up. On that note..."

Still holding her hand, he drew her toward a set of empty hooks. As soon as he took her there, she noticed a lot of the riggers shifted to a better position to watch him. It made her proud on his behalf, that they admired his skill and technique and learned from it. It helped reduce her nervous flutter as that audience shift became less subtle. Body language, exchanged comments and a lot of speculative eyes were all directed toward them.

"Hey." Des took both her hands in his as she looked up at him. "It's just us, Julie. You and me. Remember? We can stop if you want. We don't have to do this."

"I know." As she was held by his gaze, she calmed.

Things got quiet inside, because she saw and found the stillness inside him. He cupped her nape, drawing her forward as he bent to put his forehead against hers. Her fingers curled in his shirt at his waist, over the rope and chain holding the sporran, but her knuckles brushed the firm heat of him beneath.

Realizing with surprise what he'd initiated was contact between their third eye energy points, an effective and meditative way to establish intimacy, she breathed with him, and that stillness expanded around them. When he at last shifted his grip and found the hook of the dress at her nape, they might have been back in the theater again, just the two of them on stage.

As he took the dress off, he helped her step out of it. The dress's bodice took the place of a bra, so beneath the garment she wore only a gold lace thong, the garters and the stockings. His pause told her he hadn't expected that, and he held the dress at her breasts an additional moment.

"Still okay?" he asked.

"Yes." She studied the unexpected pensiveness in his gaze. "How about you?"

"Yeah." His knuckles slid along the bare curve of her full breast, the dress still partially concealing it. "Just not sure these bastards deserve to see something as gorgeous as your breasts."

Her cheeks warmed. "The only one looking at them is you. At least in my mind."

His gaze lifted to hers, his eyes flashing with hot approval. Then he set the dress aside. He detached the garters and touched her face, showing her his callused palm, a reminder that his work-hardened hands would snag the stockings if he tried to remove them himself.

"I'd leave them on you, because you look so damn sexy, but rope wouldn't be kind to them. Hold on, love. Step out of the shoes first."

In her lustful haze, she'd started to roll the stockings down without removing the shoes. Flushing a little, she stepped out of the heels, holding onto his shoulders. Taking off the stockings was a two-handed affair, but he held her at waist and hip with strong hands as she removed and tucked the filmy sheer fabric carefully into the shoes. When she set them down next to his bag, he caressed her buttocks bared by the thong. The front of his kilt brushed the backs of her thighs, he stood so close to her. As she straightened, he had his first coil of rope in hand.

He held the fall over her throat, the coil resting against her chest. At his pause, she noticed him glancing down at her shoes. She'd placed them toes out as she always did.

"It's so they can look at different scenery, since they've been looking at each other all night."

His lips quirked. He guided her head back against his shoulder, and began to run the coil of rope over her flesh. Neck, sternum, the rise of her breasts. She turned her face toward his throat, feeling his pulse against her nose and lips. His other hand stroked her body, knuckles sliding along her rib cage, the nip of her waist, the flare of her hip, and playing with the thong. He didn't seem in a particular hurry, and she lost breath and sense of time when he uncoiled the rope and wrapped it around her.

He didn't tie it. He let it coil and uncoil around her with the force of gravity, turning it into a living thing gliding over her curves. Over her breasts, under her arms, dropping to her hips, slithering between her legs. There he caught and tugged it through, tightening it so she swayed in his grip, the tension putting pressure on labia and clit. Then it loosened and fell away. He wrapped it diagonally over her, back under the thong, securing it there as he took up the other end and wrapped it around her eyes, into her mouth like a gentle bit, and around her throat. He put his fingers beneath it to twist like he'd done with the collar.

She was a swaying flower, a rose whose petals he compressed into a tightly furled bud before he allowed her to bloom and breathe with the loosening of his bindings. He took her down into a folded over position, cinching the rope around the back of her neck and thighs, holding her that way on the floor as he stroked her legs, her buttocks, the framed shape of her damp sex. He had his fingers hooked in the wraps he'd done across her back, so she felt in no danger of toppling.

The bands loosened and he straightened her again, to

position her beneath the hooks. She was already in a half trance state. He would tangle and hold her in his web a million different ways while she floated in the euphoria created by the dance between his hands and the jute rope he favored. He'd left the rope tied around her mouth, a way to relieve her of the need to talk, but she was glad he hadn't left the wrap over her eyes. She wanted to see him.

He boxed her arms behind her, forearms tied together beneath her shoulder blades. He took down her hair, combing his fingers through it. Once again, he took his time, stroking deep, tugging on her scalp, letting her feel his care along with his strength. When at last he bound her hair into a tail and attached the rope from that to her boxed arms, he left her enough slack she could look down and see what he was doing next. She was captivated by the concentrated look on his face, the energy that poured off of him as he made her his creation.

He'd secured the wraps over her arms to two of the hooks to hold her upright while he was otherwise occupied. He did a diamond harness on her body, but this time the stopper knots were elaborate, Escher-looking creations that also reminded her of the Celtic knots of his sleeve studs. He didn't stop at her hips. He left her sex unencumbered, a promising decision, splitting the doubled rope over her hips and then bringing in more rope to start a lattice-looking design that ran from the juncture of her thigh and hip to her feet, looping a double strand under the soles.

He tilted his head up. "If I tie the rope under your feet, you can't get away from me, can you? Can't outrun me."

Her heart thudded hard in her chest. He had an edge to his tone and a light in his eyes that said he meant it. The primitive side summoned for both of them. All the debris of the civilized world fallen away to make things simple and in sharp relief.

She loved the way he looked when he did this. His focus was brilliant, encompassing her and the whole creative miasma around her. She suspected he could see so many possibilities there, an aura he read to decide what he wanted to do.

Many performers used interesting ways to tap into creative energy, but regardless of the method, it always involved a focus somehow very present and yet also in an entirely different realm, the contrast the connecting link.

She loved being in proximity to that process, drinking it in. Now she was part of that live connection, in the center of the flow. It wasn't an ego thing. Being in the center wasn't about that. It was a safe feeling, a balanced one, since there could be nothing more solid than standing at the center of a circle. At the center of someone's soul, feeling as if everything around her was welcoming her, capturing her, cherishing her, taking everything from her. Bliss was the reward for her surrender.

He trailed his fingers up her torso, along the cage he'd created around her body. "I'll do this to you one weekend when we're off by ourselves together. Only I'll do a similar lattice work over your arms instead of boxing them. You'll be free to move your limbs, but this is all you'll wear. With this net tied over you, I can bind you in endless ways. Turn you into any kind of orchid I want. Hook you to my bed with your limbs spread out like a daisy, and fuck and eat your pussy, suckle your nipples. Coat you in wax or chocolate."

He cocked his head, considering, as a soft moan of reaction slipped from her lips. "I can put you down all tucked up, your forehead to the ground, arms threaded under you, between your folded-up legs. I'd bind your wrists between your ankles, so you're like a seed in the ground, not ready to split open until I cut the ties. I'd slide my cock into your tight opening, fuck you so slow, killing us both with that sweet friction, even as you'd be making those little pleading noises because you couldn't move, your climax completely at my whim."

He lifted his gaze to her face. "Ah, love, your eyes get so hungry for all of it when I talk to you like this. Stretched lips over my rope making me think of what you'll do for my cock later. That you were willing to do here in front of everyone, sweet, wanton woman."

He rose. "I'm going to put you in flight. Let your body move with what I'm doing. Don't tense and don't worry that I won't support you. Can you do that?"

She nodded.

"All right. This will help." He unbuttoned his shirt and slid it off with an unselfconscious shrug of his shoulders that sent the green spotlight shimmering over his tanned shoulders and the dragon and rope tattoos. She anticipated a Des-scented blindfold, but first he ran the soft cloth over her arms and legs, her torso, an intriguing caress and marking at once. Then he tied it over her eyes and cheekbones, across the bridge of her nose over her flaring nostrils.

"Remember what I said," he reminded her, body close to hers. "Relax. You're water, just flowing with me."

That sense of isolation with just the two of them increased, any other noise becoming the crash of ocean waves. Truth, she hadn't thought of any of the watching eyes in some time.

He removed all the rope and started anew. Around her neck, shoulders, breast and legs. She let out a breath, remembering just in time not to tense as she was suddenly airborne, hooks attached to wraps at key support points, well distributed so nothing cut into her or put uncomfortable pressures or strain on her body. Des had supported her through the lift. She'd felt his tough arm muscles and hard body against her until she evened out.

However, she knew her Dom. He relished certain types of discomfort, those that goaded desire, so she wasn't surprised he had some of that in mind for her.

She was bent mostly in half, like a diver in a modified pike position. Her thighs were tied to her abdomen, her toes pointed down. Her elbows were bound to her knees, her wrists to her ankles. She was supported by the ropes under her hips and thighs and the wraps above and below her breasts, all of the lines meeting above her back to hold her suspended and keep her back straight, parallel to the floor. He'd tied her hair in the way he favored to keep her chin up and her face lifted.

In this position he could stab into her with his jutting cock, if he moved the soaked crotch of the thong. Instead, he kept his hands running over her, reassuring, caressing, testing her muscles, tension. She wondered what she looked like and hoped he'd taken a picture. She wanted to see if he'd done something with her body she wasn't even sure she could pull off in her yoga class. But in yoga she wasn't in a daze of arousal and trance created by his touch, her muscles loose and flexible to his demands.

He kissed her mouth, caressing her cheek, her throat. He walked around her, sliding a hand along her flank. She strangled on a breath as he put his mouth between her legs. He licked her cunt on the outside of the panties, sending a jolt of reaction through her that had her trying to squirm in her bonds. The sensation was indescribable, excruciating.

"Would you come like this, my sweet sub?" he crooned at her. "Give your Master everything he wants?"

"Yes," she rasped. *God yes.*

"Good." He paused, though, something odd in his voice. He was standing again, because his fingers passed over her mouth, thumb sliding along her carotid, the thumping blood pulsing there.

He put his forehead against hers like he had at the beginning. Then, that had been to center her. She had a feeling this was to center himself, find level ground in an unstable firmament.

"Des?" she whispered. His pure, hard need pierced through everything else, took her back to that quiet place inhabited by the two of them, where she was as aware of the type of energy pulsing around him as he was of hers.

"I've never wanted to keep someone. I've never let myself...want that." His voice was thick. The clamp of his fingers on her shoulder seemed capable of piercing muscle and bone. It hurt, but she didn't think he was even aware of it. She refused to flinch, to do anything to interrupt wherever he was in his head.

"You can want that," she said softly. Her fears about being in a relationship, about having her heart crushed, none of that meant anything right now. This, someone offering her his heart, a heart she wanted, was something she would never be able to refuse, no matter what lies she told herself. She couldn't refuse the one thing she wanted more than anything.

He removed the shirt blindfold so he could look at her. When she met his gaze, she drew in a breath like a shard of glass piercing her to the core. Pain was a living thing in his eyes.

Sometimes the universe drew back a curtain and let two souls see one another directly. Such instances were so rare, and Julie had never experienced one until this. In that brief, blinding, heartbreaking and love making moment, she saw into Des. She thought he'd given her that the other night, and he had, but then it had been a glimpse. This was an in-depth look no one else had ever been given. She knew that because she had the answer his soul needed, waiting in a cold darkness she hadn't expected to see.

It startled her, but it also matched her needs and wants in a way beyond words. The bottomless glass was suddenly brimming over, able to satisfy the thirst of the whole world and one particular man.

"Des." She would have reached out and cupped his face in both hands if she could. She was helpless and immobile, and somehow that had freed something inside him, something she could answer with her heart.

She smiled at him, through tears and an aching throat. "You can keep me. I promise. It's okay. I want that more than anything. I'm not afraid anymore."

Like two children on a playground, it was that simple and straightforward. The cold darkness drew back, though the soul view remained. It was all-encompassing, overwhelming and everything she'd ever wanted to have and hold.

He was struggling with that stunning moment of vulnerability, she could tell. He hadn't meant to open himself like that, let her see so much.

"Master." She spoke in a voice thick with emotions, drawing his eyes to her face. "I want to keep you, too."

§

He untied her. Held her and she held him, a mutual aftercare, but it worked for both of them, which was all that mattered. He helped her back in her dress, and the pleasantly domestic task touched her. She was cold, but he'd anticipated that. He had a quilted flannel shirt in his duffle. It smelled like him.

When he considered it next to her fancy dress, he shook his head, as if discarding the idea of using it instead of a blanket over the satin creation, but she took it. It was oversized for him, so she was able to wrap it around herself. She did a little left and right plié, like she was displaying herself on a runway.

"Bag lady chic, complete with bare feet." She gestured with her shoes, clasped together in her right hand. Putting an arm over her shoulders, Des kissed her forehead with affection, and they went to find Logan and Madison. They were on a patio behind the building, illuminated by strung lights over a large pergola. The area was clustered with dogwoods and greenery.

Madison looked blissfully mellow, a comfortable post sub-state. Logan looked satisfied and focused on her in that way that made a man appealing to any woman. Add Logan's looks and demeanor and well...

Julie could appreciate those qualities, but her attention was absorbed by her own escort, and the reactions he'd summoned from her. Plenty of the women here saw what she did in him, because Julie caught lots of lingering looks. Let them look. He was here with her.

An outdoor bar had snacks, soft drinks, water and other non-alcoholic choices, and Logan treated them with their preference. Soda for Julie and Madison, a cider for Logan and a bottled water for Des.

As they all chatted about casual topics and the things they'd seen, Julie noticed Des was quiet, but not broody. He seemed relaxed, thoughtful, even as he remained attentive. His fingers slid through Julie's hair, caressing her bare shoulder beneath his flannel shirt. At one point, he pushed the fabric back to kiss her collarbone. When his hand dropped to her thigh beneath the table, she parted her legs, letting his grip slide up high. His gaze met hers, and she wet her lips at his look. He kept his hand where it was, fingers lightly stroking her inner thigh as her body hummed at the attention and craved more.

"So as I was saying, I think our next performance after Lila's should be *Caligula*. We'll ask Thomas if we can borrow his cows to do a bestiality scene. A bovine-human orgy."

"Oh, that sounds—" Julie shook herself out of her sexual haze and snapped her attention to Madison. "*What?*"

Madison laughed. Reaching across the small round table, she grabbed Julie's hand. "I love seeing you two get lost in one another. But I had to tease."

"Thomas's cows?" Des asked. He didn't appear unsettled by Madison's observation. Julie decided to take that as a good sign, rather than dissecting it and finding cues on how this would end up being a BDSM Disneyland fueled fantasy tomorrow.

Stop it, you crazy, dysfunctional bitch.

"Thomas's family has a farm," Julie said brightly. Maybe too brightly. She toned it down at Des's curious look. "Well, it was a farm at one time, but now they run a hardware slash general store in the middle of Nowhere, North Carolina, totally rural. But he has a cow named Kate he raised. Since they got married, he and Marcus have adopted two more and a couple of goats from a farm sanctuary organization. Even though Thomas and Marcus are both carnivores, Thomas says it's his way of apologizing for any farm-factory-produced hamburgers he's eaten."

"So have you met Marcus and Thomas?" Des asked their friends.

"I met them a couple times in Boston when they came to see Julie," Madison volunteered. "Logan hasn't yet, though he should when they come visit in a couple weeks. I'm surprised it took Marcus this long to show up after Julie told him about you."

Julie kicked her under the table, but Des felt it, since he had firm grip on her other leg. "For my screen test?" he asked dryly.

"Take it as a good thing," Madison assured him, though her quick glance at Julie said she realized she'd put it the wrong way and too obviously. *Blame it on a subspace brain haze*, her apologetic look said. Julie could hardly cast stones, but Des's expression didn't reveal what his thoughts were. She still felt very connected to him, but there was a lot happening in his mind she couldn't decipher. She didn't want these feelings they were experiencing disrupted.

"They'll love you," she said.

"It won't matter if they don't," he said, his hand sliding higher up her thigh and hooking in the thong to caress her sex as he leaned in and touched his lips to her, a deceptively mild gesture compared to what was going on beneath the table. He caught her suddenly shaky breath. "Won't change a damn thing, will it, love?"

"Um...you understand they're just friends. Practically family."

"And something a little more than that. Just making my position clear." His fingertips slid inside her and she almost choked on the surge of response that shot between her legs as he caressed her clit. His gleaming eyes said he might decide to do something unthinkable right here.

She should be responding to this testosterone bath with a snarky remark, a retort suitable for an independent woman who wouldn't tolerate a man's blatant branding, but oh God, how did he do that with those long, fabulous fingers?

She should be horribly self-conscious in front of Madison and Logan, but a desperate glance across the table showed her that Logan had shifted Madison on his lap and they were currently having a low, intimate conversation. Her friend's arm was around her husband's neck, while his large hand cupped and kneaded her breast, shaping and elongating the nipple beneath the satin bodice as she kept her gaze fastened on his face.

The table between them was small, and Logan curled his fingers around Madison's other wrist, drawing her hand back to the table. Des nodded to it, the two men in some kind of eerie accord. "Take her hand, Julie. And hold on tight."

Logan's hand slid out of view. Julie recognized Madison's jerk of response as he found his way between his wife's legs and began to play with her as Des was doing to Julie. Madison's fingers convulsed on hers. In a wash of heated lust, Julie realized what they intended. She'd never really had a girl-girl experience. She wasn't wired that way, much preferring men for her fantasies and real life sexual encounters, but this single act of holding her friend's fine-boned hand, feeling her polished nails dig into Julie's palm as her response built, spurred Julie's own.

As for her Dom, he had a laser gaze trained on her face, brown eyes glittering, mouth and jaw set. He was making an undeniable point, moving from Dom to Master in the space of a few sentences that had flipped a switch, a transition thrilling as it was unsettling.

She heard Madison moan Logan's name against his neck as he gathered her close. Julie gripped her hand as Des sent her flying up a ramp and let her go into full orgasm. Logan brought Madison to the same pinnacle as Madison clutched Julie's fingers hard enough to bruise bone. Julie wondered if either man watched that connecting point between their two women, the fingers tangling, biting, jerking, holding on as their bodies flooded with release.

They came down almost at the same time, the same gradual grade. They hadn't let go of one another. They were stroking one another's fingers, unsteady caresses. At last, Madison gave her a squeeze and slipped free as Logan murmured to her. He held out a hand to Des. "I think we're going to head for home. I'm ready to have her all to myself." His gaze shifted to Julie, who had her head on Des's shoulder, her limbs too heavy to lift on her own. "Julie, I assume you don't need a ride home?"

There was amusement in his eyes, but Julie also registered the heat. Madison's night was only just beginning. Since Des had brought her to several orgasms, but not yet allowed himself release, she might need to rest up on the way home herself.

"I'm sure I can catch a cab," she offered, then giggled, pulling Des's hair as he bit her neck, none-too-gently.

"Thank you," she said as she looked up at Logan and Madison again. They paused, hearing the suddenly serious note in her voice. "Just...thank you."

Madison reached across the table and gripped her hand, for a different reason this time. She didn't say anything, but Julie knew she understood. She didn't know if she'd find with Des what Madison had found with Logan, but Julie knew she was closer to it than she'd ever been. As terrifying as that was, she was sticking to one single resolve. She wasn't going to doubt herself tonight.

"I'll get back to you on the cow orgy thing," she said, and left them laughing.

§

She wondered if the Steak 'n Shake idea had been intended to help her refuel and recuperate. If so, it was a good plan. Julie ordered a cookies and cream shake and fries while Des had half a grilled chicken sandwich. He gave her a part of the sandwich and she traded a couple fries and a few sips of the shake with him. They people-watched and listened to the piped-in music, trying to guess song titles. She asked him about some of the people she'd seen at the party. No surprise, he knew most of them and their backstories, and she was smug when she found she'd guessed right on most of the top and bottom orientations.

They'd agreed they'd go back to her place at the theater since she had volunteers coming in tomorrow morning to paint the ceiling. Anticipating what she and Des might do there, she was glad she'd finally replaced the cot with a real double bed. It was just a cheap thing she'd picked up at a second hand shop, but she'd decorated it with a strand of colorful butterfly lights and put throw pillows on it. She was under no illusions as to why she'd made the interior design improvement when she'd had plenty other things to keep her busy this past week, but she was glad she had.

On the way there, the foolish man made her sing. He had her name her 80s song favorites and belt out as much of the lyrics as she could remember, until she was laughing too hard to continue. When she demanded reciprocity, he attempted songs like Prince's "Purple Rain." The man had a mesmerizing speaking voice...and was as tone deaf as a moose.

Trying to help him hit the right notes only led to more mirth and a mock aggrieved look on his face. As he shut off the truck at the theater parking lot, he attacked her, tickling her knees and sides as she shrieked and thrashed. She scrambled out of the truck and to the theater side door. He pinned her there, thankfully to kiss instead of tickle her, playfulness turning into something else entirely.

Fishing out her keys, she thwarted his attempts to take them and play keep away. Then he caught her around the waist, hiked her up his body and carried her over the threshold, still kissing her. They hit the wall with a resounding thud, for which he gravely apologized. She assured him her skull fracture would heal in time.

After kissing her senseless through several long, dreamy eternities, he let her down and stepped back from her, gaze sliding over the dress and everything it barely covered with possessive thoroughness.

"Jessica Rabbit," he said. "That's who you remind me of in that outfit."

"'I'm not bad. I'm just drawn that way.'" She purred the line in a sultry voice, and made a dash for the back rooms. "Have to go to the bathroom. Make yourself comfortable in my room."

He'd let her escape, but as she took care of the call of nature, she could hear him moving around her room. Then things got quiet, drawing her curiosity.

Slipping out of the bathroom and moving to her doorway, she found he'd lit several clusters of the candles she kept there for mood lighting. She didn't see him, though. She moved into the room, looking around. "Des."

The shadows in her peripheral vision moved. Before she could turn, he had her in a firm hold. His shirt was off again and he'd removed the sporran, thank God. Though he still wore the kilt, she could feel his need pressing against her beneath it.

"You left your dressing room door unlocked, Miss Rabbit," he said. "With all those photographers and fans, it wasn't a smart move."

It was easy to ride the instant surge of arousal into the role, playing the fantasy she wanted to be for him. That he'd made her feel like she could be.

"Will you hurt me?" she purred with a little jaunty twitch of her hips. He gave her flank a light slap, setting off a starburst of tingling.

"Not if you behave and do what I tell you to do."

"I'm not good at behaving." To prove it, she rotated her ass against his groin with a lap dancer's skill.

Nipping her ear, he slid his hand under the dress to caress one soft buttock. "I'll teach you to be good. And I'll tell you when I want you to be bad. Get on the bed on your hands and knees, facing away from me. This isn't going to be slow or easy. I've wanted my dick hammering inside your pussy all night."

He let her go and she moved to the bed, surprised to find herself shaking. He could sound really menacing, but below that was something else, barely restrained male lust. He could wrest orgasm after orgasm from her with a range of methods from tender to merciless. She wondered if he preferred to delay his own release because so much of his satisfaction came from taking, and taking hard. The only thing that could stop him was her. She didn't want to stop him, but it didn't mean his brutal urgency didn't scare her a little.

She climbed on the bed, facing the headboard on her hands and knees. When the mattress gave beneath her, she knew he'd put his knee behind her.

"Down on your elbows."

She complied, swallowing a moan as he brushed her hair forward, exposing her nape, and unhooked the straps at her neck that held the bodice up in front and the single thin strap following her spine in back. The bodice didn't fall free, the cloth snagging on her curves, so he finished the job by reaching beneath her and pulling it away, caressing her curves. She pressed into his touch, her nipples aching for the friction of his callused palms, but he didn't linger. He intended to finish the job.

Laying his hands on the back of the dress, he ripped it in one powerful movement to the hem, making her gasp. The whole thing fell to the bed, the fabric brushing her knees. Madison had been right. Tatters.

The thong was next. The snick of his blade told her how he was going to do it. He sliced through the elastic and pulled the thong away from her body, out of the tight crevice between her buttocks.

"Spread your knees wider."

She did it, despite her knees being made of water. She was surprised they didn't give way. She expected him to ram into her, but he wasn't going down that road without driving her ahead of him, making her relinquish her sanity.

She cried out as his mouth found her cunt, his hands pushing hard against her buttocks to lift her higher, almost taking her knees off the mattress and pressing her face into it. He sucked her clit, stabbed deep into her folds, licked and played, the beard shadow on his jaw an exciting friction against her tender skin. When he moved to her rim, she came apart at the two different yet both incredible sensations. She writhed against his powerful grip. Drawing back, he tossed the front of the kilt up over her hips, covering her as he brought his cock and bare pelvis in full, heated contact with her pussy. She groaned with animal need when he drove into her slick folds.

He kept away from her clit, making her ache and plead as he thrust, but when he seized her hair and pulled her head back, using that grip to increase the impact of his pelvis slapping against her ass, the climax began deep and took over. It consumed her body from head to toe, squeezing her muscles down on him as he spilled within her with harsh noises of release she relished. His hand convulsed on her scalp. He kept working himself in her even after his finish. It was astonishing and unexpected, how hard he stayed past climax, milking every reaction from both of them before at last he slowed and covered her with his body.

He removed the kilt without leaving her, and adjusted them to their sides. He reached over her, putting the disconnected pump on the side table, and wrapped both arms around her. His thighs cradled her ass as he pushed himself in deeper, holding onto that connection.

"Oh..." Her vocalization was a sigh of satisfaction and wonder, and he pressed his mouth to her neck, holding her even tighter.

"Same here, love. Same here."

She closed her eyes and focused on breathing, but as he

leveled out behind her, she could feel the weight of his thoughts in a certain stillness to his body. She pressed her fingers into the channels between his, across her abdomen. "All right?" she whispered. It was just the two of them, but she didn't want to make noise. She wanted the only sounds to be their breath, the sizzle of candlelight, the theater shifting on its foundation.

"Yeah. Are you? I was pretty rough."

"I loved it. Do it again. Maybe in an hour. Let me nap first."

His lips curved against her throat, but that stillness was still there.

"Sorry I was a beast," he muttered at length. "Never had one I wanted to keep. It made me a little insane. Didn't expect that."

She folded both her arms over his, held on tight. "'S'okay," she said.

Unlike him, she'd always known—or hoped—that was exactly how this would feel. There were a whole lot of lovely words other than *insane* for it.

She stroked his arm and let her breath rise and fall with his. She wasn't surprised he dropped off to sleep before she did. He'd held the reins most the night and brought her multiple glorious orgasms. The man was entitled to be tired. She liked being with him while he slept. His breath heated her throat. His body was wrapped around her, his cock still partially inside her. His nose was buried in her hair, as if he'd wanted to take her scent into his dreams with him.

As she struggled against an exhausted sleep, she realized it was the closest to contentment she'd ever felt in a man's arms. She'd never laid in bed with a lover like this, holding him and touching him with a hundred percent confidence that it was okay. Like she was inside his flesh and could feel the way he felt. She could think of him as hers.

She didn't want it to be a temporary refuge from reality. She didn't want tomorrow to turn it into an illusion. She wished she could hold onto this moment even longer, but she had to sleep. She couldn't stave it off without sitting up, and she wasn't leaving his arms.

As she curled her body tighter into the curve of his, she let herself hope that dreams really could come true. Then she slid into them.

Chapter Thirteen

They had the final showings of *Consent* during the next week. Julie was pleased with the confidence that built in her cast and crew, because in community theater the same players often came back for future productions.

Reviews remained positive, with only the occasional prudish naysayer. With twinkling practicality, Madison pointed out those would only bring in the curious, given their subject material.

Des and Missive remained the crowd favorite, though she could tell he was a little relieved when they finished the last showing. Performance really wasn't his thing, and balancing it with a full time job was draining, even for someone with a passion for the stage.

Her rope artist might not have the theater bug, but he had boundless passion in other ways. Though she wished their respective jobs let them see one another every day, she appreciated the pleasure that delayed gratification brought.

She also liked how he seemed just as happy to seize the chance to see her, even if there was no chance of sex. Like today. He'd messaged her last night that he was building a playground on Sunday with the help of some Type I kids he mentored and contractors volunteering their time. She'd barely hesitated before agreeing to drive forty-five minutes downtown to meet him there.

He'd added the text: *Sorry for the less than romantic setup, but I really don't want to wait another day to see you again. As long as you don't mind sharing time with a bunch of kids and sweaty contractors.*

How sweaty? She texted him.

Nothing that would interest you. Skunk sweat. Normal contractor sweat. My sweat is an erotic anomaly.

That left her chuckling. She picked up some lunch on the way and brought her tablet so she could run through Harris's production book details so far on *Done Right*, Lila's play.

The playground was in one of the more run-down Charlotte neighborhoods, populated by blue collar lower income working class people living in small clapboard houses. It had always been a playground, but had fallen into disrepair, and Des had volunteered himself and some of his contractor buddies to help the local church spruce it back up. A number of parishioners had turned out to work on the grading and landscaping while Des and his team, along with the neighborhood's more skilled carpenters, worked together on the playground equipment.

Since he'd texted her the "before" picture, she was delighted to see how much progress had already been made. Trash, vines and weeds had been cleared and were being replaced by mulched border areas with perennials and small shrubs, laid out beneath the several large shade trees in the lot.

Des and his crew were busy sawing, cutting, and hammering, the noise of power tools and men calling back and forth a pleasant din. They'd already put up the framework for the activities station that would have a climbing wall, parallel bars, rope bridge, a suspended path made up of tires, and monkey bars. A spacious tree fort formed the center piece. They'd wisely decided to keep an older steel set of monkey bars and parallel bars framing the new equipment, since both of those looked in good shape.

A swarm of ten kids appeared to be under Des and the other workers' instruction as he combined the volunteer activity with teaching them building skills. He'd told her four of them were his Type I kids, so the others must be from the neighborhood. She wasn't surprised that Des would include any kid interested in learning.

He looked damn good, which amused her, since he was coated in sawdust, his sweat-dampened hair scraped back with a rubber band, and he wore a paint-stained shirt and jeans. But men looked better dirty than women did. Everyone knew that, so her opinion might not be entirely blinded by lust. Though there was nothing wrong with a healthy dose of lust, especially when flavored with sheer delight at seeing him again.

He waved, telling her he knew she was there, and she settled on a bench to watch, knowing it was best to stay out of the way until he had time to take a break and say hello.

He'd pulled two of the children off to the side. Since they were standing by the old parallel bars, she could hear the gist of the conversation. He was explaining how to monitor and interpret their insulin levels when doing strenuous work like this. He had a good teaching style, conveying how important it was for them to know the information without condescending or lecturing.

"Right now, your parents probably check your numbers and stay on you about what to eat and when to take your insulin, but it's really great when you take responsibility for it yourself, and know it all so well they start asking *you* questions about it. The more you prove you can handle this, the more comfortable they'll be letting you handle it. It's your body, your life. You start taking control now, you'll be glad you did. You'll grow up to be totally cool like me."

As he said that, he'd gripped the parallel bars and turned himself upside down, hooking his knees over one of the bars. He finished the advice while hanging upside down, arms crossed over his chest, looking like a bat. The two kids jeered at him good naturedly. When one came too close, he grabbed the boy by the waist and turned him upside down, threatening to make him eat dirt.

She really shouldn't be fascinated by how his biceps bunched when he did that, or how he held the kid so easily while he himself was hanging just by his legs, but hey, she was weak. His bill cap had fallen off, his thick ponytail falling along his jaw. When he released the boy to reach down and pick it up, he put it on the head of the other child, a young girl with pink sneakers and purple hair. Julie swallowed a chuckle, realizing Des had a purple streak in his own hair. Julie suspected the girl had a temporary dye powder or spray and had talked Des into giving it a try for fun.

He was so good with kids. She wondered if he wanted any of his own. She'd always wanted to experience childbirth. Was she too old? A lot of women did it later these days. She'd be happy to adopt if she was no longer a good candidate, but she imagined a child with Des's eyes and smile, and their combined way of looking at the world.

Whoa, girlfriend. Ease up there. Way scary territory.

The slats of her wooden bench shifted beneath her hips, thankfully drawing her away from that topic. A woman had taken a seat on the opposite end. She looked about sixty and had a dandelion fluff of short white-gold hair styled around her pleasant face, combined with a bisque complexion that suggested mixed Caucasian and African parentage. She tucked a folder under her thigh as she took a sip from a water bottle.

Since she was wearing scrubs, Julie assumed she must be one of the neighbors, a medical professional about to head off for shift after checking in on how the playground was going. There were other neighbors spectating in the same way, watching from their front porches across the street, or camping out on the crumbling brick wall that edged the playground area. This bench was on the parking lot side of the playground where Des's truck and the contractor vehicles were arrayed, so Julie had had it all to herself until now.

She didn't mind the company. The woman was smiling at Des's antics with the kids, which already convinced Julie to like her, but she never needed an excuse to strike up a conversation with a new potential friend.

"He's a character, isn't he?" she ventured.

The woman glanced her way. While she'd probably given Julie a quick once-over before sitting down, that automatic evaluation strangers did before risking proximity, the woman seemed to give her an even closer look now, taking Julie's measure in an in-depth way that left Julie curious.

It was then she noticed the pattern on the woman's scrubs. Horses, galloping, prancing and rolling in small tufts of printed grass. She wore a dainty gold watch and, on the same wrist, a friendship bracelet in gold and silver thread with knot patterns that Julie recognized.

"Oh." She made an educated guess, pleased with the chance to meet another important person in Des's life. "You're Betty, aren't you?"

"I am," Betty replied in a rasping yet honeyed voice that reminded Julie of the Oracle in *The Matrix*.

Julie extended a hand. "Julie Ramirez. Des and I have been seeing each other for a short while."

"Ah, I thought so." Betty clasped Julie's hand, softening her unsettling scrutiny. "You're the mystery woman. I knew he'd brought someone home a couple times, but he's been good about sneaking you in and out while I was asleep or working."

Julie grinned. "I expect that has more to do with my schedule. I'm in theater and we're always working impossible hours."

"Sounds a lot like nursing." As the children shrieked, both women looked up to see that Des had swung off the parallel bars. He was chasing the two kids as they played keep away with his hat. He could have caught either one easily, but was lunging and missing to prolong the game.

"Lord, he's always had more heart than sense, but he's so good with those kids." Betty shook her head. "See the boy? Justice was terrified of anything even resembling a needle. Yet Des has him putting on his pump and testing his blood sugar like it's nothing out of the ordinary. None of the drama and tears that were giving his poor parents gray hairs."

"I'm familiar with Des's powers of persuasion," Julie said. "They're hard to resist. Do you know how he did it?"

The crow's feet around Betty's attractive pale green eyes crinkled. "That's a kind way of saying he's stubborn as a stump. But he can be clever, patient and kind about it, which is often just what these kids need. Took me a while to pry it out of him, since he initially said it was a secret bro code between him and Justice."

Betty shook her head. "He told the boy to imagine he was a super hero. Putting on the pump would give him powers against the evil Dr. Sharp, whose strength draws from fear of needles."

Betty considered the thin boy as Des caught him, reclaiming the hat, but in their wrestling for it, his arm ended up around Justice's back and the boy took the opportunity to give him a self-conscious hug. Des returned it in full measure, ruffling his hair.

"He told Justice that every kid who sticks his finger or puts on his pump without fear lessens Dr. Sharp's power, so he can't do bad things to make the world a darker place. I had the pleasure of being there the first time Justice put on his pump without fuss. Afterward, he was beaming from ear to ear. Des high-fived him and exclaimed, 'See, it worked. The world just became brighter, right? That was all you. Your name says it all, man. Justice kicks the ass of darkness.'"

Betty used her hands, voice and widened eyes expressively to bring the story to life. It suggested she was good with kids herself. Since Des obviously held her in fond regard from his own childhood, that came as no surprise.

Julie watched Des put Justice up on the parallel bars, spotting him so he could hang upside down. The boy laughed and then yelled as Des and the little girl tried to tickle him. She wondered if there was anyone Des wasn't comfortable around.

"So are you involved with the playground project, or just here to see Des?"

"I'm here to see Des, but he got involved with this through me. A patient from this neighborhood told me they were renovating the playground and needed skilled volunteer labor. I told Des and here he is, with his friends." Betty smiled. "He and I go way back."

"He said you were the nurse at the boys' home where he was raised."

Betty gave her another speculative look, as if she hadn't expected that to be something Julie would know. "Yes. After he moved out on his own at eighteen, I eventually went into PA work. Physician's Assistant. When he transitioned from an endocrinologist to an internist, as often happens when Type I kids grow up, he came to my boss. Now I'm his PA as well as his landlady."

"So, was he a cool teenager? Give me something that will mortify him. How can I bribe you?"

Betty chuckled. "He was a very cool teenager."

"I'm not surprised to hear it," Julie admitted. "He mentioned he dealt with a lot of health problems. My takeaway from what little he said was that he had to be a pretty remarkable kid to be as good with life as he seems to be now."

The personal note gave Julie the chance to convey the less than subtle message that Des had shared confidences with her, in case Betty wanted to be more forthcoming. She didn't want the woman to betray Des's trust, but now that she'd admitted to herself and him that she was falling in love with him, Julie wanted to know as much about him as she could.

Betty met Julie's gaze. "I believe," she said, with a look that Julie was sure had made more than one boy squirm, "this is where I ask you your intentions with regard to Des."

"That's a great combination of Southern traditional courtesy and 'don't bullshit me or I'll stomp you like a bug.'" Julie shifted closer, turning on her hip to give Betty her full attention. "I'm falling head-over-heels with him and terrified he's going to betray my heart and treat me like crap. He's made it clear that he might screw up my life entirely, but the one thing he'll never do is treat me badly."

Betty blinked. "You do brutal honesty very well. But yes, you are right. Des won't ever treat you carelessly. He's guarded himself so long because he doesn't want to hurt anyone. However, by doing that, I think he's closed himself off from having a truly two-way relationship, where he can be given the gift of someone's heart." Betty gave her another searching look. "Perhaps that's changed."

"Well, let's not go insane. It doesn't say anything about his feelings. I could be a very charming stalker."

Betty's eyes sparkled. "I think not. He doesn't bring women home, and I've never seen any of them visit him while he's working."

"Well, technically this isn't a job site. Though I have been to one of those." At Betty's satisfied look, Julie held up a hand. "Okay, don't freak me out, because being in love with him and okay with that is still new to me and porcelain fragile. Let's go back to the impressive teenager thing and you telling me stuff about him I don't know. If I've passed the initial test."

"I think you have." Betty's expression was a mix of fascination and wary amusement, but she crossed her legs, readjusting the folder beneath her thigh. "Des spent so much time in doctor's offices and hospitals," she said. "It wasn't an easy childhood, but I expect that's what made him Des and what helps him be so good with these kids. He doesn't let them feel sorry for themselves, not a bit, but he's always there with a hug or a pat on the shoulder when needed."

"Were you the one who provided that for him?"

The nurse looked surprised, but her shrewdness returned. "You have a kind heart. He needs that. I was there more than most, and it was still a sad substitute for full-time parents. He was unadoptable, as you can imagine. He accepted that early on, and the need to care for himself. He hated hospitals, doctors, people poking him and taking away his choices. I told him the best way to minimize that was to take complete control of his health."

Betty smiled at Des fondly. He was back over in the construction area, giving the kids pavers to carry to a section of the playground. "It was something to see, a nine-year-old explaining his medical history as capably as an adult. Ten-dollar medical terms tripping off his tongue like a foreign language he knew fluently. He'd tell a doctor what he'd overlooked, or show new techs how to do procedures on him more efficiently."

Betty stopped. "I have a tendency to want to talk about him to someone who thinks he's as remarkable as I do," she admitted. "You were looking at him that way when I sat down, but it wasn't naively starry-eyed. I sense you've already met his frustrating side."

"The head like a brick thing? Oh yeah. But it sounds like that may have made him what he is, too."

"It is. Our weaknesses and strengths often switch places in unexpectedly beneficial ways."

Julie considered that in relation to herself. Her heart had been broken plenty, but maybe those disappointments had been necessary for her to appreciate all that Des was, all the two of them could be. But she could ponder life paths later.

"So sick kid, orphan, it didn't matter." Julie pursed her lips. "He just took it in stride and moved forward? I'm not disagreeing. He seems far more at ease with any trouble in his past than most of my friends. And their biggest therapy issue is usually that daddy didn't hug them enough."

"It's often hard for those of us who have had family support to understand," Betty explained. "But a kid in the system, there isn't another option. You take care of yourself because numbers and time are against you getting a lot of one-on-one attention. But don't mistake taking-in-stride for easy. He had his low moments. He just never really expected anyone to be there to hold his hand through...anything."

Shadows passed through the nurse's eyes as she looked toward Des again, but when she brought her attention back to Julie, her gaze had lightened, heralding a lighter subject. "So you really expect me to buy that falling-in-love crap? Admit it. You're just using him for sex."

Julie laughed. "I admit he's extremely good at that, but no. He makes me laugh and..."

Her gaze shifted to him. He was offering each kid a supervised turn at the giant circular saw, a mother's nightmare. She'd intended to give Betty a flip response, but that wasn't what came from her lips. "I've been looking for a good man for a long time," she admitted. "He is one, and I'm hoping this will turn into a good thing for both of us. Too early to tell, but it sure feels right."

Betty touched her hand, a casual affection. "Your eyes are sparkling, so I'd say you're working a heavy crush on my boy." She cocked her head. "You're not Southern."

"No. Born in Oregon, but most of my life has been theater up in New York, Boston and Philly. I'm down here getting Wonder on its feet."

"Oh the erotic theater. I should have known he'd be involved in that." At Julie's surprised expression, Betty grinned. "I'm not a monk. Some girlfriends were gushing about it. They said I needed to buy tickets, but I missed my chance."

"Oh." Julie paused, not sure what to say to that. How would Des have felt, knowing a woman who'd served in an obvious maternal capacity to him was watching his part of the show?

"Ah." Betty's shrewd gaze said she'd connected the dots in less than a blink. "He was in it, wasn't he? With his fancy rope stuff? Oh, dear, don't look surprised. I've known about that side of his nature for a while, though we don't talk about it in great detail."

She sobered again. "At one time a whole platoon of nurses, doctors and specialists regularly prodded into Des's every day-to-day decision. Complete privacy wasn't a choice for him. It's routine to him now, but he still has to examine every choice under a microscope. Sex, exercise, job choices; anything that puts stress on his body. Fortunately, he's self-sufficient enough at this point to get by mostly with one medical care consultant. Or as he fondly calls me, 'the pain in his ass constantly interfering with his life.'"

Though Betty was keeping the conversation to generalities, it confirmed Julie's earlier suspicions, that Des's health concerns went beyond basic diabetic care.

"His rope work calms him and reduces his stress level, in one way at least." She gave Julie an unexpectedly impish wink. "I admit, I've been curious about it for a long time. Seeing him on stage, me hidden in the faceless audience, that would have been the least embarrassing option for me to satisfy my curiosity, wouldn't it? I hate I missed it."

"Well, we did tape the last show. I'd be happy to let you borrow it, as long as you promise not to post it on YouTube for millions of viewers." Julie fished out a card for her. "And if ever you want to come to another show at Wonder, we keep a few seats set by for special requests. Just tell me how many friends you'll be bringing and I'll make sure you have good seats."

Betty took the card. "How very kind of you. Oh, look out now, I've been busted. He finally noticed who was sitting with you. The first few times he looked over, all he saw was you." Betty winked at her.

Des was coming their way. Julie noted a faint tightening of his jaw when his gaze shifted between them that suggested Betty's presence wasn't entirely welcome. Did it bug him that she and Betty might be talking about him? Was he worried that one or both of them was saying too much?

Regardless, when he approached, he bent and kissed the older woman on the cheek. She put her arms around his neck, a brief intimacy and eye lock that confirmed their long history. While Julie was sure that journey hadn't always been smooth, the most enduring relationships were like that, weren't they?

"Exchanging stories?" Des said casually.

"Your ears must be burning," Julie said, just as mildly. "She was singing your praises. I'm not believing a word of it."

"Smart girl." Sitting down on the other side of Julie, so he could angle his body toward both women, he cocked his head toward the playground. "They're having a ball. And, miracle of miracles, they're actually helping. Mylo has some good carpentry skills when he's not trying to charm and hustle everyone. You here to enjoy the show?" he asked Betty.

"And to talk to you about these." Betty tapped the folder. Des's hand settled on Julie's thigh, a light grip.

"Let's do that later. I've got a lot to get done here today."

"I'm sure that's true, but we were going to talk about these last weekend. Then during the week. Then Friday."

"No, *you* thought that."

Betty's expression cooled at Des's edgy tone, but her gaze didn't leave his face. Julie sat still as a stone, not sure where to look. "You want me to do this here, in front of her?" the nurse said.

"No. I think that was my whole point."

"Then you come find me to talk before the end of the day, or I'll find you wherever you are, and I don't care who overhears the conversation."

Des's eyes narrowed. "We've already talked about this."

"We talked about it on the last set of numbers," the nurse said with strained patience. "Not these."

"They don't matter. I'm done here." Des rose. "And I'm betting your lunch break is about done."

"Desmond." Betty's tone sharpened, the way Julie suspected it would when dealing with a recalcitrant patient.

"You're not my keeper," Des snapped.

Julie suspected Betty knew—as much as she did—her sharpness was the wrong tactic to deal with Des, but the nurse's frustration level seemed equal to his. Proving it now, she rose, meeting him toe to toe.

"Closest thing you've got to one," she retorted.

Their antagonistic stance left Julie on the far end of the bench, studying Des's back and a hint of his profile, and the exasperated expression on Betty's face. Having Latin family members, Julie was used to familial conflict that was far more unsettling to those watching than those participating, but this wasn't a casual argument. It might be old, well-trampled ground, but something new had torn up the soil.

As if sensing what lay deeper than his anger, Betty softened, and touched his arm. "Des."

"Not here," he said, his jaw tight. "Okay? I'll look at it. Just...shit. And don't talk to her about this, okay? She's not part of that. No need for her to be."

He said it without looking at Julie, and strode back toward the others, clearly having no desire to engage in further conversation with either woman.

"Stubborn jackass," Betty muttered, then noticed Julie's stricken look. She sighed and pinched her brow. "I'm sorry, sweetheart. We put you in the middle of that, something I'm sure neither I nor Des intended. I didn't handle that well. I forget sometimes that he's a man grown, and doing that in front of you..."

Julie agreed it might partly be male ego, but it was also something larger, something that made her uneasy.

Betty must have agreed, because she sat back down on the bench and faced her. "I'm a good judge of people, so I took you at your word. If you want to be in his life, his health is a very big part of it, and that's the problem. He refuses to accept that being in a relationship means letting someone share that with him. I'm sure if you've become closer to him than most women do, he's given you that message."

"Loud and clear," Julie said. Betty grimaced.

"Yeah. It's debris from his childhood, where every part of his life had to be about this. Even when he realizes he's being irrational about it, it still raises its ugly head. So you have a choice. You can be on the periphery, and he'll treat you like the most special woman on the planet. I'm sure you'll have a wonderful relationship and he'll leave you with many good memories when it runs its course. But if you're okay with that, he'll have no reason to let you inside him beyond it."

Julie thought of those quiet moments together, the raw need she'd seen in his eyes. Maybe she'd gone deeper than most. Was Betty testing her to protect Des? The nurse's frankness in a world overrun by HIPPA rules about medical privacy had startled Julie, but in a quick review of what Betty had just told her, she realized she'd given Julie no real specifics. Betty's information had to do with the man himself, the kind of thing a loving, interfering maternal family member would provide. Perhaps inappropriate, but for all the right reasons.

As if picking up on her thought process, Betty nodded. "You have a special vibe to you, different from what I've felt before from his women friends. If you want to get past the pretty and romantic parts, you're going to have to push, and push hard. It will get ugly. He's a good man, you're right about that. He's also a total pain in the ass and a bully, sometimes a mean one, when it comes to protecting himself from certain things. Like reality."

She rose, picking up the folder, then hesitated. "Has he seemed okay lately? Not fatigued or eating less? Have you noticed him dropping out of sight when you normally expect to hear from him or see him?"

Julie felt a little twinge of alarm, thinking of the day she'd called him and expected he'd be on a job, only to find him sleeping in at the hotel. There'd been other days where he'd come home after work but hadn't invited her over, normally just evidence of a mature adult having a busy life.

Yet when they *were* together, it was as if being apart ten minutes was too much to him.

"Well... He texts me regularly, and my work schedule is unbelievable, so I'm not sure I can make any conclusions on that." She shifted, glancing toward Des. He was pointedly ignoring their section of the park. He wouldn't be at all happy with this conversation.

"Betty, I'm not sure if I'm comfortable..."

Betty waved a dismissive hand, taking another deep breath. "Never mind. I'm sorry. Des and I... He's never had a girlfriend, Julie, and I'll be honest. I'll trample his privacy to figure out if he's taking care of himself. I was sort of the closest thing he's ever had to a parent, and that was nowhere near close enough. He tolerates me, and I love him."

"He loves you too. It's obvious." Julie couldn't hold onto her own distress in the face of the woman's obvious unhappiness. "I do want to be part of his life. It's just, we've only been together a short time. It's..."

"It's too soon for some pushy woman to be talking to you about something this serious. You're absolutely right." Betty gave her a determined smile and held out a hand. "It was a pleasure to meet you, Julie. I think you'll be good for him. If you keep coming over, I hope you and Des will join me for dinner one night. No shop talk between me and Des. I'd love to get to know you better."

"Likewise," Julie said sincerely.

Betty took her leave without another word, pushing the folder back in her shoulder bag and walking briskly toward the parking lot. But Julie noticed there was a stoop to her shoulders that made her look older. Whatever she'd wanted to discuss with Des was weighing her down.

Julie frowned. When she shifted her gaze, she caught Des watching her. A flash of regret crossed his features, but he turned back to the job they were doing.

She thought about just leaving, but she was made of sterner stuff than that. Even if he was avoiding her, she surmised he just needed a few minutes to shake off what had happened and regain his composure.

Accordingly, she took out her tablet and went over

Harris's notes for the next thirty minutes. As she did, she kept a casual eye on what was happening with the playground and the kids. When they started planting the perennials, one of the adults waved her over. Apparently, they'd found out she was a friend of Des's and they asked her if she'd like to help. She was more than happy to do so, and put her tablet back in her car.

By the time the afternoon shadows grew long, she'd helped spread pine straw, edged the natural area with bricks, and contributed a satisfying amount to the shaping up of the park. The activities station and fort were completed by Des and his contractors. The treated wood would be painted by a different group of volunteers and next week another set of contractors would come out to resurface the basketball court. Des thanked his buddies as they headed off for their vehicles. The kids were enjoying the unpainted equipment, so when Julie returned to her bench with a free bottle of cold water and a turkey sandwich the neighbors had brought out, Des joined her.

The lapsed time since Betty's departure had erased some of the lingering hurt their argument had caused her, but he had a guarded look, as if he anticipated her hashing it out. It made her feel a little more guarded herself. However, she pushed past the desire to withdraw, paste on a bright smile and make some excuse to head off. She'd told herself she wasn't going to measure Des any longer against her past relationships. She'd experienced the pain of emotionally unavailable men, but she reminded herself Des wasn't normally like that. She refused to shut down. Instead, she initiated conversation on neutral ground, trusting they'd figure out a way to address the other from there.

"Are you supposed to take your four kids home?" she asked.

"No, their parents are coming get them at six, so I'll hang here with them until then." He paused. "Do you have to go?"

There. He'd given her an out. She met his eyes. "Do you want me to go?"

"No," he said, so simple and straightforward it released

the tension inside her. He curled his fingers around hers on her knee, tugging her hand over to his leg after he propped his ankle on the opposite thigh. Lifting her hand, he kissed her fingers. She closed her eyes, absorbing the clasp of his hand, the press of his lips.

"I was an asshole. I'm sorry, Julie. That's why I really don't want you to be a part of that. It's not my best side."

"And here I was, thinking a relationship was all about people being on their best behavior all the time."

His lips twisted wryly. "You should at least be able to demand that for the first several weeks."

"That's considerate," she said, with kindness. "But I need to say something to you, all right? Will you hear it?"

"Of course." But his eyes were wary, and she sensed that same tension in him. She put her other hand over their two clasped ones, back on his knee.

"It's okay to tell me things or not tell me things. I just want you to know you don't have to be in control all the time. I love the Dom stuff and, yes, I have a lot of sub in me, but that's not who I want to be 24/7. When it fits and it happens, it's lovely, over the top, out of this world. But I can be a partner, too."

"I know," he said after a long pause.

"Which part?"

"The over the top, out of this world thing."

She elbowed him, but the teasing helped. He slid an arm over the back of the bench and watched the kids a few minutes, not saying anything. Then he spoke. "I want you to meet someone. Okay?"

"Sure."

He whistled through his teeth, catching the attention of a pale boy with a shock of dark brown hair and striking golden-brown eyes. "Mylo, come here."

When the boy approached, he gave Julie a once-over that had her brows lifting. The kid was maybe twelve.

"Hey, don't be eyeballing my girl," Des admonished.

"Yo, you finally got yourself a hot and stacked lady, dawg. You're learning from my moves."

"And there are countless ones to learn," Des said dryly. "Tell Julie how you explain your pump to the ladies."

"Oh." Mylo lifted his T-shirt, showing her the pump holder on his belt and the injection site. The holder was black fabric with an embroidered set of fangs on it. "I do the *Twilight* soulful look on them, because I got the Edward hair, see?"

He ran his fingers through it artfully and took a seat next to Julie with a flourish. When he stretched his arm along the back of the bench, it was in front of Des's arm and close enough to press against her shoulder blades. His body canted forward while his eyes delved intently into hers. Julie shot an amused, faintly alarmed look at Des, and he gave her an encouraging wink.

"I tell them 'yeah, baby, this device, it supplies me with blood for sustenance. That way I can be close to you without the need to bite your very fine neck, except for the occasional kiss...with just a touch of my fangs.'"

"And that works?" Julie asked dubiously.

"I have a bunch of Facebook friends, all girls." Mylo straightened to fish out an honest-to-God business card. "You could be one of them. Visit my page, 'Edward Can't Touch This.'"

"Hey, Mylo, come here." The young girl with purple hair waved at him. "I need you to give me a boost on the bars. You're the tallest."

Mylo grinned. "See? Even to the young ones, I'm an addiction." He tossed Julie another outrageous ogle as he rose and made a noise that sounded like he'd tasted something delicious.

"You be good to her, Des-man, or I will."

As the boy headed back to the others, Julie choked on laughter. "Oh my God, who was that kid? His mother *so* needs to sign him up with a talent scout."

"I know it's hard to believe," Des said deadpan, "but he is a drama student." His expression became droll. "Goes to one of the magnet schools for the fine arts, which is where he gets away with such a cheesy routine."

"Hey, you put that kind of confidence behind it, a cheesy routine can make a girl's heart flutter. Add to that the hair and the charm. Wow. Glad I'm sitting down. My knees are weak."

Des made a grab for one. She scooched out of range and held up a hand. "Now, other than the fact everyone should meet that kid, why did you specifically want me to meet him?"

Des put his arm around her and drew her closer. Now that he wasn't trying to tickle her, she was amenable to it, her hand naturally falling on his thigh. "He's learned to deal with his diabetes and his life in a way a kid would," Des explained. "With imagination, by creating a role for himself. He's able to stay a kid. Though it's not always fun for him, he's got the child wonder thing happening, the belief that reality is still a choice, not a requirement."

His expression became serious. "I didn't have that. I constructed who I was on a flat concrete slab of reality and built who I was there. Rope gave me a place to step outside of that and into an alternate version of myself."

He adjusted to touch her face, slide his fingertips along her shoulder. Though he paused as if sorting out his words, he had Julie's full attention. His voice, when he spoke, was low and honest. Rough.

"When I touch you, it's different. I don't step outside myself. Instead, I go deeper in." He gave her a crooked smile. "I found wonder at last. I don't want to give up that fantasy yet, Julie, especially when I've just found it. It was why I touched you so soon after meeting you. I wanted to make sure you were real. The spider only gave me an excuse."

She looked down at her lap. "You make it really hard for a girl to be pissed at you."

Yet she only half meant it. She was still more irritated than she knew she had a right to be. Or maybe not. She couldn't quite put her finger on it but, as wonderful as hearing his words was, what had happened still bugged her, the way he'd shut her and Betty down so decisively.

"I'm sure you'll manage being pissed at me when needed," he said wryly, as if reading her mind. "I tend to bring it out in women, as you noticed with Betty."

"She loves you. Love can make you crazy." That was probably why she wasn't completely over her irritation, but she tried to shift the mood. She tipped up his bill cap and touched the fading purple streak in his hair. "I think you're wrong. I think you already discovered your child wonder side, just later in life."

"Is that your way of saying I'm emotionally immature for my age?"

She shook her head at him and sighed. "Okay, I can leave it there for right now. But when the time comes, I'll be here, Des. I won't run. I can handle it."

"That's just it." He shook his head. "I don't want you to have to."

Crap. Why couldn't he just have agreed? He had to go and push one of her triggers. *Men.*

"Why?" She got up and faced him, keeping her voice down with an effort. "Why do men have to be so proud? I get that you're a tough guy who replaces roofs for a living. You walk on your hands forty feet above the ground and drive a truck. I've been up close and personal with your balls. I know you have bigger than average ones."

His expression flickered dangerously. "It's about controlling my own life, Julie. I didn't have a mother, and I damn well proved I don't need one. Even if I did, that's not what I want from a girlfriend."

"Would you care to outline my role so I don't step outside the boundaries? Am I not allowed to care about what happens to you? Because whether or not you want to admit it, I suspect your health is a little higher on the list of things your girlfriend should know about than for the average guy."

He went to a full scowl. "The state of my fucking internal organs is not going to run my relationships or my life."

"Your vital organs *do* run your life, by keeping you alive to live it. If you refuse to acknowledge I have a vested interest in that, that I can be helpful to you, then you're telling me I'm the same as a session hookup you leave at the door of a club."

His brow creased. "Julie, that's not true. You know that."

"Yeah. Mostly." She took a breath, glancing over her shoulder to make sure their argument wasn't reaching anyone else. "I get that it takes time to let someone inside that kind of door, but you're giving me the impression if I expect it to *ever* open, I'll be waiting a hell of a long time. All because you want to hang onto control of everything behind it."

"I just told you what I want. Why can't I just have this with you for at least a little while, without having to get into all that?"

He was right. But he was also wrong. She couldn't explain why, but she was going to go with her gut, that Betty was right. She doubted Des would have let the nurse be so embedded in his life if she was an alarmist. He lived on her property, for God's sake. That couldn't be coincidental. Maybe it had boiled down to: *Okay, I'm going to need someone to help me monitor my health, but I'm choosing the person.*

"Yeah, you want the fantasy. I get it. But while Mylo is playing his charm games, he's handling what needs to be handled. Those numbers Betty is worried about sound serious. If Mylo's numbers looked like that, would you tell him to ignore them?"

"That's different."

"Is it? It doesn't sound like you have too much time to indulge reality-dodging." She tried to step back from the worry that suddenly had her by the throat, because the truth lurked in the shadows of his expression. Softening her tone, she touched his hand clenched on his knee. "Our relationship doesn't have to be perfect for it to be wonderful."

But he'd shut down. His fist didn't open, and his expression had become just as closed, his eyes shifting so he was staring stonily at the kids.

"Fine," she said quietly. "I need to get back to the theater. I'm not trying to run your life, Des. I just want to share it. If you can't let go of enough control to do that, I think we've got a bigger problem."

She wanted him to reach out to her, to stop her from leaving, but real life wasn't like that either. Each of them had to work out their own shit for this to work. So, though it hurt like a son of a bitch to do it, she picked up her things to leave. He kept his eyes on the playground, but she touched his shoulder, a quick digging in of her nails and clutch of his shirt, and then she forced herself to walk away.

"You know where I'll be."

Chapter Fourteen

Julie finished retying cables and tucked them back on the shelf of the sound cabinet. She didn't have to be doing this busy work, but supposedly it was helping her not to think about how mad she was at a certain Dom, roofer, rigger, man, child, idiot, thing.

"All about control," she said sarcastically. "Yeah, staying in control of your own death. Great. You'll still be dead. I guess you'll be in total control then. Jerk."

She sighed and wandered out to the center of the stage. Center of the world, centered mind. To her, it was the still point of the universe, a place where answers could be found. She took a few meditative breaths.

"I can't control this," she said aloud, speaking to the darkened chairs of the audience. "That's the real problem, isn't it? When you fall in love with someone, you get this mistaken notion that you have some kind of veto power over the things they'll choose to do with their lives. Maybe you do for the smaller stuff, or the stuff they can let go because they're willing to share those things. But how you live or die, I guess that falls under the single vote category. Maybe he thinks about it differently. It's a choice about how he wants to *live*."

Yeah, that was it. Sometimes she hated how the stage could speak through her so easily, making all sorts of annoying, fucking sense. Real life wasn't a play. It was supposed to be contradictory, and all about bullying the people she loved into doing what she wanted them to do because she wanted them to stay...

A lump formed in her throat, making the next words

come out thick and hard. "Stay forever."

The pain rose up to choke her, and she shoved it down. "Stop it, you moron. You don't even know what the deal is. It could be some chronic condition, not life threatening." No matter that all the information she was getting suggested otherwise. "Regardless, he's not dead yet. Not even close. Okay, yes, maybe closer than most people in terms of statistics and odds, but—"

She cut herself off at the faint vibration that went through the boards under her feet. Familiarity with the theater told her someone had entered the building. She'd locked the front, so it had to be the stage door. Her heart lifted. The rented equipment had been taken away a couple days ago, and the first read-through of *Done Right* with the cast members was tomorrow night, so she'd told Harris to take today off for a quick breather. Which meant the only one coming to see her had to be Des.

Yes, she was mad at him, but she wanted him here to yell at, to figure it out with her. To help her feel better about what he had to decide for himself, damn it. To hold him and tell him she didn't understand, but she would try, because it wasn't so much lack of comprehension of his feelings as it was fear of something happening to him beyond her control.

She moved into the wings, intending to meet him halfway. A heartbeat later she strangled on a scream as large, rough and frighteningly unfamiliar hands clamped over her throat and waist. They spun her around. A foot hooked her calf, knocking her to the floor. A knee in her back pinned her like a speared fish.

She smelled a foul odor, male sweat mixed with something else like mothballs, a noxious, untended scent. She squirmed violently and screamed, though she knew the noise dampening curtains and their lack of close neighbors made that pointless. Her hair was seized and her face slammed into the boards. Blood flooded her mouth and she was afraid bones in her face had been broken.

"Stay still and don't talk. Don't turn around and look at me, or I'll do it again. I'll keep doing it until you're still."

His voice was high and thin, at odds with the weight

pressed on her and the size of his hands. What made the falsetto terrifying was the unmistakable sound of excitement, the erratic whisper of his breath. She couldn't tell his age. She needed to fight, but he'd struck her face so hard the first time a repeat performance might crack her skull.

But you have to fight. You have to.

He didn't want her to see him. Whatever he planned, that could mean he intended to leave her alive. He had all the advantage in strength and position. Every movement sent shards of agony shooting through her back and neck. He was already putting dangerous pressure on her spine. He was a big man, she guessed, or maybe he just knew his pressure points.

"Good," he said as she became still. "Now shut up and don't talk. Don't make a sound. You do what I tell you to do. That's what you like. I've seen it, here on the stage. You like it when a man tells you what to do, ties you up. You're going to get wet for me. It doesn't matter how much you fight. I might even like it if you fight a little so I can rough you up more."

His hands were squeezing her ass, pawing between her legs. She felt sick and more terrified than she ever had, and that made her furious. But her rage would just goad him. "Yeah, you'll fight because I tell you to do it. And then I'll—"

Her attacker made a choking sound, and suddenly his weight was off her, a screaming relief. A thud was followed by a crash, then brief—very brief—sounds of a struggle, more choking.

Julie scrambled to her knees and spun. Before her was a scene she'd expect to see on stage, only this surreal drama was happening in the wings.

She recognized her attacker vaguely, and guessed he'd attended one of the shows, perhaps even sat in the front rows where her casual glance would have registered him. An overweight man with thinning blond hair and blue eyes that would have been attractive if they weren't brimming over with madness. He had a weak mouth and chin, but large hands far more powerful than the man himself looked. He was wearing blue jeans that had been opened to show a pair of wrinkled pale blue boxers beneath.

It nauseated her, but she was glad that was as far as he'd gotten. If his genitals had been hanging out, she was sure she would have vomited. As it was, she was having a hard time keeping her last meal down and not toppling over. She was dizzy from the rush of adrenaline, the blow to the face, and the wave of terror still gripping her, her mind not yet believing she was safe.

He was on his ass, legs sprawled out before him like a kid who'd fallen down on the playground. Desmond was kneeling behind him. A thick length of stage rigging was wrapped around the man's neck and pulled taut in Des's hands. While they might not be as large as this man's, she'd felt Des's strength and knew they were as strong or stronger. Particularly when fueled by the cold, still rage she saw in her Dom's eyes. She'd thought he'd been angry the day Pablo had messed up, but what she saw in Des's face now was death, plain and simple.

As the man tried to flail again, Des twisted the rope around his neck. When he choked, Des spoke in a mild tone even scarier than his expression.

"You don't want to be moving. Just like you told her, hmm? Very bad shit is going to happen to you if you fight that rope. The windpipe is absurdly fragile. Slightest amount of pressure for no time at all and you're dead. No one here's going to give you CPR, and we'll take our damn fucking time calling 911."

She had never been so glad to see someone, and especially him, who'd she'd already been hoping to see. It *had* been him she'd heard when the floor boards vibrated, because that had happened seconds before she moved to the wings. Her attacker had already been lying in wait for her, a frightening thought, but it was okay. Des was here.

Her relief made every detail about him crisp and clear. The tension in his wiry frame, the murderous fire in his eyes, the tautness of his mouth. She wanted to bury her nose in his T-shirt and take the largest breath she could to dispel the smell of the other. She felt it so overwhelmingly she knew she was in a little bit of shock, but it didn't matter. She was completely certain inhaling Des's scent alone would reverse time so this hadn't happened. But the hard shuddering of her body as she looked into a human monster's eyes told her differently.

"She wants you out of this world," Des observed. "And I'd grant her any wish she wants right now."

"I saw...they want this."

"Consent, asshole," Desmond snarled, setting off another round of choking as his grip constricted. "It was the damn fucking title of the performance."

Julie saw that Des's hold was keeping the man in an awkward position where he couldn't get his feet under him. When he started to thrash again, panic overcoming sense, she watched the rope dig into his throat.

She knew she should be doing something, but she was numb. Her eyes locked with Desmond's, and he held her in that look, helping to steady her. Blissful safety was there. He continued speaking, like the calm flow of a river.

"The more you fight," he told his wheezing captive, "The more I'll tighten my grip. Instead of you passing out and waking in jail, you'll wake in Hell with the Devil grinning at you. And that thought just makes me smile."

Shouldn't she be telling Des to stop before he killed him? Maybe she was trusting he knew what he was doing, that he wouldn't murder someone...even if that someone had tried to hurt her.

Des kept speaking to the man, though his vivid gaze remained on her face, seeing far too much. "It would make me smile because I want you dead, the way I want a good cup of coffee in the morning, a pizza on Friday night, and this woman beside me any damn time of the day. If she wants you dead, right here, right now, you're done. She's your judge, jury and maybe your executioner, if that would make her day. Hell, if it would give her no more than a second's pleasure."

The male had stopped struggling. His breath rasped, his eyes bugged out. He'd figured out his situation and his body quivered, his terrified eyes on Julie.

"So what do you say, love?" Des asked. "You hold all the power. Does he live or die?"

He was right. She wanted him dead for hurting her, for thinking it was all right. She didn't want him in the world, a reminder of how frightened and helpless he'd made her in no more than an instant, reducing her to a victim. It must have shown in her face, because Des chuckled, cold and hard. "Down you go, then."

The male's eyes rolled back, his breath rattling. Julie's breath caught and she stretched out a trembling hand, her legs still not strong enough to propel her from the floor. "I...no. Des, no."

Des eased the inert form to the floor as tears spilled down her cheeks. "I didn't mean. No..."

He put the man on his stomach and did a swift hog tie, severe enough that his chest and knees would have been off the floor if he was on his stomach. Then Des was stepping over the body, coming to her.

"I didn't want you to... I didn't mean it."

"I know that, love. He's alive." Desmond dropped to his heels and pulled her to him, holding her close. The first touch of his hands on her, the strength of his arms, was actual heaven. She'd never felt a relief so strong. "I just wanted him to piss himself when he thought you meant it. I wanted you to take back every bit of power he thought he was about to take from you."

She cried harder, and he held her tighter, but it could never be tight enough. "If you didn't mean that about being with me all the damn time, I will hurt you," she sobbed.

"Trust a woman to remember these things even in the midst of trauma and hold it against a guy." He pressed his lips to the crown of her head and answered her just the right way. "Count on it." He held her, stroked her, until the world righted itself and she had a coherent thought.

"We should call 911."

"Yeah." He'd shifted them so he had his back against the wall, supporting them. When he adjusted to dig his phone out of his pocket, he had trouble retrieving it. She shifted reluctantly, thinking she might be hampering him, but then he got it.

"Crap," he muttered.

She was still uneasy enough to react like a startled deer

to the one small expletive. Her gaze darted to the blond man, but he was still tied up. Except for a faint moan, he remained unconscious.

"Julie, love." Des curled her hand around her phone. "You don't have a signal here."

"Oh, that's right. It's awful in the stage area. It's better in the back and the lobby."

"Good. Take my phone there and call the police."

"Des..." Her faculties were sharpening rapidly, and she realized he was giving her the phone because he wasn't able to dial the number himself. His hand was shaking, and a quick look at his face showed he was pale. She put her hand on his neck and it was clammy. "You're hurt. He hurt you. We need an ambulance."

"No, we don't." He said it forcefully, and started coughing. Catching her wrist, he gripped it hard enough to hurt.

"I'm hypoglycemic. Can you do exactly as I tell you?"

She was still shook up from her ordeal, but in a heartbeat, her concern for him gave her a different focus. While she wasn't glad for the reason, she seized the opportunity with both hands. "Yes, of course. Tell me what to do."

"What every Dom loves to hear. Go call the police. Then bring me the black case in the front seat of my truck. Don't rush. You're still not steady on your feet." His brown eyes held hers, his mouth taut. "Make the call, get the case and come back."

She looked toward the man. "He's not going anywhere," Des assured her, a hard note to his voice. "Houdini couldn't shake that tie."

She believed him. She was also getting more worried about Des, because he'd slumped down against the wall as if he lacked the strength to hold himself in an upright sitting position. The shaking was worsening. She scrambled to her feet, clutching the phone. He caught her jeans leg, drawing her attention.

"911 first," he reminded her. "Police. Not ambulance. Unless you need one."

He knew her too well. She'd intended to go to the truck

first, to take care of what was happening to him, but he was right. The police were the most important thing, especially since she was going to ignore him and request an ambulance. She'd say it was for the bad guy, that she wasn't sure if he was hurt or not. If Des needed one, it would be here. He might insist the paramedics look at her in retribution. She was okay with that, as long as he had the help he needed.

She hurried toward the back entrance, not wanting to be away from him any longer than necessary, though she suppressed a shudder as she passed the shadowed areas she was sure her attacker had used to conceal himself until he'd found the optimal time to pounce.

She dialed 911 while rushing out to the truck. The small black case was there, next to his usual backpack. She told the 911 operator what had happened and that the police and an ambulance were needed.

"All right, ma'am. Stay on the line and stay where you are—"

"I can't. My diabetic friend is hypoglycemic and I have to go back to him. I'm going to lose the signal there. The police can come in the side door. I'm leaving it propped open. We're in the stage area."

She cut the connection. The operator would wisely tell her to stay outside where it was safe, where her attacker wasn't. But the operator didn't know how effective Des was at tying someone up, especially when he wanted it to be intensely uncomfortable and impossible to shake. Maybe it was petty of her, but she was glad he'd made it uncomfortable.

As she went back through the side door, she thought of the attacker's footprints being forever imprinted on the floorboards of her theater. She wasn't going to stand for that. She'd get a voodoo doctor or witch to cleanse the place. She normally didn't go for the New Age stuff, but it sounded like a good idea. There was a Wiccan craft store in Huntersville. She'd have someone come and burn sage or something.

Stop babbling, Julie. She flew back toward the stage area and then jumped back, almost landing on her ass with a little shriek as her attacker raised his head, gazing at her blearily. "Bitch," he snarled. "You better let me go or—"

"Or what?" Des came looming out of the shadows, shoving the guy's head back down to the boards with his foot. His skull made a resounding thump. She had no idea how Des had managed to get up, because he looked like a walking corpse. The shaking was affecting his whole body, but his eyes were feverish, glittering as he put the sole of his shoe on the man's throat and leaned his weight there. The man choked, tried to writhe away, but Des wouldn't let him go.

"Des," Julie said sharply, but Des didn't respond to her, holding the man's frightened gaze with one as pitiless as a shark's.

"Apologize," Des snapped. "For calling her a bitch. For all of it."

The man strangled as Des put more weight on his carotid. Julie lunged forward and caught Des's arm. He was still clammy. It was as if suddenly he'd become an old man before her eyes, but an old man still more than capable of dealing with this.

"Say you're sorry," she snarled at the man.

"Sorry," her attacker rasped, and Julie was able to pull Des away, probably because he almost fell backwards. She helped him into a seated position against her podium.

"Police?" he said hoarsely.

"They're on their way." She popped open the box and saw a syringe and vial. "What is this?"

"Glucagon. Because I can't... Christ, I'm sorry, love. I'm going to pass out. Just follow...instructions. Turn me on my side in case I...throw up."

Her gaze flew up to his face. It was as if he was speaking through cotton. His eyes rolled up in his head, and he folded over to the floor almost gracefully.

"*Des. Des.*" She looked down at the open kit. Syringe, vial. Note. Unfolding the note, she read it quickly.

Glucagon Kit: In case I pass out, follow kit directions to inject under my skin. Nothing to it. Just pinch up some loose skin and stab. I won't mind. If I'm not back in 15 minutes, do it again. Don't let me die if you can help it, but don't worry if I do. It was bound to happen eventually. If all goes well, I should be back in a few minutes. Have juice and PB crackers standing by.

Finding a loose skin part on Des was no easy task, but after she injected the liquid into the vial of powder and mixed it with shaking fingers, she realized the looseness of his jeans gave her access to the upper rise of his buttock. She injected the medicine, afraid she was hurting him, because she'd never done anything like that before, but he didn't stir. Her heart hammered nevertheless, because she wasn't sure if she was doing it right. She wasn't sure of anything. She wished the police and ambulance would get here, now, now, now.

"Shithead gonna die," the man said sullenly. "And if he don't, I'm gonna sue him for trying to strangle me. I—"

She didn't think, galvanized by something so primitive inside her she would have been afraid to look in a mirror. Lunging off her knees, she pulled a belaying pin for the stage ropes from its slot. She closed the distance between her and the man and swung, hitting him full in his fat, stupid mouth. She was pretty sure a tooth went flying. His lip split in a spray of blood.

"One more word, and I will say you got loose and I had to bash your fucking head in to save my life," she growled, brandishing the pin over him. "Got it?"

His eyes were white with fear. She spun back to Des, kneeling next to him and dropping the pin. Rethinking that, she jumped back to her feet, ran to her mini fridge and came back with a juice box. She freed the straw with shaking fingers, stabbed it into the box, and put it to the side. Easing Des's head into her lap, she stroked his hair away from his face, and thanked God when she heard the sound of sirens.

By the time the police found their way through the stage door and assessed the scene, Des was stirring. The two paramedics split up, one checking their culprit and one coming to her.

After checking the attacker out, the EMT informed the police the suspect could be taken to the station. The police hauled him to his feet and removed him, after taking an extra few moments to figure out how to get Des's rope off him. Except for feeling a relief like a weight off her chest, Julie paid little attention to the departure of the suspect. Or to the young police officer trying to draw her away from Des to talk to her about what had happened. When he realized he wasn't going to succeed until they'd figured out Des's situation, he stepped back to wait.

Des was lucid enough to explain his medical condition. "I'm good, man," he told the EMT. "Not my first rodeo. She took care of me. Just got stressed out like a fucking pansy and my blood sugar took a nose dive while the blood pressure went through the roof."

"You still managed to save the girl." The EMT was a friendly, shrewd-looking middle-aged man with blue eyes and brown hair shot with gray. "I suppose you know you should be wearing a medical ID bracelet."

"I should do a lot of things."

The EMT chuckled. "Yeah, my wife says I should eat less red meat and exercise more, and she's right. Doesn't mean I do it. But both of us should think about it, because you have a pretty girl who cares about you, same as I do."

He still insisted on taking Des's vitals and monitoring him while the police officer finally coaxed Julie a few steps away to get her side of the story. Then he had her wait in the wings with another officer while he did the same with Des. When he gestured to her to come back, she immediately returned to Des's side, taking his hand. His hold was less strong than it normally was.

"Hey, John," the EMT said. "Before you go, can you help me get this guy moved?"

Des wouldn't consent to an ambulance ride or a hospital visit, but Julie had mentioned she had a bed in back. The EMT shot Julie a reassuring look as the policeman moved forward to assist. "Your friend is an old veteran at this. His numbers are climbing again, which means you did all the right things. He's going to be weak for a little while, so we'll get him into the bed in the back and he can stay there until he's fully recovered."

The two men lifted Des, supporting him on either side, and she guided them to her dressing room apartment, where they laid him down on her mattress.

John had a couple follow up questions for her. She pulled a chair up next to the bed and answered them. She'd thought Des was out of it again, but as she relived the whole situation, his hand closed on hers. It was warmer now, and stronger, and though she chided herself for her weakness, she was glad of the support, since her hand was shaking in his. He noticed.

"You kicked his ass," he said. "Don't be doing that trembling, damsel-in-distress shit."

John smiled. "Seems like you both did a good job of taking care of each other."

"Well, she didn't have any choice," Des said dryly. "I was the one who fainted."

While he'd been forthcoming about his chokehold, she suspected they'd both left out the part where he'd given her the choice of killing the guy or not. She had told the officer she'd hit the man while he'd been tied up. She said in the heat of the moment he'd threatened her boyfriend and she wanted to be sure he couldn't get loose. She wasn't going to let herself worry about any of that now. There was plenty more to occupy her.

The EMT and policeman finally took their leave. As she followed them to the side door, the EMT gave her his card. A quick glance told her his name was Ryder. It almost made her smile, since one of her favorite Disney heroes was Flynn Ryder of *Tangled*.

"That has my cell number on it," Ryder said. "If anything comes up that really worries you, and he won't let you take him to an urgent care, you can give me a quick call. I don't live far from here and I get off shift in another hour."

"Thanks," she said. Going with her usual impulsiveness, she hugged him. "Thanks so much. To both of you," she added to the police officer.

"Don't hug the rookie while he's armed," Ryder advised. "Grateful women scare him."

John snorted. "I'm going to issue a parking ticket to that ambulance out there, ma'am. I think he's parked illegally."

He went outside, Ryder following. As she watched them

banter, and Ryder re-joined his partner in the ambulance, she was as grateful for the calming effect of their teasing as for their help.

It wasn't quite enough, though. When she closed and locked the door, she leaned against it, discovering the need to hold onto something solid and inanimate, something that wouldn't say a word about the things that gripped her and made her shake, spill a few more tears. She needed to call Madison and let her know what happened. As the theater owner, she'd be getting a copy the police report. But maybe that could wait a few minutes.

Calmer now, she returned to her room to find Des sitting up. She hurried over to him. "What are you doing? He said you need to lie down."

"I'm good. I want to sit up." He eased her away from him, making it clear he wasn't going to take any coddling. The rejection, as unintended as she was sure it was, stabbed her, because she needed to be touching him. She needed him touching her, but she didn't want to make him feel like he had to take care of her right now.

"It's a bitch, isn't it?"

He was watching her face, all those conflicts chasing themselves over her far too transparent features.

"What is?" she ventured.

"Having a guy rescue you from the bad guy and then pass out so you end up having to watch over him. It's as bad as a Dom walking away to get a beer instead of doing aftercare."

"No, it's not like that." She deliberately shifted so she was closer to him on the bed, hip to hip. He couldn't move farther away without falling off or standing up.

"You're kind of missing the point," she said. "You passed out because you expended all that energy protecting me. You saved me from the bad guy. And then you were nice enough to time the faint for after it all happened. It proved to be a good distraction. I didn't become one of those hysterical, weepy females in front of the police and EMTs. They'll go back to the station and say 'Wow, we wish all our victims of criminal violence were as cool as she was.'"

He slid his arm around her. "You remember the day I

said I don't really think about life having worst moments?"

"Yes, I remember."

He put his forehead against her temple. "When I heard you scream, I think that may qualify as one of my worst moments, not knowing if I could be strong, brave or smart enough to help you."

She lifted her head and put both hands on his face. She'd thought his hypoglycemia was a direct result of the physical stress of holding the man in that stranglehold. While that had been part of it, she realized the main cause had been far more internal. Like her, he'd likely never been in a situation like that in his whole life. He'd come to her defense with no weapon to hand except what he knew how to do with rope. He hadn't known if it would be enough, or if he'd be overwhelmed and become a second victim. Seeing all that, understanding he'd been perhaps as scared as she was, for different reasons, made her put her arms around him now and hold on, giving as much comfort as she received.

"You were everything I needed you to be, Des," she said. "And even if you hadn't been able to overwhelm him, the very fact you risked your life to try and help me meant everything."

"Though our shared final thought would have been, 'Why didn't I—or he—dial 911 before rushing in to help? Dumbass.'"

She held him tighter. "You're such a goof. But that's a very good point. Next time I'm the victim of a crime, please remember to do that."

"I have it permanently branded on my brain."

She laid her head on his shoulder and together they let out an unplanned synchronized sigh, which made Des chuckle.

"You're no victim," he said, pressing a kiss to the crown of her head. "I heard that part where you said you hit him with that rolling pin thing. Remind me not to piss you off when you have that close to hand."

"It's a belaying pin. And you need to teach me that hogtie thing."

He snorted. "I'm not sure if that's safe. I might piss you

off someday."

"You already have, and do, regularly. It doesn't matter. I still love you."

"Same goes. Speaking of which, why was the fucking side door unlocked if you were in there by yourself?"

She shook her head. "Because I was stupid. Because I was hoping you'd come to see me and say you were sorry, and I imagined this romantic thing where I'd look up and suddenly see you standing there, and you'd say something perfect. If you had to call me ahead of time and ask me to open the door, it would have ruined the scene."

"Hmm." He blew a short puff of air on her brow, stirring the tendrils of hair there. "For my future sanity, let's agree that you won't ever again compromise your safety to preserve the integrity of your internal theater productions."

"Deal."

"Good." He grunted. "As soon as I have you tied up again, I'm going to beat you. Just to make myself feel better."

"Okay. Can we stop talking about it right now, though?"

"Okay." He squeezed her. It still wasn't his normal strength, but it was getting closer. He felt solid, and he wasn't quivering any more. She curled her fingers around his hand, thinking about how he'd said he touched her hands so often when she was tied up to make sure they weren't cold, among other reasons. His had been too cold, but now they were feeling more like his normal temperature.

"Are you all right?" she asked, hoping he wouldn't get mad.

"Yeah. You took care of me just the way I needed, love." He sighed. "I guess you proved your point, about my girlfriend needing to know more about my health than the average person."

"I had to go to extraordinary lengths to say I told you so. Hope you appreciate me arranging for that sexual predator to break into the theater." Her voice broke a little as it hit her once again, what could have happened if Des hadn't come. Rape. She would have been raped. Possibly worse.

"Sshh, hey. It's done. You're good."

"So does the passing out thing happen that often?" At his curious look, she gave him a crooked smile. "Figure I'd take advantage of my vulnerable position to find out more about this stuff, when you can't get mad about it."

He closed both arms around her this time, holding her firmly against him. "You are a silly, amazing girl. And a pain in my ass. No, it doesn't happen that often. A situation like that, or a day when things just don't work right, sometimes it can bring on an attack too fast and I need someone to inject me. But it's rare. I know my body pretty well."

"Don't be selfish. I'd like the chance to get to know it pretty well myself. I didn't like your note," she added on a more serious note. "'*It was bound to happen sometime.*'"

He met her gaze. "We're all going to die, love. I don't know anyone who's gotten out of this life alive."

She'd never met someone so matter-of-fact about dying. On one hand, it gave her a sense of what living with that knowledge had been like for him. But she was going with her gut and, even if it twisted in knots at his words, at all the emotions they could be concealing, she let it guide her.

"But that's not what you meant. I can't put my finger on it, but you're different, aren't you? You're more..."

She didn't say "fragile," because it didn't quite fit. He was strong, and more than capable. But he had a disease she was fairly sure he knew was getting the best of him. The day he'd told her she had a choice of whether to go forward with him or not, knowing his health would be a factor, he hadn't directly implied it, but she knew now it had been there.

Plenty of diabetics lived into old age. Des didn't expect to be one of them.

He didn't answer her question, but she hadn't expected he would. "Want to go back to my place tonight?" he asked, pressing a kiss to her head again.

"Do I have a choice?"

"Do you want one?"

She'd intended her question as a jest, but it came out a little serious, so that his response had an edge. When she lifted her head, his jaw was tense.

"I didn't mean it like that," she said softly. "I mean...I was looking for my Dom. What he would say if I asked him that."

His jaw relaxed slightly. "No, you don't have a choice. I don't want you out of my sight right now."

"Good." She wrapped her arms around his torso. "The feeling's mutual."

Chapter Fifteen

She drove his truck, since he wasn't up for driving yet. He told her he'd bring her back in the morning on his way to work, though she wondered if he'd be recovered enough to work by then. When they reached his place, he stripped his clothes and fell in the bed, but when she paused before joining him, not sure how to explain what she needed, he already knew. He gripped her wrist and drew her close enough to kiss her palm.

"Go take a shower, love. Scald it all away. But bring your ass back to this bed. I'd like to have your soft body curled against me sooner rather than later."

A shower was exactly what she wanted, but she sat on the bed, stroking his hair and the side of his face, until he fell asleep. It only took moments.

She did want a shower and she took a thorough one, scrubbing her attacker's touch away, but she wanted to be with him even more, so she didn't linger. When she came back to the bed and laid down with her head on his chest, her arm around him, he was resting so deeply he didn't stir.

She dropped off into a sleep, uneasy, but holding tightly to him, lulled into unconsciousness by his heartbeat.

When she woke, she was alone, but he had a small house. She found him quickly. The door to what she'd thought was a closet was ajar, and a dim light was coming from the opening. She left his bed, wrapping the throw blanket at the foot over the oversized gray and red Wilder Hardware T-shirt she'd donned for sleepwear over her black cotton panties.

The room was almost a third of the size of his other

living quarters, perhaps initially intended to be a small carport for the guesthouse and later enclosed to form this room. She wondered if he'd done the work, and thought maybe he had, because the room was custom fitted for his needs. The walls were cedar paneling, and strong parallel beams crossed the ceiling. The faint fragrance of oil pointed her to several bottles. She expected he used the oil to keep the many loose coils of ropes hanging on the wall in good condition.

She passed along the wall, trailing her fingers through a waterfall of multiple colors and materials. Jute, hemp and cotton. He had a couple of nylon coils, though those were rare, because they slipped too much for the type of rope bondage he preferred. She'd paid attention the night they went to the club with Madison and Logan, when Des had told her a lot about the different types of rope that were being used, and who cared for their rope properly and who didn't.

The various hooks hanging from the ceiling for suspension work amused her, because above several of the hooks he'd fastened clip-on animals: monkeys, bears, a pink kitten. She touched a panda and sent it swaying.

But those were quick impressions, because what she really wanted to see was him. He was oiling one of the ropes at a rectangular table. The utility light over the table was the source of the room's illumination, but it was enough to give her an agreeable view of him.

He was wearing a loose pair of black jeans and nothing else. Her gaze slid over the sunburst in the middle of his back and the tattoos wrapped over his arms. He'd tied his hair back so she was able to enjoy the sharp planes of his cheek bones, the sensual lips, the flicker of his thick lashes and those compelling, brown eyes as he looked her way.

No post-traumatic nonsense interfered with the little spurt of need and yearning she felt at his expression. He'd been right. Seeing her attacker helpless and frightened, carried away in a police car, had gone a long way to making her feel in control, not a victim. John had said he already had a record, so it was likely this could put him in prison for years.

She thought of how Des had held her right afterward, his thorough aftercare, despite the physical reaction she was sure he'd felt stealing over him even then. Now that she'd had time to think about it, she was quietly amazed at the courage it had taken to do what he'd done.

He'd handed her control over the man's life or death. Even though rationally she knew it was Des's strength and direction that had guided things, that key moment had totally belonged to her. She was also sure if she truly had wanted the man dead, Des would have done it. Which made him a little scary, but maybe in the right ways. Marcus had that quality to him in even more upfront ways. However, whereas this had been a first experience for Des with this kind of violence, she'd always suspected Marcus's background had made it a far more common occurrence for him.

She studied Des as he turned his attention back to the ropes, perhaps sensing her need to orbit him without a lot of conversation yet. Her throat was still sore, but that wasn't the reason. The silence was comfortable. She drew closer, looking at the four different coils of rope he had in front of him and an open notebook which had sketches and scribblings, clippings. She saw orchids, flowers and trees, cutouts of models from glitzy magazines in different positions, juxtaposed with his sketches of rope poses and notes about the possibilities. At the party she'd heard people use the term rope artist. That was what he was.

"How did you get started in this?" she asked. "Why didn't you end up being into fire play, or get a shoe fetish?"

He smiled faintly. "You make it sound like getting a cold. I like a woman's foot in a high heel as much as the next guy. But what I imagine when I see your foot in an extremely high heel is tying your feet in the same position without the shoes. I'd bind them over your back so I could tickle the soles with a feather and watch you squeal and squirm. Maybe put you in a vat of Jell-O to see you get all slippery."

"Your mind goes into some very odd places," she said, elbowing him. He put his arm around her. "Will you answer the question?"

"I will, though I'm not really sure I have a good one. When I got into BDSM, it was a pretty mundane entry. A friend suggested I go with him to a couple play parties. He thought it would interest me, since vanilla relationships didn't really grab me. The first part of my life was a little too off the wall. I guess he realized my sexual interests would be the same."

She smirked at him and he crossed his eyes at her. "I did play with the fire stuff for a bit, and I'm not bad at it. Whip play, the precision of it was cool, and what guy doesn't want to pretend to be Indiana Jones? But I kept going back to the rigging. It absorbed me at all levels, sex and intellect, and it also quieted the voices."

He paused. "You hear that a lot in BDSM, but I think it applies to whatever thing you find in your life that grounds you. Like you and your stage. Or a singer when they're singing, a writer when they're writing. So that was how it happened. Maybe because I'd spent a lot of my early years tied up in knots over the physical crap, making sense of knots and tangled rope was soothing to me, kind of a symbolic taking control of the lines."

"You've thought this through." She considered him. "You think most things through, though."

"Yeah. I do." He held her gaze, and she knew he was talking about way more than rope. "I'm okay, love. All good now."

She pressed her lips together. She wasn't so sure about that, but she wasn't going to let this moment be about that, either. Seeing it, he continued in a casual tone.

"Now the Dom part, that was easy as breathing." He winked. "Whenever I was with a woman, I needed to take complete control. I had a couple bad experiences with women totally not into Dom/sub stuff before I figured what my issue was. Talk about awkward moments. Good women, but we were just like this..." He passed one hand directly over the other, parallel tracks going in opposite directions.

"Well, you're really good at it. I'm glad you figured it out. And, though I'm not sure I'll ever be completely comfortable with watching you do it as a performance or scene with another sub, I don't want you to stop doing that.

You should be able to grow as an artist. I get that."

She pointed to the cover of one of his books, where the subject was in a full Chinese split, her legs tied to a long pole that ran from one ankle to another, her upper torso flat on the ground and chin propped up on a chin rest. "I can't do that, and will never be able to. I don't want to hamper your art. I just...I know there's always a sexual and intimacy component to it. There has to be, for the right energy to surround it. I just don't know if I can handle you actually having sex with her, of any kind, and go forward together."

There, she'd finally said it. After what she'd faced earlier in the night, it wasn't as hard to get out, but she still hesitated to look at him right away. But Marcus was right. She wasn't a coward. She wasn't ever again going to settle for less than what she wanted. The timing might seem odd to Des to bring this up, but maybe she was still riding the self-empowerment Des had given her at the theater. She wasn't in the mood to wait. She was ready to put it to rest once and for all.

Des touched her chin, guiding her attention up to him. As he did, that grip shifted and he was holding her face firmly. "You don't have to worry about that. I've found who I want to be with, Julie."

She let a hint of a smile play on her lips, though his look gave her that lower vitals quiver. "Uh, just for verification, me, right?"

He blinked once, the sternness of his lips easing a fraction. "Unless Marilyn Monroe comes back to life, yes. Though I think your similarity to my fantasy Marilyn pulled me toward you from the first. Who's to say you're not a reincarnation?"

"She was a blonde," Julie said, amazed at being compared to the bombshell.

"She was a brunette who dyed her hair blond," he corrected her. "And I love your brown hair, so I'd rather it stay that color." He drew her attention down to the ropes, where one of her restless hands was fingering the coils. "Would you like to try doing a form on me?"

Her gaze snapped back up to him, and she saw he was

serious. Julie tangled her fingers in the coil of jute. Her kneejerk reaction would have been no, but as her attention coursed over his bare upper torso, she had a different answer. "Can I? Is that weird? I don't have any desire to top."

"It's not weird at all. Come with me and bring that rope you're touching. It should be long enough for what we'll have you try."

She did, unaccountably shy but very intrigued. She followed him to the center of the room where they stood on a cushioned mat in their bare feet. He turned and faced her.

"Okay, a rigger always coils his rope so it can shake out with minimum tangles and so he knows where the bight is, the folding-in-half point." He took it from her to show her, shaking the rope loose. His deep voice took on a different cadence when teaching, but because he was teaching her, there was an intimacy tagging the syllables that increased the density around them.

"That's because most shibari forms utilize doubled-over rope," he continued, "and that's what we'll be doing here. I'm going to guide you through a diamond pattern harness on my upper torso, all right?"

"It won't restrict your hands, will it?" She pinkened a little under his look.

"Not at all. I'll be able to touch you as much as I want. I'd never deprive myself of that." His fingers closed over hers on the rope as she followed his direction. "Here's your bight. Slide that around my neck, as if you were helping me tie a tie. Like I was one of those guys who goes into his office in a suit every day."

"I could never imagine you that way. You belong on your rooftops."

He touched her face, running his hands down her arms as she guided the rope around his neck and let both ends fall down his front and drag the floor.

"There's so much of it."

"About eight meters, which is a good length for this tie. Don't look worried. This is straightforward. You can't hurt me. Okay, I'm going to guide you through what we call a stopper knot, five of them, down the front of my body."

It took her a couple tries to figure it out, but he was patient and it was a fairly simple knot, according to him. Now that she thought more closely about the ones she'd seen him do, she realized the knots could look entirely different, even if they seemed to serve the same function.

"Like different words to say the same thing, in a bunch of different ways," he explained. "There's a poetry to rope, just like there is for spoken language."

At another time, she might have summoned a Yoda or Grasshopper joke, but the timbre of his voice, stroking her with every word, didn't encourage levity. She was content, marinating in a simmering arousal.

"Lots of rituals emphasize binding, tying and knots," he pointed out. "What you said to me a few minutes ago told me that you want to claim me as your own, exclusively. Right?"

She met his gaze. "Yes."

His brown eyes glinted with satisfaction. "I may be a Dom, but directing you to do this, seeing how much pleasure you're finding in it, and picking up on those undercurrents? You think it seems weird, you wanting to do this, but nothing is farther from the truth."

He cupped his hand under her hair, stroking. "When the final knot is done," he said huskily, "I plan to take over, Julie. You'll understand then what you doing this does to me."

He tightened his arm around her waist, holding her close to him. She'd dropped the blanket so she was just in the T-shirt. He brushed a kiss over her mouth, then eased her back. He was being so gentle with her. After the earlier events of the night, she suspected he wasn't wanting to put any kind of pressure on her, but her body was starting to stir and crave pressure. His pressure.

"Okay, once you get to the fifth knot, you're going to split the rope ends around my cock and balls, thread the rope between my legs and take it to the bight around my neck in back. You'll thread the two ends under that."

As she worked, her fingertips brushed his skin. She was standing so close to him, his head bent over hers as he watched her. "Can you be naked?" she asked when she reached the fifth knot. "I'd like to see how that looks. If that's okay."

He folded his arms over her back, sliding down to thread his fingers into her panties to grip her ass.

"If you take off that shirt so you're wearing just these. I do love your tits."

"I don't get to have the upper hand, me all dressed and you not?"

"Is that what you want to experience right now?" He posed the question seriously.

She shook her head. "I guess I was just curious if that would make you antsy."

"Who's in control has nothing to do with clothes. Not for this. Answer the question, Julie. Are you wanting to top right now?"

"No. Definitely no."

"Then don't ask me questions to test that. It means you're feeling nervous. Follow my directions, trust me, and let that go. I'll take us both where we want to be."

"Okay." As always during this, he spoke without irritation. He wasn't angry with her, just laying down clear rules of engagement. "Question, though. What would you do if I didn't follow directions on purpose, specifically to test you?"

"Bratting?" His eyes gleamed in a way that caused erotic flutters. "I'd put you on the ground and hogtie you, and I'd attach the rope to a hook so your knees were off the floor and you'd feel the strain. You'd get hot and wet over it, but you'd also have to apologize to me for trying to run things before I let that tension loose."

"Oh," she said faintly. "Good to know."

"Shirt?" he reminded her, eyes sweeping over her breasts straining against the fabric of the T-shirt. "Though seeing your nipples get bigger and stiffer under there is a pleasure, that's another man's shirt, and I want it off."

"Oh." She hadn't even thought of it that way. "It's one Thomas loaned me when I was visiting him and Marcus in North Carolina. It's his family's hardware store. He said I could keep it. It reminded me of my visits there when I was back in New York."

Initially, she'd liked it because it smelled like Thomas, a reinforcement of that reassuring, platonic crush she had on both him and Marcus, her surrogate family and best friends. Something way too hard to explain right now, when the only scent and touch she wanted were from the man in front of her.

Pulling off the shirt, she set it aside. He brought her closer again with a look and caressed her breast, teasing the nipple with his thumb. Then he let her go to detach the pump and open his jeans. He left them that way—a provocative look since there was nothing under them— as he fished a piece of medical tape and the cap for the cannula out of his pocket. He'd started to carry those two things there regularly, so that when they wanted to be intimate he could quickly cap the line and tape it against his body where it wouldn't distract either of them any more than necessary. It was little different from the pause for a condom, but she was very glad they didn't have to worry about that anymore.

That taken care of, he pushed the jeans off his bare ass.

He was temptingly erect, but he took control again, continuing to instruct her on how to tie him in the rope. She gave herself the indulgence of caressing his testicles and brushing his cock frequently as he had her run the two ropes between his legs, leaving a fist width of slack beneath his balls.

"It will draw up as we continue. Now let's do the diamonds."

She thought how it worked was cool, passing the rope under the bight, as he called it, at the back of his neck, and bringing the ends under either of his arms to thread them between the double strands in front. As she pulled those two strands apart, it created a diamond pattern between the first two knots. Another wrap around back, and then back to the front, creating another diamond, all the way down his upper torso.

He had his head tilted, watching her. On a whim, she let go of the rope to pull the band loose holding his hair and threaded her hands through it, spreading it out on his bare shoulders. He nuzzled her cheek and she closed her eyes, rubbing her cheek in his hair, against his face, showing affection the way animals did, conveying feelings without words. The motion denoted trust, intimacy, connection. He rubbed his sandpaper jaw against her, and she giggled, pushing him away with her nose, but she let her lips caress his throat before returning to the tying.

When she reached his cock and testicles and created a wider diamond that framed them, the horizontal lines running over his hip bones, she caressed his erect shaft, and ensured the lines running between his legs weren't pinching. He was right. As she'd created the diamond pattern, the slack in the rope had disappeared. She guided the doubled strand between his buttocks, letting her fingers play there, her other palm sliding along his lower back, up to the layers of muscle covering his ribs. Her fingertips traced the bumps of his spine. The man didn't have a spare ounce on him. Maybe she needed to consider the roofer diet plan, since she liked food so much.

He directed her on how to tie the form off in the crisscross pattern she'd created on his back. She still had some rope left, but he agreed without words on a momentary break, so she could lean full against him, feeling that network of rope press against breasts and nipples, her abdomen against his buttocks. She let her hand roam over him in front, exploring the harness she'd created. She closed her eyes, savoring that powerful connection, just as he'd described, and understanding why the act itself could be as powerful for a sub as for a Dom.

He put his hands over hers, increasing the sense of joining. She dragged her lips over his back. Overwhelmed was the word that so often came to mind when she was with him, but it was like being in a boat alone but not afraid, drifting in the midst of a big, powerful ocean. An ocean she didn't fear because she belonged to those waters. She could sink deep, deep down in them and never be lost or forgotten, merely held, rocked. Weightless, unbound by anything but the water itself, a hold she never wanted to escape. She slid around to his front, and found his eyes on her.

"Let's take care of the rest of the rope, all right?"

He directed her on how to draw the strands up his back and forward again, then create a network of rope that framed his shoulders, biceps, elbows and wrists. The excess she wrapped over his hands like an open glove. Every placement of the rope highlighted that part of his body, and she understood what he'd meant, about how rope tying emphasized curves and the molding of flesh. The isolating quality of the rope made her look at his many parts as unique treasures, as well as part of the whole.

She trailed her fingers over his arms and the wraps of rope over his knuckles, before she stepped back to look at her handiwork. Diamond patterns covered his chest and abdomen, while small twists and stopper knots followed the line between his chest wall and collar bone out to the round part of his shoulders. The additional rope framed his strong arms in the lattice design like he'd done on her legs at the party, ending with the triple wraps over his callused hands. Her gaze slid down to the diamond of rope framing his erect cock. Yes, she'd say he'd fully recovered from their ordeal at the theater. He seemed to be having a thrillingly virile post-trauma response to her being threatened.

Her reaction was equally primal. She wanted to go to her knees, take him in her mouth, and he saw it. "You'll be doing that," he said with dark pleasure. "But first, it's your turn. Put your arms above your head and bend your elbows so your hands are at the base of your neck. I'm going to do a two-hand tie behind your head. Curl your fingers up in a half fist facing each other. Not interlaced. Just put the knuckles against each other."

She did that under his appreciative gaze as her breasts lifted and her rib cage tilted. He went to his table and brought back another coil of rope. As he shook it out, he moved behind her. Her gaze drank in the sight of him moving in that net of rope, the way it slid along his firm flesh and rippling muscles, the framing of his erect cock.

His hands on her were caressing but swift, conveying a male demand and urgency. She felt that urgency, too. She'd never get tired of the tide of feeling—sexual, soothing, exciting, emotional—when he tied her.

He put three wraps beneath her breasts, and used them to anchor the wrist tie that kept her elbows by her ears and pointed toward the ceiling. Her half clasped hands were resting at the base of her neck. Returning to her front, he hooked his fingers in the wrap beneath her upward tilted breasts, displayed for his hot male pleasure.

"On your knees," he ordered.

His hold steadied her descent and, once she was there, he didn't waste any time. He fed his cock between her parted lips.

He was demanding, strength fully restored, and she got helplessly hotter and wetter. He'd run the excess rope between her legs, so one knot was pressed up against her clit and two big, thick ones were pushed between her labia, the final ones forming an inescapable friction against her rim. They all rubbed her as he worked his cock in her mouth.

She looked up at him. The rope she tied on him flexed with his movements, which meant he was feeling friction against his flesh from that harness, just as she felt it on her sensitive skin.

As their eyes locked, she couldn't look away. She was on her knees to him, her mouth stretched by his cock, the picture of total subjugation. She was all his, at his command, but she could tell he cherished and valued that more than the greatest treasure. His obvious desire spiked in a way that only triggered and heightened a thousand similar responses in her. She sucked, nipped and dragged tongue and lips over him. She worshipped his cock, his maleness, everything about him. He was her center, too.

She took him deeper as his thrusts increased, swallowing convulsively to control her gag reflex. She wanted him to be cruel, because he would always reinforce that with tender care. He was the sadistic and protective Dom who brought together the two conflicting things she'd always craved. Up until him, she'd ever only succeeded in finding men who possessed the cruelty, not the care that was supposed to balance it, bringing things full circle within the spectrum of her deepest needs.

He clasped her hair and drew her off of him, despite her

moan of protest.

"Drop your head back and close your eyes," he commanded, framing her jaw, the heel of his hand against her pulsing throat.

Shuddering from what she knew he was about to do, because she saw him grip his cock with the other hand, she obeyed.

Her pulse was crashing, her heart pounding. Her thigh muscles strained from the position and yet she lifted herself even more, presenting her upper torso as his canvas.

He grunted, his hand shifting to clasp her shoulder in a bruising grip that also held her up, giving her something to counterbalance her bowed body. As he began to release, the hot semen splashed against her breasts, throat, over navel and mons. Even in the midst of climax he was spreading that marking over her deliberately, a branding that had her cunt spasming from the possessive act.

The friction of the knots was an unbearable torment with all the other stimulation, her climax as close—and as far away—as her Master's command.

"Please," she begged as he finished. She knew he was staring at his handiwork with lust-filled eyes. He knelt before her, curled his hand around her hair and tipped her head back farther, a mute command to open her eyes and meet his demanding gaze. He cupped her breasts, stroking his release into her skin, using the friction of the ropes wrapped over his hands in clever ways as she made whimpering pleas before his unrelenting stare.

Then his hand dipped and he clasped the rope above the knot over her clitoris. He began to pull on it in tiny movements.

"Ssshhh," he said, gazing into her feverish eyes. "Feel that, love? All that power and response at my fingertips. You're like a star about to explode, aren't you?"

"Yes. Please..."

"Sssh...just feel... You want to please me, don't you?"

She nodded vigorously, and groaned as he sent another jagged shard of pleasure through her. "All right, then. Come, but let it come slow. Work with my fingers, and don't you look away from my face. I want to see every helpless look of suffering in your gorgeous eyes."

It rolled up just as he dictated it. In some distant part of her mind, it confounded her that her body's instincts would comply and obey him as unquestionably as her spinning mind did. A long, low cry split from her lips as she became rigid, her back a crescent against his grip. The climax that started at her clit connected to all those knots, to all the lines caging her body, the ropes, the nerve endings, his touch, his eyes, and she was lost in that ocean forever. She went down willingly in a swirling, somersaulting whirlpool that overtook her and turned cries into long, straining screams, especially as his fingers joined the knots in manipulating her flesh, catapulting her to a whole other level. It went up even higher as he pushed his fingers inside her, filling her, filling her so thick...but not thick enough...

"You," she gasped. "Please...you inside me. Please. Master."

She was falling, tumbling down the crest. She didn't need him inside her to complete the orgasm. She needed him to complete the feeling, make it whole and perfect.

God bless his understanding and his expertise, because the former had him responding immediately, and the latter made short work of loosening the rope between her legs and getting it out of the way. When he sheathed himself, he'd become erect enough again she felt the stretch of her body to accept him. She was an ocean herself, capable of pulling him in without resistance. Once there, she clamped down on him, squeezing him all the way to the hilt.

She moaned, replete. Since her wrists were bound yet no longer held to her back, she put them over his head and dropped them over his shoulders, fingers digging into his flesh. She was never letting go. They would swirl through the ocean together.

She could think of nothing better than being lost at sea with him.

Chapter Sixteen

"It's 9 ½ *Weeks*, if they'd done it the right way. You know, where a BDSM relationship is exciting, thrilling and healthy, not a spiral into a self-destructive loss of identity. As she wrestles with who she is, we keep the mystery element to him... Oh God, I'm just babbling. Do you think the cast liked it? Do you think the first read-through went well the other night?"

"Lila, I loved it, they loved it. Billie's here today and has skimmed it. He said he'd clear his schedule to be the torch singer in the night club scene."

"No way." Lila hugged her script to her like it was her baby, which wasn't too far from the truth.

"It's going to be like *Magic Mike XXL*," Julie said, beaming at the writer. "They fucked up the first one and they did the second one right. This is fabulous. The BDSM club scene is going to be spectacular. Brace yourself. Harris is friends with the lead singer of Mercury Rising, a really popular rock club band here." Julie added that, since Lila was from Asheville and might not be familiar with the music scene in Charlotte. "He thinks they'd be interested in doing a cover of 'Hurts So Good' as a live music performance during that part. If they agree, it's going to pump up the awesomeness."

And bring in even more mainstream people to check out the theater, which had delighted Madison. It hadn't been bad news to Julie, either.

"Oh my God." Lila closed her eyes. "I know I'm being an idiot, but I still can't believe you're going to do my play. I figured when I first handed Madison the finished thing a few weeks back, that would be it. She'd hate it and I'd crawl under a rock forever."

"Typical artist." Julie gave her a droll look. "You get two more seconds to indulge your euphoria, then Harris is going to sit you down and hit you with the full reality of directing a play, which is five million details to accomplish in a six-week timeframe. Make sure you have a wig, because you will tear out your hair. Ulcers are possible. You'll love every moment of it, even as you're sure you've lost your mind."

"Sounds fabulous," Lila said with wholly idealistic enthusiasm, making Julie grin. She did love this business.

"One thing we don't have to worry about is extras for the club scenes. With the exception of one who's going on a research diving trip to Panama for three months, all of the *Consent* cast are totally on board for that."

"Terrific. I'm still so thrilled that Master Horn and his sub Cherry Blossom were such a good fit for the leads. When I saw their scene for *Consent*, I was thinking, oh my God, they would be so perfect as my leads, if they have enough acting experience."

"They handled the read-through well," Julie agreed. Gavin, or Master Horn, was a little stiff, but she and Harris would work on his acting skills, smooth those out. No one expected Oscar performances from community theater performers, but there were ways to help them be more natural in their roles.

"Harris, can you sit down with her and start getting the logistics put together?"

"You bet." As Harris escorted Lila to the front row where they had a table and chairs set up, he tossed an amused look over his shoulder at Julie, because Lila continued to gush.

Julie smiled back. It had been a daring move to make their next offering a play by an unpublished and unknown aspiring playwright within the BDSM community, but it fit with Madison's mission, so it had been put on their limited spring schedule. The community response to *Consent* had suggested that risk was well-founded. Madison had already decided to offer an eight-performance run of Lila's show.

She'd also, surprisingly, received a small handful of P&Rs—picture and resume—from area community theater players willing to give erotic performance a try. Julie had auditioned a couple of them already for secondary cast members in Lila's play, and they'd been awarded the parts. They'd participated in the read-through with great results.

Julie jumped as a hand closed around her elbow. Billie chuckled. "Why you so nervous, honey-chile?""

Julie made a face. "You know why. Marcus and Thomas are supposed to arrive today."

"That doesn't explain *why* you're nervous. You've said they're your best friends."

"I know, I know." Julie sighed. "I guess it's because they are my best friends, and I'm worried how they and Des will get along. I could say it doesn't matter, that I can love them all even if they don't get along, but we all know things like that do matter and can cause major heartburn."

"Well, I for one am hoping they get along, but not for the reasons you think. This queen has to hit the road and, if it turns into a fine, macho catfight, I'll miss quite a sight. Muscles flexing, maybe some shirts torn off." Billie affected a delighted shudder. "Promise you'll take video if that happens."

"If that happens, I'll have a few bigger concerns."

Billie went to an impressive full-lipped pout. "Just selfish. Always thinking of yourself." She winked and gave Julie a strong-armed hug. "It's going to be fine, honey-chile, you know it will. Glad I stopped in today and heard about your little play. Save me a spot to sing my torch song. If that hair band that Harris knows can't work it out, I can also shed the sequins and don leather and chains to do a rock piece. I do love me some John Cougar."

"You are a treasure. I wish you could be part of all our shows, but I can't tell you how much I appreciate what you've already done." Especially since amateur theater meant all-volunteer, and Billie received nothing but Julie's gratitude for his participation.

"I have to admit, it was far more fun than I expected. I did it initially as a favor for Logan, that gorgeous piece of sadly straight ass, but here forward, I'd do it for you. You call me if you need anything. If my tour schedule allows, I'll be here. This is going to be a good place, and a great idea. You didn't know so much about that when you first came, but you know it now. Our community needs good press, a way for people to understand what we're all about."

Billie touched her nose in a whimsical way. "Maybe when you're in between performances, I can call in some friends and we can offer a one-night show to raise funds for the theater. Or for a community charity. That's always fabulous press, doing something for charity, and it does good, so it's a win-win."

"I love that idea. I so wish you could have stayed to meet Marcus and Thomas, but they're never on time. I..."

She heard a drifting of voices coming from the front foyer and broke off mid-sentence. Her heart tripped up, that nervousness she couldn't contain, along with a surge of other feelings. Damn, she really had missed Marcus and Thomas. She'd told them to give her space because she leaned on them too much, and she'd been at a low point when she'd come to Charlotte. But that feeling had passed, and she was ready to explode with happiness at the chance to be around them again.

"Oh my God, they're here." She squeezed Billie's hands, catching his amused glance as she started to dash up the aisle. She sounded as giddy as Lila. "Oh." She stopped, looked back at him. "You should really sit down somewhere." She glanced at Lily and Harris, who had overheard the last part of the conversation, probably because her voice had gone up two octaves. "You too," she told Lila. "Marcus... It's hard to explain, but just trust me. You want to have a chair nearby."

"He's gay, right?" Lila said dryly.

"It won't matter. Believe me."

"Did I hear gay? Did I hear gay? Oh yay!" Billie combined the cheerleader singsong with a little spin.

"Calm down, baby," Julie advised. "Also married and insanely monogamous. He's married to the one coming in with him, who's a pacemaker advisory of his own."

"You are a cruel woman to dash my fantasies before I can even have them," Billie complained. "I would hate you if I didn't also love you."

With a wicked grin, Julie started to trot up the center aisle, but the two men had circled around and were entering from the stage wings. They'd likely received the direction from one of the contractors working on painting and renovating the front foyer.

Julie wasn't underselling Thomas, who was ruggedly handsome in his own right. His interestingly rough-hewn face, brown hair and eyes reminded her of a young, intense Colin Farrell. When the two men were together, the energy that bound them to one another was downright overwhelming to the senses. But Marcus...

One of the paintings Thomas had recently completed for his gallery showings showed a virile, black haired angel against a night sky. One arm was clasped around the shoulders of a naked man coiled against his lower torso as they spun through the sky together. The angel's wings were silver, his one visible eye through a thick fall of hair a vivid green. It was somehow the bull's eye point, the radiant sun center of the painting, around which everything else revolved. He was an avenger, he was Lucifer, he was the promise of punishment and salvation both.

The male twined around him was an Atlas of his race, layered in muscle. The tattoo of the world on his back enhanced the symbolism. He had his face pressed to the angel's upper abdomen, his parted lips suggesting he was on the verge of tasting divine flesh.

The original painting had auctioned for nearly fifty thousand dollars, and the dozen limited edition prints sold out at eight thousand apiece. A lot of people in the art world knew that. But most didn't know that angel had been inspired by the man Thomas loved, coming out of the wings with him now.

Marcus's dark hair fell to his shoulders, his green eyes vivid. Like Desmond, he had a graceful, panther-like way of moving, but he had more mass and muscle. Not as much as Thomas, who was muscular North Carolina farm boy through and through, but enough to give Marcus a dangerous look that wasn't entirely because of his physical fitness and regular visits to the boxing gym. He wore his usual tailored and designer clothing, which only enhanced that all-there sharpness he had.

His charisma was a ten foot field around him, and Thomas's aura intertwined with it, increasing the wattage. The easy-going handsome male artist wore faded jeans and a crisp blue fitted button down shirt that had to be a gift from Marcus, because it was upper scale designer wear. Thomas dressed neatly, a good Southern boy, but he could care less what the tag inside the shirt said, as long as it was comfortable and drew Marcus's attention.

He didn't have to worry about that. He'd been the center of Marcus's attention from the very first. Even now, Thomas was charmingly oblivious to his own appeal, though Julie was glad he'd finally realized just how much Marcus needed and loved him.

That silly line, one person completing another, was never as obvious as when she looked at the two of them. Marcus's dangerous sharpness had had an empty painfulness to it until he'd married Thomas. Whereas Thomas had nearly driven himself into an early grave when he couldn't find balance between his love for his family and his love of Marcus and his art. They'd helped one another overcome the obstacles and accept the bond that was inevitable between them.

Ironically, it was also part of why she'd finally had to escape from New York, because looking at what she wanted so much for herself every day and nearing forty without it had been too much.

That decision had brought her here, to Des. It was too convenient, too rom-com, so when she looked at it that way, it was petrifying. And that was what scared her about Thomas and Marcus's visit, wasn't it? They were the truth-finders. They would know. They could confirm she was the recipient of a miracle, or prove it a lie, and she'd be back to where she'd been before, vowing she'd never go down this road again.

Look how well that resolve had worked.

"It's so wonderful to see you two idiots." She ran up the side steps onto the stage and flung herself into their open arms, a three-way hug so welcoming, unexpected tears choked her. Their tight hold suggested the feeling was mutual. She slid back before she completely made an ass of herself, and dashed at the tears.

"Hey." Thomas caught her face, his thumb passing over her cheek. She thought he was gently admonishing her for her tears, but when he inadvertently pressed on her sore cheekbone, she flinched, and remembered.

"I told you on the phone I had a mishap on the stage. I'm always getting bumps and bruises."

"You ran face first into a wall on purpose?" Marcus asked, turning her face to study it. "Even for you, that's a little extreme."

"Okay, I didn't lie." Or rather, it was almost impossible to lie to Marcus when he pinned someone with that don't-bullshit-me look. "It *was* a mishap. A guy broke in and attacked me, some lowlife jerk who thought BDSM was an excuse to attack women. Des was here and took care of him."

"Not soon enough," Thomas said darkly.

"Well, he wasn't here when it started, but he was here before it went anywhere. That was the important thing."

She held onto both of them. It said something about how well Des had helped her get over it that she hadn't even thought about the lingering bruises on her face, but in the face of their concern and barely veiled desire to murder someone, she realized she needed to cover some ground, fast. "Seriously, guys, I'm all good. I'll tell you the whole story, but it's thanks to Des I didn't even think to mention it. Haven't even had one nightmare."

They exchanged a look. She caught the light brush of Thomas's hand over Marcus's forearm. Thomas would tear apart anyone that hurt her, but he was the one most likely to rein it back first and hear what she was saying. His touch brought Marcus down a couple notches. Still, she made a mental note to make sure no one told them about the Pablo incident. As scathing and scary as Des had been about it, she expected they'd be equal storm centers about that. And Marcus...forget it. Pablo would need a protection detail for the rest of his life.

"We have so much catching up to do," she said. "About

things way better than that. Let me introduce you to some of my other lifesavers."

She drew them over to Harris and to Lila, who came up the stairs on the other side of the stage to join them. She explained the woman's new play to them so that Lila was blushing and fluttering, her already elevated pulse rate around Marcus and Thomas probably skyrocketing. Julie knew she shouldn't take such pleasure in seeing women so unbalanced by the two, but it was one of her small joys in life.

She was aware Billie had moved up onto the stage, too, only he'd pulled a chair into the center of it. He had his impressive legs in tight jeans crossed as he cooled himself with a white cardboard fan. It was printed with large purple letters: *Baptist Mothers for Family Sanctity, Tent Revival, March 10-13, 2000.* It had to be one of his own props, though she had no idea what orifice he'd pulled it out of. Regardless, Billie hadn't wasted a good stage opportunity. Julie smothered a laugh at his bright-eyed gaze on Marcus and Thomas. "Told you," she said to the drag queen.

"Oh my my my, yes, honey-chile, you surely did. Mm-mm-mm." Billie emphasized the last syllable and rose, extending a hand. Despite his more masculine travel attire of a fitted dress shirt over jeans, he could still project his female side admirably.

"I was prepared to like you simply because you are Julie's friends, but I see so very many other reasons as well." He let his gaze travel over Marcus and Thomas appraisingly while Julie rolled her eyes. Marcus returned the handclasp before Thomas did the same.

"You must be Billie Dee-Lite," Thomas said. "Julie says you've been a lifesaver."

"I prefer to be the ass saver. So much more fun." Billie winked. "You are very special to this dear girl. So glad I got to meet two of the three fine men who have won her love. She's already won all of ours. We're never letting her come back to your godforsaken part of the world."

"Trying to keep a New Yorker out of New York is like keeping a rabbit out of a lettuce patch," Marcus advised.

"We always find our way back."

"Depends on just how tasty the lettuce is down south." Billie swept his gaze in such a provocative direction, Julie elbowed him.

"Oh my God, please behave."

"That Puritan ship sailed a long time ago, honey-chile, and it's never coming back to this port. I only welcome heathens and pirates now. Those with debauchery on their mind get tied up to a very special dick, I mean dock."

He looked at Marcus. "I'd love to tie this one up, but I can tell he does the tying. That'd make my heart go pitty-pat if I was a sub, like little Harris over there. But this one..." He let his attention slide over to Thomas and Julie hid a smirk as Thomas damn near blushed. He was very much Marcus's submissive, but he wasn't into being public about it. "He likes it when you take control," Billie purred, "and that is a morsel that just begs to be devoured."

"That ass is taken," Marcus warned with humor, but a gleam in his eye. "And everything attached to it. Don't make me get rough with you. Wouldn't want you to break one of those pretty nails."

Billie waved the glossy set, painted purple with silver flecks. He dressed as a male for traveling, but he always wore makeup and nail polish.

"I live for the rough stuff. And I hope that ass is taken quite regularly, else it would be a waste." He winked at Julie. "As much as I'm enjoying the view, this girl must hit the road."

Billie leaned close, brushing Julie's cheek with his lips. "Don't you worry about a thing, honey-chile," he murmured. "You just let them and Des exercise their delicious male testosterone and work it out. Bat your eyelashes and enjoy being the center of all that big, bad male protectiveness. Take video if that catfight happens."

Julie rolled her eyes but watched with fondness as Billie Dee-Lite made his other good-byes and then sauntered away, a predictably dramatic exit stage left. He gave Harris's ass a playful pinch as he passed him. Thomas and Marcus were watching him with equal parts fascination and amusement, the usual reaction to all the contradictions that were Billie.

"So how long are you guys going to be in town?" Julie asked. "Where are you staying? I have a little one-bedroom apartment nearby."

Madison and Logan had insisted on her renting a nearby place that wasn't as isolated. Since the theater was taking off, she knew it was time to clear out of the dressing room area, regardless, but she'd stayed one additional night here, just to prove her attacker hadn't made her afraid to do so.

"I haven't had a chance to make it my space yet, but I do have a sofa." The only decoration so far was a set of chimes Des had bought her at his preferred farmers' market, which she'd put on the small balcony she had on the third floor. At the end of a long day, she'd sit out there with a cup of tea, put her feet up and listen to their music change with the angle and weight of the breeze.

"I could take the sofa while you guys take the bed," she continued. "The bed's a queen. We could slumber party. Well, I mean..." Abruptly, she realized she had a variable she hadn't had when last she saw them, and that was the possibility of Des spending the night.

"Des might be there, but as long as you guys are all okay with sharing one miniscule bathroom..."

Thomas looked at Marcus. "Did we give her permission to have boys sleep over?"

"She's blushing," Marcus said, studying her with amusement and something more serious.

"Shut up, both of you. This is new to me. I'm not used to juggling guests with...someone I'm seeing."

"It's okay. As lovely as those accommodations sound, I was able to scrape up enough to get us a suite at the Marriott for the week. That recent artist I signed is making a decent amount of commissions. When I can get him to work."

Thomas snorted. "I'd get more done if my spouse wasn't so needy and demanding."

Julie latched onto Marcus's words. "A week? You'll be here a whole week? That's fabulous."

Marcus shrugged. "We figured we'd pitch in here and help out with your new play, visit with you and get to know

Des."

"Oh God, that would be so wonderful. We're really short on set work help right now, with my student volunteers involved with exams. Thomas's handyman skills would be invaluable."

"And mine wouldn't?"

Julie lifted a brow. "You're great for hauling and lifting, but handyman work is not your forte. Remember my toilet?"

"I can't help that it was possessed by Satan. I told you to call a priest, not a plumber."

"Regardless, I have a much better use for you. I need you on publicity and community relations. I was trying to figure out how to juggle the radio and TV spots we've booked, because poor Madison got a cold and sounds like a frog right now. I can give you the basics and let you run with it. You're as good as Steve Martin in *Leap of Faith*, getting everybody out to the tent revival."

"I take it he wasn't available?"

"All booked." She beamed and then impulsively flung herself back into their arms, holding on tight. "I love you guys. I can't wait for you to meet Des, though I'm scared to death about it. I want you all to like each other so much, I probably need to let you three get together on your own so I don't turn it into a disaster by trying to control all of it."

"Have you ever known Marcus to let anyone else take control?" Thomas pointed out.

"I think you know the answer to that," Marcus rebounded, tossing him a look. Julie raised a brow as Thomas flushed this time.

"Do tell?"

"Nope, that one stays between him and me," Marcus informed her firmly. "The hint was just to torture you."

"You love your small torments of us lesser mortals."

"Exactly." Marcus pinched her ass and she punched his solid stomach. "How about you show us what we can do for you right now? It'll take your mind off what we'll do to Des if he's not good enough for you."

She smirked, but as she led them backstage, she couldn't help adding, "He's good enough for me. Really. He's...we fit."

She stopped and faced them. "Honestly, I think I want you guys to like him so much because I do. I'm a big girl and I know even if you don't hit it off, that doesn't matter as much as what he and I feel for one another. But I love you guys and...I love him." She shook her head. "I adore my idiot family, you know I do, but the two of you are the ones I want to approve of him, dumb as that sounds. I've had appalling taste in guys, but he's different. God, I know that sounds lame and meaningless."

Thomas and Marcus exchanged a look full of multiple meanings, then Thomas reached out and clasped her hand, Marcus taking the other. "You don't have appalling taste in men," Marcus informed her with a direct look. "You just have a very good heart. If this guy is good for you—and he seems to be—I think it will be easy for us to get along. Anyone who truly loves and cares about you will get our vote."

"That doesn't mean we won't bust his balls," Thomas added with a worrisome twinkle in his eyes. "That's required. We have to at least throw him in the trunk and make him think we're going to stake him out in the woods for possums and fire ants to eat his eyeballs."

"You can take the boy out of redneck country, but you can't take the redneck out of the boy," Marcus said fondly.

"Does the Maserati even have a trunk?" Julie demanded. "One bigger than a toddler?"

"Oh, he finally let the Spyder go. Mercedes CLA Class. Much more leg room. And a decent trunk."

Julie widened her eyes and put her hand on Thomas's arm as she did a mock stagger. "He got rid of the Spyder? I never thought I'd see the day."

"Well, he is over forty now," Thomas affected a stage whisper behind one hand. "He's starting to grow out of that sports car thing."

Julie laughed as Marcus went after Thomas, probably intending to take him to the floor and pummel him. Thomas ducked behind her, holding her by the shoulders to use her as a human shield, while Marcus resorted to tickling to get her out of the way.

She shrieked and squirmed away, but threw her arms out in front of Thomas to protect him. "Be nice," she told Marcus. "You need him to take care of you in your old age."

"Oh, you are both *so* dead."

§

She'd arranged for Des to first meet Marcus and Thomas at a Chili's for dinner. She figured the casual atmosphere, good food and busy bar would be a good combination for the three men.

Des had texted her that he'd meet them at the restaurant. She, Marcus and Thomas had time for a round of beers and a half hour of catching up before he arrived.

When he came in, her heart did its usual little tilt, the way it did each time they were apart and she saw him again. Evidence like that supported her resolve that this time things would be different. Even the few times she'd imagined herself in love, she hadn't experienced the light-as-air reaction to a man as often as she did with Des.

Giving Marcus and Thomas a smile, she slipped away from the booth to retrieve him, since the restaurant was crowded and he might not locate them. It also gave her the excuse to put her hands on his shoulders, lift onto her toes and kiss him without any self-consciousness.

He'd showered, and smelled clean and damp. Over his dark blue jeans he wore a Doctor Who T-shirt. It showed the Tardis as if it was the center point of Van Gogh's *Starry Night*.

Gathering her close, he pressed his face into her hair. "You smell so pretty," he said. "Just as pretty as you look. I missed you today."

He said that almost every time they'd been apart, but it wasn't rote. He seemed to mean it every time. They really were kind of gone over one another. As much as she wanted to rein it in, chide herself not to be silly, or to risk too much, whenever she saw him at the end of the day there was no choice but to react honestly, because he did the same.

She drew back. "You look pretty special yourself. Love

the T-shirt. I may have to steal that one."

"Since it's a size too small for those gorgeous breasts of yours, I'll look forward to seeing you in it."

She elbowed him but took his hand, threading back through the crowd toward their table. Marcus and Thomas watched them with observation skills an FBI behavioral analysis unit would envy. "Guys, this is Des. Desmond Hayes. Des, these are my best friends, Marcus Stanton and Thomas Wilder."

"Pleasure." Des shook Marcus's hand first, giving him and Thomas an equally assessing glance. "She's been so happy you guys were coming to see her."

Julie noticed Thomas was studying Des peculiarly, his head cocked. It wasn't unusual to see Thomas looking at someone with a particular intensity, because he was always composing future works in his head. Des would definitely qualify as appealing subject matter. She wondered what Des would think if he inspired Thomas's next masterpiece, since his focus was often gay erotic art. Des didn't have any problem being around gay men, but he was damn straight in his own preferences.

When he caught her looking, Thomas lifted a shoulder and his expression cleared. "We've only recently heard good things about you. You've been keeping her tied up these past few weeks."

"In more ways than one," Des said agreeably. He earned a sharp look from Marcus, which he met with a clear-eyed Dom-to-Dom look that gave Julie a little flutter. He'd taken that opening on purpose. It was a "Yeah, you're her friends and I hope we'll all get along, but I'm not going to walk on eggshells or kiss your ass to get your approval." It was also a not-so-subtle way to confirm she'd told them about his preferences, Dom and rigger. She'd told him she had.

Yet remembering his reaction at the party when they'd talked about Marcus and Thomas with Madison and Logan, she realized the message Des had just sent had been a reinforcement of that, as much for her as for them. She didn't know if that made her feel better or more nervous.

Des hadn't intended it as a juvenile joke, either. He'd delivered it with a straight look, tempered with the friendly handshake. Marcus was still considering him while Thomas moved in to smooth things.

"We've missed her, too," he told Des, and glanced at Julie. "New York needs your humor to keep it from taking itself too seriously."

"You were supposed to be holding up that end of things with your clear-eyed Southern perspective."

"Marcus has been keeping me too busy. Josh warned me what it would be like to be married to my manager and I just didn't listen."

"Now you're stuck with me for life," Marcus said lightly, caressing Thomas's nape.

Julie slid into the booth and Des took the seat next to her, his hand settling on her thigh as she curled her hands around his biceps to hold onto him. Under the lamp hanging over the table, he looked a little tired. The roofing job had been a big one, though. A couple of their usual guys had been unavailable, and the home was an eight thousand square foot estate with two guest houses they'd also wanted re-roofed.

The waitress arrived to take Des's drink order and he requested a Redd's Wicked Ale for Julie and an ice water with lemon for himself. Initial conversation was easy. Thomas asked Des about his day, and Des offered some high level details about the roofing job, which he confirmed had turned out to be a bear.

"Somebody married a Victorian monstrosity to a Cape Cod and it had a baby. That thing had about twenty different roof lines and steep peaks, dormers out the ass. We'll get good money for it, but I don't think the guys ever want to see one like it again. The lady who owns it is a theater buff, though." Des tapped his water against Julie's bottle. "I told her about Madison's new place. Made it sound very trendy and on the wild side so she'd bring her friends. Might make her hair fall out when she sees a show."

"Or she'll love it," Julie rebounded. "Middle-aged and older professional women are the ones who particularly love classy erotica. They just don't have a lot of places they can see it that are comfortable for them. That's part of what we're trying to change."

"You're doing great," Thomas said, and nodded to Des. "She showed us how things were going today at the theater."

"She and Madison have done a hell of a job bringing it all together," Des agreed. "They've created a lot of good buzz in the BDSM community here, because while no one cares about converting anyone, it'd be nice not to worry about so much ignorant backlash if it gets out a person is involved in the scene. Not a problem for me, but I know it's a big issue for a lot of people, particularly those going through divorces and kid custody battles."

Marcus gestured with his beer. "Plenty of otherwise intelligent people used to think that the word homosexual was synonymous with pedophile. So, here's to things that are changing."

They clinked their drinks together for the toast, and Marcus shifted subjects. "So, your opening salvo aside, I understand you're quite a rigger. Did a little research on you. You've got a top notch reputation."

Des inclined his head. "I'd say sorry about the salvo, but I'm not, unless it made Julie feel uncomfortable. That wasn't my intention, love," he told her, as if it were just the two of them at the table.

"It's all right. Billie Dee warned me the three of you would have to do some yard dog circling stuff. Just warn me if anyone's going to try and mark me."

Thomas chuckled, but he looked at Des seriously. "That all may be true, but the real truth is we love her. We look out for her."

"With that common ground, it doesn't sound like we're going to have any problems." Des lifted a brow in Marcus's direction. "Will we?"

Green eyes held brown for a long moment. When Thomas's foot pressed on hers under the table, Julie caught his amused gaze, as he mouthed one word. *Breathe.*

Marcus inclined his head. "Sounding like we won't. So tell us more about your rigging work."

"Oh my God, he's amazing. You should have seen what he did in the first performance..."

Des didn't seem to mind that she jumped in to gush. He leaned back in the booth and adjusted his arm along the seat rest, his fingers playing in her hair and caressing her shoulder as she spoke. When he asked them to do so, Marcus and Thomas shared some of their experiences with the BDSM world in New York. At length, Marcus put her back in the hot seat.

"How about you, Jules? How are you doing in this brave new world?"

She glanced at Des, whose encouraging expression told her she could share whatever she wished without offending him. "Des has helped me understand a lot more about the psychology, so I can help my performers shine even more. For my own self..." She thought about it, aware of their eyes on her, but particularly Des's.

"I think I've found something that I want to keep exploring," she admitted. "I love having Des...do the things he does to me. It feels great, not to have to play games, to have everything laid out so bare and honest. It's scary sometimes, but it also feels peaceful. And wild and passionate, at the same time. If that makes sense."

She looked up to meet Thomas's understanding gaze. "It's exactly like that," he said. "Congratulations. Marcus was sure you'd embrace your submissive side with the right incentive and environment. Looks like you've got both here."

"So is there a secret handshake now that I'm in the club?" she asked. She felt a little shaky at having said so much to them. But the honesty had been the right tactic, because Marcus's gaze was less speculative and more relaxed, on both her and Des.

Though she'd known Marcus was a good friend, this version of his caring was new. During that look between him and Des, he'd almost intimidated her. Probably because his protective *and* Dom sides had hooked up and been on full power. She guessed her reaction was proof she did embrace a submissive side, though it was the Dom at her side that commanded her deepest responses and brought those cravings to life.

"Yes, there is a secret handshake," Thomas said

seriously. "We'll show it to you at the special initiation rite where we'll sacrifice a nubile virgin."

"Okay. When does that happen?"

"It's like a rave." Marcus said. "You'll get a text telling you where to meet."

"Don't think I've ever tied up a virgin," Des said.

"You mean the BDSM world isn't overrun with innocent virgins?" Julie smirked. "Imagine that."

They ordered an appetizer while waiting for their meals, and the conversation started running the normal gamut for people getting to know one another. As she relaxed, she enjoyed watching Des handle himself with her friends. Since he was comfortable with almost everyone, she wasn't surprised to see that he, Marcus and Thomas were bantering in no time like guys did when they found common ground.

Thomas was an artist, and Des was almost as serious about his rope craft. Marcus had an appreciation for all art forms. They didn't leave her out, bringing her back into the conversation to talk more about how the latest performance went and how the theater would do going forward. After she laid out the current projects, Marcus was studying her thoughtfully again.

"Sounds like you won't be coming home for some time."

"I'll make runs up to help Belinda, though she's doing a good job without me. She'd probably be okay with me turning it over to her permanently. The board we set up when we incorporated as a nonprofit love her."

"How about your parents?" Thomas asked. "When will they be back in the States?"

"Probably not for another six months. Mom is in love with Singapore right now. She wants me to come visit her there, and I probably will when our schedules match up. She'll be thrilled if I can ask her for a plus one ticket." Julie glanced at Des. "Want to go to Singapore in about six months, if I haven't managed to scare you off?"

"Can I use the ticket even if you have?"

"Sure. I'll tell them to put you in the cargo bay."

"Ouch." He flicked her hair off her brow. "You think your Mom will like me?"

"Oh, don't waste your energy." Julie grimaced. "She'll wish you were a hedge fund manager or a distant relation to the British royal family. She keeps hoping that in my little theater 'hobby' I'll meet an intensely rich and well connected investor. He'll whisk me away and let me live in luxury while I give him two point five children before I die of boredom or a Xanax overdose. But once she gets over that, yeah, she'll air kiss you just like she does me."

At Des's concerned look, Marcus lifted his beer to draw his attention. "Julie loves her mother. She just has her firmly planted in a reality scape that gives no quarter."

"It's the best way to love Mom," Julie said practically. "Dad is so vague when it comes to dealing with family, you don't need to worry about him. He likely won't remember your name two minutes after he meets you. He goes through life like a rubber duck dropped square in the middle of a lake, floating along with no real direction when it comes to family. But he's sharp with money. He's connected to a Spanish royal line that goes back centuries, so there's always been family money. He hires really good people to keep it making money for him and supporting us—Mom, my brother, sister and me—in the way he wants."

At his quizzical look, she grinned. "Yeah, I guess I can trust you now. I doubt you're a gold digger. My family's loaded. In my twenties, I went through this rebellious phase where I was determined to earn my own way, not rely on their money. Dad, as mild-mannered as he is about everything else, nearly had an aneurysm. It took me a while to pull my head out of my ass and realize it had to do with him, not me. He had no problem with me working long hours and establishing a solid reputation in theater business. He just couldn't handle me doing something as lowbrow as accepting a paycheck for it."

Des blinked and she laughed. "Yeah, I know how it sounds. But he was much happier when I went from paid stage work to community theater, and that was our compromise." Julie imitated her father's smooth Spanish accent. 'Go find something meaningful, *querida*, something that engages your passions. Change the world. Just honor your father by allowing him to care for you while you do.'

"He still fusses because I don't care anything about having a house or a fancy car, all the things my siblings have, but he's come a long way since our initial fights about it. Oh, and just a side note. Mom was a short-lived B-film star. She's a knockout still."

"Turtle and rabbits," Des recalled. "Except for the knockout part. Now I know where you got your looks."

"That was so the right thing to say." She curled her hands around his arm again and hugged it to her breasts. "Seriously, we could have a great time in Singapore, so think about it. We'd have to do some family stuff, but then we could tour Malaysia or Indonesia. Mom and Dad would pay for everything, so the only lost income would be from any jobs you missed. And remember, it's not a pride thing. It would genuinely hurt them if I didn't let them handle the trip for both of us."

"I've had the pleasure of meeting Mr. and Mrs. Ramirez, and everything she says is dead accurate," Marcus added. "Her father has a very Old World sense of honor, but it's oddly touching. And unchangeable."

The conversation moved from there to other, less personal matters. Commercials on the surrounding TV screens, more about Marcus and Thomas's life up in New York and Julie's, when she was living there. She noticed Des was participating, but as their dinner moved into the second hour, he was getting quieter, doing more listening and smiling, though there was a slight strain to his face. His appetite was off, because he only ate half of the small meal he ordered, the rest untouched on his plate. He wasn't feeling well.

She was sure of it, but there was no way she could draw attention to it without ruffling his feathers. That was the problem about getting so close to someone so fast, while at the same time not having enough of a foundation to justify acting...well, wifely. A scary word to pop into her head, but she couldn't deny the drive.

When Marcus asked her about dessert, she shook her head, though the Oreo cake looked fabulous. "To tell the truth, guys, I'm a bit beat. It's been a long day. I think I'm going to call it a night soon…"

"No, don't do that." Des stroked her leg. "I know you want dessert."

"Want and need are two different things. My ass does not need that."

"I've seen your ass. Cake does lovely things for it."

Julie snorted, but caught the warning look in his eye. To hell with it. She went with honesty, putting her hand on his arm. "If you've had a long day, it's cool if you want to head for home, okay?"

He coiled his fingers around hers and leaned in to brush his lips against her ear. As he spoke against it, she noticed Marcus and Thomas doing their best to look as if they were involved in conversation with one another, to give them the illusion of privacy. "I don't want to go to bed without you, love," Des murmured. "I'm all right. Just quiet."

He lifted his head, looking toward Marcus to restore the four-way conversation. "How long have you two been together?"

"What do you mean?" Thomas asked blandly. "He's just a good looking piece of ass I picked up on the plane. Looked like he needed someplace to go."

Marcus grimaced at him. "Yeah, because North Carolina would be the destination a top grade piece of ass like me would choose for a good time."

"Well, top grade maybe ten years ago. Now…"

Julie yelped as Marcus reached across the table and gave a lock of her hair a brutal yank.

"Little bitch," he pronounced. "Des, you need to beat her. A lot. I'll hold her down."

"I can do the holding my own self, but thanks for the sanction," Des rebounded.

"Doms encouraging Doms," Thomas said to her. "Beware and run."

"We only keep picking at you because you've been so sensitive about this ever since you hit your forties." Julie sniffed at Marcus. "You'll be beautiful to the day you die and you know it. Even then everyone will want one last time to admire your corpse."

"Just make sure Thomas isn't in charge of dressing me,"

Marcus said, taking a sip of his beer.

"I have a flannel shirt and a pair of overalls that will look great with those overpriced Italian shoes you like." Thomas grinned and answered Des's question. "We've been together a while now. Long enough to feel like we're starting to get the hang of it."

"Looks like it." Des rotated the glass of water in his hand and sat back once more. He linked fingers with Julie's on the table and squeezed, an admonishment as if he anticipated her trying to interrupt.

"Here's the deal." Des's gaze shifted between the two men. "I love her, but I'm not a great bet in the grow-old-together department. I expect she's told you some of that. She says none of that matters and that she wants to give us a good run. I'm selfish enough, and want her enough, to listen. Plus, I think past a certain point it doesn't really matter anyway, does it? Your heart gets stuck on someone. So I guess what I want to tell you straight up is I'm a selfish bastard. I may break her heart because my body gives out, but my heart won't. If I hurt her, it won't be because I don't love her enough."

Julie stared at Des. That heart he was worried about breaking was in her throat. A cheerful cacophony of noise continued around their table: people eating, talking, laughing or watching TV at the bar. The clink of metal and glass added to that rushing undercurrent. Life kept moving on, but things here were quiet, reflecting the stillness inside her as Des shifted his gaze to her, his grip sure and firm. She lifted her chin, telling him...she agreed. She accepted.

Marcus's foot was pressing against hers beneath the table as Thomas reached over, covering her and Des's clasped hands. He'd meant it for her, but didn't seem to mind including Des. Des looked mildly surprised by the affection, but then Marcus spoke, drawing their attention.

"You asked us how long we've been together. Long enough to recognize when someone else has a good start on it. She knew we didn't have to approve of you for her to decide to want to be with you. She's an accomplished, brilliant woman. But we're family, and I've learned that a family's support can sometimes be the difference between success and failure when you're trying to make a relationship work."

Marcus exchanged a meaningful glance with Thomas, full of past history, then brought his eyes back to Des. "You seem good for each other. You have our support, both of you. Unless you turn out to be a dick, and then we'll rip yours off."

"Fair enough." Des toasted him. "Because I'd feel the same way about anyone who hurt her."

"That's the right answer. Just be good to her. She's earned it, a hundred times over. If what she's said is true, sounds like you do, too." Marcus tapped his glass. "Take her home, Des. You both look like you need to call it an early night. We'll be around a few days. If things go right between you, you'll have a lifetime to get to know us both."

Chapter Seventeen

She'd been right about how tired he was. They'd dropped off her car and he'd taken her back to his place in his truck, but he'd said very little, though it was as he said. He was quiet, not unhappy. He held her against him as he drove, letting her chatter and making accommodating grunts as needed.

Once they reached his place, he stripped down to his boxers, drew her to the bed and removed all her clothes but her panties, which seemed to be his preferred nightwear for her. She'd have to talk him into letting her wear something more come wintertime, though usually he had excellent ways to warm her up.

Tonight, he gathered her close and told her he'd had a good time with her friends. While his cock was semi-hard at her proximity, showing an interest in sex, she didn't push it and he didn't either, almost immediately falling into slumber.

He held her close through the night. Though a couple times her shoulder started to ache or she had an itch, she ignored those things, not wanting to do anything to cause him to let her go. As she lay there, the need to hold him even more tightly than he was holding her had her keeping her arms wrapped around his back, her face against his chest.

She was typically overly paranoid about things, so she told herself to ignore a niggling uneasiness, even as she kept rousing to listen to him breathe, to wonder at how deeply he was sleeping. She thought of the things they'd said and done at dinner, Marcus's serious tone and the look in his green eyes. When they'd parted that night, he'd hugged her and offered words that both reassured and unsettled her.

"We're here for whatever you need, Julie. Always."

She'd turned to Thomas for his hug and found him watching Des with that same curious look. Her Master was currently paying their check because he'd refused Marcus's offer to pay for all. "Okay," she told Thomas. "I know that look. I get first dibs on any paintings you do of him. And a big family discount."

"No, it's not that." Thomas's brow creased. "He's just really familiar to me."

"Maybe you saw him in one of the clubs you and Marcus visited while you were traveling. He does several rigger conferences each year."

"Yeah. Maybe. Hey, on that note, let me get a shot of the two of you on my phone before we part ways. You know Daralyn and Les are going to want to see the guy you're dating."

When Des returned, he was amenable to a picture, standing beside her in his easy, friendly way as she laid a familiar hand on his chest and smiled for the camera.

As she drifted off into sleep now, she dreamed of Thomas's picture. There was a fading on the edges of Des's side. She tried to get Thomas to sharpen it, to take it again, but he said it was too late. It was fading, and she had to figure out a way to keep Des in the picture...

She woke from the disturbing dream. It was daylight and, since she didn't have to be at the theater until later in the morning, it was okay for her to sleep in. It still felt strange and overindulgent after the round-the-clock schedule she'd been keeping these past few weeks between the theater's demands and Des.

She was alone. She cleaned up in the bathroom, using the contents of the toiletry bag she'd brought to wash her face, brush her hair and teeth. Donning a knee length purple knit skirt and a pale green cotton baby-tee, she accented them with silver hoops and a silver and jade stone choker before she went in search of her Dom. She left her hair down, brushed out thick and shining, because he liked it that way, though she pocketed the barrette she'd need when the humidity kicked in.

Through the window, she saw him outside, bagging up leaves in Betty's yard. She was glad to see him awake and looking restored, but as she started to open the door, she saw Betty was with him. From their body language, it was clear she was about to interrupt a heated conversation. She hesitated, torn between defusing it with an untimely interruption, and letting them work it out. When she decided on the latter, she couldn't shame herself into closing the door and not eavesdropping. That dream was still too close to the surface of her consciousness.

"I don't want to talk about it," Des said stubbornly.

"So you've said. You've been a broken record for the past two weeks. Des, you can't ignore this."

"I'm not ignoring it."

"Yes, you are. Your numbers are not good. You've held out on intense insulin management longer than most with the type of insulin resistance you have, but your kidneys are starting to show the strain. You're going to be facing dialysis soon and you know it. Not years from now; in a matter of months."

His jaw set as Julie's breath caught. Betty stepped closer, and her expression softened, but not enough to dilute the steel in her eyes, her determination to get through to him.

"I know you've started taking fewer jobs and working less days of the week, which is good for your body, but you can't ignore the signs. You don't want to wait until you're in full renal failure. You can do dialysis at home, you know that. A few times a week, at night. You just hook yourself up at bedtime."

"You think you're telling me something I don't already know? That I haven't studied this shit a million times? Once I start dialysis, that's it. Dr. Greeley said it might work for me a few years. And then it won't."

"Which is why you should do what I've suggested a million times. Sign up to get a kidney."

"I'm not a good candidate. They've told you that before."

"Your earlier health problems made you a bad

candidate, but you've beaten those problems and manage your diabetes better than any patient I've ever had. If we were determined, we could get the donor list people to consider giving you one. You are extremely disciplined. You would take very good care of a donor organ. A kidney is one of the easier organs to obtain, relatively speaking."

"For most people. They've never stopped saying what they said at the beginning. My body isn't typical. It's likely to reject anything less than a close genetic match, and I have no family. Even if I had, it would give me what? Maybe another decade before it fails."

"Ten years is a lot better than six months if you do nothing," she snapped. "Why are you so fucking stubborn about this?"

"Because my whole life has been about this."

"Don't give me that adolescent self-wallowing crap," she retorted. "You went out and made yourself an incredible life."

"By calling my own shots."

"Des, I'm not your prison warden. You're still calling your own shots. This is all your own choice. Get on a list, start dialysis. Some people do dialysis for fifteen years or more. A kidney can give you a decade. So a potential of twenty-five years, and who knows what other developments will happen during that time. Fight for yourself. Fight for your life."

"I do that. I've done that." He threw down the rake and rounded on her. "And it's not enough. It's never fucking enough. There's always going to be something else."

"Yeah, there is." Betty crossed her arms over her chest. "So why don't you tell those Type I kids you mentor to just give up now? Before they ever experience a senior prom, or a first love, or a trip to Disneyworld? Just fuck it, go ahead and die because life might be harder for you than other kids. What is the problem? Why are you acting this way?"

"Because I'm sick of it," he exploded. "You don't get it. You can't get it unless you're having to deal with it every fucking day. I'm tired of having to always be on guard. Check this, watch that, eat this, don't eat that. Hyperglycemia, hypoglycemia. Carry a damn suitcase with me everywhere to manage it all. Weigh every fucking decision I make against how it will affect my diabetes, my pancreas, my kidneys..."

"You've always done that." Betty studied him. "Nothing has changed. Except her. That's it, isn't it? Julie."

Julie told herself to go away before she heard where this was going, but she couldn't make herself move, could barely breathe, in the face of Des's anger.

Des kicked the bag of leaves he'd just packed. The plastic exploded from the force of the impact and leaves scattered around his work shoes. He marched away from Betty, muttering, snarling to himself, and he rubbed both hands over his face. Julie had seen that densely packed energy around him before when he was fully in Dom mode with her, an exciting, sexual energy. Right now it was painful and volatile. Betty held fast, but even she looked a little pale in the face of his rage.

As he gathered his thoughts, Betty glanced over and saw her at the crack of the door. Julie didn't draw back. Betty could out her there, or Julie could do the right thing and close the door, but they both made their choice. Julie didn't close the door and Betty shifted her attention back to him as if she hadn't seen her.

As Des turned to face the nurse, there was a defeated look to his expression Julie had never seen before. "We've just started, Betty," he said, a note of despair in his voice that wrenched her heart. "I didn't intend...I told myself I'd never drag someone I care about into this. And I did it anyway. She deserves better than someone who started life broken."

"You listen to me." Betty set her jaw and stepped closer, gripping his forearm. "We're all broken in some way, Desmond Arthurius Hayes. It's how life shapes us for one another. If Julie Ramirez sees what I see, she knows what a treasure she's found. And if she's a good person with a loving heart, you deserve her."

Des shook his head, pulled away. "No one deserves this. God is a heartless bastard."

"You're being a selfish idiot who can't handle being out of control," Betty said with gentle ruthlessness.

"Being out of control is the one thing I've always had to accept. But I don't have to accept it for her."

"That's her decision, not yours."

The portent in Betty's voice was as clear as a whispered cue through a mic. Summoning her courage, Julie stepped out the door. It was a little chilly and she shivered, crossing her arms over her body, but she met Des's eyes without flinching. "I shouldn't have been listening, but I'm not sorry I did. I feel like I do deserve you, Des. Meeting you has been one of the luckiest moments of my life."

He looked torn between anger at them both, and then a desperate, helpless fury captured his expression. "You should have respected my privacy," he told Betty. "And shut the hell up when you knew she was there."

"Des," Julie said sharply, but he shot her a withering look.

"I shouldn't have gone down this road with you. Just...fuck. Please get the hell out of here. I need you...I just need you to be gone right now."

He pivoted and strode away, headed down the path toward the barn. Julie stood frozen, certain this was how it felt to have a spear shoved through her gut, pinning her to the wall behind her. Betty stared after him, her mouth tight. When she noticed Julie's reaction, she climbed the porch steps to put a hand on her arm. "Here, honey. Come sit here."

She directed Julie into a rocking chair. "Breathe. You've gone pale as a sheet. Put your head down if you need to. That bastard. That stubborn, wonderful, pigheaded asshole."

Betty rubbed her back, a soothing touch. "He didn't mean it. You know he didn't. He's been over the moon about you since he met you. I've never seen him react to a woman the way he has you."

Julie pressed her forehead into her arms and straightened. "You warned me, right?" she said with a shaky laugh. "You said it would get ugly when we got into this territory. I guess I just thought we'd gotten through it."

Betty shook her head. "He's always been able to keep relationships at an arm's distance. I guess that's why he's into all that rope stuff. He can get sex and intimacy without commitment. You've kind of messed that up. In a good way."

"Doesn't feel that good at the moment."

"That's because he has his head up his ass," Betty said tenderly, glancing toward the barn. "For truly understandable reasons, though I take issue with him striking out at you. But he'll give himself hell for that himself when he settles down." Betty sighed and touched her hand, a simple, practical stroke. "He's angry and he's scared, that's all."

"I know. I mean, I don't know that, but I can tell he's upset." It still hurt that he'd struck out at her, especially after everything they'd shared up to now.

Some relationships weren't given a lot of time before they had to face the "for better or worse" clause. Maybe someone else in a relationship less than a few weeks old would cut and run in the face of that demand, but she'd waited a long time, not only to feel this way about someone, but to have him feel the same way about her.

"Where's he going?" she asked Betty. "He's getting company, whether he wants it or not."

§

He was clearing out a shed behind the barn that appeared to be filled with old construction materials. She supposed it was his way of dealing with his emotions, the same way she'd reorganized cords in the sound cabinet the day she'd been frustrated with him.

She took a seat on a nearby stump, watching him. He noticed her, but didn't say anything for a few minutes, pulling boards out and tossing them with a resounding clap on the ground outside the shed door. He was wearing work gloves, which she was glad to see since a lot of the boards had nails sticking out of them. Bugs skittered off the boards and she lifted her feet, letting a spider of an unsettling size scuttle away.

"So what's the real reason you're not on a donor list? Even if it's not a genetic match, why let that stop you? You told me you don't let a doctor or anyone else tell you how long you have to live. And as Betty said, you're pretty darn healthy. Except for the whole kidney failure thing."

She wasn't sure if the mild tease would be useful or not, but anything that would get him talking was worth a shot.

Desmond stopped, yanking off the gloves and tossing them to the side. "You know what being on a list means? It means there's someone below you, someone who will be waiting for a kidney longer. Maybe a kid, maybe a middle-aged woman who wants to live long enough to retire and have that house at the beach she's always wanted. Maybe a loser who's never done much with his life but, when he gets the gift of a kidney, it opens his eyes and he realizes how much more he could be and do, and he becomes the center of someone's world as a result."

He swiped a lock of hair out of his eyes that had come loose from the band holding it back. She wanted to stroke it away from his face herself, but she curled her hands on her lap, waiting him out. "I have no family," he said. "I'm a roofer and I'll always be a roofer, because that's what I like. I'm a guy who gets his freak on with rope and topping beautiful women. I know who I am, I like my life, I like the people in my life. I've figured out my shit. I don't need more time on that. Someone else might. I'm not going to be the one who takes it away from them, just because I'm scared of dying."

Every word pummeled her. It was unbearable to hear him write himself off, as if her feelings for him didn't matter, as if she didn't matter. Then he pinned her with a blazing gaze.

"Or because the very thought of not having more time with you makes me want to shove every damn person on that list out of my way. Just to get a single moment more together."

Before she could fully wrap her mind around the words, the fierce, frustrated way he said them, he had her on her feet and pushed her against the outside shed wall, kissing her in that hot, take-over way he had. His body pressed between her legs, his other callused hand gripping her thigh and pulling it up against his hip so she had to let him against her core.

They were surrounded by barn, forest and pasture, so they had their privacy, sort of. She hazily wondered if he was going to take her right here. The remarkable thing was she'd let him, her whole being hurting for and craving him. It made his anger contagious, so that she was shoving at him, pinching, scratching, slapping.

He seized her hair, yanking her head back and biting her lip. He was rough with her, pushing her to her knees, holding her against the wall with his work shoe against her abdomen, the heel firm between her legs, eyes glittering as he unbuckled his belt and stripped it with a hard yank. He opened his jeans and reached down to scoop her up and hold her against the wall.

He had his hand under her skirt, the underwear ripped away, and then he sheathed himself in her. When she snapped at him, caught between a snarl and a moan, he pulled out, turned and pushed her down over a dilapidated table, clearing a brace of old paint cans sitting on it with a sweep of his arm, sending them tumbling into the grass.

"If that's the way you want it," he muttered. She hissed a creative curse at him that insulted his manhood.

"Baby, you know that's not the truth," he said, slamming back into her, violently enough she cried out. "Yeah, there's no fucking problem in that department. Keep fighting me. You'll lose."

She did fight him, and he held her down, and they climaxed at almost the same moment, her strangling on her cries and him grunting with visceral satisfaction. Then things got quiet, and he settled over her, arm over her chest. Where she would have bitten him a moment ago, now her tear-stained mouth was pressed against his forearm, sticky with sweat and grit. His forehead rested between her shoulder blades, and his other arm was banded around her waist. As clarity returned, she registered that he was holding her so tightly she almost couldn't breathe. He was shaking as if he was going to come apart.

He wouldn't let her hold him, but he held onto her. She wondered if he was using her as an anchor, one that wouldn't tear loose, something that he could depend upon in the midst of the storm, not something that would surround and hold him. He was a rigger, after all. That was his job.

When she realized the heated slickness on her back were his tears, she went still as her heart cracked inside her. How could she bear to stay if she was going to lose him?

"I love you," he said against her flesh, and she closed her eyes.

That was why.

"Des, I could give you a kidney. We could check and see..."

"Oh, Christ. No." He pulled away from her so abruptly he left her cold and aching, though he courteously eased her skirt back down, smoothing his hands over her buttocks. She heard him adjust his own clothes, then he turned and sat her on the table with one easy hoist, though his arms were tense and he averted his face, wiping at it self-consciously with the back of his arm. "Shut up and don't bring that up again."

"Why not?"

"Because that's not happening. You're not going to have an organ cut out of your body for a guy you've just met. We're not going to have that between us."

"So it's better for me to stand over your grave?"

"For me, yes." At her stricken look, he stepped closer, his abdomen brushing her knees. "This is why I've avoided relationships. Julie, I want to share my life with you, I want to love you, be in love with you, but my body, my choices, are mine. If I choose to die because I won't take someone else's damn kidney, especially yours, that's my choice. If you can't be with me because of that choice, I get it." He swallowed, his expression taut, drained. "It sounds fucked up, but it is what it is."

"Is it a control thing?" She didn't want to fight any more. Her stomach hurt, and her body vibrated from his violent possession that said so much about the emotions churning between them, but she needed to know. "You're my Dom, so you refuse to rely on me to keep you alive?"

"You make me feel alive, in a way I've never

experienced. I'm ready to ride that ride as long as my body can handle it." He dropped to one knee before her and grasped both her hands. "But I won't let you give me a kidney. All I want from you is your love."

She swallowed over jagged glass. Taking the hem of her shirt, she lifted it, touched it to the tracks of tears he hadn't been able to brush away with his arm. His expression flickered, revealing raw pain, and a weariness that made her think he wanted to put his head down on her lap and let her hold him. She would have done it, but his expression shut down and hid that need away. He closed his hand around her wrist to stop her cosseting and the moment was lost.

"You want my love on your own terms, where you don't end up feeling like you owe me." She tried to pull away, but he wouldn't let her.

"No. I just don't want that to have anything to do with why we're together."

"It doesn't work that way," she said. "You don't set terms when it comes to love. It's all or nothing, do whatever you need to do to be together, to love one another. It's messy, and ugly, and angry and beautiful and perfect, all rolled up in this messy ball like spaghetti. *That's* the way it's supposed to work."

He blinked. "I never thought of love like pasta."

She wanted to snarl at him, because he was trying to make a joke, but she was too messed up right now, brimming over with the need to scream, to cry, to punch him. She jerked her hands away and shoved off the table. "You're right, I need to get out of here. But you don't get to say we're done. You're not going to break my heart because you're too stubborn to let someone help you."

He caught her by the shoulders before she could move past him and gave her a sharp shake. "And how is being less than who I am going to help?"

"I don't know," she shouted. "But I can't figure out how you being dead is going to make things any better. Can you?"

At his tight look, she bolted, hurrying up the path back toward his house. Yeah, she'd go, because she needed to get away from him and think some. It wasn't until she was in his place, packing her overnight bag, that she remembered he'd driven her here. Well, fuck that. She'd call a cab if she had to do so.

Then she heard his truck starting. Moving to the window, she saw the vehicle trundling up the gravel drive. What the hell?

A knock on the door resolved that question. When she opened it, Betty stood there with a pained smile on her lined face. "He said since I ruined your morning, the least I could do is give you a ride back to your place. He figured you weren't interested in riding with him."

"I think the reverse is true. But he's being an asshole. You didn't ruin my morning. Maybe I can get the answers from you he won't give to me." At Betty's hesitant look, Julie shot her a dubious look. "Really? You're going to resort to being tightlipped now? I'm here, I'm interested, and I want to help. "

Betty's green eyes sparked with grim humor. "I think I'm starting to like you."

"Well, don't make any hasty decisions. I'm in a really bitchy mood."

"That's why I know we'll get along."

§

By the time Betty dropped her off at the theater, Julie had rethought wanting to be told the things she was told. Desmond had fought this battle all his life, struggling against myriad complications that had stacked the odds against him, over and over. He and his body had overcome those challenges each time, often with great personal cost. His erratic health history had interfered not only with relationships, but with college and career choices. It had impacted unexpected things, like getting business loans approved, and less unexpected things, like medical costs and insurance coverage.

It made her understand better the brick wall of dark emotion she'd hit, the frustration that had made so much of what he said initially seem insensible. He was fighting with himself now, and she hadn't know which questions to ask or the things to say to help him untangle it. She'd been too focused on her own personal cost. So first she had to deal with that, right?

She tried working, but she couldn't. She told Harris in a voice she knew was suspiciously choked up that she had to go out for a while, and she wasn't sure when she'd be back. She got in her car and drove without clear purpose, but she wasn't surprised to see where she ended up.

She walked into the empty church, relieved to find it unlocked and her the only person in the nave. She had no idea what denomination it was. The white clapboard structure had beds of petunias and pansies on the outside, so it had felt welcoming.

As she walked down the main aisle, she soaked in the hushed, calming energy, and studied the blocks of color on the stained glass windows. She wondered why so many churches used stained glass, what the history was behind that. She'd have to look it up.

Her gaze went to the plain wooden cross mounted over an altar up front. More fresh flowers were gathered at its base. As she slipped into a pew, the simple beauty of it caused tears to well up in her eyes. That, and Betty's words.

Renal failure... He seems mostly fine, but that's the way kidney failure can be... Several months at most before he has to start dialysis... Prognosis for the effectiveness of dialysis differs from person to person... Attitude is everything... He refuses a kidney...

She was weeping, and she hated being weepy. She much preferred to be angry.

"I finally have someone who loves me the way I always dreamed about being loved, and You want to take him away. What did I ever do to You that You hate me so much?"

Her voice echoed through the chamber. Normally she spoke in a low voice in a church, like everyone else. But she wanted to be heard. She demanded to be heard. She glared at the cross. Everything here was supposed to be soothing and comforting, but it all felt like a mockery. She'd debated religion in countless coffee shops with lofty cynicism and academic boredom, but when it came to facing the foxhole, she was like anyone else. She was a child blindly seeking comfort... Or a lost adult realizing all the wishful thinking for an attentive, loving Divine Force was just that.

No. *No.* It wasn't wishful thinking. Rainbows and flowers, summer storms that electrified the sky, lizards that could look exactly like the plants on which they were resting. All the complexity of the human anatomy and musicals like *Seven Brides for Seven Brothers, Camelot* and *Man of La Mancha.* Those things didn't come out of a void.

She had a great life, she knew she did. She shouldn't feel this way. But it didn't matter. She was going to have it out with Him, Her, It, and she'd do it on Their home turf.

"What kind of sadistic asshole are You?" she demanded. "Sure, Julie, you can have the prince, but just not for long? What is your fucking problem? And why would You do this to Des? This great guy who's just...he's so wonderful..."

"Miss?"

She turned to see a middle-aged black man with a kind face. He wore jeans and an Oxford shirt in a pale lavender color, but he had that air that told her he was one of the pastors here, lack of robes or collar notwithstanding.

"This is between Him and me," she snapped. "It's a private conversation. Did anyone ask you to butt in?"

The minister eyed her. "A conversation conducted at the top of your admirably strong lungs?"

She blinked, realizing the echoes of her last syllables were still vibrating off the walls. She had been yelling. "Oh. Sorry." She wasn't. Her fists were clenched and her throat was tight, her eyes burning with unshed tears. "It's okay. I'm okay. I'm sorry. I just need to sit here for a while. Um, can I still sit here?"

"Would you like someone to sit with you?" he asked.

It was such a compassionate offer, the tears spilled out, but she shook her head. "I think I just have to think it through. I promise I won't scream anymore."

"Well, it's just you, Him, and me." The minister nodded. "If you need to shout a bit, I'll leave you to it. Just don't resort to violence. My office is around the corner there." He pointed. "I'm Jerry. If you need a human counterpoint, come find me."

"Okay. Thanks. I mean it. Really."

He gave her a searching look. "Sometimes, after you get it all out, just sitting here quietly helps. It's been my experience that He offers His best solutions when someone is actually listening."

Jerry retreated on quiet footsteps down the aisle. Julie moved to one of the pews and sank down in it, contemplating the altar again, the bright flowers. She knew Jerry's advice was sound, but right now, she felt like she was going to shatter. If she kept thinking about this, she might just resort to breaking things. She should leave. But something about the quiet of the place made her want to stay. She typed in the name of the church, the street it was on, and two more words.

Please come.

Then she set the phone aside and tried not to think. Her hands were shaking and her heart was pounding, so she focused on calming down, not on trying to make sense of it. She needed to get a grip before she could make sense of what defied comprehension.

He was quick, she'd give him that. She wondered if he'd showed up at the theater after she left to help out Harris as he'd promised, which meant he hadn't been far from here. She had her eyes closed, but she knew his scent, that combination of hair and body products that enhanced every powerful, sexy inch of him. But right now, he wasn't some absurdly handsome man. He was just her friend.

Marcus slid in to the pew, his arm along the edge behind her, pressing against her shoulders. He didn't say anything, waiting her out.

"Do you believe in any of this?" she asked, her voice hoarse from a strain she couldn't define.

"More than I used to."

"Because of Thomas." She didn't need him to confirm the obvious. "What if Thomas got sick and died? Would you still believe? Or would you believe but be really pissed? Sign a deal with the devil to bring it all crashing down on everyone else, because you were hurting so badly you wanted everyone else to suffer, too?"

"Probably," he said truthfully. "Though I might take a minute to at least try to look at it the way Thomas would. That I'd had the opportunity to love someone the way he and I love one another, and too many people never find that."

"Yeah. It's hard to understand that scarcity." She bit her lip. "I've met very few people who don't deserve to have love in their life, or who wouldn't be better people if they did. So why is it so hard to find and keep?"

Marcus sighed and twirled a lock of her hair around two of his fingers. "Because we're human, which means we're innately self-destructive morons who refuse to attain the level of enlightenment needed to maximize the miracle of someone just as messed up as ourselves wanting to love us."

She met his serious green eyes. "Oh my God, who put together that string of bullshit?"

"You did. When you were drunk on your thirty-fifth birthday."

"Great. A drunk single woman with a degree in drama queen and too damn much higher education."

He touched her face. "What's going on, Julie?"

"He's sick, Marcus. Seriously sick."

She gave him the highlights she'd gotten from Betty, along with the things she'd learned since meeting Des. "Now he's mad at himself and feeling guilty for dragging me into all this. He told me at the beginning, mostly, but I don't think he expected it to suddenly get this bad, this quick. So he pushed me away, told me to get lost."

Marcus raised a silken brow. "I hope you told him to fuck off, you'll leave when you're damn good and ready."

"Sort of. He left before I could dig the shrapnel out of my chest and get that far." She drew endless circles on the blue denim stretched on Marcus's thigh.

"You have that uber-Dom, large and in charge thing happening. He's different, but the right kind of different for me. He's the quiet fire that's always going to keep the home fires burning. That's what I always wanted..." A hint of a painful smile touched her lips. "Well, with some of that dangerous bad boy thrown in, just enough to make it all fun. He has that, too. I hope you'll stick around long enough to see him do a rope session. It's something else."

Marcus nodded agreeably, though he remained quiet. Just listening.

"I told him I would give him a kidney, and..." She stopped as Marcus winced. "Yeah, that's the same reaction he had. What the fuck?"

"Because he's a man. Because he's a Dom. Because he's in love with you, Julie. Despite how much ground you've covered, you're still just starting on this road together. You say he drew hard lines about his health from the beginning, which means he didn't want it to interfere with the falling in love part. Now this has come along and your first, very well meaning offer to help is to have an organ cut out of your body for him."

"Yeah, I get it. It's pride."

"Don't get a tone." He shook his head. "Pride isn't the surface emotion a lot of people think it is. It can be, but in this case, I think it's connecting to a lot of deeper issues. Control of his own life, his perception of himself, and how others perceive him."

"I love him, Marcus. I know we're just on the front end of it, but I do. I don't doubt it at all, and I think he doesn't, either. Which is maybe why he's acting like this. If we'd just been playing at falling in love, he could convince himself I could just walk away and he could too and he could die without hurting anyone..." She stopped, her voice breaking, and Marcus's arm moved fully around her shoulders, drawing her close so he could kiss the top of her head.

"I know you love him. I can see it. You were glowing like a lamp when you introduced him to us. It was in your voice, in the way you touched his arm. And you're right, it's not one-sided. He was measuring us up the same way we were measuring him, making sure we were the good friends you thought we were."

"So Billie was right. Dinner was a sexist testosterone exchange, the 'Let's all make sure the mindless female knows what's best for her.' How charming." She poked him.

Marcus pursed his lips. "We are what we are. I expect Des knows just how intelligent you are, just as we do. Yet when it comes to someone we love, we respond to any threat, not with rational thought or the right words, but with our hearts."

"Yeah." She thought of the kidney offer and winced now, too. "What do I do to make this right?"

"You didn't do anything wrong." Marcus said it firmly, tipping up her chin and giving it a tap of reproof. "Go see him after you've calmed down, and he's had some time to do the same, and talk it out, figure out how to go forward. That simple. No blame on either side."

"No matter how pigheaded and stupid he's being."

Marcus snorted. "Yeah. I'd probably dial that back."

"He's the Dom I've always wanted and didn't know I did," she said softly, looking at her hands in her lap. She gave Marcus a glance from beneath her lashes. "Don't get me wrong, I still wouldn't kick you out of bed or anything."

"My feelings are bruised, but I'll recover. As long as you feel the same about Thomas."

"Absolutely. I'd take him down in a heartbeat and eat him with a spoon."

She fended him off when he tried to tug her hair, but that was a distraction. He pinched her side, hard.

"Ow. Meanie." She smacked his arm, but then he captured her hand and tangled it with his, resting the knot of their fingers on his knee. Sobering, she dropped her head on his shoulder. "What if I lose him? I don't need a man to feel safe, but Marcus, he makes me feel so safe and loved. He's so strong and warm. He's this force all around me when he ties me up, when he talks to me a certain way, looks at me a certain way... I know I probably sound stupid."

"Not at all. As a Dom and a man, he'd get a fierce joy out of hearing you say it, so you should say it to him sometime."

"But how could I survive losing that?"

"The way you survive anything with that indomitable personality of yours. Your superpower, Julie, is your ability to overcome any storm to find the sunshine again and share it with others." He sighed. "And failing that, Thomas and I will make the sacrifice, convert to bisexualism and you can become our sex slave."

"That's good to know. I'm going to cry for a little bit now and then I'll be okay."

"All right." Marcus folded his arms around her and held her closer as the sobs surged up. "I'm right here, baby. I'll hold you until you're okay. But from here forward, this is Des's job, so he better get his fucking act together."

Chapter Eighteen

She thought it out. After she left Marcus, she felt better about things and, after she made a few more stops, that good feeling continued to build. When she finally texted Des, she didn't know if he'd answer, but she counted on him having had some time to calm down, as Marcus had said.

Where are you? I want to come see you.

About five minutes later, when she thought maybe she'd been wrong and was struggling with a sinking feeling as a result, her phone pinged with an address. Nothing but an address, but it was enough.

It was out in Huntersville, but she used the forty-five minute drive to listen to some upbeat tunes, pick up a pair of oatmeal cookies from Showmar's and consume them with a Coke Zero, and keep in the right frame of mind. Everything was going to be all right. She remembered Marcus's arms around her, him saying that to her. He wouldn't say it if it wasn't true. Marcus didn't lie to her.

She wasn't typically clingy, but she was glad he and Thomas would be around all week. She grinned, thinking of Thomas painting backgrounds. If they could add to the playbill that the sets were painted by Thomas Wilder, that would draw in even more patrons. Everything about the theater effort so far had seemed blessed by good fortune. It was also how she'd met Des. She wasn't going to let one setback turn it into a Greek tragedy. She wasn't going to let him turn it into a Greek tragedy.

Okay, remember what Marcus said. Dial back shrew mode.

The address wasn't a house, as she'd expected. It was a park. Latta Plantation Park was accessible from a side road that took her past a couple horse farms and the Carolina Raptor Center. She sent him an additional text to locate him, and found him at the picnic area and kayak launch by Mountain Lake.

He was straddling a picnic bench and facing away from her, staring out at the water. Scooting up behind him in the same position, she slid her arms around his waist. She threaded her fingers up under his untucked shirt, stroking his tense abdomen, the fine hair that arrowed down between the layers of muscle, and laid her cheek on his back.

"It's a nice view here. The lake's not bad, either."

It was nowhere near her strongest material, but it was heartfelt. When she'd driven up and seen him sitting there, his hair loose on his shoulders, his long-fingered hand resting spread on the table top, the denim of his jeans stretched over ass and thighs, his T-shirt delineating the set of his resilient shoulders, her heart had been like a rag wrung out of all its blood.

What if I lose him?

What if you spend your time with him worrying about losing him? How pointless would that be?

He didn't move at first, just kept looking out at the water as she stroked him, pressed her body to his. But then his shoulders lifted in a sigh and he closed his fingers over hers.

"I figured you'd said 'fuck that insensitive asshole' and I'd never hear from you again," he said.

"No, you didn't. You knew this was just a bump in the road, just as I did."

"More like a crater."

"Nope. Just a bump." She pressed a kiss to his neck where the stretched T-shirt gave her access to flesh. He sighed again.

"Don't be cheerful like that. The 'rah-rah, it's all going to be okay' floor nurse routine."

"Does Betty do that?"

"No."

"Then why would I?" She nudged him. "And what's wrong with a little optimism when clouds are dark? No one fusses about turning on a light when it's nighttime, right? It's just good common sense."

He chuckled, though his shoulders slumped briefly. She squeezed him, hard. "Turn around and look at me, Des. Please?"

She backed up enough to let him put his legs under the table. His eyes were weary and sad, which concerned her, but she'd made him laugh. She took it as a hopeful sign.

Des ran a hand over his face. "All the stuff Betty said, it's true, and I agree with her, 99% of the time. But I get tired of dealing with it, you know, and I can't always be upbeat and rational about it. Sometimes I need to get selfish, childish and stubborn. I need to be pissed off and frustrated and say dumbass things. I have more times of late when I don't feel good, and it makes me less easy to get along with. That's a lot to dump on a girl you've just met and you're trying to impress, you know?"

Julie recalled her earlier thoughts in the church, when she'd thought about life being so much worse for so many other people, but sometimes something sucked so badly you just had to stomp your feet, be pissed off and childish to deal with it. While it hadn't felt great to be in the debris circle of Des's detonation, she did get it. And she could forgive and love. Reaching out, fighting the fear of rejection, she laid her palm on his chest.

"So you're telling me you're not perfect? You're human? That's a real let down."

"Yeah, isn't it?" His attempt at a smile was so painful it twisted her heart. "Actually, the way I behaved was closer to subhuman. I'm sorry, Julie. You didn't deserve any of my shit. And—"

She shook her head. "Stop right there. That was perfect. You're going to ruin it by saying something like 'this is why I can't be with anyone,' and that's just so wrongheaded thinking, Des. You're a great guy. You're my guy. I love you. After all the crap relationships I've been in, I should be more cautious and shouldn't trust my feelings at all, and the funny thing is, I haven't, not for a long time. But in this scary short time, I crossed a line with you and suddenly I trust them again. I've run the gauntlet. I know what I want and don't want in my life. I don't have to debate endlessly on it anymore."

"So how about if your guy is having to do dialysis five nights a week? Or hey, you're in the mood for some great sex, but I feel like shit?"

She pursed her lips. "How about all the wonderful times I'd miss with you if I only keep score on those times? What about the gift of letting me be part of your life, the person who supports and loves you through that? That is a gift, Des, whether you realize it or not. Don't be such a Dom. Give up some control. Come to the dark side and be like the rest of us mere mortals."

When his expression darkened, she tightened her fingers on his T-shirt. "Because I'll tell you one thing up front. When I get sick, your ass better be at my bedside, putting cold compresses on my feverish brow, massaging my feet, asking me if I need a blanket..." At his amused look she tossed a mock scowl at him. "Oh yeah, you laugh, but ask Marcus and Thomas. I am a clingy, needy sick person, and a total wimp. A cold is full scale, I'm-going-to-die, bubonic plague. I am the biggest baby in the universe. Fortunately, I don't get sick too often, because Marcus said he'd smother me with a pillow and call it an assisted suicide."

"Okay, note to self. Call Marcus and Thomas when you get sick."

"Jerk." She punched his shoulder, pleased when he grabbed her wrist, the hint of a true smile on his face this time. She curled her fingers around his, holding on, and leaned in to touch his face. "We'll get through this, okay? We, you and me, and all our friends. I'm not the only one who loves you, Des." Freeing herself gently, she turned and pulled a small sheaf of folded papers from her bag.

"What is that?"

"Well, while you were off being all broody, I was making rounds and reaching out. I didn't tell anyone anything specific, so don't get that scowly look. I told them you were going through a tough time right now and words of encouragement would be appreciated."

She handed the small bundle over. The one on top was a crayon drawing on construction paper. It showed a male stick figure walking on his hands on a roof line, a big bright sun behind him. Below that, childish scrawl proclaimed, "You are the sun."

"That was one of your roof groupies, Tina. She said one day you were up there and the sun was right behind you, and she thought 'Des is the sun.' So she wanted me to tell you that 'You're like the sun. You make things shine brighter.' This is an email from Billie, and a couple from folks at Logan's club, and the stage hands at the theater today..."

She hadn't had time to do much more than a quick call out, so the notes were short, but she knew the content wasn't what was important as much as the sincere good wishes that had gone into them. "Oh, and there's a case of your flavored water in the car, from the guys you work with. One of them, Diego, said a case of beer or a carton of cigarettes is what really says 'best friends forever' but since you don't smoke or drink, the water is as close as they could get to that message."

Seeing his pensive look, she closed her hand over his. "You're allowed to be special to people. You're allowed to want your life, to fight for your life. The rest of us will be really happy to have you around. And if you and I don't work out, we don't work out. I'm not going to think, 'Well, hell, he's sick. I have to stay because of that.'"

At his look of surprise, she shot him a shrewd glance. "You think I didn't realize that was part of what was bugging you? Des, I want to be with you for you. Healthy or sick. Guilt isn't glue; love is."

"Nice. You can put that on a mug." He didn't say it in a snarky way, though. More as a way to cover whatever was going on behind his thoughtful brown eyes, though she noticed her comment made his shoulders drop down a notch.

"I try to make everything I say imminently quotable, so when someone writes my biography they'll have great sound byte material. It worked for Ben Franklin. They've done whole books of his sayings." She tapped his chest. "Apology accepted. If you'll accept mine for jumping in with both feet and trying to fix, instead of trying to listen."

She took a deep breath. "I can't promise I'm going to be reasonable and understanding when you want to do things your way that might lead to...bad outcomes. I'm selfish. I want you around. But I will try to be as supportive and caring as possible."

"Okay." He looked out toward the water again. The sunlight limned his jaw, reflected off his hair, making her want to touch, but she restrained herself, knowing he needed to talk. "I want to hang around for you, Julie. I want to see where you and I go. But when I realize that by doing that, I could just deepen this thing between us, make it worse if...the worst happens...I feel like a real shit. Then I just feel shitty about all of it. I used to manage that fatalistic feeling pretty well, but in some weird way, getting something as amazing as you, as what you and I are finding, has opened it up again."

"I asked God what kind of sadistic son of a bitch He is, to do something like that, so you're not alone in that feeling. Though since you're a Dom, maybe you understand Him better."

"I think you're thinking of a different kind of sadist. I like to dole out pleasure and pain together."

"Well, that's what this is, isn't it?" She touched his face. "The greatest of pleasures bring the potential for the deepest pain. Maybe that's the way it works."

"Maybe." Des closed his hand over hers. He paused long enough she could sense he was struggling with something difficult to say, so she waited him out. "You remember that day at Bob Evans when you thought I was keeping you at arm's length? I didn't really understand why you thought I was bullshitting, but I realized this morning it was because I was bullshitting myself."

He met her gaze. "I've kept relationships at a distance so I wouldn't hurt people, but I never thought that I might be shielding myself. I didn't want to get so close that saying good-bye would hurt me too much. I don't want to say good-bye to you. But I'm a sinking ship, Julie. That's the truth."

"Oh Des. You're not a sinking ship. You made it to shore. Here. Inside of me. You can keep me, remember? I'm all yours, no matter where you go."

All these years, she'd wanted someone to reassure her of that, that she was something they'd want to keep. In the face of the near violent need she felt in him, a black hole that needed her touch to fill it, to shine light inside it, she let go of any shortcomings or perverse insecurities. She stepped toward what love truly was. A completion for another soul that needed her help to anchor, to ground, to stave off fear and realize everything he was. She was someone who deserved someone she could keep. So did he.

"I wasn't expecting you," he said slowly. "I really wasn't. You remember that day we talked about who we'd want to walk into Heaven with? No one came to mind. I've felt alone most of my life, and I've embraced that feeling, moved past the fear and owned it. So I guess I'm more afraid of wanting to need someone like that, to allow myself that weakness, because I've always had to live without it. But I've thought about it a lot since our discussion."

Her throat was so thick with emotion she wasn't sure how she was able to talk. "So did you decide on Betty Grable or Marilyn Monroe?"

"Tough choice. Maybe Sophia Loren. In a gold dress, with a figure made in Heaven, shiny brown hair..." He stroked it, as they both remembered the night at the party.

"I'm in love for the first time in my life, Julie. I've started in that direction before, but I've always been able to pull back. I can't seem to pull back from you."

He drew a breath. "So I'm going to start the at-home dialysis, like Betty suggested. It'll be a few times a week, and I can do it at night, when I sleep."

"Sounds good. Do it for the people who care about you. It's only a few hours of your life." She modified and gave him back the words he'd given her, when he'd wanted her to go to the urgent care.

His wry expression said he recalled it, though he gave her a direct look. "The first couple times, I'd rather do it on my own, to see how bad it's going to be."

"Okay." She accepted that, though it took some effort. "But maybe if it's driving you a bit crazy, you could call me while it's happening. We could chat a few hours. I know how restless you can get if you have to stay still too long."

"Okay." His fingers clasped hers. "Will you take a walk with me?"

"Of course I will. Anywhere."

He rose, offering her a hand to help her up. As they stood facing one another, she rose on her toes and slid her arms around his shoulders, holding him tight. "I'm sorry for anything I said that was mean," she said softly against his neck. "But I won't be sorry for loving you. Not now or ever."

His arms wound around her, and he held her just as tightly in answer, putting his face against her hair. "I'll hold you to that," he said.

She eased back only when his grip slackened. She was pleased when he took her hand, shouldering the pack he'd had at his feet. He drew her across the parking lot, his destination apparently a trail marker. It was a good thing she'd worn sneakers, because as they hit the trail, his pace increased.

"Where are we headed?"

"It's a surprise. Can you be away from the theater for a while?"

"All day if needed. I told Harris I had some personal things to handle. Thomas and Marcus are here a few more days. Lila freaked when she realized Thomas was painting some the sets."

"Hmm." He stepped off onto a side trail little more than a deer path, and took her down into a ravine, steep enough he spotted her as they slid down the incline. From there the growth grew even denser. He held branches away from her face as he directed her beneath and around them. Another few steps and the foliage opened into a small clearing with a trio of maple trees and a creek trickling through, a musical gurgle of sound. A frog startled by their appearance hopped back in the water with a small splash. There were moss-covered rocks clustered around the creek, and the area had a damp, green smell to it. Sunlight filtered through the interlaced tree branches enough to balance the coolness, but there was a hushed quietness here that reminded her of the church.

"So are you about to tell me you're a serial killer, and this is where you bury your bodies?"

His lips curved. "You did say you always wanted to meet one, but no." Closing his hand over her wrist he knelt, drawing her with him. "See here, where the grasses are pressed down? This is where a deer sleeps, maybe a couple of them. A mother and a fawn. Maybe even a male-female pairing, though they don't really mate for life like other animals do. They can still dream together. Everyone likes having someone like that."

"Yeah. But I like the mated pair idea. Let's pretend they mate for life."

"Okay." He took the hem of her shirt in both hands. "Raise your arms, love."

That telltale flutter in her stomach told her that her Dom was taking over. She obeyed and he stripped off her shirt, his gaze sliding over her breasts in the plain pink bra, the fabric thin enough to show the shape of her nipples. He ran a knuckle over her cleavage and then pushed her jeans off her hips. He took her pink underwear with it, removing her shoes and socks, then her bra. She was standing in the forest naked before his avid gaze.

"Turn toward the tree in the center of those three maples and put your arms over your head. Do it now." His manner became crisp and decisive, brooking no conversation. A primitive part of her understood. After the overload of vulnerability, he was re-asserting control to bring him balance. Thinking of what she'd said to Marcus about safety and heat, it brought her balance as well. She could handle the times he might be vulnerable, where she would have to be the one that brought reassurance and comfort, but knowing he had this reservoir, and a natural instinct and desire to use it whenever he could, was all that mattered to her.

He bent and unzipped the front pockets of the tote. She wasn't surprised he kept coils of rope in the pack, as well as things for his diabetes. He did a quick tie, wraps above and below her breasts, her wrists bound to a branch. A yoke around her throat ran down to the back wraps and secured there, holding her body up straight, her arms bound and her breasts thrust out. He put her face forward against the tree and ran ropes around her upper torso, then dropped to tie her ankles, holding them spread and bound against the tree.

She had enough slack for him to work his fingers in between the trunk and her body and play with her nipples, pinching them and rubbing the tips against the rough bark as she shuddered and her hips bucked against his pelvis, pressed against her bare ass cheeks.

"I'm thinking I should become one of those guys who lives in the woods, off the grid, and keeps his woman naked all the time," he said gruffly in her ear. "I'm not feeling very civilized right now, Julie. I want to remind you I'm your Dom at a level I don't usually go. Can you handle it? Can you handle everything I'm feeling right now, every fucked up, needy, want to fuck you and beat you feeling I have?"

"I want to feel all you're feeling," she responded, her voice unsteady. "Master."

Master. It was a whisper that went through her vitals, through her rapidly beating heart and suddenly constricted lungs as he bent and picked up a long stick, about an inch in diameter at the thickest end. He examined the rough, knotted length, the narrowing of it at the end that he tested by pulling on it. In the corner of her eye, she saw how it snapped back, giving it a whip like flexibility.

No further words, no explanations. He slapped her with the switch and she jumped at the sting, then made a tiny whimper as he followed it with a firm rub over her pale buttocks.

"God, I love your ass. Just as full and gorgeous as the moon. Going to fuck it and your cunt. After this."

She jumped again at the next slap, cried out. He fished in the tote again, and produced a rubber ball. It was too big to swallow, but not too big to get past her teeth as he worked it into her mouth.

"Don't want a hiker to hear you screaming and call the police. Now you can beg for mercy all you want."

No safe words, none given or needed. She trusted him, knew he'd know if she couldn't take anymore. The times he'd hinted at giving her more pain, this was the real deal, that side of his nature fully unleashed. She screamed against the ball as he worked up the intensity, crisscrossing the strikes, using different rhythms, patterns, force.

Her body writhed against the tree, further roughness. He alternated his blows with strokes of her flanks by his strong hands. He pinched and caressed her between her legs, taking the slippery honey there on his fingers and painting it on her rim.

"Des." She shrieked against the ball as he hit her several times more. It was exquisitely painful now, her whole body shaking, nipples hard and abraded against the bark, her pussy dripping, her buttocks clenching at the blows, which just seemed to inflame him further.

Tossing the switch away, he dropped to one knee, parting her buttocks to lick her rim, stab his tongue into it. She came apart, crying out, flinching against the tight hold of his hands over the welts he'd left on her ass. When he stood and opened his jeans, the metal tick of the zipper had her shuddering with another wave of sensation.

"Beg me to fuck you. To hurt you some more."

"Please...anything for you. Anything. It...God, it feels too good...and awful."

Her words were muffled against the ball, but he understood the pleading note, because his dark, pleased chuckle ran tingles up her spine and deep into her ass and cunt. He removed the ball, collecting the saliva from the corners of her mouth with his fingertips.

"You'll just have to bite back those screams yourself, love, because I want to hear every word that spills from your lips as I fuck you."

He pressed his cock into her pussy, working his way into the tight angle, the head of his organ sliding along the front wall of the channel. When his body was flat against hers, he thrust his cock in her in small movements, his other hand sliding around her throat.

"Your life in my hand, love. Is it mine to have? To take?"

She understood his savagery to the root. He needed to

hurt her, to hurt them both, to torment them both. "To have and to hold..." she whispered.

He paused, then thrust deep into her, as she whimpered and his grip tightened further. "Please...Master," she begged. "Please."

Let me have all of you. Please trust me, love me. Fight for me. Fight for your life. Know I can't find this anywhere else, with anyone else. I've just found you.

His fingers slid over her clit as he pushed in deep, withdrew, slow, sliding movements that took her even higher. She begged him for mercy, and received none. He kept taking her higher and higher, teasing her with his fingers but not letting her have the friction she needed to go over. Then he withdrew and slid his cunt-slickened cock into her rear passage, slowly stretching her, invading deep as he let his fingers replace his cock inside her pussy, a thrust and retreat that had her crying like a bird, her head tipped back on his shoulder, her whole body swept with a need so strong she thought she could die from it.

He buried his fingers in her again and kept them still as he began to rub her clit with more diabolical intent. At the same time, he pumped more fiercely into her ass, increasing the discomfort with the pleasure.

"My sub. Her gorgeous ass is all mine, isn't it?"

"Yes," she gasped. "Yes, Master. All of it. Oh God...I can't...please."

"Come for me now."

She did, her response gushing over his fingers, her muscles clamping over his cock, making the climax all the more intense, particularly as her squeezing hold brought him over the same edge. They cried out, grunted, and moaned together, two people clawing and straining to be as close to one being as possible. Their bodies were joined, but it felt as if their hearts and souls had come together too, crashing and pounding, clinging to one another in a storm.

She'd thought of the many ways their paths could have intersected before this, and hadn't come up with anything she could have done differently to make it happen sooner, or work as well as it would work today. They'd been meant to meet in the here and now, after they'd each experienced the lessons they'd needed to make this work with one another.

So that was that. This was the time they'd been given. Whatever might happen to Des, that was the unknown. Their relationship, on the other hand, was meant to be.

There'd be no more turning back, for either of them.

Chapter Nineteen

Des wiped the sweat off his forehead and dropped to a squat on the roofline. This job, roofing multiple houses in the same subdivision, had taken him several hours out of Charlotte. He'd been away for four days. It would be the last time he took a job like this. He missed being with Julie. He also couldn't work at this pace anymore. If he hadn't committed to the job a couple months ago, a favor for a development manager who'd given him and his guys work when times were far leaner, he wouldn't have done it. He'd limited himself mostly to supervision on this job, more so than he'd ever done before, but this last day he'd pitched in, determined to be done with it and get home tonight.

He'd started the dialysis a couple weeks ago, and Betty wasn't seeing the results she'd hoped. They'd gone with the peritoneal dialysis, which he could do at night in his sleep and had equipment that could be easily transported, a nice rolling case he'd brought with him here. However, she was thinking he might respond better to the hemodialysis, though the data was inconclusive that one was any damn better than the other. Hemodialysis would require the surgical insertion of a fistula in his arm. They'd put in a catheter for the peritoneal dialysis already. He was starting to feel like a cyborg.

She wanted to push the damn kidney transplant thing again, he could tell. He knew she and Julie had been talking, because one night Julie had oh-so-casually mentioned some articles she'd been reading. He'd tried not to let his normal defensiveness assert itself, but he hadn't been altogether successful, and she hadn't been altogether successful in not being pushy. He'd told her he'd be working out of town the next few days, so he'd call her again when he got back. And that was the last time they'd spoken.

He was an official dumbass. He wanted to hear her voice. He wanted to curl around her in bed, bury his face in her hair, and keep at bay everything that seemed to be closing in on him, way too fast. Fuck, he'd had this under control for a long time, with a fuck-it, whatever happens, happens, mentality. But it was frayed at the edges. He should tell the guys they had to finish without him, and head for home. He felt like he needed to be home, with a sudden urgency he couldn't explain. He needed to be in his bed, with her. God, he felt like shit.

"You roofing this whole thing by yourself?"

The familiar voice surprised him. He rose so he could see the front lawn, where Marcus Stanton stood looking like a Michelangelo sculpture in Armani, the silver of his Rolex and his ebony black wings of hair catching the sunlight.

"We just finished this one. The other guys went for a dinner break. I was taking a breather, doing some thinking."

"It's a good place to think." Marcus's gaze coursed over the expanse of new shingles, the sunset sky building in rose and gold color behind Des.

"So why are you here?" Des asked. "Found some talent to recruit?"

"There's talent to be recruited everywhere, but no. You're about thirty minutes away from our North Carolina house. Julie told me you were at this job site. I need to talk to you. Well, we do." He gestured to his car, a gleaming Mercedes, where Thomas was sitting in the passenger seat. He lifted his hand in greeting as Des noticed him. "But Thomas and I agreed I'd talk to you first.'

Surely Julie hadn't worried so much about his phone silence he'd sent her friends after him? He'd been texting her, for Christ's sake.

His irritation must have shown, because Marcus's expression hardened slightly. "If you don't want to come down, I can come up."

His tone raised Des's hackles. "I didn't ask for company."

"Coming up it is, then." Marcus disappeared beneath the roofline.

"Climb up on this roof in those fancy shoes, you'll break your neck," Des called down.

"Yeah, and that one will be on you."

When Marcus's head emerged over the roofline, Des sat down on the peak, eying him. "Did Julie send you?"

Marcus gave him a puzzled look. "Why would she?" At Des's surprised expression, his eyes narrowed. "Did you two have a fight?"

"None of your business, and not exactly."

"When was the last time you talked to her?"

"A few days ago. I've been busy."

"Hmm. I would kick your ass off this roof if it wouldn't scuff my very expensive shoes." Marcus settled his hip on the top rung of the ladder, a half seated position. "I asked her where you were, she told me how close you were and I casually mentioned we might stop by to take you out for dinner."

Des studied his expression. The man could play poker in Vegas, because he wasn't giving anything away, but Des relied on his gut rather than physical cues. "Why didn't you tell her the real reason?"

"I'll let you answer that, after I tell you why I'm here. Julie told me you have this thing about not wanting to take a kidney that could go to someone else."

Before Des could react to that, Marcus waved a hand. "I get it, but only because if Thomas needed a kidney, he'd probably feel the same way you do. I'm a stubborn, selfish bastard, myself. I'd want the chance to live. But since you're just a stubborn bastard, let's look at it this way. You believe in fate, destiny, powers bigger than yourself, magic, Harry Potter?"

Des arched a brow. "Religion?"

"What the hell does religion have to do with God?" Marcus snorted. "Let's just say for a minute you answered yes, which I'm sure you would, because you sit up on rooftops on your break to commune with something. And you love our girl, and you can't truly love someone without some kind of belief in a power bigger than yourself."

"My girl. Not yours."

Marcus showed his teeth in a Dom-eating feral grin. "She's yours when I decide you're not going to be a dumbass. Stop changing the subject. I need to run something by you. Give me your opinion on the odds of this hypothetical situation ever happening." He settled on the ladder as if it was a comfortable chair. Des gave him points for the deception, because he knew the aluminum rung had to be cutting into the guy's perfect ass.

"You meet a girl from New York, who came down here because Madison happens to be friends with her and happens to need help with her community theater. You fall in love with her, and she introduces you to her two best friends. All around the time your kidneys are about to give up the ghost."

"Sounds like a Murphy's Law kick in the teeth."

"I haven't reached the Twilight Zone punch line yet. Since Thomas met you, you've felt familiar to him. He's not the New Age type, so he's not talking past lives. It wasn't until we came home here and showed his mother that picture he took of you and Julie that we figured it out. You look like his aunt, Elaine's sister, Christine."

Des felt an odd lurch inside of him, which he immediately ignored. He had no idea where this was going, but it couldn't be going where it sounded like it was.

Marcus tossed him a look. "Still sitting? Good. Well, here we are at dinner, talking about the chances of two people looking like they're related who aren't, when Elaine tells us one of the dark Wilder family secrets. Christine was a prescription drug addict, who basically drifted through life until she died of an overdose. But one of the things she confided to her sister on one of her rare visits home was that she'd given up a baby and never told anyone about it."

That lurch became a precipitous dip in his chest, but Des set his jaw. "That doesn't mean anything."

"No. That in itself doesn't. But Thomas contacted Betty, who has your blood work on file. He had her do a DNA test, and your markers, or whatever they call them, line up. He's your cousin, Des. Your mother was his Aunt Christine."

The roofline wavered, the sun suddenly much brighter and hotter. Des curled his fingers around the roof's spine, for the first time in his life feeling like he was up way too high. He closed his eyes.

"Des?" Marcus's voice was sharp. "You okay? Shit, I knew I should have told you to come down."

"I said no. Not your fault. Yeah. I'm fine." Des opened his eyes, willing it to be a true statement. "This is bullshit. It's bullshit." His voice sounded hollow, like through a megaphone.

"Yeah, that would be my reaction. But let's trace our steps back to the Fate crap. What are the chances one of Julie's best friends ends up being your cousin? And it just so happens that cousin is probably going to be a great match for the kidney you need, and he wants to give it to you. Hell, he'd cut it out and hand it to you right now if I let him. That is a lot of 'just so happens'. You turn your back on that, I wouldn't blame the Powers-That-Be for skewering your ass with a lightning bolt right here, right now."

Des struggled past the unlikeliness of it all and focused on what he could handle thinking about. "You can't be fine with the person you love giving up an organ."

"It's not my choice, it's his. No matter my feelings, I'd be just as clueless as you if I ignored a coincidence so close to a divine miracle that for a moment I almost believed there was something greater than my own awesomeness."

Des clasped his arms around his knees, his jaw set. It was too soon, too...abrupt. Yet how else could something like that seem? The real problem was he'd fought this idea for so long, denied himself the option. True, he'd started giving it some more thought, though he hadn't revealed that to Julie. She and Betty had been wearing him down. Well, his desire to be around as long as he could for Julie, to make her happy...that was what had worn him down.

Marcus shot him a look. "You may not want to take up a spot on a donor list, but Thomas has a kidney he's willing to give to you and only you. Unlike you, he accepts this big cosmic mash-up."

"Have you told Julie any of this?" Des demanded.

"No. This was your decision, and we didn't want to get her hopes up if we were wrong about Thomas's match or your interest in it."

"If I decide not to do it?"

"Then she'll never hear it from us. I won't hurt her needlessly." Marcus gave him that hard look again. "But I hope you won't, either."

"What if something goes wrong with his other kidney? How're you going to feel about this conversation then?"

Marcus shook his head. "Is that what this is really all about? You'd prefer to die than to feel obligated to anyone? Refusing to be the receiver, ever, is a form of selfishness. It's called self-imposed martyrdom, and there's nothing more annoying. But, hey, if you decide to go that route, you'll be the proudest, most selfless guy in the whole cemetery. Julie's heart will still be broken."

Des clenched his fists and stared off at the sky, the drift of clouds, a sunset so deep in colors it made his eyes and chest hurt. "Fuck you."

"Yeah, I get that a lot. Not usually from straight guys, though."

Des shifted his glance at the creak of the ladder. Marcus had removed his shoes and stepped onto the roof. He made his way up the slope to Des. "Hell, those shingles are hot."

"Not as hot as they'll be in August." Des was impressed by Marcus's balance and confidence, the way he didn't overbalance or seem nervous, like so many people did when they first walked a roofline. He settled down next to Des, shoulder to shoulder.

"Nice view up here."

"How'd you learn to walk a roof?"

"I engineered some creative escape routes in my youth."

Des sighed. "It's not that I'm not appreciative. I know I'm coming off like a shit—"

Marcus waved a hand, stopping him. "I get it. Really, I do. But see, people like Thomas and Julie, they don't. They've always had people telling them what to do because those people love them. Not because they're trying to assert power over them, control their lives or make them helpless. Though with a strong personality, it can seem that way sometimes. You need to meet my mother-in-law," he added with a twist of his lips.

Despite the humor, when Marcus met his gaze, Des saw a dark history behind the green eyes, much darker than he would have assigned to the well-dressed, wealthy and confident male. He detected something feral and predatory there, a creature who would kill to survive. Then Marcus blinked and his expression was casual once more, though Des was sure the reveal had been intentional.

"I lived on the streets in my teens. I should have been dead a hundred times over. I lost people out there I loved and, until I met Thomas, I genuinely thought my heart had died with them. But it didn't. And I almost didn't realize that until it was too late."

Marcus shifted to lie back on his elbows, tipping his head to look at the clouds as Des had done. "This is where people like you and me end up being the village idiots," Marcus mused. "We're so focused on no one controlling our destiny, no one telling us what to do. That's because we've been helpless, we've been controlled by fate. But as a result, we miss that the person who loves us is trying to give us a gift of themselves. She or he is trying to say, 'you matter so much, there's nothing I won't do to keep you safe, well and happy.' Yeah, we can differ on methods, but letting someone help you keep on living, that one's clear cut. Right?"

Des swallowed. Marcus gave him a piercing look. "Let me put it another way. Are you her Master or not?"

Des stiffened. "That's private."

"Doesn't look all that private. To another Dom, it's as obvious as your ridiculously low body fat ratio. So if the answer to the question is yes, then you do what you have to do to be around to take care of her. Right?"

Marcus straightened, getting to his feet so he could begin working his way down the roof. "You don't owe me any answers, Des. I'm giving you information. What you do with it is up to you. But I'm hoping you're as smart as she thinks you are."

He'd reached the ladder again, and started down it, holding his shoes and socks, but stopped when his upper body was still visible. "Well, let me correct that. Most of us aren't as smart as the people who love us think we are. But if we love them back, we do our best to try and fake it."

"Yeah." Des couldn't argue that. His brow creased. "Julie's family...they didn't sound like they were really there for her much. Emotionally, I mean."

"Yes and no. They're like a bunch of toddlers, everything periphery to their perpetual self-absorption. Yet, her mom still flew home from Europe when Julie had to have an emergency appendectomy. And her dad insists on paying for her upkeep, though there are homeless people with more fixed costs than that girl." Marcus shrugged. "Families all care, in their own warped way."

"Yeah." Desmond looked back up at the drifting clouds. "You never answered my first question. What happens if Thomas's other kidney goes bad?"

Marcus stared at him between the rungs of the ladder. "If you hurt Julie, if you don't appreciate the gift that life has given you, I'll personally cut it out of your body so Thomas can have it back. Otherwise, there are plenty of people in the world who don't deserve to live that can give up a kidney. I'll find them."

Des blinked as Marcus's head disappeared beneath the edge of the roof. "He meant that shit," he muttered.

"Of course I did," drifted up from below the roofline. "Asshole. Go talk to Julie. Do the right thing. Stop being a prick."

Des shook his head. He paused, pride warring with a whole lot of other emotions, so that when he spoke, it came out a harsh bark. "Marcus."

Marcus reappeared. Des wished a million things could be different, but Marcus's words had reminded him there were a few key things that he didn't want to change. He swallowed pride, a jagged lump the size of Texas.

"I'm feeling a little out of it. Can you and Thomas help get me to the ground so I don't break my neck?"

Marcus's expression switched to instant concern and Des shook his head. "I'll be fine once I get down there and rest and eat something. Just overdid it on this job."

"Well, then, we'll take you out for some dinner. And we can go to Elaine's—"

"No." Des shook his head. "Not right now. I can't... You're making me rethink something I've always been sure I'd never do. Thinking about a family I didn't know I had on top of that, dealing with it today..."

"Yeah. I get it. No worries, man." Marcus's empathy was clear, helping Des relax, but he wasn't done yet.

"I want to talk to Thomas about this, one on one, no interference. All right?"

Marcus's green eyes reminded him of Betty's no-nonsense sharpness. "You got it, but it was Thomas who insisted on this, Des. Believe me, my influence was more on the 'are you fucking mental' side. Initially."

"And now?"

Marcus lifted a shoulder. "We find ourselves agreeing to all sorts of insane things to honor the people we love. To give them the gift of our faith, and trust that sometimes they might know a little more about things than we do." His lips quirked. "Though if we're smart, we don't tell them that. Else they'd become unbearable."

§

A meal and a night's rest had restored his strength. Though Des had protested fiercely, Marcus and Thomas hadn't stopped with offering him dinner, probably because he'd only eaten the amount of it needed to prevent dangerously low blood sugar. His lack of appetite only increased their worry. Thomas had driven Des in his truck the several hours back to Charlotte, Marcus following in his car.

"You look like shit," Marcus said bluntly. "We're going to get you home."

Des and Thomas had their talk, though it was clear that Marcus had spoken the truth. Thomas had no concerns about donating Des his kidney. He also didn't bring up much about the familial connection, sensitive enough to realize—or Marcus had cued him to it—that Des wasn't really ready to discuss that.

Des had eventually nodded off, sleeping through the offerings of the radio station that Thomas turned on as background noise. When he woke, Betty was leaning over him through the open window.

"I'll take care of your dialysis tonight," she said. "You'll feel better tomorrow."

He was unable to refuse. He pushed down that familiar demon of helplessness, of being far less of a man than Julie deserved. Thomas helped Betty get him into the house, his arm strong and sure around Des's waist, Des's hand gripping his broad shoulder. His cousin. This was his cousin.

No, still not going there. But as he glanced at Thomas, at the serious brown eyes and straight nose, he wondered if they shared any common features.

"Thanks," Des said. "Thanks to you both. Sorry about this."

"Nothing to be sorry about."

"Well, I wouldn't say that." Marcus had rolled in the case with the dialysis equipment and was at the foot of the bed. He gave Des a humorous look. "I did tell you that Elaine Wilder was your aunt. The horror of that is enough to put anyone on his ass."

"My mother is going to put something up your ass."

"She says worse about me all the time. Your mother has a gutter mouth these days."

"From your influence."

As the two men bantered back and forth, Des was aware of Betty hooking him up, her mouth thin and eyes worried, but when she caught him looking, she stroked a hand along his face, a maternal caress.

"Just rest, Des," she said quietly. "I'll handle this tonight."

He drifted off. When he woke, a few hours from dawn, Marcus and Thomas had gone. Betty was asleep on his couch. She'd removed the dialysis hook ups when it finished cycling, shut everything down and prepped it for the next treatment. He would have done that. He usually did that, usually did all of it himself.

But as Marcus said, family cared about you when you needed it. He spent the next couple hours staring into the darkness, thinking about how he'd find the courage to fight for family and love for the first time in his life... And fight for his life, one more time.

§

Des came into the theater. The audience area was dark, but with the stage lit, he didn't have trouble finding Julie's silhouette. She was watching the ongoing rehearsal, leaning against the seat in front of her. Lila and Harris were handling most of what was going on, but she'd watch and give her opinions. She would enhance without taking over, provide direction where the path was murky. He'd watched her do it during the prep work for *Consent*, offering suggestions to Harris, to the tech people. She had a grasp of the whole picture invaluable for making the resulting production the best possible offering.

She wasn't always nice about it. She could be a bitch when needed, stepping in when someone was going the wrong direction and needed a firmer hand. She knew her ultimate responsibility was to owners, investors and, most importantly, the audience. Turning out quality, art, was her focus. Not control or power. She understood that beauty happened with the placement of rocks at the right spots in the stream. She directed and altered the flow, so sunlight could sparkle in a different pattern upon it, or so a tree's roots wouldn't be eroded by the water creeping up the banks. Yet she retained her appreciation of water as water, maintaining the integrity of what it was.

He loved taking all that passion and submissive response and doing the same with his rope. Shaping, driving her to a churning peak, seeing the many different ways she would overflow, respond to his will. Yet he was always dipping into the same deep immutable pool, the soul of who she was.

He'd been a bastard. Marcus was right. She'd forgive him, because that was part of who she was, too. But he had no intention of taking that generosity for granted or abusing it too often. And not just because Marcus would cut his kidney out with a dull edged knife if he didn't.

Des slid down into a seat four rows behind her, wanting to take time to savor the way she was when she thought no one was watching. The slight movements of her shoulders and head were like an alert, smooth-feathered bird.

She picked up a notebook, scribbling in it, and set it back down, leaning forward to fold her arms on the chair in front of her, showing her sharpened attention for the next scene.

Onstage, the hero walked across it as the heroine stared at him. Master Horn and Cherry Blossom were good choices for these roles, a handsome couple, but not so pretty that they didn't look real, or glamor over the strength of the Dom/sub dynamic happening between them. Des had watched them in a club environment, and they could be mesmerizing.

From the conversation back and forth between Lila and the director, Des knew the setting of this scene was supposed to be a colorful marketplace in the islands, with a small cluster of extras shopping around the hero and heroine. As they approached one another, the movements of the others would slow, all people on stage except them frozen.

Harris spoke. "Lights will dim and our center stage characters will be spotlighted, as if time has stopped."

Master Horn slid a large hand over Cherry's shoulder, wrapping his fingers in her streaked blond hair to tilt her head back. Their eyes locked. "I'm going to take you home now. Tie you up so you can't move. Then I'm going to whip you. Your ass, your back, your thighs. I'll press myself up against all those marks and, when I'm balls deep in you and start thrusting, that pain will become pleasure. You'll beg for more. Because surrender is tearing yourself open, taking pain and asking for more. Nothing is sweeter or more terrible than cracking open your soul and giving it to someone you trust. Do you trust me?"

"Yes," she whispered.

"Then get on your knees to me here. In front of all of them. Now."

She sank down, his hand still in her hair. She pressed her lips to his thigh and stayed motionless, cuing the end of the scene.

The performance would be powerful because it would be real. The flogging scene would happen, and her excited reaction would be genuine. Des had read that part of the script, because it preceded a rope tying scene Julie wanted him to check out, both for his insights on its safety and improvements to make it more dramatic. Horn wasn't a rope guy, so he welcomed the expertise.

This show would likely generate more controversy than the first. *Consent* had been an amalgamation of talents the audience could mostly absorb with pleased fascination but the detachment of viewing a circus, a fantasy come to life. This script dealt with issues and emotions everyone experienced, kinky or vanilla. It would be impossible to stay detached and not see the connections between this power exchange in the BDSM world and the give and take in every relationship.

Julie leaned back in her chair. Des wanted to move into the row behind her, take down her hair, stroke his fingers through it, put his teeth against her throat and cup her beautiful breasts.

He had the right to do all of that as her Master, her lover, her Dom. But the man had some bridges to mend first. He wanted to wrap his arms around her, press his face against the side of hers and hold on to that still, precious moment as long as he could before the world ruined it. That had been the root of his problem, hadn't it? He wanted that perfection, nothing about his health and his life destroying it.

During those early dawn hours, he'd realized that he was going to have to accept a new definition of perfection. It was going to sometimes be messy, heartbreaking, tedious, frustrating... It was going to be everything that sharing a life with someone was and meant, like Julie had said. Glorious heaven and hell, and many other places in between.

"I missed you," she said abruptly, not turning around. "Jerk."

Of course she knew he was here. He almost smiled. Rising, he came down the aisle and moved into the row behind her, sitting down so he could cross his arms on the seatback next to her and look at her profile. She kept her eyes on the stage, though currently the actors were discussing some kind of issue with Lila, their words indiscernible as Julie and Des's conversation would be to them. Two different plays in progress.

"I missed you, too. So much it hurt."

"Good." She set her chin and he almost smiled again, except it was blocked by the ache in his chest. He trailed his knuckles down her face, then spread his fingers out, settling them over her throat. The way she responded to that, not softening yet not drawing away, sent a hard jolt of longing into heart, stomach, groin.

He felt the jump of her pulse, that awe-inspiring reaction. Initially, he'd wondered if her response to him was just a first sub experience thing. It could be, but the offering of her love wasn't a first-time experience. Either he was too selfish and fearful to let her go, or he trusted what they both seemed to feel around one another. Trust was always a harder and bigger leap for a Dom than a sub. But he'd better find the balls for it or she'd kick them into his throat. Yeah, she might let him cut her loose, but only if he was hobbling.

He did smile now. Leaning in, he spoke against her delicate ear. "I'm going to do the kidney transplant, Julie. I'm going to try really hard to make it work and last, so I can be with you. Unless you've decided I'm too much of a bastard, in which case I'll skip the whole surgery thing and just die. Not that you should feel any pressure to be with me because of that."

A quiver went through her, the initial reaction to the news, along with all the emotional debris that went with it, but he was proud of his girl, how quickly she rallied. She masked all that to give him an indifferent sidelong glance.

"How long before I have to decide one way or another? I'd prefer to be mad at you for another month or so, if you can put off dying until then."

"Oh, well, it's imminent. Any minute now, so you'll have

to decide this second."

"I'm calling Betty to verify that. I'm suspicious of your motives."

"You should be," he said and tilted her head back. He rose to get the best angle at her gorgeous lips. She was resistant at first, all those tumultuous emotions coming to the forefront in the bite of her nails through his shirt, the stiffness of her body, the punch she tried to land in his midriff. He caught that, prying open her fingers and shifting his grip to her wrist to hold her while he kissed her like the desperate man he was. When her nails dug in for a different reason, her captured hand curling over his, her lips softening, he groaned into her mouth.

He destroyed her hair by tunneling his fingers in it, and kissed her even deeper. He could have dragged her over the seat, taken her then and there, but the shadows weren't deep enough and the distraction of those on stage wouldn't be prolonged enough. Plus, while the male need to steep himself in sex to heal the wounds of the past couple days was strong, she needed something different first.

Stepping over the seat, he sat down next to her and wrapped her up in his arms, pulling her onto his lap to get as much of himself around her lush, trembling body that he could. "I'm sorry I was such an asshole. I'm sorry for wanting you to be with me through all this. I'm sorry for every moment I'm going to be a jerk about this stuff. I'm going to have to learn how to stop being a fucking island fortress about it. It just feels like such a lousy gift to share with the woman I love."

"Men are so dumb," she said against his chest. "You couldn't give me a better gift than that."

"Women are bizarre." He felt her lips curve against him. He didn't want to ruin the moment, but he knew this was part of what he'd just promised. Full disclosure.

Taking a breath, he eased her back. "There's more to it. And I want you to understand something. If you don't want me to do this, I won't. I'll get on the donor list and wait for another." Even if a genetic match was likely the only chance he had. "And I can do dialysis for a while." Even though Betty said he wasn't responding as well to it as she'd hoped. "Okay?"

None of those caveats mattered. He would watch her reaction closely and, even if she tried to hide it, he wasn't going to do anything to jeopardize her relationship with the best friends she had if... Well, if he ended up meeting all expectations for a shortened life span.

"You remember that my best chance is a genetic match, which is different from most people who need a kidney, because most the time they don't need to be as specific as other organs."

"Because you're special," she said.

"Because I'm a fucking health disaster," he corrected, though he stroked a hand down her face for her staunch loyalty.

"Turns out, Thomas may be my cousin. Actually, apparently is my cousin."

Her eyes widened. "What?"

"He thought I looked familiar, and..." He gave her the details as her gaze stayed fastened to his face. He could practically see the thoughts whirling behind her eyes, digesting the impossible the way he had.

"I thought he was staring at you so funny that night we had dinner. Oh my God. And Thomas, he didn't even hesitate..."

Her eyes filled, confirming what he knew. She was blessed in friends. He spoke gruffly, not ready to show how much it had moved him, particularly yesterday. Marcus might be the Dom in that relationship, but it was Thomas who'd been immovable on taking Des home, not taking Des's no for an answer.

"Thomas said Elaine, his mom"—Des's aunt, something he was still trying to wrap his mind around—"could tell me more, when and if I'm ready."

"Des. Wow." She put her hand over his, and he gave her time to let it sink in, so she could marshal whatever questions she'd have. "I know you probably don't want to hear this right now, but what are the chances? You meet me, and Thomas, one of my closest friends..."

"Yeah, Marcus pointed out the same thing when he told me about it. Fate, destiny, all that good stuff."

"Did he call you?"

"He came out to the job site. He and Thomas both." He was prepared for her to be upset that they hadn't talked to her first, but he saw it hit her with another blinked-back round of tears.

"They didn't want me to know in case you said no. Those idiots." But love saturated the insult, and her hand was tight around Des's. Then her eyes brightened and she touched his face.

"You have to admit it's a damn good sign from the universe. Kind of hard to say no to it."

"Tell me about it." He gave her a crooked smile. "I'm new to all this, Julie. Betty, my doctors...I'm not saying I got to where I am all by myself without help. That'd be the height of ego. But I'm not used to the level of emotional support, the sharing that comes with family, a woman who wants to be with me through all of it. I don't know how not to view it as..."

"Interference? Someone trying to run your life, tell you what to do, control things? Yeah, welcome to family culture shock." She dimpled. "I have faith in you. You'll get used to it. You might even move from tolerance to actually liking it, after a few decades. It grows on you, like an affectionate fungus."

He chuckled, but sat silently for a time, gathering his thoughts. Her fingertips glided back and forth across his chest, her eyes on him. She didn't speak, waiting him out, giving him time.

"I'm sure about Thomas's feelings, but how do you think Marcus really feels about it?" Because he knew exactly how he'd feel if Julie had decided to donate her kidney to someone.

"He'll be worried as hell and masking it," Julie said bluntly. "Thomas is what makes him human, and whole. But if Thomas can help, that's what he's going to do, and he'll do a good job all on his own making Marcus okay with it, don't worry. Marcus is a different kind of Dom from you. You have it as this simmering undercurrent delicious to feel, like being surrounded by a cocoon of vibrating energy, even when I'm not with you. You turn it up when it's time to let it out to play. Whereas Marcus..."

"It's usually at a nine, even at low level. Yeah, I picked up on that. Doms do take each other's measure. Have you ever watched the two of them have a scene?"

"Oh God, no." Her expression was comical. "I imagine it, which gets me stirred up, but I think they'd be horribly uncomfortable with me watching. Their favorite dungeon in New York is men only. Marcus will go to co-ed. He says he doesn't really give a shit about gay men's hang ups about doing scenes in co-ed clubs, but I think it's still a comfort zone thing for Thomas. I get it."

"Would it turn you on to watch them, if you could do it without embarrassment on either side?"

She snorted. "It would turn on anything with a pulse. I take it we're done talking about life and death decisions for a while?"

"We are." He squeezed her hand. "I haven't seen you in four days. I have bigger issues."

"I'm not fooled. You're trying to distract me with sex so I'll forgive you for the cone of silence."

"I would never try something that devious and underhanded. Besides, you already forgave me. You're a saint that way, forgiving the inevitable shortcomings of those around you."

"Mm-hm." She did a credible imitation of Billie Dee-Lite and earned a smile from him as he recognized it.

"Not bad."

"Well, it still needs work. But I think you actually have to be a formidable black woman to pull off the intonation. That 'who do you think you're fooling' and 'boy, I will so kick your ass' combo.

"Or a formidable black drag queen."

"Exactly." She paused to trace his cheek and jaw. "I know it can't always be perfect for us," she said seriously, "and I know you have to be your own person. I know I can be a steam roller when I'm worried and want to take care of someone I love. So we're going to hurt each other again. I'm not naïve. I just need you to understand that when you pull away and close down, it leaves me all alone with years of built up insecurity about guys who walk away from me emotionally and physically."

"I know." He closed his hand over hers. "I'm sorry, Julie."

She glanced down at where his hand tangled with her other one in her lap. "I try to manage that shit on my own, but one of the things I like about you is how open you seem to be to me and my feelings. So I'll work on being better on my end if you could add one thing to that Billy Joel song."

She watched him figure it out, and he loved the pleasure in her eyes when he did. "The part that says when he's deep inside himself, not to be too concerned, because he doesn't really need anything while he's gone?"

"Yeah. If you could just send me a hug or two when you're in that place, stick your head out now and again, that would be great."

He met her eyes. "Even if I'm deep in my head, I still need you, Julie. That's how I knew when I fell in love with you. For the first time in my life I need someone so much I can't turn it off and convince myself otherwise."

She slid her arms around his neck, holding him close and turning her head to his mouth, offering him a marvelously predictable hot, toe-curling kiss. He quickly took over, fist in her hair and in the back of her shirt, finding bare flesh beneath it and telegraphing his desire. They'd need to find somewhere private really soon.

"Good answer," she said against his lips.

Chapter Twenty

Marcus leaned against the wall, watching the nurse flutter around his lover, doing her job while blushing and smiling at Thomas's uncalculated charm. His sexy, slow smile, the way he called all women *ma'am*, how he tried to accommodate her while she was trying to do the pre-surgery prep, were all part of what Marcus found appealing about him.

Yet there were far, far deeper and broader things that bound the two of them together. During the time Thomas had left him to care for his family, during the struggle to reconcile their own needs with that, Marcus's gut had ached for everything they could be to one another, a chance they'd had for far too brief a period.

Now past the worst of those challenges, the two of them were married and Thomas's art career was in full swing. Yet Marcus felt like he'd experienced only the tip of the iceberg of how deep their bonds went. He loved his farm boy more every day, a condition only exacerbated by Thomas feeling the same way.

His initial reaction to Thomas's decision to give his cousin a kidney had been no, no and *oh hell no*. He was the selfish one. He knew that and didn't apologize for it. But he'd learned it didn't matter who he was to Thomas as Master or husband, friend or lover, there was an inviolate area of choice that belonged to Thomas alone. It was an essential part of who he was, and as much a part of what Marcus loved about him as anything else. Goddamn it.

Marcus knew he was a prick for wishing he hadn't visited Des to give him the option, persuading him toward this. But fuck, he loved Julie, and Thomas had asked him to do it.

"You're good at convincing people to do things they think they'd never do," his pet had said, his brown eyes knowing and understanding Marcus's dilemma, but trapping his conscience in a corner on it regardless. He'd make Thomas pay for that later in a variety of ways. There would be a later. He wasn't going to be a drama queen about this. Thomas would never let him live it down.

Almost no one who donated a kidney died during the surgery. Very few had any complications afterward, and Thomas was strong and healthy as a draft horse, especially now that they'd gotten on top of that ulcer he'd developed some time ago.

As the nurse took her leave, Thomas's doe-brown eyes came back to him. "You look like a glowering statue over there," he observed. "Or a stick of dynamite about to go off. Not sure which."

"I'm missing a whole day of work for this. And don't get me started on how far behind you'll be on those three pieces you owe me for the San Francisco show."

"You don't care about any of that." Thomas held out a hand. "Come sit on the bed with me."

"There are many things I want to do on a bed with you. Sitting is not the first one that comes to mind."

"It's the hospital gown, isn't it? The way the pale color leeches all the pigment out of my skin and how the sack-like shape and gap in the back show off my ass. It makes me irresistible."

Marcus came and sat on the bed, bracing his ankle on his opposite knee. Thomas's hand fell naturally on his thigh and their fingers laced. "Your mom should be here soon with Rory," Marcus said.

"Yeah, he'll take any opportunity to drive, now that he has the hand-controlled van. I told you that we should have called them afterwards, or just waited and brought it up at Easter dinner. 'Hey, I did two gallery showings and we visited Monterey. Here are the pictures. Oh, and by the way, I donated a kidney to Julie's soulmate.'"

Marcus arched a brow. "Under normal circumstances, I

have zero fear of your mother. Telling her we didn't give her so much as a heads up before they put you on a table, cut you open and took a major organ out..."

He cut himself off when a mortifying and terrifyingly strong wave of emotion hit him. He was squeezing Thomas's hand so hard he was likely going to break it. "I shouldn't be here."

"You have to be here. I need you. It's in the marriage rule book." Thomas wouldn't let him pull away. "Do me a favor. Hold me in that way you do really well, that convinces us both everything's fine."

Actually that was the feeling Marcus got when Thomas was holding him, but since he was supposed to be the alpha and Master here, he had enough pride not to say it. Though from Thomas's knowing look, Marcus figured he already knew it. But he did wrap his arms around Thomas. His pet sat up so it wasn't like Marcus was lying in his arms like some swooning heroine. He knew this helped Thomas as much as it helped him. That was what the whole marriage deal was about, too.

Thomas let out a sigh and relaxed against him as Marcus threaded his fingers through the curls at his nape and tugged. Then he trailed them past the tie of the gown and stroked the bare line of his spine.

"It's going to suck, being out of commission on the sex side of things for a while," Thomas said.

"As long as you can get on your knees and give me blow jobs, I'm good with it."

"Asshole." Thomas put his lips against Marcus's neck and bit lightly, but it sent a bolt of response into dark, savage places Marcus knew were too close to the surface. His farm boy was fanning the flames. "Let's get in a quick fuck before this all goes down."

Marcus chuckled, though his fingers dug into Thomas's back muscles as his submissive's lips and tongue dragged over his carotid. Marcus had fucked him endlessly last night and, though he hadn't always been gentle, he'd been thorough.

"You are pushing it," Marcus muttered, drawing his head back. He gave Thomas a warning look, though the moist look of Thomas's lips was way too distracting. He attempted a casual tone.

"If I entertain that idea for even a millisecond, that's when your mother and Rory would come in. Your mother would have a heart attack and Rory would swear we'd burned out his retinas."

Still, Marcus slid his hand under the covers, under that blissfully loose gown, and closed his hand around his sub, his slave, his heart and soul.

His gaze flicked up. He knew Thomas had only been half teasing, but it was still a surprise to find him fully erect. Thomas gave him a strained smile. "You should have seen yourself while the nurse was prepping me. Face all stern, you leaning against the wall with your arms crossed over your chest. You're wearing jeans today and you didn't shave this morning, giving you that rougher, more dangerous look."

When Thomas nipped his neck again, Marcus found his footing. Using a grip on his hair to pull him away, Marcus pushed him to his back, reinforcing the motion with a harsh command. "Stay down."

Thomas's eyes widened and flicked to the closed door, but he'd started this and Marcus would finish it. He had ears like a cat's. Plus this wasn't going to take long.

He raked up Thomas's gown and bent over him as Thomas sucked in a breath. "Marcus."

"Just lie there and take it. You're mine to do whenever I want, right?"

Thomas nodded, his jaw tight, long fingers clutching the covers. Marcus put his mouth over him, went down on that hard, rigid organ that pulsed under his tongue and lips. He knew this body better than his own, knew Thomas deep down was a little worried, a little scared, as anyone would be. His Master could make sure he knew it was all right, no matter how bone deep terrified Marcus was of losing him, of something going wrong. This act, meaning so much more than just mouth, hand, cock and orgasm, could calm things for both of them.

Those who thought going down on a man was a submissive act had never done it this way. Ordering the man in question to be still as he held all control and took away rational thought with the strong suction of his mouth, the clever dance of his tongue, the sweet, sucking sound that escaped his lips—it was like crack to a Dominant. Marcus flicked his gaze up to see Thomas helpless and shaking, lips parted and eyes half closed. Marcus slid his fingers around to Thomas's fine ass, dug into the muscular cheeks to push him harder into his mouth. He knew Thomas's triggers, playing around the edge of the corona, tickling, licking and stimulating under the ridge, feeling the vein pulse and bunch beneath the pressure of his lips.

"Marcus..."

"Not my fucking name," Marcus growled against him. "Not right now."

"Master." Thomas's hand dropped to his head, to tangle in Marcus's hair and Marcus allowed it, because they both needed the closed circuit of contact for this current to build and achieve the desired effect.

"Now," he said against him, and his pet surged up like a taut bow, as obedient and wild as Marcus could wish. He released into Marcus's mouth and he swallowed him down, sucking and stroking, gripping him with his hand, wanting to give him the best damn blow job he'd ever had in his life. If the worst happened and Thomas woke up on the other side, Marcus wanted his reaction to all the pleasure of Heaven to be a shrug and one three-word statement:

"I've had better."

Yeah, one of these days lightning was going to hit him. Though right now, feeling hard as a rock and quivering inside as much as Thomas was outside, Marcus felt as though it had.

Marcus shifted off him, but stayed leaning over his body. He had his sub's gown rucked up so he could fondle his cock and balls, make him twitch and jerk because he was so sensitive. Thomas grimaced, knowing his Master was doing it on purpose, but he didn't try to get away. He just did those little quivers, his brown eyes alive with fire and fastened on Marcus's face. "I should do something for you."

"Yes, you should. But you'll do it later. An IOU I fully

intend to collect." Marcus bent and pressed a kiss to Thomas's upper thigh, then found himself staying there, his cheek to the muscled flesh as he slid his arms around Thomas's ass, thighs and waist to hold him firmly against him.

"My sticky cock is going to get stuck in your beautiful hair."

"Won't that be a picture for the nurse?"

Thomas stroked his hair, moving it away from the area of danger. Marcus could feel the care and caress in his touch. His pet's breathing was deep, erratic, his thundering heart trying to return to a resting rate. His femoral artery pulsed beneath Marcus's cheek.

"Remind me again why we're doing this?" he spoke against Thomas.

"Because we love Julie, and because this guy is family. And because it's the right thing to do."

"Yeah. Bollocks on all of that. I love you, Thomas. You're the good one of the two of us. You're going to be fine, because you know I'm Satan, and if anything goes wrong I'm going to unleash a plague on the world."

"Bollocks right back," Thomas responded mildly, as Marcus released him to prop on one hand and look at him. "You're a good man and you always have been. You take care of your family, and that's been a shifting definition all your life, to anyone who needs you. Me, Julie and my family, which is now your family."

"No matter what Rory says," Marcus added, his standard quip. He paused. "Do you believe it, what you said earlier? That Des is the right one?"

"I think so. You've seen her with other guys. I never really had the chance to do that, but this feels different from what I heard about her other relationships. Real and deep. They have a good shot."

"Yeah."

Thomas trailed his fingers through Marcus's hair, those clever digits that created masterpieces. "I worry about her, though. After waiting so long for someone who will treat her right, she could lose him."

"Yeah, she could. But she's already figured out it's better

than not having had that gift. She'll embrace it a hundred and twenty percent because of that."

"Her change of heart surprised me at first," Thomas admitted. "I was pretty sure she'd accepted being alone, and had moved relationships lower on her priority list. Her life is so full. Complete. You know how she is. Good friends, good life, and she positively glows when it comes to the theater and the career she built there. I expected her to struggle more with whether or not it's worth it to get herself tangled up with someone."

"No you didn't." Marcus caressed Thomas's abdomen, lips curving as he squirmed when he hit a ticklish spot. "You know Julie has wanted to be deeply, totally in love with the man of her dreams all her life. Even if she'd convinced herself she'd given up on that, it happens when it's going to happen, and you don't get a choice. It's like planning to adopt a Yorkshire Terrier and coming home with a St. Bernard. Love chooses you, and Julie's natural state is to love or be loved. And she's got a moderate sub side, so..."

"She has no choice but to adopt Des and let him sleep on her bed."

"Wasn't that the way it worked for us, *pet*? I saw this scruffy-looking, starved artist and I had to bring him home."

"If I remember, you did let me sleep in your bed, from that very first night."

"Well, you begged, with those soulful brown eyes."

"Softy. Oh, fuck, I hear my mother's shoes. Get off the bed so I can pull my gown down."

To Marcus's amusement, they scrambled like a couple of guilty teenagers putting things to right. He nearly vaulted back to his position against the wall, arms crossed over his chest. A quick glance said the erection he was nursing had subsided enough to miss notice, though the sparkle in Thomas's eye, the grin on his face, could likely spur it back to life in no time.

Yeah, that was the effect his sub had on every part of him. Even as he wished the cost wasn't all of them being here in the hospital, Marcus was glad Julie had finally found that. He'd given himself his own answer to why they were here. Whatever was needed, you did it, because love was worth it in a way nothing else in life could ever be.

§

Julie held Des's hand as the male nurse gave them a heads up. "You're all set, Mr. Hayes. We'll be back to take you to surgery in a few minutes." He was a young man, slim with blond hair and friendly blue eyes. Though Julie was concerned by his youth, he seemed to know what he was doing as he prepped her Master for surgery. She was being silly, she knew she was, but she expected they were used to that. Thank goodness she had Betty with her to keep her from being an idiot. Julie was confident Betty would step in if any care Des received was anything less than it should be.

"When he's in post-op, they'll call our desk and let us know it's time for you two to meet with the surgeon," the nurse told Betty.

Betty had his healthcare power-of-attorney, but Des had already updated his privacy paperwork so Julie could be in on everything discussed today. She was pleased with that further evidence he was trying not to shut her out of anything, though it didn't really help alleviate any worries about how today would go.

"Thanks, Sal." Betty rose. "I'm going to go to the nurses' desk, give you two a couple minutes. I'll be back." She winked at Julie and touched Des's arm. "You've got nothing to worry about. This is the easy part."

She followed Sal out the door, comfortably chatting with him about the current gossip on the floor, since Betty was a regular visitor to this part of the hospital.

Julie knew she was right about this being the "easy" part, though that drew her mind to what could happen in the aftermath. She'd had a crash course in everything transplant-related these past several weeks, and anything else she could learn about managing diabetes. She did it on her own time, not wanting Des to think that she thought she was going to have to be his fulltime caregiver. But to her way of thinking, it was like him being there when

Pablo's scaffolding had failed. He'd known how to help and what to do when it mattered.

Kidney transplant surgery was now fairly straightforward. Thomas's recovery should be a hundred percent if there were no complications, and complications for a healthy male donor were rare. Regardless, Marcus would watch him like a hawk during the recuperation period and make sure he followed every rule to the letter.

Des's challenge would be his body accepting the kidney. He'd be put on drugs to try and prevent rejection, drugs that would lower his immune system significantly, and that he'd be on for the rest of his life. His diet, already fairly structured, would become even more regimented. If his system rejected the kidney, he would go back on dialysis and either have to do that permanently or try again with a different kidney. Though if his body rejected one that was a close genetic match, it wasn't likely to accept another.

Yes, there were possible bad outcomes. But through the many things Julie had learned, the details she'd internalized, she held onto one message with both hands, the one Betty had hammered into her. *This is a good step, the right step. The best chance he has to keep living anything resembling a normal life.*

She ran an appraising eye over him. He was quiet, deep in his head somewhere, understandably, but the pressure of his hand said he was also with her. His hair was tied back for when it would need to be scooped up and tucked into the paper hat he'd have to don for surgery. They'd also put similar boots on his feet. He'd made the nurse smile when he'd asked for both of those things to happen at the last possible moment.

"Don't want Julie to see me like that. She'd be taking pictures and using them to blackmail me."

"That gown is looking good on you," Julie said now.

Des glanced down. She'd only brought it out a few minutes ago, when the nurse had said it was time for him to change, so he hadn't had time to tell her what he thought of it. The nurse had responded to it with "that rocks", causing Julie and Betty to exchange an amused look. It also made Julie wonder if Sal was in the BDSM lifestyle.

The surgical gown was black, with tan-colored rope knots scattered among the silhouettes of voluptuous females tied in various poses. "Shibari surgery wear," Des commented. "I can't believe you found this."

"It wasn't me. Billie and Pablo helped find the cloth, and I sewed it. I've worked as dresser plenty of times, enough to do basic seamstress work. Fortunately, a smock isn't very form fitting."

He smoothed the fabric. "It's pretty damn awesome, Julie," he said in a low voice. "I'm going to tell them they better not mess it up or lose it when they strip me like a newborn up there."

It gratified her to see how touched he was. He didn't say 'get blood on it,' though she heard the slight hesitation as he averted that direction. Her hand involuntarily tightened on his. She wanted to climb up on the bed and hold him so tightly he'd need oxygen, but he'd cared for her, held and reassured her more than once these past several weeks. Today was her turn to be the sturdy brick wall.

"They better not. I won't hesitate to take a megalomaniac surgeon down a peg or two because he couldn't be bothered to fold up a smock and put it on a shelf where it would be safe."

"I'd pay good money to see that." He paused. "You said Pablo helped?"

"Yeah. I would have told you about him coming by the theater earlier, but the gown was a surprise and I didn't want to tip my hand. Billie suggested the vendor and placed the order, then had Pablo pick it up and bring it to me, since Billie's on his circuit up in Virginia. If you'd come by while Pablo was there, I was going to throw you off the scent by telling you he's been so wracked with guilt about the nearly-killing-me thing he wanted to give me a backrub followed by intense oral sex."

"That's a very thorough apology. I'll keep that in mind next time I piss you off."

"I'll think of a way for you to piss me off so it will happen sooner rather than later."

She ran her fingertips over his smiling lips, along the creases by his eyes. She couldn't help herself. He was so handsome, even fatigued and pale as he was too often these past few weeks. This was going to help. It had to. She kept her tone cheerful.

"Seriously, when he brought the fabric by, he gave me a sincere, face-to-face apology. He said he knew he should have done it a lot sooner instead of sending his chickenshit text—his words, not mine, though accurate—but he'd been too embarrassed. For a few weeks after that, he'd had the jitters about doing any more rope work, because it really hit home how right you were about what could have happened."

It was Des's hand that tightened on hers this time. She saw his memory of the incident in his gaze, felt it in the strength of his hold on her. "About fucking time," he said. "Asshole." But he said it without too much rancor and, since she knew the reason he hadn't held onto his rage against the young rigger, she bit back a smile.

"Hmm." Lifting his hand to her cheek, she cupped it around her jaw so she could nuzzle it. His eyes centered on her, his fingers caressing her. Ever since the important decisions had been made, about this surgery and their relationship, things had been different between them. She didn't think it was too romantic or fanciful to call it a connection beyond words. That quiet core came with a constant, humming fullness of emotion, a bond that could only be expressed in weighted, tender, passionate stillness. She leaned in to put her lips to his, a lingering, soft gesture full of future promises. When she eased back, she didn't go far, because he'd slid his arm around her waist to keep her close.

"The 'asshole' told me you came to see him a few days after my accident," she said. "He said you introduced him to George, who mentors riggers at Logan's club, and Pablo is now learning under his supervision. I think that was the best possible balm on his feelings to help get him back on the right path."

"I wasn't doing it to make him feel better. Just to help him be better. And save lives."

"Well, that amounts to the same thing. It's when you feel like you've been written off that it's hardest to regain confidence. Not everyone has your discipline or inner strength."

"You do. Because you're here, willing to take a chance on us, even if—"

"There is no 'even if,'" she interrupted firmly. "Every relationship is fraught with risk. Ours just has a few less common ones. Some knots and loops that will bind us all the tighter, if you want me to put it in relatable terms."

His lips curved, the brown eyes lighting. "All right, Miss Stubborn. But don't make a habit of interrupting me, or I'll take a belt to you."

She sniffed. "One mule knows another. It takes a brick to get through your thick skull."

He grinned fully. "Did you slip off to give Thomas a hug when Sal there was checking my vitals?"

"I did. I gave him one from you as well, since I know you two are manly men who don't do hugs."

"You know, if I die on the table today, I won't have to worry about meeting the rest of the family."

"Yes, death would be far less terrifying than that." She made a face at him and pinched his arm. "I promise you have nothing to worry about. You'll love them, and they'll love you."

Though he'd spoken with wry humor, she knew the man who'd faced so many things that would scare the daylights out of most people was genuinely unsettled about meeting Thomas's family...Des's family. He hadn't wanted to meet them before the surgery. He hadn't really wanted to talk about why, though she expected it was because he had enough variables to juggle in his mind. She was glad that Thomas's family had accepted his decision without complaint, though Elaine had had the last word, as she often did in arguments with anyone, except Marcus.

"Elaine said to tell you she's looking forward to meeting you. She also wanted me to give you this right before you went into surgery. Now seems as good a time as any."

Julie straightened to put her arms around him and give him a firm, lingering hug. "She told me to make sure it lasted at least ten seconds, because the best hugs do," she murmured.

She saw the surprise in his face, and a mix of emotions that suggested what all was happening deep in his head wasn't as calm as it appeared on the outside. She looked down at their clasped hands, giving him a moment to manage his reaction. "She also said you don't have to worry about anyone's expectations. She just wants to meet her nephew."

"Well, regardless, best to meet afterward." Des cleared his throat. "Because if she finds me detestable, she'll wonder why the hell she's letting her boy give up a vital organ."

He said it with his usual dry wit, but Julie wondered if there was some truth to his worry. Just in case there was, she punched his abdomen and pronounced her opinion of that.

"Idiot."

He fended her off. "At least aim for one of the trashed kidneys. I might need the rest of my internal organs."

"You will."

"All right. Don't get feisty." Catching both her hands, he drew her out of her chair and startled her by dragging her onto the bed with him, so he had her cradled against his side.

"Be careful of your IV."

"It's on the other side. I've managed a pump for years. I can handle some attached tubes."

He tipped up her chin and kissed her hard, palm smoothing down her back to cup her buttocks. She'd worn snug jeans with a gauzy pink and fawn colored top over it and a camisole beneath. She was all silky curves from the waist up, and tight, thin denim below. He conveyed his appreciation with hands and mouth, until she felt arousal not only stir, but jump up a couple notches.

The last time he'd made love to her, his energy had been low, but it had been all the sweeter because they took it slow, a mutual caressing and lots of kisses that progressed to her sliding on top of him, guided by his grip, the shift of his body. He'd huskily commanded her to lower herself onto his cock. As she did, he'd wrapped his hands around her wrists, holding her in sensual restraint, her arms on either side of her, wrists pressed to her sides as she rose and fell, the pinnacle building until they shuddered through it together.

Now he broke the kiss but held her hard against his body. Taking her hand, he guided it beneath his gown to grip him firmly, her fingertips brushing his balls, her fingers coiled around his semi-turgid shaft. He pushed into her hold, closing his own hand over it, then brought her palm back to a more public-appropriate location on his chest.

"Just wanted to go in with a reminder of what's most worth living for."

"And, since you didn't have a bag of carrot sticks close to hand, you made do with the second best thing."

"Ah, a woman who understands me."

She chuckled and held onto the humor, though it took effort when she heard a gurney and a blink later saw an orderly and Sal at the door, along with Betty.

"That's my ride," Des said, helping her off the side of the bed as he sat up. Squeezing her hand, he rose, tall and strong, her Master, her Des. He brushed a kiss over her lips. "See you in a bit, love."

"You bet." This wasn't a life-threatening surgery, not the actual surgery itself, so she wasn't going to cry. She smiled for him. Though he didn't smile back, seeing all the things churning inside her, she knew he was glad to see her smile. He leaned in and spoke against her ear.

"You'll do something for me?"

"Anything."

"And here I am going into surgery." His eyes sparked at her. Then he sobered. "It doesn't matter what happens during or after this surgery. I made this choice, and Betty's right. It's the best one I've got to have a normal life with you. So whatever happens, there are no regrets. We're rolling the dice and seeing if we'll get lucky. Got it?"

"Got it."

"I love you. I look forward to saying that to you every day for the rest of my life." He touched her face and straightened as Betty slid into the room.

"Hey, I've got cupcakes," she said, waving two she had

on a brightly colored plate. "A patient's family dropped them by for the nurses. Homemade yellow cake, butter cream chocolate icing."

"You are a very cruel woman," Desmond said. "You hear my stomach growling?"

"You've always said my main joy in life is torturing you." Betty set the treats aside and wrapped her arms around him for a hug as Julie stepped back to give them room.

"No one does it better." But he held onto her an extra moment and Julie heard what the nurse whispered to him.

"I'm so proud of you, son," Betty said.

"Same goes," he returned, touching her face. "I've always been glad you're in my corner. Even when I don't act like it."

Betty's eyes glistened, but she covered it by moving around the bed and helping Sal, taking the IV off its hook and handing it to him to transfer it to the gurney as Des boosted himself onto the transport.

"I'll give you a twenty if you do a two wheeler around the corner," he told the orderly, a large black man whose name tag said Paul. Paul gave him a dubious but humorous look.

"You're only wearing that gown, man. Not sure I want a twenty bad enough to take it from where you have to be hiding it."

"Smart man." Des did a fist bump with him and stretched out. "But if you change your mind, I'm good for it."

As the nurse adjusted the covers, Des looked toward Julie again, then shifted his glance to Betty. Now the look on his face was one she recognized, the face of her Master, protective and in charge, despite all evidence otherwise. Her heart swelled in her chest, creating pain and joy at once.

"Take care of my girl, Betty. Don't let her worry."

"I won't. I love you, stubborn boy. See you in a bit, with your fancy new kidney."

"The kidney of a famous artist, no less." Des linked his hands behind his head and tossed Julie an arch look. "It might elevate my rope work to a whole new level. At the very least, I'll probably piss more artistically. Like in loops or swirls or something."

"Just so long as you keep it inside that porcelain circle," Julie said dryly. "Else this relationship won't last."

He winked. "That ship is going to sail in a few seconds anyway, because Sal's taking out the booties and paper hat. My irresistible sex appeal will be shattered beyond repair."

"You're going to totally rock that look," she said fiercely.

Though of course he looked as foolish and sweetly vulnerable as every patient did. Julie managed to brave face it until they wheeled him off and the door closed with a quiet whoosh. Betty's arm slid around her as Julie bit back a little tremble of reaction.

"He'll be fine," the nurse said firmly. "They took your friend up a few minutes ago. Why don't we go hang out in his room with his family? I'll let the nurse desk know where to find us. Dr. Pindar is the absolute best at this in the Charlotte area. Des is in great hands."

"I know. I'm just being stupid. Why didn't I say I love him, too?" She would have chased down the gurney like a melodramatic novel heroine, but Betty caught her arm.

"Because he already knows. And because you'll tell him when he wakes up, when it will mean even more." Betty touched her face. "You remember when we met, you told me you've waited a long time to find the right person for you?"

Julie nodded. Betty looked toward the door as if she, too, were following the progress of the gurney with her ears. "What you may not realize is, despite how much he tried not to let it happen, he's waited a long time for someone, too. No matter how much more time this gives him, Julie, you're the one who saved his life. You gave him a reason to want to live for himself." She linked arms with Julie. "And in my book, that makes you a real life miracle."

§

Betty's advice was sound. Julie, Marcus, Rory, Elaine and Betty hung out in Thomas's room, providing one another needed support and company. Though Des had checked into the hospital the night before, it was Betty's pull and Marcus's wealth that had obtained Thomas an assigned room before his surgery, and Julie was grateful for the gathering space. Daytime TV droned in the background while they talked and made runs to the cafeteria for bad, high calorie snacks. They discussed the hardware store, how Les was doing in medical school, Julie's impressions of Charlotte...an assortment of random topics that helped fill the time and turn minds away from worrying.

Eventually, Elaine started asking Julie and Betty questions about Des. Julie could see Marcus was absorbing the information as intently as Elaine, probably to fill Thomas in later, but he was curious for his own sake.

Julie was part of that rapt audience when Betty offered a more detailed picture of the boy and young man Des had been. Though the shrewd nurse kept them distracted with the stories, Julie saw Marcus check his watch more than once. A couple times he rose and paced the hall when it was obvious he was too restless to be still. The first time he did it, Elaine caught his hand as he passed her and squeezed. He answered that pressure and bent to drop a kiss on her head.

"Don't go far," she said. "You know Thomas doesn't want you smoking."

Despite her own worries, Julie hid a smile. Elaine knew enough about Marcus to know he smoked when he was tremendously agitated.

"I'll just be out in the hall," he said, brushing her cheek with a light knuckle, his way of reassuring her.

Betty handed the ball back to Julie and she entertained Elaine and Rory with her stories of Des's "Slinky" routine on the roof, his Type I kids like Mylo and people at the theater like Billie. She tactfully stayed away from the specifics of their performances. Julie was sure Elaine knew it was erotic in nature, since she avoided asking for details a person would normally ask about the productions. However, Julie knew she wouldn't be comfortable with open discussions about it, so she tactfully stayed away from that. As always, though, Elaine was supportive, lauding Julie's success in getting the theater up and running.

"Do you have any other pictures of Des?" Elaine asked her at length.

"Oh, I..." She didn't. She didn't have a picture of him. Not even the one Thomas had taken at the restaurant that night. Why hadn't she told him to send it to her? Here she was, doing what she was doing, feeling for Des the way she did, and she didn't even have a snapshot of him on her phone.

"Hey." Betty put a hand over hers, as if sensing the tsunami of emotion the simple request had provoked. "It's okay. I do. I have plenty." Reaching into the canvas tote she had with her, printed with whimsical purple flowers on the outside, she drew out a slim photo album that looked new. "I copied the pictures I've collected of him over the years and made you an album, Elaine. I figured his aunt and cousins would want them, or at least be interested."

"Oh." Elaine's face lit up. "How very kind of you."

Marcus had returned from his latest pacing, so he moved next to Julie as Betty shifted to sit next to Elaine. Rory rolled his wheelchair over to the other side of his mother to see, since Betty put the photo album in Elaine's lap. Marcus slid his arm around Julie and brushed his lips against her temple as the two women began to talk about pictures of Des, starting from his first intake picture at the boys' home, and the infant pictures from the hospital. Julie wanted to see them, too, but right now she needed Marcus's strong arm more.

"I know he's going to be fine today," she said softly, combatting the coil of desperation in her gut. "There's more potential for complications afterward, really. Infection, rejection, all that. But that's the thing. I can't stop worrying about a million things that might have made yesterday the last day we had for him to feel like himself, be himself, be the person I love... We're still so new to all of this."

God, was that what worried her? That he'd come out of that surgery no longer Des?

She hadn't meant for anyone else to hear her, but Elaine had incredibly sharp ears. She stopped and looked up. "Loving someone isn't like loving a painting, dear. It's like loving a garden. A lot of hard work, and some things thrive, while others wither and die, but those fertilize the rest. And things always, always change, from season to season."

She reached over the album to take Julie's hand and hold it. Betty watched the interchange with quiet approval and agreement in her expression.

"But your love for your garden, all it's been, and all it can be, never changes." Julie could tell from Elaine's fond, wistful expression she was thinking of her late husband. "You can't predict how it will work for you and Des. Only time and God can help you figure that out. Just don't lose your faith in love. It's one of the strongest, most wonderful things about you, and I'm sure that's a big part of what Des sees in you as well."

Hearing the wisdom of an older generation was as reassuring as Marcus's arm around her shoulders. Elaine gave her hand one more pat before returning to the album. "Look at him there. Twelve years old... Oh my."

Elaine's eyes abruptly filled with tears, alarming all of them as she fingered the teenage picture of Des. In the earlier pictures, his hair had been short, an incompatible look with his features, though Julie suspected short hair was a requirement of the boys' home. But in this picture, it was starting to grow out. His eyes were the same in every photo. A penetrating brown that conveyed his depth of character even in a two-dimensional medium.

"Mom? You okay?" Rory put his callused, large hand on her thin forearm. He'd grown into a handsome man like his older brother, and was tanned and callused in all the right places from his work at the family hardware store he managed, despite only being in his twenties. His physique made it clear he didn't let being in a wheel chair keep him from hard work.

Elaine nodded, withdrawing a small album from her own sizeable purse. Opening it up, she displayed a young girl around the same age as Des in his picture. The likeness was so remarkable, the only thing that distinguished them seemed to be gender. "It's no wonder Thomas saw the resemblance. Look at the two of them. It almost made the DNA test unnecessary. There's no doubt they were mother and son."

"You're right, Mom. He looks a lot like Aunt Christine. I remember she always had peppermint drops."

"Yes." From the press of Elaine's lips, and the flicker in Betty's eyes, Julie suspected there was a less-than-innocuous reason for that. If his mother was a drug addict, she likely had bad teeth. Julie thought about Des's subconscious preference for peppermint scent in his own home and wondered if he'd internalized that olfactory memory as an infant.

There was no unkindness in Elaine's voice as she gave her son the simple one-word answer, only sadness as her fingertips slipped over the picture. "She was never a happy child, not like you, Thomas and Les, but she was artistic and dramatic. She'd create costumes out of scraps of cloth and old jewelry our mother had. She'd stroll through the house like a fine Victorian lady, or a princess. One time she imitated a British accent and pretended to be Queen Elizabeth for a whole week."

"Ah, a method actor," Julie said.

A touch of gratitude crossed Elaine's expression as Julie pulled her out of the shadows. "Yes. That's exactly how she was. She loved to pretend to be someone else."

Sal appeared at the door and five sets of eyes immediately snapped to him. "They're in recovery now," he said. "Dr. Pindar said he'd come here to see all of you once he cleans up, but the surgical nurse told me everything went exactly as planned. No problems for either of them."

"Thank God," Elaine said, as Betty echoed the same sentiment. Rory stroked his mother's arm and Marcus's grip on Julie's hand increased, a silent message of hope and reassurance. She'd hold onto that, and use it however she needed for Des.

As she looked around at Betty and Thomas's family, including Marcus, she knew neither she nor Des would have to stand alone in that. She'd teased Des about family culture shock, but there was nothing better in the world to have when you really needed it.

Especially when the family in question had hearts as big as these.

Chapter Twenty-One

Des moved in and out of a post-operative haze. Only vaguely aware when they moved him back to his room, he was nevertheless pleased to feel Julie's hand on his arm and her lips briefly on his face. He could smell her scent, so as he drifted in and out, he knew she was in the guest chair recliner. Betty came and went, her and the new shift nurse, an attractive black woman who smelled like lemon, checking all his vitals and making him do the spirometer to improve his breathing when he was conscious.

He knew he was starting to wake up for real when he was aware enough to register the catheter that would help the transplanted kidney's communication with the rest of his plumbing. The newest member of his organ team had better get up to speed soon, because he wasn't going to tolerate having his cock stuffed with a tube any longer than necessary.

He had the pressure cuffs on both his legs to prevent blood clots, and an IV in his arm and neck. They made him feel tied down, antsy, but he pushed that away. Another temporary condition only.

A glance at the clock, the light through the blinds, and a somewhat muzzy recalculation of the passage of time told him it was close to daybreak. He guessed it was early morning rounds, based on the sounds of rolling carts, beeps and murmurs, and the movement of nurses up and down the hall in their squishy shoes.

The recliner was empty, but the blanket wasn't yet folded, also confirming the early morning hour. At the sound of a door opening, he turned his head and saw Julie coming out of the bathroom.

She was a welcome sight, and a charming one, in pajama bottoms with kittens printed all over them. Her soft, stretched vee-neck T-shirt made him want to touch her generously wobbling breasts. Since getting erect with an installed catheter was not a good plan, he forced his thoughts elsewhere.

He lifted a hand, drawing her attention. "Hey there." His voice was thick, unused, and he cleared it as she beamed like the sun.

She immediately came to his side and closed both her hands about one of his. "Welcome back."

Before the surgery, there'd been some fear and tension in her expression, despite her best efforts to conceal it. She didn't have much of a poker face, his love. But he was glad for it, because the range of emotions he read now were heartening. She was more relaxed, and very happy to see him.

He knew the surgery had gone well, because he remembered Dr. Pindar discussing it with him in post-op. However, typical for anesthesia, things that had seemed clear then had turned into a dreamlike haze. He'd have to ask Julie or Betty for a recap. But he'd retained the most important thing. Step One was a success.

Maybe they all knew it was the easiest step against what might be ahead, but he'd take it as a good sign. He was going to let Julie's optimism bolster him. Though he'd possessed a will of iron and enough self-discipline to direct an army battalion his entire life, he hadn't always been optimistic. Just stubborn. For her, he wanted to be optimistic.

"So..." She gave him an mischievous look, drawing a chair close to the bed. "Since you have a gay man's kidney, are you having any urges to fulfill a couple of my guy-on-guy fantasies?"

He chuckled, and winced. Her eyes darkened and she placed her hands on his torso as if she could soothe away the pain. "That could backfire," he advised her. "What if having a gay man's kidney makes me want to be gay?"

"Based on how you were looking at my breasts just now,

I think I'm safe."

"Caught that, did you?"

"I think you'll be ogling my breasts when you're ninety. And did I thank you for that?"

He lifted her hand to his lips, kissed it with decent accuracy. "I feel like I have fur in my mouth. Can I have something to drink?"

"The nurse said not at first. We can use these wet swabs on your lips and inside your mouth if it feels dry, but not even ice chips until the doctor gives the okay."

"Nazis."

"I know, right? They say it's for your own good, but I think the Inquisitors said the same thing when they were racking heretics."

He smiled, despite the discomfort of dry lips. "I missed you, love."

"I was here the whole time." Her fingers tightened on his, but her eyes shone with care and love. It was a good feeling to be basking in that light. "Oh, here, let's do the spirometer thing and get it over with. She told me to push it on you like a drug dealer coaxing six-year-olds to do crack as soon as you surfaced."

He remembered the nurse walking him through it, but he let Julie show him again, because it meant she curled her fingers around his hands and caressed his face as he brought the mouthpiece to his lips. When he sat the device down, he laid his head back on the pillow, feeling lightheaded.

"Julie?" At the light rap on the door, he opened his eyes. An older woman he didn't know but was pretty sure was Thomas's mother, based on similarities in their facial features, peered around the panel. "Marcus just relieved me and I wanted to see—oh." She startled when she realized Des's eyes were on her, and she smiled, a partly nervous, partly pleased and anticipatory look. "I'm so sorry."

"It's all right. I'm awake."

"So I see." She smiled more warmly. "I'm Elaine."

"I figured." Des cleared his throat, feeling ridiculously awkward. Elaine hadn't expected he'd be conscious, though now that he was, she looked eager to stay. But he could also tell she was struggling to not seem too eager and spook him. If he wasn't ready to talk, he expected she'd go away without offense, but he didn't know what he was ready for.

Julie filled in the sudden silence in her comfortable way, bless her.

"You talked Marcus into going back to the hotel?" she said to Elaine. She included him in the talk with the angle of her body, still sitting on the bed, but she spoke in that way people did around a recovering patient who might not yet be up to talking.

"Oh, I'm sure I didn't, though he let me believe that." Elaine offered a self-conscious chuckle. She wore dark slacks with a blue tunic top over it that pinned at the hip, accentuating a trim figure. Her dyed ebony hair was long but pulled back in a sleek twist. Her hazel eyes had a touch of blue-grey to them when she turned her head toward the light. Des wondered if she looked like his mother. Since Thomas had been cued into his parentage by comparing Des's looks to his aunt, not his mother, Des guessed that Elaine and Christine had drawn from different gene pools within the same family.

"He was probably in the cafeteria the past few hours to catch up on his work emails and texts," Elaine continued. Her Southern accent was country rural, soft and pleasing. "Staying as close as he can without making me think he doesn't trust me to watch over my own son. I hope he took a little nap down there, though, because I don't think he got much sleep. Thomas woke up about an hour ago."

"Des has only been up a few minutes. I'll go tell the nurse he's awake. Would you like to sit with him a few minutes while I do that?"

"Oh, well, if he's waking up, I don't want to intrude on you two. I can come back later."

Julie had looked his way as she made the offer, confirming he was okay with her suggestion. He wasn't sure, but Elaine's kind attempt to give him an out, combined with the way her eyes were fastened on his face, drinking in his features, decided him. *Don't be an asshole. Or a coward. What are you worried about?*

Exactly what he'd said before the surgery. Though he'd posed it as a joke, and Julie had gone along with it, the wisdom in her lovely brown eyes had told him she knew the truth. He didn't know how he'd feel if Elaine didn't like him. Didn't matter how old he was, an abandoned kid would run toward the edge of a cliff to avoid another dose of familial rejection.

"No, it's good. Please..." He gestured Elaine farther into the room, coughing a little, the after effect of the breathing exercise.

Julie picked up her robe, shrugging into it and freeing her long hair from the collar. "I'll be back in a few minutes," she told Des, leaning over to brush her lips over his. He put his hand on her shoulder to hold her, bring her back down for more of that, just an extra minute. When he at last let her go, she ducked her head, hiding her flush as she hurried from the room.

She'd handed Elaine a cup of water with what looked like big Q-tips in it before she departed. Elaine moved the rolling table close and set the cup on it so he could reach for one of the swabs and roll it across his lips and in his mouth. Fortunately, he was able to do that on his own, but she helped him find the controls on the bed and raise him to a more upright reclining position. It felt better to sit up and be somewhat in control of his faculties, though he had to close his eyes a few minutes at the return of the dizziness. They had him on some good painkillers, because he wasn't too uncomfortable, but fortunately he also wasn't loopy. He hoped.

She'd put her bag on the chair and he saw a photo album in it. "You've been sharing pictures?" he asked, looking for a way to start the conversation that might put them both at ease.

"I thought...well, you don't have to look at them. In a way, I brought them for myself. It sounds silly, but I felt like by bringing pictures of the woman who bore you, I was bringing Christine with me to meet the child she never had the chance to know."

He blinked. "That was...an odd way to refer to her."

Elaine's lips tightened. "She wasn't your mother. Betty

was probably the closest thing to that for you, wasn't she? God bless her. But I'll call Christine your mother if you wish me to do so."

"I don't. I guess I'm just surprised...that you'd realize that I wouldn't be comfortable with that. She was your sister." He was usually more lucid than this, but maybe this halting, gentle way they were both handling one another was how it should be. Julie had left only the bathroom light on, so it was dim and quiet in the room, cocooning them in their own world.

Elaine took a breath. "She was my sister, and I loved her deeply, even though I didn't know how to help her. It took me a long, painful time to realize both those things could be true. Would you like me to talk about her? We don't have to do so. You've just been through surgery. We can certainly talk about other, easier things."

"No. I think it might be easier to talk about it now. While I'm on painkillers."

Elaine reached out to touch his hand, then thought better of the familiarity, folding her hands back against her. He didn't disagree with her decision. He wasn't sure if he was ready to be touched by his aunt, but he regretted if his lack of encouragement pained her. She straightened her back, though, and gave him a brisk nod that told him she wasn't that fragile.

It almost made him smile. Yeah, she'd raised three kids and, from what he'd heard, she held her own with Marcus. Knowing she wasn't going to break if he said the wrong thing relaxed him a little more.

She sat down in the chair Julie had pulled up beside the bed. "Christine had an artist's personality. When I first recognized it in Thomas, I worried so much about him because of her, but he had a steadiness, a grounding, she never had. Nothing was ever right for Christine. She had this vision of how her life was supposed to be. Whatever didn't fit with that, she simply denied, shut away, or blamed it on someone else."

She shifted back in the chair and crossed her legs, tucking a stray wisp of hair behind her ear. She wore an inexpensive wedding set and her fingers had slightly swollen knuckles from arthritis. While her nails were neat and polished, he could tell she worked with her hands. Thomas had mentioned on that drive back to Charlotte that his mother loved gardening.

"Would you like me to go on?" She was watching his face. At his agreement, she continued.

"Our parents were simple farm people, but they took her to a psychiatrist on the recommendation of a guidance counselor. He put her on drugs, anti-depressants, things like that. She became addicted to any drug that could change her mood." Pain crossed Elaine's features. "She'd steal my father's painkillers for his knees, so he had to keep them locked up in the gun safe. She left home at eighteen and would come back on occasion when she had nowhere else to go. The only one she'd tell anything was me. To my shame, I took that as a badge of honor, keeping her secrets even as I knew that she'd become poison to herself."

Elaine shook her head. "Thomas was ten when she came to stay with me for the last time. After three days, I told her I would get her into a treatment program, but if she wasn't willing to do that, she had to leave. She'd become so unstable that I didn't trust her around the children. My husband saw it. 'Lainie, I love you,' he said, 'but she shouldn't be around the kids. We both know it. If it's too hard for you to tell her to leave, I will.'"

She blinked over the memory of a beloved husband, her hand dropping to her wedding set without conscious thought. Des felt an odd twist as he always did, seeing those subtle yet unmistakable signs of a family connection that extended over years. He'd never had that, but he was hearing about the family that had contributed to his own life's path. No matter how painful the tale for both of them, he realized he did want to hear it.

He'd always claimed that it didn't matter if he knew or not and, in a way, it didn't, but knowing who his mother was had always been a puzzle. Her pieces added to the picture of his own life. It might not change who he was or how he viewed himself, but would give him a greater sense of balance, however hard it was for him to explain why. Perhaps it was because of what he saw in Elaine's face now.

That sense of being part of a whole, not a piece cut away and drifting alone.

"She refused, of course, but that was when I learned about you. She broke down and cried, and said if she hadn't been forced to give up her baby, maybe she would have been happy like me. At first I thought she was lying, a sympathy ploy to convince me to let her stay longer. Like most addicts, lies came as easily to her as truth, and all too often became the same to her. But as it all spilled out, I realized, to my horror, she wasn't lying."

Elaine's eyes became distant as she recalled the conversation with her sister. "She told me you'd been born sickly. In her twisted mind, she took that as more proof that God hated her. She said God could have given her something perfect and beautiful to love, but he gave her something she couldn't care for, an excuse to leave you with the hospital and the social workers."

Elaine paused, recalling herself, and put her hand over Des's on the blanket. Her touch was soft and cool. He was more ready for it now, but his fingers twitched in reaction, so she drew her hand away.

"Forgive me, son. Perhaps I shouldn't have told you that, but nothing in those words she spoke were true. You were a gift she should have treasured. Your health was merely her excuse."

"Yeah. And her fault. She abused her body, and my body paid the price."

Des had no anger over it. It was just simple logic. But when Elaine flinched, he put out a hand, palm up. She glanced at him, then laid hers in it, like a butterfly landing. It worked better that way, him initiating the touch. He closed his fingers over hers, gently, wondering at touching her. But the feeling that rose in him was too powerful, too undefined, and he didn't want to lose control. He drew back.

"Like you said, she blamed others for the things she did. I'm not a child, Elaine. Maybe when I was little, I went through the 'why didn't my parents love me enough to keep me' phase, but I had good people at the boys' home who looked after me. I'm not really into religion, but I do believe there's Something out there, and whatever she was so willing to blame gave me the smarts to embrace my life instead of being bitter about it. Most the time." He smiled at her. "You know, once when I was in the hospital, Miss America came to visit the children's ward? She was wearing this silky floral dress. When she bent down to stroke my head, I could look right down the front of it. I was nine. I was old enough to appreciate the gift."

Elaine tsked at him, but her eyes twinkled, telling him he'd succeeded in easing her mind. "Mind your manners, young man."

He sobered. "Seriously, she was nice. And I thought, wow, if I hadn't been in the hospital today, I wouldn't have met her. It was around about then I started realizing that, no matter what shit I had to deal with about my health, there were plenty of good things out there for me. I just had to pay attention so I didn't miss out on the opportunities to have them. Fortunately, my first goal—to marry her—didn't work out, so I didn't find myself off the market when I met Julie."

"She's a very special woman."

"She is." Des read the speculation in the older woman's face. "I won't hurt her. I love her."

"Then you'll definitely hurt her." The wisdom and experience of it showed in Elaine's hazel eyes. "That's the way love works. She'll hurt you sometimes, too. But love is all about forgiving one another, learning to love, laugh and grow together. Build a life together. Is that your intention?"

Des blinked at the shift. Though Elaine had been tentative in their discussions of Christine, Des now found himself in the laser sights of a woman who operated on a code many would consider outdated. But she'd obviously taken Julie under her wing and would protect her in the ways she knew best.

Despite being bedridden and not at his best or most stubborn, he rallied enough to give her a direct look.

"I think that's something she and I should discuss first before I make my intentions known to anyone else."

"Hmph." Another long stare, and Des considered it lucky he didn't relapse, holding fast against it. Then

Elaine's lips curved, and her eyes sparkled anew.

"You'll do, Desmond. You have backbone." She rose, gripping his hand and holding onto it this time. "If you don't already have a tradition of your own, I'll expect you for Christmas with the rest of the family. Julie usually stays at Marcus and Thomas's house, right down the road from us, and you're welcome to do that, or you two can stay in Thomas's old bedroom. My house is open to you."

I'll expect you for Christmas with the rest of the family. Never in his life had those words been said to him. Maybe it was the surgery, the painkillers he was on, or other debilitating factors that made him susceptible to sucker punch triggers, but his chest got tight, his throat thickening. "Um...I...that would be..."

Her eyes softened, and she bent down to kiss his forehead, her thin, cool hands cupping his jaw. She pressed her cheek against his, trapping the moisture that had leaked from his eye and absorbing it into her own creased skin. She straightened, combing her fingers through the wisps of hair at his brow.

"You have no idea how much you look like her," she said, her own voice thick. "I lost my sister, Desmond, long before she actually died. I prayed for her every day, but when she told me about you, God forgive me, I prayed even harder for you. Though I knew giving you up was the best thing she ever could have done for you, I prayed that you'd end up with someone who loved you. I've prayed for you every day since she told me about you."

She was killing him. As he tried to nod, her hand gripped his again, her eyes suddenly brilliant in their intensity. "I know you're a grown man, and you've dealt with all these things, and obviously dealt with them well. You are a generous, kind person. However, I want you to know something. If she had come to us when she was pregnant with you, Robert and I would have taken you in a heartbeat. You would have been raised as one of our children, just as loved as any of them. I didn't have the chance to do that, but if you want a family now, you have one."

Okay, Marcus was right. The woman *was* evil. When his

shoulders shuddered and he turned his face away, she wrapped her arms around him. Though she was careful not to disrupt his IVs, she held his face to her bosom so he could bury those tears there. He had his arm around her fragile yet oddly sturdy body and, while he held on tighter than he should have, she never flinched. She cradled him in her arms in a way he'd also never experienced. As he wept without thought or analysis, she cried, too.

His body would heal from this surgery, but Elaine had just helped heal a wound to his soul.

§

He didn't really remember running down, but the drugs and the stress of the surgery overcame him. He recalled her settling him back on the pillows and using a damp cloth to wipe his face, her fingertips combing back his hair again. She admonished him about using the word 'shit' earlier, telling him he needed to watch his language. It made him smile. He slept.

He was aware of Julie coming back, sitting with him, gripping his hand, the press of her mouth against his, an entirely welcome sensation he tried to prolong, but his arm was too weak to lift. It was okay, though. Her clean female scent stayed close.

When he woke again, she was curled up in the guest chair, asleep. Marcus was laying a blanket over her, and Elaine was saying something about wishing she could bring him back some breakfast since hospital food was so horrible. He was all for that.

"Eggs and hash browns," he mumbled. "And take Julie with you. She needs to sleep in a real bed. Don't let her wear herself out. I'm fine here."

Elaine came to the bed and pressed a motherly hand to his brow. "She's as stubborn as you are, but they said you'll be able to have a liquid diet tomorrow and get the IVs out. If you're up to it, you'll be able to get up and move around a bit. That will go a long way toward convincing her. They won't let us feed you anything but what they approve yet. Have to take care of that special kidney of yours."

"Bet Thomas will get hash browns," he said sullenly, but he took a closer look at Marcus. As Elaine had hinted, he had the lined tiredness in his otherwise perfect face that said he'd been camping out in another room the same way Julie was camping in his.

"Is Thomas okay?"

"He's great. We'll get you together for a visit in the morning."

"Tell him thanks. Thanks...to all of you."

Des saw Julie's eyes open and he couldn't look away. He wanted her in the bed with him. He wanted her close.

"Let's give them a little time to snooze. We'll go back to Thomas." Elaine, picking up the vibe, eased her and Marcus toward the door. Des felt a little guilty about making them feel like they had to leave, but he did have one question he wanted answered first, that he asked as they reached the door.

"How do you know I'm a generous, kind person?"

Elaine blinked. "I've interrogated your closest associates. Waterboarding was used."

He snorted but Marcus tossed him a look. "Believe her. She could wear a California redwood to a stump."

"Hush," Elaine told him, though her lips pressed against a smile. "I talked to these two and Thomas about you. Particularly Julie. That wonderful girl thinks she's been in love before, but I disagree." She glanced toward Julie and back at Des. "You love someone worthy of being loved, and it's clear to me she's deeply in love with you."

As Marcus held the door for her, he gave Des a nod before the door closed behind them.

Des looked toward Julie immediately. "Can you come here?"

Her lips tipped up. "What, a request? No Dommish orders? No 'get your ass over here now'?"

"Not my style."

"I beg to differ. It's your style. You just don't use the words. You use 'the look.'"

"Well at the moment they've got so many chemicals running through my system, the best I can manage is a cross-eyed, drooling stare. But since there are three of you,

I'm having all sorts of good fantasies. Get all of your asses over here."

She giggled and put the footrest down, coming to him with the blanket still wrapped around her. He expected it was chilly, as it always was in hospital rooms, though he wasn't feeling it, since they had him swathed in a bunch of blankets.

He was able to move over enough for her, though, so she could slide in on the side that didn't have all his hookups. As soon as she pillowed her head on his shoulder and settled her body against his, his world centered in a way that he knew without question answered Elaine's question about intentions.

"I'm going to marry you," he said.

"Oh?" She sounded drowsy, but happy at the prospect. "I can go for that. Are we doing this right now, or is there time to get a dress?" She paused, and she didn't have to say anything for him to know she was thinking of the night in the theater.

"Is that the one you'd like to wear?"

"Yes. I'll get it altered to fit me a bit better. Otherwise it will slide all the way off my boobs at the reception when I step on the hem and cause a wardrobe malfunction, but...yes."

"Good."

"Good to the wardrobe malfunction or the dress?"

"Both." He put his arm around her. He was weak, Christ, he was weak, but that would change. The one good thing about having a tidal health history was knowing these things ebbed and flowed. He'd be strong enough to lift her over a threshold by the time they were married. He'd make damn sure of it.

"So...Elaine. She's a bit scary. She said she expects me to join them for Christmas this year."

"Of course. You're part of the family, aren't you? I was going to invite you to Marcus and Thomas's as my plus-one. Sounds like I'll be yours. Don't tell me you're going to refuse. It takes a braver woman than me to say no to that woman."

"Are we sure she's not a Domme? I'm thinking she has

stilettos and a whip hidden away somewhere."

"If she does, when she passes—hopefully decades from now—we better get them before her kids find their hiding place. Thomas would be traumatized for life." Julie glanced down, amused, noticing he was winding his pulse-ox line around her wrist. "Just can't help yourself, can you?"

"I was going to ask Sal if he'd bring me restraints. Figured I could cuff you to the bed, make sure you don't go anywhere while I was sleeping."

"I won't go anywhere," she said. Suddenly sobering, she curled her fingers around his wrist with her other hand. "And you aren't either. You hear me? I don't care about statistics or anything else. You're going to hang around long enough for me to grow old with you. Better or worse and all that."

"Good thing I asked first. I'm pretty sure not only is the man supposed to be the one to propose, but a Dom would definitely be the proposer."

"I'm a pushy sub. You've said so. And a New Yorker." She smiled, but then she shifted uncertainly, as if doubting herself, or his feelings on the matter.

"I do. I will. I feel like we already are." Des touched her face, stroked it. "If I should go before you, it won't matter, Julie. I'm not taking a boat anywhere you can't go. Whether it's a day or fifty years from now, I'll wait right there on the other side. You're worth the wait to me. You always will be. I knew it the first time I saw you."

She blinked back tears. "You're just saying that because I let you touch my breast within a minute of meeting me," she said.

"Well, yeah, there is that." He considered her. "You know, I haven't given you flowers in a while. I liked the liquid nitrogen scene Tony did with Charlotte. Would you like it if I gave you flowers that way? Leave the blush of a rose's petals against your fair skin when the bloom explodes into a million pieces?"

"I'd like anything you'd give me. The first date we had, you took me to see flowers."

"Actually our first date was my daring spider rescue. The notorious breast-touching-excuse incident."

She chuckled, held him tighter and he kissed the top of her head. "We're okay, love," he murmured. "We're okay."

§

Four days later, they let him come home. Julie had been as glad as Des was to be back in his bed. And, as much as she'd enjoyed his reaction to her surgical gown gift, she was happy to have him back in his jeans and T-shirts. Though it might be a while before he did handstands on a roof again, she was okay with that.

Des's post-surgical instructions forbade him from lifting anything heavier than a cinder block for several weeks, or exerting himself too strenuously, so he coordinated his roofing jobs by phone and very brief visits out to job sites. He had good people working for him, so his income didn't suffer.

While he hadn't lied to her when he told her he had few expenses, Julie had learned his medical insurance, available to him only because he paid a high premium and maintained a sizeable deductible, didn't cover everything, like the expensive pump supplies. He'd learned to keep all his other bills low to meet those costs.

Yet like her, there wasn't much he needed in life except the pleasure of day-to-day living. He was at least able to minimize the doctor visits he disliked so much, because with Betty nearby, the nurse handled a lot of the follow up monitoring that would have been done in an office, including staying alert for any warning symptoms of rejection.

Julie had one-heart stopping night when she rolled over and discovered he had a fever. In a blink, she'd concocted all sorts of emergency scenarios involving organ rejection or life-threatening infection, but it turned out to be fine. Over his protests, she'd woken Betty to check on him. After a brief interrogation, the nurse learned he'd let some of his Type I kids come visit him and meet her horses the day before, and Justice had a cold.

Betty designated Des the stupidest man alive—which she said was a very notable distinction, since anything with a penis was incurably stupid—and determined he'd simply caught the boy's bug. He'd been relegated to bed and chicken soup for the next three days under the pain of her wrath.

For the time being, Des was supposed to minimize contact with immune system risk factors, like groups of children. Julie knew that, but she'd been at the theater when he'd decided to invite the kids over, so she hadn't been able to run interference. Not that it would have helped much, since Des was getting more recalcitrant with every passing day. Whereas he'd take a certain amount of mothering from Betty, he tolerated zero levels of it from Julie.

However, though Betty was scathing in her discussion with him, she'd called Julie later to give her some even-handed advice. "He's going stir crazy. Once the cold passes, if he'd be a help to you at the theater and no one there is an adolescent petri dish, see if he'd like to go to work with you."

Julie hadn't attempted to snow him as to her reasons. She simply asked him if he'd like to come with her to the theater to get out of the house. With a searching look, he accepted.

It turned out to be the best solution for all of them. Not surprising to her, he was a big help, and it came at an opportune time. Lila's play had opened and run with better than decent ticket sales for all showings. Harris and Madison had picked up the extra slack and made it happen while Julie's care and attention were focused on Des.

Audience reception was so strong to *Done Right*, they decided to ride its momentum. The next production they'd planned had hit a scheduling hitch, so they bumped it further down the schedule and decided to do a follow up play Lila had already written, set in the same world.

Julie was pleasantly surprised to find Des was willing to do anything needed to help, even mundane clerical tasks. One day he sat with her at a table in the front row, assembling promo packets for her student volunteers to pass out at the area colleges, local community organizations and anywhere else potential audience members would be. As she'd sat across from him, working on her computer and emailing press releases to the local news outlets, she'd secretly watched and savored his efficient way of working while he bantered with the tech repairing a couple of lights along the stage edge.

Lila was directing this play as she had the first, with heavy support and guidance from Harris and Julie. During rehearsals, Des provided good input to her on how the Dom/sub dynamics would come across to an audience. He also supervised volunteers on scene building—after Julie made it clear she would eviscerate anyone who let him do anything he shouldn't.

He didn't appreciate such overprotectiveness and was quick to inform her of it, not always in kind terms. She understood there was a line he didn't care for their relationship to cross, but she also couldn't help caring about him and being protective. Fortunately, through their arguments, they learned to understand one another somewhat better.

"You're not going to get to be bossy much longer," he warned her in a lighter moment. "You'll be back at my mercy and then I'll make you sorry."

"Yes, I'm a terrible girlfriend for looking out for you," she retorted. Yet she longed for that time as much as he did.

However, his recuperation period brought a bolstering reassurance about the substance of their relationship. While she'd never thought it was based only in sex and BDSM, before his surgery those things had been new and exciting enough to overshadow learning other things about one another.

He didn't care much for TV, but they both loved good films. He liked *Fast and Furious* type action films, while she was a classic film buff. They found common likes in older movies such as *Forrest Gump* and *Regarding Henry*. They also enjoyed choosing the worst of the B flicks— double ZZ basement finds, as Des called them—to dissect over popcorn.

They returned to Daniel Stowe gardens and wandered the trails, enjoying the flowers, sitting by the water and talking about everything. They never ran out of topics, though she equally liked their comfortable silences. One night when Betty deemed he was doing well enough to be out in a crowded environment—and he was chafing too much at the prolonged restrictions to keep him at home— they joined Logan, Madison, Troy and Shale at a karaoke bar and each tried out the mic, with hilarious results.

Though Des tired out before midnight, he tipped his chair against the wall behind him and enjoyed watching the others. She leaned against him, hand lightly on his thigh, and feeling glad to be there with him.

They talked about deeper things, too. Elaine, his mother, her relationship with Thomas and Marcus. When her friends had headed back to their North Carolina house after the surgery, Thomas had told her they'd be there for at least a month. She knew there were plenty of good doctors to handle his follow up in New York, so she suspected they were staying close in case anything came up with Des. She appreciated it, even as she hoped it wouldn't be necessary.

The one thing she and Des didn't talk about much, though Julie knew it was on both of their minds, was the future. A healthy kidney like Thomas's might last Des eleven years, but she worried about when it would give out. At that point, he might be on dialysis permanently. But that was the future, and he wouldn't let her talk about it, not now. As his strength returned, he had other priorities in mind. One night, he let her know it in unmistakable terms.

§

"It's a full moon tonight," he mused, looking at the play of its light coming through the window, creating a silvery-white beam on the bedspread. Julie lay in his arms, a luxury during his healing that was becoming blissfully routine again. Her fingertips slid over his bare chest and he turned his head to nuzzle her temple. There was a different quality to the caress, more firm, questing, and she drew in a breath as he moved down to her cheek, nudging her jaw so she lifted her chin and he kissed her throat. Her arms wound over his shoulders, fingers sliding through his hair.

"Des..."

"Love the way you say my name like that," he murmured. "Look at me."

She lifted her head to meet his gaze as his fingers took over from his mouth, stroking her throat, tracing her collar bone, his palm moving over her heart and holding there, a pressure that made her aware of her heartbeat and the sudden concentration in his brown eyes.

"For just a second there, you let it all go. Your body took over, your soul, that submissive side that surrenders to me. It's time to let the rest go, love."

Her brow furrowed and he shook his head. "Do you have to talk about how you breathe? No," he answered the obvious question. "Because you just do it. I told you from the beginning, I've carried this with me my whole life. I live the best way I can to ride the train as long as possible. I don't want to miss a bit of the scenery because I'm too focused on where the train will end up. I need you to do that, Julie, now more than ever. Your worry is killing me."

She was wearing a silky baby doll that he'd talked her into buying and wearing to bed, with the droll observation, *"Just because I can't use my cock right now doesn't mean I don't like to keep it entertained."* He slid the thin strap off her shoulder so he could finish his caress of her collar bone to the point of her shoulder unimpeded. He brushed his knuckles over her breast, teasing the ripe curve. His heated eyes remained on hers.

"When I see you worrying, I worry about you, and all this scenery gets ruined for both of us. If this is going to work, you have to enjoy the train ride with me and not get bogged down. Sounds selfish of me to demand that, I know, but if you can do that, I promise that attitude will take us both to a better state of mind. A synergistic reaction like some other things we enjoy. Hmm?"

She smiled tentatively, through a swirl of reaction from his touch. It made sense, didn't it? After all, yes, she could lose him, but he could lose his life. If he could figure out how to handle that reality without being obsessed with it, so could she.

"I'm just new to it," she said. "I can do it. I just need practice."

"I can help with that." His mouth curved, and he placed her in the full block of moonlight. "Lift up."

When she complied, he put a pillow under her back, making a tempting bridge of her body. Her heartrate kicked up. Being around him on a normal day was like being around an aphrodisiac. Since he'd started to regain his strength, they'd made a concerted effort to ignore their smoldering chemistry, but his expression said he planned to turn up the heat.

"Take off the gown and the panties. I want to see my sub."

She complied. She didn't want to fall back into worry so readily, but he wasn't yet cleared to have sex. Was he planning on pushing that envelope? Would she be able to deny him?

"Ssshh. Your thoughts are making a racket," he chided her. "I want to watch you, love. And we're going to do it my way."

He left the bed, a visual gift in his loose pajama bottoms and nothing else. He'd lost some muscle tone and weight, but not much, his lean torso as wiry and interesting to her as it had ever been. The surgical scar still gave her heart a little jump. Reaching out, she grazed her fingertips over his flank as he bent over his dresser.

He turned, holding a handful of rope. "Lace those wandering hands behind your head. I'm turning you into my own personal pin-up."

He tied her wrists and fingers above her head. Running the ropes over her butterfly spread elbows and upper arms, he did an elaborate breast harness that constricted and lifted the curves, putting them on lush display for his avid gaze. Next he brought the ropes beneath her, through her thighs. He spread her knees, bent and tied them in the same butterfly shape, giving her a true hourglass look. He did an elaborate rope harness over her pelvis with more slender rope.

When he was done, he hooked his fingers in the slim rope, stroking the small knots over her clit and labia, watching the way she squirmed, lifted, undulated. He'd left her enough movement to be a man's wet dream, struggling and quivering, her limbs, breasts and hips bathed in moonlight. Her throat arched and her wet lips parted.

"Des," she pleaded as he put his fingers inside her. His jaw was tight, his gaze relentless, that shift that let her into the darkest room of his soul. It was a dungeon where he wanted to possess her completely, take her to this.

"Your gorgeous wet cunt. Fuck, I want to be ramming into it, reminding you I'm boss. Sounds cavemanish, doesn't it?" he mused. "But that's the way weeks of this shit makes me feel. That's what's coming for you, love, when I get full strength. Just some merciless, caveman, Master-slave, nothing PC about it, fucking. I need to drown you in a boatload of Tarzan."

"Okay," she agreed, breathlessly. "But you don't have to do this for me. I want to come when you're ready, when we can go together..."

He chuckled, a dangerous sound. "This doesn't have anything to do with what you want. I'm not being selfless, love. You'll know that before it's over. Watching this happen, turning you into some wanton little sex slave on my bed, may turn me on so bad it'll give me an aneurysm, but you don't call the shots. You're going to come for me. Again and again. And again. When you're exhausted, limp in my arms like a pretty little hen buffeted by a storm, I'm going to do it one more time. I want you to be begging for mercy, and not getting any from me. Fair enough?"

"Doesn't sound like fair is your goal." She was surprised her voice was more than a squeak.

"No, it's not. Clever girl." He bent, suckled her clit as she jolted at the sensation. Rising to go to the dresser, he returned with a vibrator about six inches long. He fixed it in the small net of rope he'd created over her clit and labia, cinching the lines to hold it there.

"Now see, this will roll a bit," he explained with lustful satisfaction. "You'll have to keep squirming to hold it where you want it as you get more and more excited. It'll also give you a little breathing space as you come down from one climax and charge up the hill to another. But I won't let you take too much of a breather. No cheating."

He turned the vibrator on, and the rhythm was one that would push her up, and drag her down. As she tried to wrap her fragmenting mind around that, Des bent to cup her breasts and leisurely suckle her distended nipples. The excruciating sensations were coming from everywhere. She rolled and pitched like she was on a turbulent sea.

When he at last sat back, his lips moist from nursing her, he drove her even higher simply by watching her with a man's undisguised hunger. He had an impressive erection against his pajama bottoms, but he seemed to ignore it, focusing on her, taking his satisfaction from his control, what he could do to her.

She toppled over the first orgasm, and it was a rough, tumultuous one, fueled by several weeks of desperation and worries. Mortality had been beating down both their needs and this was a defiance against it, an answer and challenge at once.

She cried out her response, the unrelenting pulse of the vibrator giving her no quarter. The more she squirmed the higher it took her. When his fingers slid between it and her soaked cunt, she mewled in relief and jerked as he brushed his fingers over the lips of her sex, communicating a muted form of the vibration through his fingers.

"That's it, my beautiful sex slave. Your Master wants to see you do that again." Lowering his head, he cleaned her with soothing strokes of his tongue. Tears rolled out of her eyes, reflecting what she was feeling. He rose to kiss them away, bracing himself over her. She couldn't explain why she was crying, and he didn't ask, but it wasn't because he didn't notice or was being callous. She suspected they both understood why.

He changed the vibrator rhythm to a gentle roll against her clit. He worked it against her sensitive flesh in slow circles. As he did that he was kissing her body, rubbing his sandpaper jaw against her tender skin. He rose to kiss her gasping mouth with leisurely thoroughness. Then he went down again.

Never had she had a lover do this, this unhurried, you-are-my-universe kind of lovemaking where he fed off her every reaction, making it all about her, but all for his own pleasure. She could do nothing but be lost in him, ache for him and love him. There was no conflict here, just two souls dancing forever in a world belonging to the two of them.

Climax after climax. He hadn't been bluffing. He used the vibrator, his mouth, his fingers, the demand of his voice. His piercing eyes, dark as an abyss, insisted, his body looming over her haloed by moonlight.

When he at long last decided he was done, a couple hours had passed, and she was a dish rag. No, dishrags had more starch to them. She was as malleable as water, perspiration glistening on her naked body, her lips parted to gulp in air, all her pulse points thudding with a replete lassitude.

He adjusted her bonds so he could turn her over on her stomach, bringing her knees beneath her, tying them together, adjusting the pillow so her ass was in the air, her cunt framed by her thighs. She heard another drawer open, and smelled the fragrant scent of the heated lubricant he'd used on her before. She wasn't able to resist anything and, when she felt the broad tip of a dildo at her rear entrance, she had no resistance. By the time she registered how thick it was, he already had it past both rings of muscle and was easing it deeper into her passage.

"Oh God, Des. That feels..." It was uncomfortable, unnerving, but she was so loose, it wasn't burning. Though the potential was there, a little fizzling sting around her rim. He adjusted the ropes once more to hold the toy in place. She heard a metal clink, and his belt brushed against her ass.

"I decided you needed a reminder. I want to own your soul, Julie. Okay? Give every bit of it to me, so I'll know I didn't fuck this up, dragging you into this."

"It's already yours," she said, voice breaking. She wanted the pain and punishment. How had he known it? What she heard in his voice said maybe he needed it, too.

He reached beneath her, adjusted the vibrator once more and turned it on to that mind blowing rhythm that made it impossible to stay still. She let out a moan of protest, it was too much, but when the first crack came, she was already lifting into the blow, and the vibrator stroked over her clit, sending an impossible shard of pleasure through her.

She shrieked on every strike. The hard sting, the clutch on the dildo in her ass, and the vibration in her cunt, combined to break her down into whatever he needed, whatever they both did.

Once again, astoundingly, he took her back to climax. This time she was sure it tore open her soul. When it was done, the dam had given way and she was fierce in the grip of a cathartic cry, working out and knocking loose every worry or fear she'd let build up in her all these weeks.

"That's my love. My sweet sub. My girl. There you are."

He'd untied her, was rubbing her back and legs, turning her in his arms, wrapping her up in a blanket and him, holding fast. She put her hand over his, and knew what Elaine had said was right. Whatever she'd felt before, it hadn't been love, not truly. She'd never let herself be lost in someone so completely.

"Ssshh, easy love. Easy, girl. I'm here. I'm a monster, but I'm here."

"Not." She sniffed. "Perfect in every way. Master."

"Sssh. Sleep. It's okay now. Sleep."

She had no choice in that, either, since she'd left behind her own will hours ago and wanted only to obey his every word, give him everything he wanted. She held onto him and was pleased that he didn't let her go, either.

He was right. There was no room between them for any more worries. Only love, and it could fill and overflow their hearts and souls until they swam in it all the way to Heaven.

Chapter Twenty-Two

A week later, they received an invitation from Marcus and Thomas to stay overnight at their North Carolina house. Elaine wanted them to come for dinner because Les, Thomas's sister, was coming home for the weekend from medical school at Duke University. She hadn't yet had a chance to meet Des.

While she'd normally look forward to any visit with Marcus and Thomas's family, Julie chafed at the timing. The day they were supposed to go was the official day Des had an all-clear to resume all normal activities—including sex. She'd figured Des would prefer to have the privacy of his place to tear her clothes off and do all the things that he'd been threatening, but Des told her to say yes to the invite.

As they left Charlotte that day, Des agreed privacy would be optimal, but he gave her a wink as he took the exit ramp onto I-85.

"They're going to give us a private bedroom, aren't they? They live in the sticks, but it's not like *Little House on the Prairie*, everyone in a one-room cabin."

"You just admitted you've watched *Little House on the Prairie*."

"Everyone has watched at least one episode of *Little House on the Prairie*, no matter how much they deny it," he said staunchly. "Melissa Sue Anderson was hot. And don't get me started on Ma." His gaze slid over her. "I wouldn't mind seeing you in one of those cute farm girl dresses with the little boots and stockings."

"There's something deeply twisted about you."

She chuckled as he grabbed at her knee and she scooched farther against the passenger seat to avoid him. Even as he teased her, though, she wasn't fooled. Something was up. He had something planned, but he wasn't in the mood to share, even when she probed. But he gave her a nice surge of arousal when he leveled a more direct gaze on her.

"Come here and stop hiding over there."

She moistened her lips and slid back to the center of the seat. He settled his palm on her leg, sliding up to her upper thigh and then turning his hand so he cupped her between her legs under her skirt, fingers playing over her labia like a violin and sending a quick little shudder through her. "You just sit like that for a while," he said conversationally. "Find us something on the radio while I drive."

"Sadist."

His eyes glinted, but he kept his hand there until she found a station he preferred. "You feel wet," he said. "I'd like to keep you that way all day, but..." He gave her a firm stroke that made her draw in a breath and put his hand back on her thigh. "That's just a reminder that things will happen when they should happen. All right?"

"Okay." She curled her hand over his. "I'm rethinking wanting you back to 100% again. You may drive me crazy. Crazier, that is."

He shot her a grin. "Sit back and enjoy the ride, love."

Elaine fed them a repast that would put a Thanksgiving dinner to shame. So much so that Julie was afraid they'd need to postpone sexual activity for a week unless she did a marathon jog from here to the state line. Since she abhorred all types of formal exercise, her serious contemplation of the idea said just how desperate she was.

It wasn't that she needed this first time to be acrobatic, rock-her-world kind of sex. She just wanted her Master's cock deep inside her, his body pressing her down, his arms around her. She needed that link and connection as much as she needed air, and the more she thought about it, the scarcer the air seemed to be getting.

It didn't help that Des kept touching her, putting a possessive, stroking hand high on her thigh under the table. Or laughing at Marcus's and Rory's banter with his sexy timbre. Or getting that attentive look in his brown gaze as he listened to Elaine. She wondered if his frequent touches were a way of communicating his own urgency, but the difference between her and him was he fed off of denial, fueled by his sub's frustration. The only thing that might keep her from murdering him was that she couldn't have sex with a dead man. Though if she got any more sexually frustrated, her moral barometer might drop precipitously.

Des had shifted his hand to the back of her chair and was playing with her bra strap under her shirt when she was beaned by a biscuit.

"Hey, girl with the idiot dreamy look on her face," Marcus said. "Pay attention. Might as well be freaking newlyweds," he grumbled to Thomas. "When she's not looking at him, he's looking at her."

"Yeah, not like anyone else we know at this table," Les said, rolling her eyes at him and Thomas. She winked at Des. Though when not smiling she looked like the serious overachiever she was, Les was a pleasant girl with brown hair and hazel eyes like her mother's. She became even more animated when Daralyn, a family friend who'd lived with them for the past few years, was here, but Daralyn had a field trip with her community college this weekend. Something Julie was happy to hear because, though she loved being around Daralyn, the young woman was painfully shy and needed to be more socialized.

Marcus sent Les a mock frown. "I have a very important something to tell you both," he said to Julie. "I acquired the information at great personal cost."

"You had to give up hair mousse for a week?" Rory asked, wide-eyed.

"Shut up, crip, or I'll let the air out of your tires," Marcus advised.

Elaine tsked at their byplay. Yet Julie noticed the men were keeping the humor clean if tasteless so she didn't have to resort to outright admonishment.

"Spill. What's this valuable info?" Julie asked.

Marcus glanced at Thomas. He had his arm stretched

behind Thomas's chair, body canted toward him, foot propped on the cross piece beneath. Unlike Des and Julie, they'd already been able to resume carnal relations, but from the hawk steadiness of Marcus's gaze, Julie suspected he didn't yet consider them caught up from the deficit. But when had Marcus and Thomas *not* been like that? Honest to God, she was going to have a meltdown if she couldn't have Des, or he could have her, two minutes ago.

Des was more than partly to blame, and not because of his attentiveness today. The man had used his Devil-cursed self-discipline to tie her up and do a repeat of that wonderful night several times, a scintillating reinforcement of the Dom and sub bond, as well as the other bonds between them. As much as she loved that, the aftermath had been even more precious. He'd held her so tightly, a quivering mass of "fuck it, I want to live" energy that broke the heart and made her love him all the more.

"I had to call Tyler," Marcus informed her.

She returned fully to the present with a mock dramatic gasp, putting her hand to her heart. "Oh my God, you're right. Thomas, how could you let him make such a terrible sacrifice?"

"I will dip your hair in rubber cement while you sleep," Marcus said.

"Enough," Elaine said, putting pecan pie on the table. "Tell them your news. I've been fairly bursting with it since Thomas told me last week."

"He's such a tattle tale." But Marcus relented, meeting Des's gaze. "There's a study going on right now. It puts pancreatic cells in this biomaterial that withstands immune system attack. When the cells are injected into you, the cells can maintain their ability to detect low blood sugar and produce insulin in response. What healthy pancreas are supposed to do. Encapsulated islet cell therapy, I think it's called." He glanced at Les, as if he'd confirmed some of the medical terms with her.

"Regardless, Jon will be able to explain it much better," Marcus added. "I understood every third word, but the important gist is there's a lot of optimism surrounding the study. It's ready for human trials."

Julie raised her brows. "How did you find that out?"

"He called Marcie," Thomas supplied.

"Oh." Julie beamed and explained to Des. "Marcie is a friend of Marcus and Thomas's. Well, let me step back. Initially the common friend was Lucas Adler. He's a big CFO for this major company out in New Orleans. Marcie is his sister-in-law. When she was working in New York on an internship, she, Marcus and Thomas hung out together so...they could show her the ropes in the area."

From the flicker in Des's eyes, she knew he understood. Marcie was a submissive, and Marcus and Thomas had been her introduction into the New York BDSM scene. "Anyhow, she's now married to Ben. Does that make her a sister-in-law squared?" she asked Thomas.

Thomas laughed. "While the Kensington guys are a lot like brothers, they're not actually blood-related, so no. Lucas and Ben both work for Kensington & Associates, run by Matt Kensington."

He directed his further explanation to Des. "Five of them run the executive management team: Lucas, Peter, Jon, Matt and Ben, and they're thick as a pack of wolves. Anyhow, Jon is their Leonardo da Vinci when it comes to mechanical stuff and cutting edge research. He has contacts with all sorts of other geniuses, people involved in everything from the next shuttle launch to cancer research. Marcus asked him to dig around and see if there were any reputable studies that might fit your situation."

"Studies like that are tough to get into," Des said.

"Yeah, they can be, but like anything else in this world, it's who you know," Thomas pointed out. "The study is being conducted by a Tampa research center. One of the top researchers involved founded a juvenile diabetes camp and foundation. Tyler Winterman is a big donor and honorary board member."

"The light dawns." Julie chuckled. "I bet that hurt."

"Yeah. I merely gave up a kidney. Marcus having to call Tyler and ask a favor, *that* was the real sacrifice," Thomas said.

Julie beamed at Marcus. "You do love me."

Marcus sniffed. "Piss off, both of you." At Elaine's sharp

look, he lifted both hands. "I could have used a much worse expletive. They're picking on me."

Elaine bit back a smile, and Julie exchanged an amused look with Thomas. She could tell it was a quiet pleasure to Thomas, the rapport that had grown between his husband and mother. Especially since at one time they'd been as close to sworn enemies as two people could be.

"Mom." After Marcus's news had been revealed, Celeste had left the table to retrieve homemade ice cream for the pie. Now she poked her head back into the kitchen from the cellar door. "I can't find the vanilla. Where'd you put it?"

"Daralyn might have moved it to the smaller freezer when we were reorganizing down there. Let me come look." Elaine rose and joined her daughter. Des's hand slid higher up Julie's leg, his thumb putting pressure on the juncture between hip and labia. Covering his hand with hers, she dug her nails into his flesh and gave him a look.

"Asshole," she mouthed. He winked, but he shifted his hand back down and spoke aloud.

"Marcus and Tyler aren't friends?" he ventured.

"It's complicated," Thomas responded.

"For those of us who like to fantasize about guy-on-guy, there's a whole homoerotic Julius Caesar versus Alexander the Great thing going on there. Total fantasy on my part"— she raised her voice over Rory's mock gag and dramatic stuffing of his fingers in his ears—"since Tyler is as straight as a pencil. Their relationship is basically built on power tripping, art bidding wars and one-upmanship."

She glanced at Thomas, whose set expression suggested he wasn't thrilled with her musings. She put a hand on his arm. "I don't want Marcus to be with anyone but you. It's just a fantasy I think about. Can't help my thoughts."

"That's fine," Thomas said evenly. "You can have the fantasy. Just as long as *he* isn't having it."

"Not likely," Marcus said. "Tyler's ass is so tight you couldn't get a pencil dick up it anyhow."

"Sounds like you'd have no trouble then," Rory observed. Thomas smacked the back of his head.

"Hey! Mom's not here," Rory protested.

"That's why I did it. So she was represented."

"You couldn't get either to admit it under torture," Julie told Des, "but Marcus and Tyler actually like each another."

"No we don't," Marcus said automatically. In Elaine's absence, he was doing a quick check of the messages on his phone, something she didn't care for them doing while a meal was in process. He pocketed it as her feet heralded her return and smoothly resumed the discussion in progress.

"I gave Tyler some of the basics of your condition and he passed it on to the study director. They're interested in bringing you into the program, to see the impact their work has on a more challenging case. And the great thing is this research center has connections to a lot of other studies happening in the field of diabetes research, so if you get your foot in here, it might lead to other things."

Marcus met Des's gaze. "I didn't investigate all this to make you feel pressured to do it, but if you'd be interested, there's a window of opportunity."

Julie held her breath, waiting for Des's response, but she needn't have worried. While Des still wrestled with being handled versus cared about, he was getting better about understanding the difference between the two. Proving it, he extended his hand across the table.

"Thanks, man," he said quietly. "I appreciate it a lot."

"Well, she is right. I love her, pain in the ass that she is. And she loves you. I even find you mildly tolerable. I think we should get rid of Rory and replace him with Des." Marcus tilted his head toward Elaine. "He'd be a much cooler son, I promise."

Rory snorted. "If we'd replace anybody, it'd be the obnoxious Yankee that Thomas dragged home. Des at least was born in the right part of the country."

"I was originally a mid-westerner. God help me," Marcus said.

"Still a northerner, dude. Check your geography."

Marcus bared his teeth at him and turned his attention back to Des. "Tyler also has a couple guest houses on his Gulf property. If you decide to do it, you may be down there for a few weeks, or have to return for follow ups. He said you're welcome to use one of them whenever you need it. As long as I don't come, so he doesn't have to put up with me."

Julie gripped his hand at the same time she closed her other one around Des's. "Liar. He'd welcome you just so you could fence post."

"That's riposte, which is a maneuver in fencing," Marcus said, while her eyes danced. "Proof how far a liberal arts education will get you."

"I like my word better. It included both ideas, which is clever and outside the box. That's what a liberal arts education will get you."

"If you find enough business graduates to fund your clever and outside the box ideas," Marcus retorted. But he squeezed her hand once more before they separated so Elaine could put down the vanilla ice cream. The scoop was already tantalizingly embedded in the creamy treat. Julie eyed it and took a deep breath. Maybe just a small sliver of pie...

§

Despite the waning afternoon, a nap was in order once they returned to Marcus and Thomas's house. Des told her he'd join her soon. Marcus was going to take him to his office in the refurbished barn to conference with Jon and the research director on the study particulars.

While she was staying as informed as possible about everything that could help Des with his health, he preferred to stay in the lead and consider his own reaction to new data before bringing her opinions into the equation. She tried to respect that most days, and today was easier than most, since she was having trouble staying awake. He gently but firmly suggested she go get her nap, and she decided to comply without complaint.

While she tried to stay awake until he came to join her, the day's travel and a million other details caught up with her. Her intended short power nap turned into a deep sleep. Thomas and Marcus's guest room, tucked into the back corner of their old farm house, was designed to be a nap heaven. Her sleep was more restful than any she'd had in a while, except for the nights when Des had given her those thorough sexual workouts.

She'd wondered if that was partly why he'd done it. Even when she was watching out for him, he was watching out for her, too. It was nice.

She had little memory of anything over the next couple hours except the ceiling fan turning slowly over the open canopy of the wood-framed queen-sized bed and the sun fading away over the fields behind the house. The window allowed the bed to be bathed in a square of natural light. Eventually, she felt Des's arms around her, his lips against her cheek. She nestled into the curve of his body with a sound of contentment and drifted. Despite her earlier desires, she was deep in dreamland, and it was nice just to spin there with him.

When she finally stirred, the clock on the bedside said ten p.m. She'd anticipated waking up an hour ago and sharing a glass of wine with Thomas and Marcus on the front porch. The time startled her enough she would have shot out of bed like a guilty Goldilocks, but Des's arms were around her. She realized it was the quiet whisper of her name that had brought her out of sleep. "Julie. Wake up for me, love."

She pressed her face into his throat, pleased when he cupped both his hands around her skull, stroking her hair. "Want to see something worth seeing?" he asked in that same low voice.

"Are you naked?"

His lips pulled into a smile. "Almost." When she opened her eyes, she saw he was on the top of the covers, stripped down to his jeans. He rose and offered her a hand to help her slide out of the high bed.

As she did, his gaze passed over her, registering strong approval. She'd removed her skirt and blouse and put on one of his snug T-shirts as nightwear so she didn't wrinkle her clothes.

"Nice as this is..." Des put his hands on the hem of the T-shirt and lifted it over her head, revealing her unbound breasts, leaving her standing in her lacy panties. He brought her closer, hand slipping inside the filmy fabric to knead her flesh as he kissed her, a wake-up call that had desire returning in one deliciously slow surge.

When she would have put her arms around him and drawn him back to the bed, he brought her to the window. There was a window seat there with a cushion, and he guided her up onto it, putting her hands on the sash and applying pressure, telling her that was where he wanted her to leave her palms. "Look," he ordered.

She glanced out over Thomas and Marcus's back yard, framed by live oaks and pines. It had the backdrop of a field that had once been farmed but now provided a few acres of pastureland for their three cows and two goats. The chickens were in their roost for the night. But those brief impressions weren't what he wanted her to see. It didn't take her more than a blink to find out what he did.

She drew in a breath. She'd told him she'd never watched Marcus and Thomas in a scene. The closest she'd come to it was the night she'd shared a bed with them for her birthday. Then she'd had the pleasure of curling up behind Marcus, daring to trail her fingertips down his back while he took Thomas next to her. She'd told Des she would be too embarrassed to watch them...while they knew she was watching. She assumed they'd be the same way, but apparently they'd figured out something, based on what Des whispered into her ear.

"They know we're here. I thought if you could get the chance to watch them in a way that worked for both of you, you might like it."

"How did you get Marcus to agree?" She swallowed a moan as Des's palms glided over her breasts, light as the touch of air.

"Sometime in the future, when I'm doing a scene with you, he and Thomas want to watch. It will be at a distance like this."

"He...they wanted to do that?"

"You sound surprised." He bit her neck. "They may be gay, but the three of you have a special relationship. I think they like the idea of you and all your curves bound up..." His fingers trailed up her bare spine then over her shoulder, around it, so he could press all five digits into the curve of her left breast, take possession of it. She leaned back into him, breath accelerating as he stroked the nipple, caressed the flesh around it. "Deal?"

"If I say no?"

"Then I have to close the blinds."

"Doms are manipulative, blackmailing sadists."

"Yeah, we are." He kissed her throat again, letting her feel his teeth first as a graze, then latching on hard. As she whimpered, he drew her back against his body, a straining bow notched with an arrow of sensation right down the center. His jaw tightened, teeth digging in as he banded his arm beneath her breasts. He pressed his pelvis against her ass, and she closed her eyes at the size of his erection.

"Please..."

"First, you watch. I want to know just how hot watching your friends gets you so I can punish you accordingly."

His tone was serious, making her shiver.

The one-level house was on a high enough foundation she had an elevated view. Marcus had Thomas stretched out on a blanket spread-eagle, his feet toward the field, his eyes blindfolded. His arms and legs were staked out with rope, and he was entirely naked. Marcus was circling him, dressed only in jeans as Des was, but, as Julie watched, he opened and shucked them off, so he could straddle Thomas and feed his cock between his lips.

Thomas's fingers clenched in his bonds. Since his body was turned diagonally toward Julie's view, she could see how stiff his erection was, how it jerked at Marcus's provocation. Her pussy dampened even more as she watched Thomas suck on Marcus's cock, the hollowing of his cheeks, the flex of muscle on both men's bodies as they moved in rhythm with one another.

She whimpered as Des slid his fingers between her legs, playing in her slipperiness beneath the crotch of the panties. "Please take off all your clothes," she whispered. "I need you inside me so badly, Des."

"I know you do. I'd kill anyone who tried to stop me from fucking you tonight, but we'll get there. Watch."

Thomas's muscles bunched as Marcus at last pulled away. In that pause, Des removed her panties, then continued to stroke and play in Julie's cunt, sliding fingers inside her then out, his other hand trailing along her arm, her neck, the side of her breast, then back up to grip her throat and hold her fast. She could do nothing but watch and grip the window sill, her body shaking as he rubbed his denim-clad erection against her backside.

"Spread your knees wider," he commanded.

She obeyed, wanting to beg, wanting to do anything he said. Marcus rose and moved down Thomas's body. She gasped as he slapped Thomas's cock with his open hand, doing it a couple times before he gripped Thomas's testicles, turning his wrist enough to suggest he was putting some twisting pressure on them. When Marcus said something to Thomas with erotic menace on his face, Thomas's lips parted, his tormented body straining up toward his Master.

As he did that, Des clasped both her breasts and started putting upward pressure on them. It was an uncomfortable feeling, the kind that spiraled arousal through her as she stretched against him, trying to keep her eye on the tableau as her own Master had ordered.

"Feel that," he muttered. "Does it turn you on for me to demand too much from you?"

"Yes," she breathed. "God, yes."

Marcus had released his sub and was freeing Thomas's ankles, but only to bind his thighs and calves together. He untied his arms and rolled him, bringing Thomas up onto hands and knees. Marcus stripped the belt out of his jeans, a thick strap even at this discreet distance. Julie felt a trickle of trepidation for Thomas, even as she suspected he'd respond to it the way she had when Des had done it to her. Anxiety at the pain, but an inexplicable eagerness for it.

When Marcus struck Thomas, she was amazed at the force. Her fingers convulsed on the ledge again. Thomas had started to put his head down and Marcus said something that brought his blindfolded face up so Julie could see the reflexive pressing of his lips, imagine the grunts coming from between them at each blow. Des reached in front of her and pushed up the window, cracking it so she could hear Thomas's guttural moans on the breeze.

"Des, I'm dying here."

"It's beautiful to watch." He eased several fingers into her wet pussy again and began to thrust, slow and easy. She shuddered and cried out on each penetration, moaning at the withdrawals, begging for more.

"I need you...your cock. Please."

"I like hearing 'please' from your lips. Keep begging and I'll keep thinking about it. Are you still watching?"

"Yes. Oh God, poor Thomas. It looks like he's...ah..." She nearly choked as Des did something that sent a tight spiral straight up her core. "Oh, God..."

"I suspect he's enjoying every damn minute, no matter how hard Marcus is hitting him. At least his dick looks like it is."

"Do you like...watching them?"

"I like watching a Master work. I love watching you get so stirred up by all of it. Now be quiet. Focus only on that and this..."

She heard his jeans open, and nearly sobbed in relief as the head of his cock pushed against her opening. While she'd imagined the first time since his surgery to be with him on top of her, in the bed, just the two of them in an isolated bubble of reconnection, there would be time for that. Right now was right now and she wouldn't trade it for anything. There was a lot of scenery she could anticipate on a train ride with him.

She didn't expect the climax to detonate when he first breached her slickness, but as she choked on a surprised wail, he slid in all the way to the root and gripped her neck again. He had his arm banded around her hips so she could barely move, the climax forced to happen in a tight warren of space and limited motion, making it all the more intense.

Especially when Marcus set aside the belt, knelt behind Thomas, gripped his flexing ass cheeks and thrust into him, so fast and deep it suggested he'd already been well-lubed. Thomas's lips stretched back farther, his head still up.

Marcus seized his hair in one hand, using that and the hold on his hip to ride his bucking mount thoroughly and hard. His muscles rippled, hair fluttering along his shoulder blades. The set of his mouth and glittering green eyes said he planned to take everything Thomas had and demand more. Looking into Marcus's face, Julie saw what she often saw in Des's at this moment.

They wanted it all, everything to the depths of their sub's soul. Total possession and even beyond that, something so all-consuming there were no words for it. If there was reincarnation and multiple lives, they wanted all of those. When death came, they intended to leave a brand on the soul of their sub that declared: *this one is mine, through all eternity.*

She let out a sound that expressed that truth, that told Des he could have that. That he already did. He was staying so still, letting her spasm and clutch around him, whimper and cry out through the orgasm. It wasn't enough. She needed more.

She saw Thomas climax, jetting into the blanket, and Marcus followed right behind him, head tipping back. Hearing the grunts of the two men as they found completion together, she sighed with pleasure. She let go of the window sill to grip Des's hands on her body, dig in with little bites of her nails, trying to tell him what she needed, but he already knew.

He withdrew from her and turned her body in the same motion, lifting it in his arms before she could protest or worry. It was clear from the stern set of his face he would tolerate no nursemaiding from her right now.

He laid her on the bed and stood back, staring down at her body with a peculiar look on his face. "Spread your legs," he said softly. "Cup your breasts, and look at me. Show me you're all mine."

She opened her thighs, knowing her labia and clit were swollen and wet. She cupped her breasts, her nipples stiff and large. Her pulse jumped in her throat as his hot gaze covered her. She realized then he wasn't wearing his pump, and he'd removed the injection site. Today was the day he'd change it out, so he'd wanted nothing between them this first time. She wet her lips.

"Stay in that exact position until I tell you that you can

move," he said. Putting his knee on the bed, he positioned himself between her spread legs, taking hold of his cock and slowly stroking himself over her cunt, allowing a couple drops of pre-come to splatter on her clit. She shuddered but held her position. His eyes lifted to her parted, moist lips.

"As tempting as your mouth is right now, I'll take advantage of that later. You'll use that to slick me up right before I fuck your ass. Every time I've tied you up and brought you to climax these past few weeks, I've thought about all the ways I want to use your body, love. It's a good thing you had that nap, but even after I tire you out, I'm going to fuck you in your sleep. I'm going to make sure you know you're mine no matter where you are."

It so matched what she had just thought, it raised the hair on her neck, but in a good way. Thank God, he finally fed his cock into her cunt again, a slow, deep sinking until he adjusted to brace himself over her. His gaze raked her body, the way she was still holding her breasts on display for him. Her thighs trembled against his hips, her body held in an excruciating stasis for him.

"Tell me what you want, Julie."

"I want to put my arms and legs around you. I want to hold you so I can feel our hearts beat together. I need you so close. Please."

"All right. But you let me do the moving, like you're a puppet and I'm holding the strings. I'm going to tie you like that sometime, so you have to move with the pull of the ropes, letting me direct every movement."

"I'd love that." She could imagine that as one of the upcoming performances, except she didn't want him to do it with someone else. Maybe...maybe she'd do it with him. She didn't care who was watching.

He lifted her legs, directing her to clamp them around his bare hips and ass. He bent and kissed the top of her breasts, dipping his head enough to wrap his lips around each cherry-sized nipple in turn and indulge a suckling while she panted and her pussy squeezed down on him. She could feel the telltale quiver of his thighs, the tautness of his ass, evidence of the restraint he was putting on his own desires.

Lifting his head, he took her right hand from her breast, kissed her palm and guided it to his side. Then the other one. He met her gaze.

"You can move and hold me however you like now," he said quietly. "I love you, Julie. No matter what. No matter how good or bad it gets, I love you."

"Same goes," she said, her voice shaking. She slid her arms up to his shoulders, tightened her legs around him as he pushed deep into her. She pressed her face into his neck, holding on as he began to thrust. So much control all these weeks, but suddenly, in the space of an indrawn breath, it broke free. Her cry was as raw as Thomas's as Des pushed her legs higher up on his back so he could slam into her more forcefully, testicles slapping against her perineum, sending shock waves of pleasure through her. He gripped her ass in both hands, shortening the thrusts to make them even more potent, rubbing against her insides, drawing her up the side of that cliff with him again.

He rolled them so she was straddling him and he was bringing her down on him with a hard hand on her hip and another tangled in her hair, his gaze all over the bouncing movement of her breasts. He reared up to capture a nipple in his teeth and bit, making her yelp at the pain but tangle her fingers in his hair to hold on, take it, take anything he needed to do to her. He rolled her to her back again and braced himself above her, slowing it down, then speeding it up. He was obviously taking full pleasure in being inside her once again as he drew closer and closer to release.

He was her anchor in a world that was spinning and quaking. He came down on her again, let her wrap her arms around him once more. It was as if he couldn't get enough of every position, every view. It told her he wasn't making empty threats about what the rest of her night was going to be like. But she was okay with that. With all of it.

She held onto him, spoke incoherent messages of love into his ear as their bodies rocked and moved together. He responded in kind, and she pressed her cheek against his face. "Des," she whispered. "Master. Please give all of yourself to me. Please."

He was close, she could tell he was, but she also sensed a struggle in him. This close, so open to one another, she understood. He was having to hurdle an obstacle that had come with the surgery, some wall of uncertainty about the strength of his body, the full recuperation of it. She could feel it in him now, that struggle, and she slid her hands down his back to grip his flexing buttocks and gazed up at him.

"Master," she whispered again. "Please come for me. I need to feel you release inside me."

His brown eyes were fiery heat, and his lips stretched back in a snarl, a ripple going through his body as he finally let go. The climax was hard and long, a pulsing, heated wetness that sent her spiraling off into a jolting aftershock.

When they at last slowed, she was gasping and he had a satisfied set to his mouth. It filled her with anticipation, and a contentment so deep she didn't ever want to leave this moment.

Almost. She wouldn't let him go, willing him to lay his full weight on her.

"I'm too heavy."

"Not for just a minute. Please."

He complied, though he propped his elbow by her head so she didn't have all of it. Though he was lean, he was a very solid one-seventy again, so she appreciated the consideration, despite perversely also wanting him so close he crushed her.

"Thank you. For all of it. And the thing with Marcus and Thomas. Why...?"

"Because I wanted to give you something." He spoke against her hair. "Something no one else could give you, to thank you for...everything. I didn't want to just fuck you like some kind of rabbit, this first time."

"I would have been totally fine with that. I was almost fine with it on the table in front of the whole family this afternoon. It was a close thing."

His lips pulled against her face in a smile. She closed her eyes, held him tighter. "But this was amazing. Do I need to thank Marcus too?"

"This was a Dom-to-Dom thing. The acceptable

etiquette is to act like nothing happened, unless you and Thomas want to have some gushy sub-bonding over how wonderful your Masters are."

Julie chuckled, her muscles rippling along his cock, still within her. "First, Thomas would agree with me that neither of you needs any more ego stroking. Second, I think that's more a girly thing. Thomas will probably be better if we don't talk about it. We never really talked much about the New York thing, either. It just was, a very nice *was* that needed no embellishment or analysis."

"Good decision." Des let out a contented sigh and rolled, taking her with him so she was spread out over his body, her thigh over his, arm over his chest, face against his neck.

She ran her fingers lightly down his side, to the upper rise of his firm buttocks. "Did all these nicks and scars come from roofing? You're like a New York cab."

He gathered her to him. "Some of them. I was an adventurous kid, too."

She rested her hand on his chest, threading through his chest hair and moving up to trace his throat. He glanced down at her, cocking his head at her absorption. When she brought her hand up to his jaw, he met her with his hand palm to palm, fingers folding together. She loved him. So much.

"I love you, too," he said, and it didn't surprise her that he'd heard and answered what she'd said only in her heart. He touched her chin. "So you think a sliver of that no-sugar pie Elaine had us bring back to the house would be good right now?"

"You can't possibly be hungry. I should hate you."

"I bet I can talk you into some more of that homemade ice cream. I'll just spread a couple tablespoons on your pussy and have it that way, warming up everything I make cold."

"Well, if you put it that way, I could have a spoonful."

He grinned. "Then go get it, woman. Wait on me like a proper sub."

She snorted and tugged his chest hair. "If you think you found yourself a service sub, think again. I'm in this for the sex."

He turned his head and nuzzled her neck, adjusting to his hip to push her back. He pinned her wrist to the bed as he kissed her throat and bit her. When he raised his head, his eyes were intent and sharp.

"Get your pretty ass out of this bed and bring me what I told you to. Else you'll be very, very sorry."

Her pulse leaped at both tone and look, and she swallowed, a quiver running through her. Her lips parted, but before she could think of what to say his own quirked, his eyes gleaming.

"You've got some service sub to you, love. I can promise you that."

He put his mouth back on hers, silencing whatever indignant response she could have summoned, which she suspected wouldn't have been much, given all her brain cells had seized up at his command. When he finally lifted his head, though, she'd rallied.

"I've got some news for you," she said. "Tit for tat. You can say you don't care much about being called Master, or giving orders about touching or not touching, because you have your rope do all that for you. But you have quite a bit of that kind of Master in you when you want to use it."

"Well, you bring out the desire for variety in me." He nipped her ear. "We'll have a while to explore all the different things we can be for one another. Things neither one of us may have anticipated."

"More than a while," she said, refusing to allow any fatalism to infiltrate this moment. "A lifetime." Sobering, she touched his face. "Say it for me. Please."

"A lifetime," he said, capturing the hand and pressing a kiss to her palm. When he lifted his head, she saw the hope for it in his own eyes, that hope reflected and feeding off hers. "A lifetime, and then some."

A delightful warmth spread through her. With a quick kiss and a provocative wriggle, she slipped out of bed, evading his grasp. Throwing a grin over her shoulder, she grabbed up a robe on the way to the door. "Our lifetime starts with a bowl of homemade vanilla ice cream and leftover pie. How can that not be a good sign?"

Epilogue

Lila's second play was a hit. Even though a couple sexually repressed critics panned it and another group tried to challenge their permitting, Madison had the continuing staunch support of the two county commissioners, one of whom was in the lifestyle himself. But ultimately, Wonder's success rested in the hands of word-to-mouth recommendations. Since those were overwhelmingly favorable, the naysayers couldn't pose a real threat.

Julie went to sleep exhausted in Des's arms but happy and content. Madison was already planning a couple more productions and an impressive schedule for next year. Julie had agreed to stay on as managing director and Madison was going to start paying Harris a modest salary from ticket sales.

"I'm taking you somewhere, love. Just keep dreaming."

She blinked, coming back to the surface and registering that it was between one and two in the morning. She was groggy but receptive to the kiss Des placed on her lips. No theater success was complete without being thoroughly ravished by one's Master, after all, and Des had seen to that with great detail, part of why she felt boneless and in a dreamy Elysian Fields as he bundled her up in a blanket and picked her up off his bed.

"Where are we going?" she mumbled.

"It's a surprise." He was taking her car, so he'd reclined the passenger seat. As she settled in, she noticed he'd put a tote in the back that looked like it had some snacks and a change of clothes for her, which was good, since she was naked under the blanket.

"Don't get stopped for speeding," she said.

"If I do, showing the cop what's under that blanket will get me off the hook."

She snuffled a laugh into the blanket. "Unless it's a girl cop."

"If it is, one of my most prurient fantasies could come to life." Tucking a bed pillow under her head, he kissed her before he circled around the front bumper and took the wheel.

She fell back asleep easily and didn't wake until dawn. When she did, it was to the cry of seagulls. She opened her eyes to find she wasn't dreaming. They were at the ocean.

The car was parked and she was alone, the windows down so she could inhale the fresh sea air. When she pressed the lever on the seat so she could sit all the way up, she saw they were parked at a public beach access, where the low rise of dunes and gently waving sea oats gave her a panoramic and peaceful view of the ocean at sunrise. The sky was a mellow hue of rose-grey and pink, the sun close to making an appearance.

Des was close by, not a surprise since she knew he'd never leave her unguarded in the car. He was standing on the hard-packed sand closer to shore. His hands were tucked in his back pockets, hair fluttering over his shoulders as he contemplated the view.

She understood why he'd wanted to look at it by himself first. There'd been so much unsaid, when they'd talked about seagulls and a postcard from a mother he never knew. But she suspected he could stand some company now.

Deciding she didn't care about the clothes, since it appeared to be just them on the beach, she wrapped the blanket around her and left the car, trudging over the sandy path through the sea oats.

When she'd opened the car door he'd turned, warming her heart with his awareness of her. His brown gaze caressed her from mussed hair to her bare feet framed by the trailing blanket. Turning back to the view as she approached, he lifted his arm and she slid under it.

"Good morning," he said, gathering her close and

kissing her forehead as she nuzzled his throat.

"Good morning. Where are we?"

"Cherry Grove. North Myrtle Beach."

"Like the postcard Christine left you."

"Yeah." He stroked her shoulder, pushing the blanket away enough to find skin and coil his fingers in her loose hair. "I was wondering if she stood at an access like this while she was pregnant with me. If she was thinking about what to do. Maybe she intended to drive home to Elaine, ask her for help, but she reached Charlotte and lost her nerve or something. Maybe she needed a fix and the city was just too tempting. Whatever."

He lifted a shoulder, banishing a darkness she suspected he hadn't intended to summon. She put her hand on his chest, tugged on his T-shirt.

"All that may be true. But when she stood here, maybe she thought about how it could be if she was different, if life was different. Maybe she had one pure moment, you know. I think everyone does that. No matter how many bad choices you make, there are these blinks in time where you wish you could be the kind of person you should be. Maybe she thought about being a good mom, about loving you. And if she did, that's good. That's cool. That one moment's enough. Right?"

He touched her face, his eyes caressing her. It made her want to hold him tighter. He made her knees weak, and she knew he'd make her feel that way now or in a hundred years. And he could make her laugh when her heart was breaking.

She opened the blanket, wrapping it around both of them as he held her and found her mouth, parting her lips and sliding in to stroke her tongue with his. As he became more demanding, his hands closed around her waist, sliding down to cup and fondle her ass until she was pressing more insistently against him.

He broke the kiss, glancing ruefully at the rows of beach cottages that flanked the beach access and gave way to high rise timeshares and hotels. "Much as I'd love to take you right here on the sand, I think we might get busted. Want to sit and watch the sunrise?"

"I'd love that." She beamed up at him, reaching up with both hands to cup his face. He uttered an amused oath and grabbed for the blanket, salvaging her modesty.

"Woman, you have no shame."

"I trust you to take care of me."

His mouth firmed. "I will, you know. Even if I can't promise that you won't sometimes have to take care of me."

"Progress." She lowered her hands to his shoulders, fingers curling inside the neck of his T-shirt. "Taking care of each other is kind of the point. I want to take care of you. I want you to take care of me. I want to finally know what it is to love someone until the end of our time here on earth. To know what those old couples walking on the beach hand-in-hand know."

He brought her down to the sand with him, holding her cuddled up against his side so they could watch the sun start to break over the horizon. As it spilled the light of a new dawn upon them, Julie lifted her face to its warmth, even as she savored the feel of Des's warmth and life next to her.

She thought of sitting with her feet in the Hampton Inn pool. That hadn't been so long ago, but the paradigm shift since then made it feel like a lifetime. She was certain she'd found now what she'd hoped to find then, in the complex yet intriguingly simple man beside her. Even better, she thought he'd found it with her.

Glancing up at his profile, his absorption with the sunrise, she thought that type of gift made a change of heart possible. Des had said he'd embrace life for her, and she'd hold him to it, because she fully intended to live the entirety of hers with him.

For better or worse was beside the point. There was no *worse*, not as long as they lived that life together.

"You kidnapped me. You owe me breakfast," she whispered against his throat.

"I can think of a lot of things I'd like to do to you as my kidnap victim," he responded, his arm still around her. "Breakfast wasn't at the top of the list, but I'll feed you before I check us into a family-run cheap oceanfront hotel and have my way with you."

"Hmm. Will it have a pirate's lair kind of name, like the Porthole Pelican?"

"Absolutely. Or Bob's Beach Hut."

She grinned. "I want hash browns. And coffee to wake up."

"Baby, I have ways of waking you up that will put caffeine to shame."

He tugged her onto his lap then, finding his way under the blanket as she held onto it and him as much as she could, enjoying the sunrise, the gentle roar of the ocean, the touch of his hands and the promise of a new and glorious day.

A steady heat, holding fast for a lifetime against the coldness of the world.

She couldn't ask for more.

THE END

Afterword

Author's Note: *Don't read this before you read the book, or you'll get some major spoilers!*

Obviously, the main purpose of this book—and what I enjoy most as a writer—is to tell a love story. I hope you've enjoyed Des and Julie's. However, I did want to insert this follow-up note about Des's diabetes and kidney transplant. Type I diabetes and kidney failure are serious issues that can affect all aspects of a person's life, and the lives of their caregivers. I hope I was able to convey that in *Worth the Wait*, but I freely admit there are many details I generalized or left out in order to balance the flow of the love story with the reality of these conditions.

Also, while I made my usual attempt to research and confirm the details were accurate (and any shortcomings in that regard are my fault, not that of my wonderful sources), I also balanced the "must dos" with human nature. My conversations with Jeanie, a caregiver to a diabetic teenager, and the very helpful blogs put out there by people with Type I, gave Des the license to, on occasion, do inadvisable things. Such as disconnecting his pump beyond the recommended time period, or having a food that's not on the approved list (grin).

Another note on timing. Dialysis and transplant preparation usually take more than just a "few weeks" to put in motion, but for the purposes of the book I contracted the schedule a bit. However, with his connections through

Betty and his worsening condition, it is possible the time frame could have been stepped up for Des. On the kidney transplant, the availability of an appropriate donor could also have accelerated the schedule.

Anyhow, if at any point my decision to leave out some details made these conditions seem less serious, my deepest apologies to those who know just how challenging they are. I'll close by expressing my admiration for how people like Des make the most of their lives. Seizing love and appreciating life to the fullest, no matter what physical obstacles are placed in their way, leaves the rest of us no excuse not to do the same.

Oh, and for those who want to tease me about the *deux ex machina* of how Des found a kidney, I fully accept that it was very much an HEA romance kind of thing. But that's what makes writing (and reading) romance so much fun! Lol...

READY FOR MORE?

Check out Joey's website at storywitch.com where you'll find additional information, free excerpts, buy links and news about current and upcoming releases in the Nature of Desire series and for all of her other books and series.

You can find free vignettes and friends to share them with at the JWH Connection, a Joey W. Hill fan forum created by and operated for fans of Joey W. Hill. Sign up instructions are available at storywitch.com/community.

Finally, be sure to check out the latest newsletter for information on upcoming releases, book signing events, contests, and more. You can view current and past editions and subscribe to receive upcoming editions at storywitch.com/community or click the link under the Community menu.

About the Author

Joey W. Hill writes about vampires, mermaids, boardroom executives, cops, witches, angels, housemaids... She's penned over forty acclaimed titles and six award-winning series, and been awarded the RT Book Reviews Career Achievement Award for Erotica. But she's especially proud and humbled to have the support and enthusiasm of a wonderful, widely diverse readership.

So why erotic romance? "Writing great erotic romance is all about exploring the true face of who we are – the best and worst - which typically comes out in the most vulnerable moments of sexual intimacy." She has earned a reputation for writing BDSM romance that not only wins her fans of that genre, but readers who would "never" read BDSM romance. She believes that's because strong, compelling characters are the most important part of her books.

"Whatever genre you're writing, if the characters are captivating and sympathetic, the readers are going to want to see what happens to them. That was the defining element of the romances I loved most and which shaped my own writing. Bringing characters together who have numerous emotional obstacles standing in their way, watching them reach a soul-deep understanding of one another through the expression of their darkest sexual needs, and then growing from that understanding into love - that's the kind of story I love to write."

Take the plunge with her, and don't hesitate to let her know what you think of her work, good or bad. She thrives on feedback!

Find more of her work by following her on Facebook and Twitter, and check out her website for more books by Joey W. Hill.

Twitter: @JoeyWHill

Facebook: JoeyWHillAuthor

On the Web: www.storywitch.com

Email: storywitch@storywitch.com

Also by Joey W. Hill

Arcane Shot Series

Something About Witches
In the Company of Witches

Daughters of Arianne Series

A Mermaid's Kiss
A Witch's Beauty
A Mermaid's Ransom

Knights of the Board Room Series

Board Resolution
Controlled Response
Honor Bound
Afterlife
Hostile Takeover
Willing Sacrifice
Soul Rest

Nature of Desire Series

Holding the Cards
Natural Law

Ice Queen

Mirror of My Soul

Mistress of Redemption

Rough Canvas

Branded Sanctuary

Divine Solace

Worth The Wait

Naughty Bits Series

The Lingerie Shop

Training Session

Bound To Please

The Highest Bid

Naughty Wishes Series

Part 1: Body

Part 2: Heart

Part 3: Mind

Part 4: Soul

Vampire Queen Series

Vampire Queen's Servant

Mark of the Vampire Queen

Vampire's Claim

Beloved Vampire

Vampire Mistress

Vampire Trinity

Vampire Instinct

Bound by the Vampire Queen

Taken by a Vampire

The Scientific Method
Nightfall
Elusive Hero
Night's Templar

Non-Series Titles

If Wishes Were Horses
Virtual Reality
Unrestrained

Novellas

Chance of a Lifetime
Choice of Masters
Make Her Dreams Come True
Threads of Faith
Submissive Angel

Short

Snow Angel

CPSIA information can be obtained
at www.ICGtesting.com
Printed in the USA
LVOW03s2225120617
537890LV00011B/603/P